DARK THINGS

Sukanya Venkatraghavan is an Indian writer and winner of the *DNA-Hachette* Bestseller Hunt (2014). Her first brush with fantasy was as a film journalist, covering the glamorous yet daunting world of Bollywood with publications like *Filmfare* and *Marie Claire*.

Currently based in Mumbai, Sukanya lives with her husband and a large congregation of cat and owl figurines collected from all over the world. *Dark Things* is her first book.

W0232901

DARK THINGS

SUKANYA VENKATRAGHAVAN

hachette
INDIA

For Rohith, who used his magic for good...
You are loved and remembered always.

First published in 2016 by Hachette India
(Registered name: Hachette Book Publishing India Pvt. Ltd)
An Hachette UK company
www.hachetteindia.com

SRD

Copyright © 2016 Sukanya Venkatraghavan

Sukanya Venkatraghavan asserts the moral right to be identified
as the proprietor of this work.

All rights reserved. No part of the publication may be reproduced, stored in a
retrieval system (including but not limited to computers, disks, external drives,
electronic or digital devices, e-readers, websites), or transmitted in any form or
by any means (including but not limited to cyclostyling, photocopying, docutech
or other reprographic reproductions, mechanical, recording, electronic, digital
versions) without the prior written permission of the publisher, nor be otherwise
circulated in any form of binding or cover other than that in which it is published
and without a similar condition being imposed on the subsequent purchaser.

This is a work of fiction. Any resemblance to real persons, living or dead, or actual
events or locales is purely coincidental.

ISBN 978-93-5009-922-3

Hachette Book Publishing India Pvt. Ltd
4th/5th Floors, Corporate Centre,
Sector 44, Gurgaon 122003, India

Typeset in Garamond 11.5/15
by InoSoft Systems, Noida

Printed and bound in India by
Manipal Technologies Limited, Manipal

MIX
Paper from
responsible sources
FSC
www.fsc.org   FSC™ C043100

✳ 1 ✳

Someone once told me a beautiful story. A princess had been cursed to sleep forever and could only be awakened by true love's kiss. Then, one day, a prince came along and kissed her, and they lived happily ever after. I liked the story, though I didn't think it was quite that easy to wake up from curses of that kind. But I liked the idea that a kiss could bring someone back to life.

Because, you see, usually when I kiss someone, they die soon afterwards. I live in the exact opposite of a fairytale. I kissed the man who told me the story. He kissed me back passionately, as if it was the last thing he'd ever do.

Turned out, it was. He died a few hours later. So, now do you understand? The story amused me. But I couldn't believe in it. It is easier to believe in the curse of the evil witch than in the kiss of true love.

Just like it is easier to believe that monsters and ghosts exist than Gods do.

Of course, monsters exist. They roam the earth. They scope the sky. They haunt the underworld.

And monsters don't look anything like monsters. They look like you and me. In fact, they look more like me than anyone else.

What do I look like?

My mirror – the little thing made of some ancient metal and mercury – tells me I look like dark magic. Sometimes, when it is in a charitable mood, it says I am pretty, like a vial of poison. Beautiful, like blood. Tempting, like a secret.

Sometimes my mirror will tell me what colour my eyes should be that evening. And, at other times, it will just cloud over and not speak to me at all.

I was wearing soulful brown eyes that day. The kind that make men want to rescue me.

He was tracing the twisted flickering of my lashes on canvas in a manner no man had, in even the deepest moments of passion.

'Maybe strangers see your soul the way you yourself don't. That's what happens when you flirt with serendipity,' he said as he sketched me, his long fingers smudged with charcoal. This was right after I had said the drawing looked nothing like me, even though it did.

There was no place for serendipity in my life. It was pretty straightforward. I had rules and timings, and consequences if those rules were not followed.

But it had rained that day. I liked it when it rained. It washed away the borders of my life, however temporarily, and I could allow time to stretch itself out just a tiny bit.

So, when the sky decided to storm loud and heavy, I found myself running for shelter. I liked doing normal human things like running from the rain when I could. At other times it was a fun game, dodging lightning and riding rainclouds.

I ran towards the nearest shelter I could see – a few tents in the middle of a ground that sported a large banner with the words 'Art Festival' on its gate in bright lettering. I hurried into the compound, with its gaily coloured tents and stalls where people were selling things or making them. That's when I saw him.

He was sketching an old man, his long fingers moving nimbly across the canvas. I paused in the rain and watched him until he began to sketch a little girl. When she left clutching her drawing in her little hands, a delighted smile on her face, he sat back for a moment, looking satisfied.

Following a strange impulse, I walked up and sat down. He looked at me for a few seconds and then picked up a pencil.

I let him sketch me because I was curious. For once, I wanted to know how someone saw me, and not the other way around. I watched his dark hair fall over his eyes as he traced the pencil on the canvas.

'Are you finished?' I asked after some time had passed. He seemed to be taking longer with me.

'A sketch is always unfinished,' he replied. 'It just depends on when I choose to stop.'

I glanced at the canvas, still unfinished but brimming with life. *My* life. My face... Only this looked like me in another lifetime, with a soul that actually functioned.

'You've got my eyes wrong,' I told him instead.

He took a step back, frowning at the charcoal face on the easel, and then turned to look at me.

'I haven't got them wrong. I just see them differently,' he said, his black pearl eyes boring into me.

I accepted his theory in silence. My charcoal eyes had a compassion my real ones did not. He had infused them with a soft light that made me uncomfortable. I have seen my eyes, all my eyes, in all their emotions. None of them are soft.

I relaxed my pose for a minute and looked around at the people milling around, a whirring, humming blur of colour and noise. A lot of people looked towards us, drawn by the tall artist and the subject. And as always they lingered, looking at me as if I had cast a spell on them.

He asked me to resume my pose and I turned back, angling my face just as he wanted. I watched as my hair flowed down my shoulders with long single strokes of his pencil. He tilted his head to a side and looked at his drawing. *Not like a painter*, I thought. More like a writer, rereading his words. I peeked over his shoulder and gasped.

He had pinned me down on canvas. I wanted to stay there forever, in a charcoal eternity of how he saw me.

'Done,' he said finally.

The charcoal me stared back unflinchingly, as if she was the keeper of my secrets.

'I like her.'

'Do you want her?'

'No, I already have me. You keep her.'

With that I walked away with a smile. He came after me, leaving his stall, his long hands buried in the pockets of his jeans as he smiled boyishly, the setting sun behind him infusing him with a golden aura. *Like a God who walks the earth*, I thought, and then laughed inwardly at my private joke.

I walked away. I had to. I liked this guy.

I wandered about in the rain until it was time for my assignment. As the reflection of city lights in muddy rain puddles twinkled, I felt a strange sense of longing. He wasn't the first guy I had walked away from. But he was the first guy who had seen kindness in my eyes, even if it was only in charcoal. As if he could see deep inside me, even though I myself had never been able to understand who I really was.

Serendipity, he had said. I thought of the word as I set my eyes on him at the hotel. Somehow, he looked taller in the dark of the night. I couldn't help but gaze at his long beautiful fingers, the ones that had sketched me with such surreal grace. I liked the face he had given me earlier in the day. It was a face I would cherish for a long time. I wondered what he had done with the sketch, whether it was still hanging on the cloth wall of the stall at the art festival.

Of course, he didn't recognize me. I was on assignment, after all. Sporting my favourite look – pale skin, green eyes, long black hair and a figure that was slender, yet full – I looked very different from the woman he had met this morning. I even had a tiny mole just above my upper lip. I felt my imprint, the frangipani-shaped magical tattoo on the inside of my wrist, glow faintly in anticipation.

He smiled at me, a slightly puzzled look in his black pearl eyes. I could see his lashes – long, curling lashes – sweep up and down as he blinked slowly, and a strange magic unfolded within me.

I wanted to pick him.

I didn't want to pick him.

See, this is why I hate coincidences.

I returned his smile, haughty with a tinge of flirtation. Then I walked past, just slightly brushing his hand. I had to make contact. I couldn't bewitch him without touching his skin. Strangely, as we touched, for a fraction of a second, I felt a tug. Like someone had latched a hook onto my core and pulled.

In fact, my core, the thing that kept me alive, was tingling. Lust glided through my blood, a shimmery opaque creature with crumbly wings.

I want to pick him.

I don't want to pick him.

Because if I do, he will die.

I could have walked away. He would feel the bewitching for a few hours but it would eventually fade. If I didn't do anything about it, it would flee quietly from his bones and he would wake up the next morning feeling a little disoriented and dull. And that would be it. He would live. I could make that choice.

And yet, my core felt a desire for his secrets. I wanted them. Beating, pulsating, dark, untold, unknown, unspeakable... I craved for them.

I wanted to pick him.

I turned with a calculated sway of shoulders and hips. My hair whipped around me like a gentle rainstorm and my eyes glinted with magic. The bewitching had worked, so the moment I turned, he did too. I could see his black pearl eyes, that had earlier in the day held wry amusement, were now glazed over with my magic. I felt a hand grip my elbow. I turned to look at him.

'I'm sorry, but have we met before?' he asked uncertainly.

I was surprised. *How did he know?* Recovering quickly, I replied, 'Do you say that to every pretty girl you meet at a party?'

'No, just the ones I'm sure I've met before...'

After a moment, he shook his head as if dispelling the thought. 'I'm Dwai,' he continued.

'Dwai? That's an interesting name. Is it Indian?'

'Very much so. What's yours?'

I told him. It didn't matter what name I gave. He wasn't going to remember it anyway. And tomorrow he wouldn't be alive to mention it to anyone.

'That's an interesting name too.'

'Are we going to stand around talking about our names all night?'

His lips twisted into a wry smile at my question. I ran my finger lightly up his arm, deepening my bewitching. He hooked his arms around my waist and pulled me closer. I brushed my lips against his.

The more I touched him, the deeper he would fall under my spell.

When we pulled back, I batted my eyelids and the lights in the hotel corridor went dim.

Before I could say, 'Let's go get a room here,' he grabbed my hand and started to walk. I began scanning for his secrets. I was thirsty. I wanted one. Any one.

Give me something… Which friend of your mother's seduced you when you were fourteen? Who did you run over on the highway while driving drunk on New Year's Eve ten years ago? Come on…something, anything.

But I got nothing. It was like hitting a brick wall. I couldn't even penetrate the first layer, get to the easy ones. This one kept his mind locked very tight. I was intruiged.

We walked down the dim corridors until he led me out of the main entrance and down to the gates, into a waiting cab. His place was a short ride from the hotel, he told me. I was surprised at myself. I almost never let this happen. I stuck to hotel rooms as far as I could. Private homes could be tricky. You were never sure where you might find traces of old magic. But I didn't feel like resisting. We held hands in the cab and I squeezed his palm tighter in the hope that I might get something.

Still no luck. Strange. It wasn't easy to resist my magic.

He turned to look at me, his crooked smile in place, and for a second I wondered if the bewitching had worked at all. Then I looked into his eyes and I was certain my magic was melding slowly with his blood. But for some reason my core was uneasy. I fought off the feeling and smiled back instead.

His home was dark. He fumbled for the light switch, his

fingers clumsy from my bewitching. The light came on, ochre and bright. I dimmed it a little. He didn't notice. I realized that people in the building opposite his could look in through the window and I cast my eyes towards the curtains. They slowly drew close.

His face was lined with strange shadows from the fragmented light. It made me think of someone else. No, not right now. I moved closer to him and his eyelids flickered almost as if he was struggling with my magic. I reached out and placed a hand on his chest.

'What are you doing to me?' he murmured. I didn't reply. Instead, I kissed him. As he pulled me closer, I could feel his heart beating against my chest. His black pearl eyes had deep copper-flecked irises. I closed my eyes and reeled us both in into my bewitching.

8

✢ 2 ✢

Something was wrong. I knew this as soon as I closed the door of the apartment behind me, but I couldn't put my finger on it. I had left him spread-eagled on the rug, his dark lashes curled upwards, almost touching his brows. His mouth had been curved in a smile. I had watched him for a while before leaving.

If I knew what regret felt like, I would say it was this.

Dwai…short for what I will never know. I couldn't find it inside him. In fact, I didn't know what I had found really. See, the thing is, once I took someone's secrets, they became a blur to me. I could only remember them for a flash of a second. Then they were gone. Which was usually a good thing except, this time, I was curious about my prey. I wanted to know more about him, but the information was locked inside of me. Only one person had that key.

I thought about how it had felt, being with him.

Like diving deep down into the ocean, I thought. I had felt my core hit the flat, hard surface of the water and then sink into its inky depths. Millions of creatures had flitted around me but I hadn't been able to clasp my fingers around even one. I had swum deeper and deeper, and all I had felt was nothingness. How was this possible?

I looked up at the sky that was still troubled and stormy. I could fly and lose myself in the clouds. Anything to avoid this uncertainty I was feeling.

I tried to lift myself into the air but sank back to the ground. Mild panic rose in my chest. *What was happening to me?* I had never failed to fly before. Summoning up all my strength, I tried again. This time I managed to rise into the atmosphere, even though my core was still shaky.

You can fly without wings, of course. I did. But I liked picturing a pair of shiny dark satin-feathered wings rising out of my shoulder blades like smoke in the sky.

Being what I am, however, I don't need wings. Being what I am, I can also shape-shift. Steal your secrets. And kill you.

I am a daughter of the night. A keeper of dark things.

Secrets are dark things. They don't exist in the light. They glow faintly in forgotten corners, in mysterious mind-nooks, in lost memory maps. Secrets are the shadows of the soul.

Often, I am your last and best-kept secret. The one you die with, the one that killed you.

9

3

The sky was tinged an odd scarlet. The moon looked swollen and poisoned with red. A blood moon. I don't remember ever having gone out on a blood moon night in the five hundred years that I have been around. Strange, because there must have been quite a few.

We had been doing this for a very long time. Five centuries, to be precise. That's a long time to be seducing and killing, for holding someone else's secrets in your core, for however brief a time, before they were retrieved. By her. My mistress.

It was for precisely this reason that I now had to head back to the place I called home as fast as I could. I could feel the pull of the moon tonight. It carried with it an unsettling magic. A strange feeling rose in my chest, an odd vibration. I tried to ignore it but it was like a bee, buzzing around inside me.

I began to fly lower because I wasn't sure I could stay airborne for long. The odd thrum inside me was now like a dragon's heartbeat. It must be what I had taken from him. It had to be. But this had never happened before. Not in five hundred years. I must have done something wrong. But what?

It was a little after midnight. The air was still and the streets were empty but for a few stray cats and dogs who stared at me as I floated through the air above them.

Except…

The feeling came out of nowhere, as it had for more than half-a-century now. My skin prickled.

I was being watched.

I tried to rise higher in the air and fly faster but failed.

Whatever or whoever this was couldn't fly, this much I knew for sure. Shadows took on forms and I looked around. There was no one there, neither monster nor man. And yet I knew I was being followed. I had to stay in the air. I had been lucky enough to escape once but I might not get a second chance.

Whoever this was wasn't giving up on me.

In the distance, I could see the old house that held the portal back to Atala. When I reached the building I lowered myself to the ground but not without a quick look around. I felt the presence still lurking around me.

The old house had lain unused and abandoned for over fifty years now. The portal was the tiny window right next to the broken door. If a human looked in through the window, they would just see the dusty insides of a forgotten house. For Yakshis, however, the window was a gateway to Atala.

The rats around the house saw me and scampered away, their noses twitching. I climbed into the portal with a quick glance behind me and, after walking down a dark corridor for what felt like ages, I was finally at the gates of my home.

Atala, a dark realm tucked away under Prithvi. Atala, beautiful, like a magical creature that has never seen light. Atala, home to the darkly ones, the dire creatures, the night sirens.

I paused outside the magnificent gates into the Palace of Vishara. The two skulls on top of each gate turned their bejewelled sockets towards me and a familiar chill ran down my spine. Even after hundreds of years, there was no getting used to this. They turned to face each other and nodded slightly. I had clearly passed their inspection. The bone and iron gates, fashioned like two great hands clasping each other, opened. One had to pass through them quickly or they would close, the fingers impaling you in certain death. I stumbled past them and into the darkness that was Atala. In the distance, the Palace of Vishara gleamed like a goblin's eye, oval-shaped and ominous. My home.

I walked through the grounds, the smell of blood in the air. It was the frangipanis. No, not the kind you find on Prithvi. These were carnivorous. After all, blood wasn't hard to find in Atala.

'Ardra!'

I turned. It was Vina, one of the Yakshis and my best friend in the palace. She hurried towards me, her long black hair trailing behind her lovely face like a sheet of wind.

'Where've you been?' she asked. 'I've looked everywhere for you!'

'I...' I started. The thrum in my core was drowning out everything else.

'Yes, yes, I know, you have a habit of wandering off on your own. But something has happened. Again.'

'What?' I asked, my core pulsating wildly. Did she know I had gone out to take secrets and that something had gone wrong? I was ideally supposed to be making my way to the Retrieval Room now, where Hera would be waiting for me.

'One of the Yakshis...she's been missing for a couple of days. And...' she drew in a deep breath, 'the slayer...he found her. They found her burnt bits in an alley.'

I went cold. The thought of the slayer coming after me was paralyzing. *No*, said a voice inside me, *he let you go once. He wouldn't come after you again.*

'That's horrible,' I said, my voice sounding strange even to my ears.

'There was no sign of him, of course. And only last week three vampires were killed. He's really on a rampage.'

Vina kept talking animatedly as we walked down the passage towards our chambers. When we reached, I made an excuse to get away. I had to get to the Retreival Room and something told me that she musn't know I had taken secrets that night.

I continued down the corridor until I reached the large ornate doors I was looking for. Reluctantly, I opened them and stepped inside.

To my utter surprise, the huge throne was empty. Where was Hera? She had never missed a retrieval before. *She must know I have secrets with me – she always does.*

Unsure of what to do, I slowly tiptoed into the room where our secrets were retrieved. It was a large space with pitch-black walls and no windows. A single chair adorned the centre of the room, a stark throne made of ancient metal.

The thrum in my core returned. Dark shapes on the wall sprung myriad arms and legs and crept across the floor towards me. I closed my eyes, trying to shut out everything, including the beast in my core.

She isn't going to come, I realized. *What the hell is going on?*

I paced across the room uncertainly for a few minutes and then swiftly turned on my heel and headed back towards our chambers. As I entered, I saw some of the Yakshis huddled together, weeping. Vina was with them, talking animatedly. She barely noticed that I didn't join them, choosing to climb into my blood red pod and lying down instead. My hand mirror was by the pillow and the strange creature within peeked out warily at me.

'What?' I snapped. 'Everything is fine.'

'Of course it is,' it replied lazily.

I turned my back to the mirror and shut my eyes. I could hear the babble of the Yakshis outside my pod.

Why hadn't she come? I must have made some mistake. Was it not my night to go out?

I fell asleep with uneasy dreams of long shadows, bloodstained Yakshis and deep black pearl eyes with a hint of a smile in them.

4

When I woke, there was no one in the chambers with me. I felt a strange hollow feeling in my core, as if someone had stuck a spade into me and dug something out clumsily. Had the secrets been retrieved? No, that wasn't possible without her.

I slipped out of my pod and, ignoring my mirror that was making snide noises, made my way to the common hall. A huge statue of Lord Mara, the God of lust, stood in the corner, but there were no Yakshis to be seen anywhere. I couldn't tell if it was day or night but that hardly mattered in Atala. Here, it was always dark. I looked out of one of the tall bejewelled windows and saw the sun skulking behind the shadows of the dark purple sky that hung over the palace. Yes, Atala had a sun, but it was always in eclipse. It looked charred around the edges, always burning but forever shrouded in darkness – a big black orb that neither gave light nor life. The sun was always positioned right over the Palace of Vishara because that's how she liked it.

She...Hera. Queen of Secrets. Of dark things and everything unspoken. The Empress of Atala.

I was afraid of her. I didn't know why but I had always felt like she hated me.

I dreamt of her often. Snakes in her hair, dead suns in her irises, she would rise above Vishara and swallow the sky. I would stand and stare at her as the snakes hissed and lunged for me. I always ducked and moved away just in time but in that sliver of a second, I would look down upon my heart and find a gaping hole there. Before I could scream, I would wake up. I always woke up before I could scream.

Did Hera not care about her Yakshis? Would I die if the secrets were not retrieved? Could they retrieve secrets after the keeper was dead? Why did my core feel empty? I didn't know. We were not encouraged to ask questions in Atala.

And then I remembered. She sought me out especially on full moon nights but never when the moon was red. In fact, as far as I knew, no Yakshi had ever gone out on those nights.

I turned a corner and saw Vina and Mantri in deep conversation. Ugh. Vile, oily, creepy Mantri was Hera's Chief of Guards. Well, I suppose anyone would be creepy if they had two heads of which only one talked and the other looked like it had been stitched on with its mouth sewn shut. Sometimes when I looked at his heads and I watched one talk, I felt like the other one was struggling against its stitches, trying to undo them. His shapeless form smelled like old cabbages and cockroaches lying dead in dusty corners. Only Vina talked to him voluntarily because she wanted to remain in his good books. You could get away with a lot if you had him on your side. I, on the other hand, couldn't stand him, and I knew the feeling was mutual.

I was about to back away slowly when Vina looked up and saw me. She made a subtle gesture asking me to join them but I shook my head. I didn't want to deal with Mantri right then.

I began walking aimlessly until I left the main palace hallways and reached the open ground outside. I wasn't really sure where I was going but I wanted to get away from the palace and be alone with my thoughts. I looked up to see a flock of mrig pakshis flying across the sun, creating a ripple of silver and gold around it with their golden heads and silver bat-shaped bodies. Half-bird, half-bat, they belonged to Atala, as strange as the land they inhabited with their mewing cries and featherless wings. I paused to watch them fly around the curve of the sun and disappear, perhaps into the Black Dwarf Sea that surrounded Atala. Wine-coloured and uninviting, the sea was where planets came to die. No one had access to the jewelled beach except Hera. It meant there was no way out of Atala, unless she wanted you to leave it.

The birds reappeared suddenly in the cloudless Atala sky and I started to follow their path. I walked on, crossing the grounds into the gardens of Vishara, abloom with jewelled plants and ghostly trees that seemed to whisper in the wind. Sometimes I would pause, trying to fathom what they were saying, trying to talk to them, but most of the time they only rambled on like senile old ladies, the wind carrying their whispers far and wide. Today, however, I walked on. There was a sense of foreboding in my core that I couldn't understand.

After a while, I heard a noise and stopped. It was only then that I realized where I was. Lost in thought, I had turned the corner where the garden gave way to a large thicket of trees surrounding a tower. I wasn't supposed to come here. This was the forbidden part of the palace – no one but Hera was allowed here. I stood transfixed for a few seconds. And then I heard it. A whisper. But this wasn't the trees; this was something else, something more sinister. It sent a chill down my spine and something inside me screamed. I felt a rush of emotion unlike anything I have felt before. *Fear, it's just fear*, I told myself.

I stepped behind a tree and forced myself to steal a glance upwards. The tower window was open and I thought I could see a figure behind the iron bars. I should have run then, far away from whatever this was. But a horrid fascination had gripped me and I stayed. A soft, strange rustle came from the tower. Perhaps whatever it was had sensed my presence.

'Run!' urged my brain. But something kept my feet glued to the ground. Another rustle set off an odd flutter in my core. I drew in my breath. What was this thing? Could it see me somehow? Would Hera find out I had come here? The thought of her finally woke me from my reverie. I turned on my heels and raced across the grounds towards the palace, finding my way back to my chambers. I climbed into my pod and sat there, my breath coming in rasps and my heart thundering. What was that sound? Who did it belong to?

I wasn't sure how long I stayed in my pod. At some point I fell asleep. Slinky, crawling eerie creatures skulked across my dreams. Hera towered over Atala, snakes in her hair, a one-eyed raven on her shoulder. A mrig pakshi flew above her and she looked up smiling. She flicked out her tongue, long and forked, and caught the bird. In a flicker it disappeared into her mouth. And then there was that sound again. It brushed all over my dream like a vulture's wing...

I woke up with a start.

⊹ 5 ⊹

There was one other recurring dream that had haunted me for years – more a memory really. I will never forget how those blue eyes, bright with fury, had speared into me as I wondered what it would be like to die...and how rapidly the anger in those eyes had changed to puzzlement and then wonder. I didn't die that day, but even now, almost half-a-century later, I see those eyes in my dreams and when I'm awake, I can feel his presence around me. I still don't know why he let me go that day.

It had been a particularly cold winter's night sometime in the early 1900s. I had just exited a jazz club with my prey. The air was dewy and the city lights danced faintly in the distance. My prey was enthusiastic and drunk, humming along as we walked down the wet road to his home. He hadn't noticed my eyes changing from green to brown and then back to green and my Yakshi imprint, the frangipani tattoo on my wrist, glowing in the dark. He didn't even blink when I lifted my feet off the ground and floated alongside him. He broke into a loud song and laughed as he tottered ahead of me. It was just another night of seduction and secret-taking for me.

I felt his aura long before I actually saw him. He appeared as a shadow around the corner and when he stepped into the light, I instantly knew who he was.

The slayer, as he was known, had a reputation for ruthlessness. He had been hunting monsters for centuries and had never failed. No one knew who he was or where he had come from, just that he had appeared one day, a lone figure in a long trench coat and a hooded face armed with a sabre. No one had heard his voice as no one had lived to tell the tale after encountering him.

Except me.

That night, he had advanced towards me with lightning speed, even before I could think of rising higher into the air or changing into my warrior form. I had never seen anyone move so fast. I could feel the force of his strength as his body came closer to mine. I was sure I was going to die. He would slay me with his sabre or I would explode into flames in the way Yakshis were known to do when he tried to capture them. Clattering footsteps told me my prey had fled the scene, leaving me backed against a wall with the slayer advancing upon me, one hand clutching a gleaming sabre. His eyes gleamed a deep sinister blue in the moonlight as his other gloved hand closed around my throat. *Why wasn't I self-combusting yet?*

And then, as I gazed into those mad, determined eyes, I felt a jolt of magic that seemed almost primal. The fear I had been feeling until just a moment ago vanished and, suddenly, my core felt calm.

No, I choked, bringing my arm up to free my neck from his clutches. *NO*.

He grabbed my arm with stinging force and I gasped. When he flung it against the wall brutally, I let out a snarl of pain. I could feel the bones in my wrist snap. His eyes travelled from my face to my arm and then back to meet my angry eyes. Something in his forbidding expression changed. I heard him draw a deep breath, his eyes growing wider in shock. He let go of my neck and, as I saw his hand clasp his sword tighter, I thought, *This is it...this is the end.*

To my utter surprise, he took a step back, flinging the sword away in what I could only call frustration.

'Run,' he rasped. 'Run, before I change my mind.'

I didn't run. I swarmed up the wall and took flight. As I rose into the air, I looked down to see a dark lonely figure kneeling on the concrete, his sabre gleaming a few yards away. He didn't look up as I flew out of sight, still unable to believe what had happened.

All I knew was that the slayer could have run his sabre through my chest that day but he didn't. He let me go.

I never told anyone about my encounter. Not even Vina. Something told me it was best to keep it to myself.

In the coming years, he would chance upon other Yakshis, and every time this happened, the Yakshi would self-combust. He never got the chance to question or kill one. They simply exploded into flames, crumbling into ashes in front of his eyes. This was the way Hera built us, so that no one could capture us unless they had her command to do so.

And therein lies my other question: Why didn't I self-combust? Why didn't I burst into flames when he gripped my neck?

I remember Hera's rage when some of her Yakshis were lost in this manner.

'It is him, I know,' she roared, her robes flying as she paced. 'He's trying to find passage into Atala.' She let out a growl of rage.

The crone, Dakini, sniggered as she always did. 'Strange are the bonds that bind you, O Mistress of Phantoms,' she said snidely. Hera gave her a stinging look and walked away.

The crone watched her go and then muttered under her breath, 'What you leave behind will come after you, for after all, you are bound together by heart and destiny.'

The monster slayer and Hera seemed to have shared some mysterious past. But Hera had likely crossed a lot of people and had enemies everywhere, so I wasn't surprised.

Years passed and while I never encountered the slayer again, I started to feel like I was being watched. I knew someone was stalking me from the shadows every time I was on Prithvi. Sometimes, when my imagination got the better of me, I would see a glint of blue in the dark – eyes that held a certain recklessness. I haven't felt safe ever since although I haven't been attacked either.

Of all the questions that haunt me about my own existence the one that stumps me the most is, why did he let me go that day?

✥ 6 ✥

The night was thick as a velvet quilt as we wove in and out of the sky, our laughter ringing loud and clear. I was happy after a long time. Sneaking out of Atala with Vina that evening had given me a sense of freedom I rarely experienced. She was very good at things like this. She had a way of bending the rules and never getting caught.

Vina was one of the more powerful Yakshis in Atala. She had a thirst for secrets, for seduction, that even Hera recognized. Vina was in awe of Hera, as were most of the Yakshis. 'I think she is the most powerful witch in the world,' she said to me once. 'So powerful even the Gods leave her alone.'

Of course, this was only speculation as there weren't any Gods around anymore. One of the most popular rumours in the supernatural world was that the sky city of Aakasha was a ghost town since the Gods had abandoned it. Which meant that Apsaras or Gandharvas, the heavenly beings who loved to sing and dance, were not there either. Apsaras had once been famous for their powers of seduction, the greatest of kings and sages having fallen under their spell. The Gandharvas, on the other hand, were known for their knack of charming young women. Moreover, they were supposed to be natural healers.

But there was a great silence about the existence of either for centuries, so much so that it seemed doubtful they ever existed. For all it was worth, it just seemed like a beautiful story out of the Old Books, one big fancy myth.

But we were myths for anyone who didn't believe in us, too. And Prithvi's penchant for the supernatural had declined. Nobody believed in anything that was even slightly out of their realm anymore. Of course, this made our job even more amusing. Mythical sirens from a strange realm walked around on earth seducing mortals. Humans didn't believe in us almost until the last breath was drawn out of them.

There were so many rumours about Hera and Atala. Some of the Yakshis seemed to think the realm was a part of Prithvi that had broken away during one of the wars with the Old Gods. Others believed Atala had been home to the Asuras until they abandoned it for deeper, darker realms, leaving Hera to claim it for her own. Some whispered Hera had created the realm in a day as the result of a boon from the Gods, and that Vishara had been built in the blink of an eye from a single sapphire.

Whatever the truth was, Atala was my home. It also housed exiled Rakshasas who were under Hera's control and a motley crowd of supernatural beings who flitted between Atala, Prithvi and other lesser realms.

So much of Hera herself was shrouded in mystery. No one knew what she was exactly. It was strongly believed by Yakshis like Vina that she was a very powerful witch – the kind that takes really powerful dark magic to become. It was generally believed that the universe's magic had weakened considerably, leaving the old witches less powerful than they would have liked to be. Yet Hera was more powerful than ever. Where she got this power from was a constant source of debate and rumours.

'Whatever it is,' said Vina. 'I would sure like to know the secret.'

We were sitting on the steps of an abandoned temple on the top of a cliff, watching the city lights blinking below us. This was one of our favourite haunts.

'The secret to being so powerful...' Vina continued, her eyes gleaming in the starlight, her peacock imprint glowing as it did whenever she was excited.

'Have you heard of Blood Queens?' Vina asked suddenly. I could sense the exhilaration in her voice.

'No, what are they?'

'The most powerful witches in the world. They rule over different things. For instance, the Blood Queen in the realm of Ice and Skulls rules over valkyries and vampires, chaos and cold. And the one before her was even more powerful. She ruled over the Night.'

'And you think Hera is one?' I asked.

'Is one, or will soon be one,' said Vina. 'Her powers are strange, Ardra. Stranger than most witches. She is locked in Atala. I know she doesn't have free passage to other realms. And, yet, she is so powerful. Have you seen her after she has retrieved secrets? Have you seen her in the subsequent days? She emanates power. If anyone can be a Blood Queen, it is her. And I think that is what she is trying to do, along with that old crone.'

I drank all this in. It seemed like a bizarre story, but then again, it was no stranger than our own existence. And, in our world, anything was possible.

'So, what do you have to do to become a Blood Queen?'

'I'm not sure. I think it needs some really complex magic. And some kind of sacrifice.'

A memory resurfaced in my mind and I nearly gasped. A

few centuries ago, I had been wandering around in the palace when a strange glow from one of the rooms had caught my eye. I should have turned back then, yes, but I didn't. Instead, I followed it and watched as the glow became stronger, exuding belligerent magic. Soon, I could hear low chants in the crone's voice. When I peeked into the room through the door, I saw Hera standing naked over a bubbling cauldron.

'Will it work this time?' she had rasped, as the smoke from the cauldron swirled around her.

'We must try everything, we must...' the crone had said, pulling something towards the cauldron. Something unwilling and terrified, gagged and bound. I hadn't dared to go closer but I had caught a gimpse of a tail. A beautiful long tail reflecting the colours of the ocean.

A mermaid's tail.

The crone had begun chanting once again, this time louder and more frenzied, as Hera circled the cauldron. The mermaid whimpered.

I retraced my steps and hid behind a marble column near the door. I could hear the swish of a knife followed by a muffled scream. And then a horrible blubbering sound filled the corridor as if something was being drowned in the cauldron.

I ran, never looking back.

'A secret for your thoughts,' Vina clicked her fingers in front of my face.

I watched my friend as she rose in the air playfully, none of her thoughts as dark and troubled as mine.

'What sort of a sacrifice do you think it entails?' I asked, hoping my voice was even.

'Who knows?' said Vina, twirling in the air. 'Can it be worse than taking someone's secrets and killing them?'

Could it? Could one act of horror be worse than another?

Could certain monsters be more inhuman than others? And what did being human mean anyway? The stories I heard on Prithvi about what humans did to one another were sometimes so unsettling that it felt as if the lines between our worlds were blurring.

'Look at what's happening on Prithvi, for instance,' Vina continued breathlessly. 'Have you heard that something has been attacking humans in increasingly brutal ways? I mean, we know that this has been happening for centuries but they seem to be getting worse – so much so that the humans have begun to take notice. I mean, this *thing* preys on humans, eats their innards, peels off their skin and places it on backwards. They are bound to notice that kind of brutality! That itself breaks the laws of the supernatural world. What do you think it could be? Not a werewolf or a vampire, definitely. This is something else. Some dark creature we've never heard of? Maybe it's the slayer.'

For a second I wondered if she was right but something told me he would not kill innocent humans, least of all with such brutality. No, he was after the supernatural beings that caused harm on earth.

And then I remembered the thing in the tower. Its energy was unreal, even for a supernatural being. I wanted to tell Vina about it but something held me back.

There was a mild splash in the sky above us. It pulled me out of my thoughts. Vina was still twirling in the air, oblivious. I looked up at the star-sequinned sky above me. Something was shooting through the air. Or someone.

I slid off the cliff, flying a little higher than Vina. I could see the hazy outline of a man clearly now. He was dipping in and out of the clouds, heading towards earth.

'Vina…'

'What?'

Now the outline was lost in the dusty haze of the night.

'Nothing,' I said, deciding to first confirm what I had seen for myself before telling anyone.

'All right, nothing it is,' she said. 'I'm going down there for a while. You should head back to Atala.'

We said our goodbyes mid-air. I watched as she swooped down like a graceful bird in search of prey. I paused, wondering if I should follow my hunch. I had never seen a flying man come out of the sky before. He had a lithe grace and an aura of magic that felt alien and yet somehow familiar.

Just then, the night sky rippled and I saw him again, weaving in and out of the clouds. I rose higher in the air; I had made up my mind.

Swooping through the air, I dashed after him. I was curious, my core thrumming with excitement.

The clouds parted just as he came into my sight. He was diving towards the earth and as he did I caught my first real glimpse of him. His long pointy face, with pale blue eyes and long brown hair, looked handsome yet vapid.

He must have sensed my movement because he turned suddenly. His baby blue eyes widened in surprise as he saw me hovering in the air a few metres away from him. He then turned swiftly and shot back towards the sky.

'Wait!' I hollered.

He didn't pause or look back. I raced after him.

'Wait... I just need to ask you something, that's all.'

If he had heard me through the deafening wind, he chose not to acknowledge it. Instead, he flew faster, racing upwards with unbelievable speed. I saw the surface of the night sky shiver as he approached it. As I watched, it let out a quiet rumble and a little circular opening appeared in the sky. A portal. I didn't even know there were portals in the sky. Where did they lead to?

The man finally paused by the portal and turned. Keeping his eyes on me, he pulled himself into the portal and disappeared, swift as an arrow.

'WAIT!' I shouted and dived right after him towards the circular opening.

A sharp electric crunch hit me as something within the portal fought back against my invasion. Spikes of energy slit my skin and I screamed. The portal began to shut in a slow grinding motion and, as it did, the spikes became stronger, more brutal. I heard a dull thud as the portal closed and vanished from the sky and I was thrown back with such force that I had to shut my eyes.

I plummeted to earth.

⚔ 7 ⚔

Have you ever fallen from the skies and hurtled towards the earth? I bet not. Well, it didn't matter whether you were mortal or monster, when your body hit the earth, it hurt like hell. I lay there on the slightly damp ground for a few minutes, not daring to open my eyes. Something wet and sticky oozed around me and I felt a warm liquid making its way from my forehead to my eyelids.

Blood.

How I managed to make my way to the old house, I don't really know. I dragged myself through streets that were relatively empty; I managed to glide through others. My semi-conscious mind kept replaying the moment the massive portal in the sky had sent ripples of shock through my body, sending me careening out of the sky.

Finally, I spotted the old house, a comforting and familiar sight. I tried to climb into the window but collapsed onto the ground. Thick midnight-blue blood, a Yakshi's life-force, was dripping from my arms, legs and forehead.

I leaned against the wall and slumped down, staining the old plaster with my blood. I needed to see a healer and stem this flow or I wouldn't be alive for too long. I tried to get up but my legs couldn't carry my weight. So I sat where I was, drifting in and out of consciousness.

I sensed him before I saw him. He appeared as a tall blur in the darkness, his sabre glinting by his side. I tried to get up and crawl through the window before he could reach me but my body wouldn't budge. *This is some way to die*, I thought.

As he drew closer, his scent wafted towards me. To my surprise, it was a deep, beautiful golden scent, pure and warm. He, the monster slayer, dangerous and ruthless eliminator of the supernatural, smelled of sunlight.

I tried to open my mouth and say something, perhaps shout a warning asking him to stay away from me, but no words came out. I shook my head and tried to crawl away, even though I could feel the terror slowly fading from my bones.

My eyes were blurry with tears of pain as I saw him kneel before me. I noticed the mild surprise in his eyes as he took in the wounded Yakshi sitting in a pool of her own blood. Like all those years ago when I had seen him, his face was covered with a hood. All I could see were his azure-blue eyes.

He leaned closer now, his eyes on my frangipani imprint that was glowing weakly. Then he slowly took off his hood. He was beautiful in an almost ethereal way, his face chiselled to perfection. His neck and collarbones were marked with intricate wave-shaped markings that glowed faintly, like precious stones under water.

I couldn't take my eyes off him.

'What happened?' His voice washed over me like a memory, except this time it was quiet and firm. It didn't seem like the voice of someone who wanted to drive a sabre through me.

Our eyes locked and my core shook with a furious emotion I had never experienced before. His eyes then travelled to the rivulets of blood flowing from my arms and legs.

'I was attacked...' I managed to say.

'By what?' he asked, his eyes fixed on my imprint. When I didn't reply, he said, 'Can you walk?'

I shook my head. He made no move to touch me.

'Get away from me,' I rasped, the pain suddenly melding into waves of uneasiness. 'Get aw...'

Blackness.

❊

A ball of light flooded my irises. My whole body was racked with pain and I could feel a raging fever tearing through my insides. I tried to get up but I was too weak.

He was sitting next to me.

'Where am I?' I wanted to say but the words came out in the form of a painful whimper.

'Don't,' he said.

I slumped back on what I realized was a bed and closed my eyes again. Everything faded from my consciousness and only a pair of jewel-blue eyes remained, watching me. The image was oddly comforting.

He was flying through a sky studded with stars and glowing planets. When he extended his hand, I took it. We flew together through the constellations. I could feel his eyes on me, sharp, piercing, tender. I felt oddly at home with this stranger.

But he was no stranger. 'That's the difference between a dream and its memory,' he said, as he slowly faded into the stars. I shouted his name but I was alone among a thousand galaxies…

I woke up with a start.

Was it dream, driven by delirium? *Or was it a memory?*

I sat up, not sure where I was for a second. The room was bare, save for a battered couch facing the bed I was lying on and a table in the corner, on top of which lay the jewel-crusted sabre.

'How are you feeling now?'

Startled, I turned to see him sitting at the other end of the bed, his jewel-blue eyes searched my arms and face for wounds. I mumbled something incoherent.

'Here, drink this,' he said, handing me a goblet of a clear liquid with bubbles the size of marbles. I hesitated.

'I promise I'm not trying to poison you,' he said, a faint smile touching his lips.

I felt myself blushing and quickly tipped the contents into my mouth without question. A warmth spread through me instantly.

'Better?'

'Yes.'

He regarded me with an intensity that was disconcerting.

'How did you get hurt?'

'I…I fell from the sky.'

'People don't just fall from the sky. Something happened.'

'Why should I tell you?' I spat, gathering every ounce of strength I had. 'You…you tried to kill me once.'

'Tried' being the key word here, I thought.

His answering silence was unflinching, uncomfortable. *He is not going to kill you*, I thought, almost to reassure myself. *He is not...*

With that thought, I fell back on the bed, unable to keep my eyes open any longer. Even as sleep washed over me, I was still acutely aware of his presence next to me, watching me closely.

I woke up to darkness outside, as the solitary window in the room told me. I heaved myself off the mattress and stood up. Spotting a bowl of fruit placed on a stool near the bed, I reached for an apple. The sweetness coursed through me, making me feel slightly better. I was still weak, my wounds now resembling fading blue spiderwebs on my arms. I touched one and winced. It was still raw. I spotted a sink in a corner that I hadn't seen before and limped up to it slowly. Opening a creaking tap, I held my face under the lukewarm water for a long time. When I turned, he was standing right behind me. My core jumped to life.

He wasn't human, this tall creature of incredible beauty and force. And he wasn't a monster. He was unlike anything I had ever set my eyes on.

'You scared me,' I said, suppressing the urge to scream. He turned abruptly and walked towards the open doorway that led outside.

'Why did you rescue me?' I asked. 'That's not what you normally do to my kind...'

He turned and his jewel-blue eyes fell on my Yaskhi imprint. My core was thumping hard now.

'Is she there?' he asked, his jaw tight and grim.

'Who?'

'She, that wicked bitch...'

He meant Hera.

'Don't call her a bitch,' I said, almost involuntarily. It was what I had been taught since I had been made. 'She's a Goddess.'

'Your loyalty is wasted on her,' he spat.

His anger was fire, its flames burning dangerously close to the surface.

'Who are you?' I asked, sounding a lot braver than I felt.

His eyes flashed, haunted and wild. 'You have no idea who I am?' he asked in a low voice. 'None at all?'

'No,' I frowned. 'Except that you tried to kill me about half-a-century ago. And that...' I stopped.

I was afraid to say the words out loud. It meant confronting the fact that I knew he had been stalking me for years.

'And...that Hera hates you. Obviously. But I don't know who you are.'

He walked towards me rapidly. As he did, he pulled a pair of leather gloves out of his coat and put them on. Then he grabbed my hand, turning my wrist so that the frangipani faced upwards, its glow stronger than before.

'This...' he said in a voice racked with emotion. 'Do you know what this is?'

'It's my imprint,' I said, my breath coming raggedly. 'All Yakshis have an imprint.'

His grip around my wrist tightened for a second and then he let it go, unleashing a roar that was almost animalistic in its agony. My eyes started to blur again. He was saying something now but I couldn't comprehend what it was over the roaring in my ears.

The room started to spin and I shut my eyes, not sure if I was standing or falling. I felt him standing completely still next to me, , not attempting to catch me, or hold me, or touch me...

When I came to again, I was alone. When I got my bearings, I realized that I had to get away from here, away from him. Whoever he was, he wasn't good for me. Not as a slayer, not as a stranger, not as anything.

I clutched my throbbing head as I considered my options. In the state I was in, I wouldn't make it to the portal. A wild desperation gripped me and I swung my legs off the bed and stumbled to the door. He appeared on cue, a dark sliver framed against the doorway.

'Where do you think you're going?' he said roughly.

'Let me go,' I whispered hoarsely. 'Let me...'

I brushed past him wildly, thinking he would grab me and force me back inside, but he did nothing of that sort. He stared at me, a look that was feral and somehow familiar and then, to my surprise, he stepped out of my way.

'Go,' he said.

I could feel his eyes scorching my back as I ran out the door as fast as I could. I realized he was living on the top floor of an abandoned building just outside of the city. I managed to fly to the bottom, some of my wounds beginning to bleed again. I could feel the heat rising in my eyes as my fever shot up once more.

I have no idea how I reached the portal. He hadn't come after me, and as I crawled past the gates of Atala and into the palace, I wondered if it had all been a dream. I managed to find the infirmary and struggled into one of the beds.

After that, I remembered nothing.

❧ 8 ❧

Perhaps a healer had attended to me, because when I came to, my arms were swathed in bandages. I remained in the infirmary for about three days and when I finally left, my arms were completely healed but my core was heavy. The slayer seemed to have reopened a wound I didn't even know I had.

'I don't know what has gotten into you lately,' said Vina, clicking her tongue in disapproval. 'And you won't tell me how you got those injuries either.'

She was the only one who had missed me and had come looking for me. When she found me at the infirmary, she instantly understood that no one else could know I was there – even though I refused to tell her how I got them, my injuries were clearly not the usual kind. If she had noticed I was absent for a whole night before returning to Atala, she didn't mention it.

'Do you want to sneak out again?' she asked, her eyes gleaming.

'No,' I replied. I didn't feel like going out and I didn't want to talk to anyone either.

'Suit yourself,' she shrugged and walked away.

I just wanted to be alone, perhaps hide in a secluded part of the gardens till I felt more lucid. I was also having recurring nightmares of Hera and the slayer. What had he sparked within me? It felt so familiar, and yet I couldn't quite place it, my memory strangely foggy and uncertain.

An oily nasal voice shook me out of my reverie. Mantri stood before me in the corridor, smirking like a lowly sea serpent, his two-headed body illuminated by the little light streaming in from one of the palace windows.

'Well, well, if it isn't Ardraaa,' he drawled, his four eyes taking in my figure. My Yakshi attire of a black leather bustier and pants didn't help. All of us wore the same thing when we were in Atala. We looked like moving pieces of darkness in our uniforms. I always waited for my assignments simply so I could wear something else. I loved the clothes I wore on Prithvi. They made me feel less ordinary.

I nodded at Mantri and attempted to walk past him when he put a slimy arm out to stop me.

'Why have you been missing, my precious?' he hissed. 'Where have you been hiding?'

'I haven't been hiding. I was...' I trailed off. I didn't want him to know what had happened.

'You were in the infirmary for three whole days. You think only that conniving friend of yours knew? I'm aware of everything that goes on here.'

'Then why do you ask?' I said curtly.

'Tsk. A lowly succubus dares to talk back to me? You know what I'm capable of, don't you?'

He always called me a succubus. It's the lowest name anyone could give us. It reduced us to base creatures and nothing else. I watched him, malice dripping from the corners of his twisted mouth, the other one pursed and silent, his four eyes shining with glee, and I felt sickness rising to the back of my throat.

'Yes, Mantri. And, no, you don't scare me.'

'I wonder what our mistress will think of your injuries,' he said silkily. 'It is entirely possible I might accidently let it slip in our conversation when she summons me next.'

'As I said, you don't scare me. Go ahead. Tell her. Where is she, anyway?'

'How dare you ask of her whereabouts? It is sacrilege.' He glared and took a step closer. 'There are ways, you know, of keeping secrets in this place. It isn't dissimilar to how you take them.' The implication was obvious.

'I have to go,' I said, attempting to walk past him once more. He gripped my shoulder and pushed me back, pinning me harshly against the window. He brought his heads close to mine and I could see head number two's mouth clearly as his hands closed around my neck. Its lips seemed not so much stitched together as glued together in one long sticky line. I was so fascinated by it that I barely heard what he was saying.

'...you are up to? I saw you that day, near the forbidden part of the palace. And I also knew of your blood moon sojourn. Nothing escapes my notice, succubus. Do you know the consequences of what you did?' I heard the last slimy trail of his threat.

'And what is it that you think I did? Let me go, Mantri, or…'

'Or what?' he sneered.

'What do you want?' I said, panting. His hand was still around my neck but it was his smell that was choking me.

'Let me tell you what I want to do with you,' he cackled, his other head rolling its eyes in glee. His face was twisted with lust.

'You really think Hera will care if one of her wormy little succubi went missing? I doubt she will even notice. When

I'm done with you, your beautiful body will be fed to the mer dogs. Not a trace will remain of you.'

Maybe some of the others would give in during moments like these, but not me. As a slithering arm wound around my waist to pull me closer, I sprang into action.

A moment later he was on the floor, clutching his crotch, his face twisted in pain, spluttering expletives. Aah, that gave me immense pleasure. I wondered if I should throw in a punch or two, but stopped. The consequences, well...

I took a deep breath and walked away, stepping past his heads; the dumb-mouthed one sniffed in disdain as my heel brushed its nose.

I headed back to my pod, shaking in anger. 'Don't mind him, dear,' said my mirror when I picked it up. 'You have other troubles to attend to.'

'Indeed I do,' I murmured, closing my eyes. Fatigue washed over me and I slipped into an uneasy sleep that brought forth myriad dreams. I was walking along an empty passage, covered in blood. The frangipanis craned their necks and kissed my shoulders. I could hear their hushed whispers in the wind. They wanted my blood. The passage got darker as I walked on, shadows appearing on the walls and pillars. Two-headed creatures; growling, slithering mer dogs; electric sky portals, beasts in forbidden towers; slayers with jewel-blue eyes who smelt like sunshine; Hera...

I turned a corner and realized it led to the forbidden part of the palace – the tower with the Thing. 'Stop, Ardra! Go no further,' the frangipanis seemed to whisper.

'Go on, go on, Ardra! The Thing in the tower has been waiting for you,' said the shadows. I walked on, a deep sense of dread creeping into me. *It's just a dream*, I said to myself. *No one can hurt you in a dream. Go on up the tower, see what lives there...*

The tower. Those spiralling steps and that voice, no, noise…

I kept walking towards it and I felt that odd rustle in my core. As I made my way up the staircase, the frangipanis behind me began to hiss. My legs suddenly felt like lead. Each step was heavy, as if something was pulling me back.

You can go back now. You can choose to wake up…

But I kept going. When I reached the top of the staircase I felt a painful tug in my core, a familiar feeling of uneasiness. Odd lights danced before my eyes. I thought I could hear the frangipanis urging me to return but they were so far away. It couldn't be them…or maybe it was – anything could happen in a dream.

That odd rustle again… This time it was clearer, sounding like something scaly and rough brushing against a wall. Was there something scaly and rough inside the tower?

My hand brushed against the massive door, and as I did, spikes sprang up – sharp long spikes laced with poison.

Wow, Hera, you really don't want people to see what you have up here, I thought. I was feeling oddly brave. Maybe it was easier to feel brave in a dream.

I could feel the thing on the other side of the door. It was crouching, restless and dark. Maybe it sensed me. What was it? A giant mer dog? Hera's pet monster?

'Hera already has a pet monster – you,' said the frangipani, or was it a voice inside me?

I felt something flickering to life, like an eyelid fluttering open, and a sharp stab of pain inside my head…

Flicker, flicker, flicker.

My hand reached out for the flower-shaped knob and I found myself admiring the beauty of the door, with its jewelled tapestry and carved edges…and no spikes.

Where had the spikes gone? Had my dream removed the spikes?

That sharp jolt of pain again.

Suddenly, I could hear a voice on the other side of the door — a voice that seeped into my core. I opened my eyes in terror as I realized I wasn't dreaming any more. And I wasn't in the tower. And this wasn't the door with the spikes. This was another one, one which I didn't have access to. And that voice…it was Hera! I was outside Hera's room.

✢ 9 ✢

I was standing outside the most dangerous room in the world and I wasn't dreaming. Nothing would save me if I were found here. I would be burnt to char by her fury because Hera hates intruders. I should have turned back then. And yet…

The door was ajar, just a crack. This time I didn't need the shadows on the wall to urge me on… I was awake and fully aware of what I was doing.

I stayed and listened. Simply because I had to. It wasn't idle curiosity. It was this sense of urgency I felt that told me I was about to learn something important even if I didn't know what it was. Suddenly, a shroud of darkness covered me from head to toe and I knew the shadow creatures had found me. They would protect me, these creatures that looked like shapeless hats with saucer-like eyes, made of dark dank corners and sunless dungeons. They always found people who needed to be hid. I found them depressing and sad but today I was grateful for them.

Hera's voice wafted through the door like an icy draft. A shiver shot up my spine and I knew then, almost as a premonition, that I was very afraid of what I was going to hear. I could see her through the crack in the door and even the slivered Hera, the parts of her I could see terrified me. She was impossibly tall and I could see a golden snake in her flaming fire-like hair gleaming like an adornment. She was beautiful, but in the way of a force of nature gone rogue – as if something exquisite and perfect had turned on itself, creating a creature that was full of darkness and terrible beauty.

She paced up and down impatiently in front a huge silvery orb with bronzed arms rising from inside to frame it. A beautiful mirror; old, very old and burdened with so much magic. The mirror was positioned right where I could see it and I drew in a deep breath as one of the arms slowly pointed a finger towards the door – at me – and something within the mirror seemed to wink, as if my eavesdropping was a cosy secret between two girlfriends. My core stopped and started as the mirror shrugged, its surface rippling as it did.

A one-eyed raven flew around the room, a scrawny bird named Gaggii that belonged to Hera.

Hera looked into the mirror and the surface fogged up. Sepulchral creatures seemed to lurk within. They swirled around her, whispering, as she traced the beautiful contours of her face, running her long fingers over its striking features. She caressed her under-eyes and the creatures in the mirror cackled.

Someone behind her coughed politely. Gaggii cawed and flew to Hera's shoulder.

Hera turned, her face lined with disdain. The humped, bent-over thing that had coughed hobbled closer to her.

I realized it was Dakini, the old crone. The oldest crone, with the soul of a vulture. She had once belonged to a realm that no longer existed. The story goes that when her home was burnt down and she had nowhere to go, Hera took her in. Since then they have been queen and crone, steeped in dark magic and sorcery. The crone would do Hera's bidding, however horrible the command.

The crone stood as close to Hera as she was allowed.

'It didn't work. You said it would…' Hera's voice was low and furious. 'That werewolf was a waste of time…'

'I never said it would work, O Mistress of Desire. I said we must try. Again and again we must…' said the crone.

'It was never going to work with an ordinary hybrid was it? You simply wasted my time, you old bag of bones. And on a blood moon night, too.'

The crone sighed.

'The Unspeakable demands a sort of penance, O Queen. An ardent persistence…'

'I wish you wouldn't call it that,' spat Hera. 'The Unspeakable is a banned thing…'

'What store do you keep by the laws of this world, O Queen? They mean nothing to you…'

'Nothing,' murmured Hera. 'Nothing at all. And yet every time I fail…' she traced the lines of her face. 'This happens. Tell me how to stop it.'

'Stop it?' The old crone sniggered. 'The oldest magic cannot stop what the heart has started. Especially one as poisonous as yours.'

Hera darted her a sharp look.

'Oh, I meant that as a compliment, O Queen of Desire. Poison has its own potent beauty, doesn't it, an insidious eternal power of its own. And yours is a curse from a powerful magic gone wrong. Oh that black night of mistakes. To stop this, O Queen of Desire, and to become *that*, you will need to do the Unspeakable. Again. We need to achieve two things. And both can be done with one tricky spell. If not, those lines will flow like rivers on your face, and one day those rivers will dry up and you will be nothing but a withered landscape. An ordinary dark goddess...'

'Dakini!'

'A werewolf has tainted magic within him. It is a useless exercise and I had warned you. We need someone pure and good. We need a...'

Hera raised an eyebrow.

'A what?' Her voice cracked like a whip.

Dakini lowered her voice and whispered something into Hera's ear. I couldn't catch the words. All I heard was a sharp intake of breath and Hera's little shout of anger.

'*NO!* I can't. It's too risky. And even if we wanted to where would we find one? There hasn't been one in the last 500 years.'

'We must look high and low. The spell failed last time because we created one. Now we need another to undo it.'

'A ridiculous, impossible idea. We may not care for the rules but the other realms do. What you intend will never happen. Leave, Dakini! And don't return until you have a better plan.'

'A better plan? Your entire life, your ambition, now hinges on one mistake. You have spent 500 years trying to reverse its effects. The secrets help, O Queen, they do. But for how long? Prithvi grows weaker. It fails to sustain magic of any kind. How long will your girls bring you dark things enough to fire your power?'

'Ask yourself that, you incompetent hag. And now I have to hide in here on blood moon nights, for the spell will be fatal to me if I, even by mistake, allow a secret-taking.'

'Aaah…Mantri mentioned something, O Queen. The girl, she…she was out on the night of the blood moon.'

'WHAT?'

'It's of no consequence now. But I shudder to think… There must have been some mistake in the log books.'

'Did she take secrets? Because that would be…'

'No, it seems she returned empty. Nothing happened.'

'Nothing happened! Had she taken secrets and had I met her to retrieve them…' Hera whispered, her voice trembling a little. 'Think of what might have happened. This is because of your own incompetence,' she roared.

'I have always warned you in time, haven't I? You are so forgetful, O Queen. I warn you from stepping out on blood moon nights. Oh, the long shadows of spells gone wrong!'

Hera lunged forward and caught the crone by her throat. The crone gasped and spat, 'Your mistakes are bigger than your ambition, O Queen…'

A snarl of anger escaped Hera and she threw the crone back with force. The old witch hit the ground with a brittle sound.

'And whose foolishness was that a result of? Whose lethal carelessness?' Hera growled.

'Whose indeed? A foolish jealous woman and her need to conquer everything, even love…'

The last two words seemed to have struck home as something shattered as it fell to the ground and the room filled with hissing wails and shrouded screams. Hera had destroyed her mirror and the creatures within. Some of them slipped out of the silver water that was gushing out of the orb, screaming and moaning. Some of them evaporated as they touched the diamond floor and others flailed about gasping and coughing.

Hera kicked a couple of them to the side and they dragged themselves out of the room, slimy and mournful.

I heard a roar, and a blast of iciness engulfed the whole place. Hera was angry. Angry and sad.

'Have a heart, Your Highness...' sniggered Dakini.

Hera swung around, her eyes flashing with madness. 'Out, you ugly old piece of rubbish! Leave and do not return until you have the answers. And as for the Unspeakable, mention it again and I will rip your tongue out and feed it to the mer dogs.'

The crone cackled with laughter. 'You amuse me, O Mistress of Phantoms. *"Feed my tongue to the mer dogs."* I was there when they were thought of, when this place was just a piece of rock and you were deciding whether that sea should be a sea or a jungle full of ghosts. Feed *me* to the mer dogs, indeed.'

With that she walked out. I could hear advancing footsteps and I shrank back into the shadows as Dakini tottered out muttering 'silly girl with her childish ideas'.

She paused in the passage and sniffed. Could she smell me? My Yakshi blood? She paused and looked in the direction of the shadows that hid me. For a second I thought she had seen me, but she walked away, leaning on her stick, sly-eyed and mean-mouthed, her leathery robes trailing behind her like a mangy coat.

I stayed there in the shadows, everything that I had overheard replaying in my mind. Nothing that was said in that room made any sense to me, and yet I felt like I was meant to understand. And what was that about the blood moon? The last blood moon was just a few days ago – the night I went out. Something was terribly wrong here. And that last sacrifice I had witnessed with a mermaid had been on a night when the moon was red.

Is that why Hera didn't meet me that night? I thought. *Because something about that blood moon would prove fatal to her? They had no idea that I had taken secrets that night...*

Something tugged at my feet and I was pulled out of my thoughts. It was one of those slimy creatures from the mirror. It was dying and I could hear its deep rasping breathing as it clung on to my leg with its slimy tentacle-like hands.

'Let go,' I whispered. '*Let go...*' The creature made horrible dying sounds and one of the shadow creatures whimpered.

One strange creature dying on me was enough; I didn't need another frightened to death around me as well. I had to get out of there. I tried wrestling my leg out from the mirror creature's grip but it held on tightly, its breathing getting hoarser. *Great, my leg is going to be its tombstone.* I put a hand out to soothe the whimpering shadow creature and as I did it shrank back against the wall with a little screech. I looked up from the dying mirror creature and right into Gaggii's one black beady eye.

The raven had seen me.

☩ 10 ☩

I stared back, unflinching and in that second I felt no fear, no trepidation. But I knew that if Gaggii had seen me she would tell Hera. And that would not bode well at all.

So I ran. It seemed like the stupidest, weakest thing to do, to run from Hera and her raven but that's what I did. The shadow creature was still with me, screeching and mewing and then it bounded ahead. I didn't turn back but I could hear Gaggii cawing. The shadow creature had engulfed Gaggii in temporary darkness, allowing me some time to try and get away. She would, of course, shake off the poor thing and run to her mistress. If I could just get to the portal before she got to me...

I flew past the skull gates and to the portal outside, the weird shield-like object that hung outside the gates. I couldn't believe it – I had made it. And the shadow creature had returned to me and that could only mean Gaggii had managed to fend it off and head back to Hera. I didn't have much time.

I ran towards the portal and then stopped in my tracks.

Mantri was leaning against the portal, smirking, a bit of drool leaking out of his mouth. The other head was rolling its eyes and bobbing with a telltale air.

'Well, well...if it isn't my favourite succubus. Twice in the same evening! Lucky me. Heading for a night out on the town, are we?'

He threw a glance at the shadow creature on my shoulder. 'And would that be your date for tonight?'

'Let me pass, Mantri. We can save this chat for another time...'

'Another time?' He drawled on, his oily voice gleeful. 'I may be mistaken but I believe there will be no other time. Your time is up. Hera just sent me a signal. You think that I would just be hanging out here for fun?'

Damn!

I took a step forward. The coward that he was, he took one backwards. I could take him easily in a fight but I didn't have the time. I could only do one thing. So I did it. I flung the shadow creature at him. It went hurtling, squealing at the top of its voice, and hit him with a force of darkness he wasn't expecting. I ran to the portal but he had closed it. *Damn, damn Mantri.*

And so I ran again. As I dashed past the frangipanis with their whispering blooms and the tall trees with the jewelled flowers, I realized I was once again heading in a direction my feet, my dreams, seemed to take me automatically. Towards the tower. The shadow creature caught up with me again and I could feel it picking at my clothes making pitiful noises. It didn't want me to go up the tower. No one in their right senses would. I reached the bottom of the tower and paused. Why? Why the tower? I couldn't possibly escape from there. And yet...

I was surprised no one had come after me. No guards, no obedient Yakshis, no Gaggii. It was almost ominous, this lack of interest in my escape except that of Mantri's.

I decided to go up the tower regardless. Some strange monster instinct, call it a Yakshi's seventh sense, told me to go to the room at the top. I started ascending the stairs with a calm I did not recognize. I paused again after two flights and the shadow creature made a gulping noise.

'It's okay,' I murmured. 'We are going to be okay.' I felt a strange feeling wash over me. The kind that made me uncomfortable, gave me nightmares. *I should turn back. I should go back, and find a proper route of escape*, I thought.

The shadow creature picked at my sleeve again. 'Stop it,' I said. 'I've decided to turn back...'

Just as I said that, the creature dashed in front of me and quivered there, shaking its head frantically and whimpering. 'What is it?' I asked. 'What are you trying to tell me?'

It took hold of my hand and pulled it frantically. I realized it wasn't pulling me backwards. It was egging me on. It was trying to tell me something.

'You know something, don't you? You know a route of escape up there.'

The creature nodded in enthusiasm. 'If you're wrong and this is a trap, I will feed you to the light wells,' I threatened, and the creature let out a loud squeal.

'Ssshhh, I was joking. Now let's see…'

I started to climb the stairs again, but when I was outside the door – the one with the venomous spikes – I hesitated. I had been here before, in a dream. And yet when I had opened my eyes I had found myself outside Hera's chambers. Was this some sort of a trick? Some sly magic designed to fool anyone who might attempt to find out what lay on the other side of the door?

I put a hand out and touched the wolf-head door knob. The spikes sprung out, making a sharp sound. As I turned the knob, the spikes moved forward to attack me – but I was too quick for them. I pushed the door open and darted in.

That was close.

The shadow creature tugged at my sleeve. 'Yes, let's find the portal, if there is one here. Come on!' I took a breath and looked around.

The room was empty. But it wasn't the lack of things that struck me – it was the sense of desperate desolation I suddenly felt. I felt sad, so immensely sad in this room that I thought my core would break.

It was a white and circular room, the starkness somehow making it seem even more bare. There was only one window – the window through which I had spotted someone or something moving in the room the day I had wandered into the forbidden part of the gardens. I looked around for something that could be a portal but I spotted nothing.

'Come on, let's do this fast,' I whispered to the creature. 'Let's do this before whatever lives here spots us.'

But as far as I could see, there was no sign of any life here. The room at the top of the tower was sad and forlorn and empty. The shadow creature wafted ahead in front me, and I realized it was going towards a door at the other end of the room. A tiny door, so white, so inconspicuous, that I had almost missed it. It had a little wolf-head knob that whirred and turned as soon as I touched it.

Don't go in, my Yakshi seventh sense whispered, but I ignored it and walked into room on the other side.

The portal I had been looking for was in the corner of the room. Except it was also a human corpse. With a gaping hole in the middle of it. Shutting my eyes, I found myself hoping that this was a dream...just a horrible nightmare.

I am a monster and I have seen some pretty terrible things but a human corpse portal is not one of them.

Before I could take another step, I heard a thick rustling behind me and I froze – something was just outside the door.

The shadow creature squeaked and pulled my hand frantically, propelling me towards the corpse portal. I heard the door creak open behind us but I couldn't bring myself to look back. I could feel it behind me – heavy, scaly, its breath making that rustling sound that I was now so familiar with, like the racket of a hundred crickets.

The shadow creature was hysterical by now. Whatever it was, it advanced slowly, like big beasts approach their prey. I could see a giant shadow on the wall and just as I was about to turn and face it, the shadow creature pushed me and I fell right through the portal, hurtling towards Prithvi, just as a great big growl bellowed behind me.

I landed in Prithvi with a thud. Clearly, the shadow creature was stronger than I had imagined. Wincing, I sat up and looked around. I was on a deserted railway track. There wasn't a soul around except the rats scurrying along the tracks. I pushed myself up, picked a direction and began walking, wondering what to do next. I couldn't return to Atala, that was for certain. I would be killed even before I could reach the gates. In that moment, I felt utterly alone; there wasn't a single person I could turn to. Vina belonged to Atala and Hera, and enlisting her help would only put her in danger. I thought about the shadow creature and how I had become used to its company – and how it had saved my life.

A feeling of sorrow washed over me I remembered the white room. And the thing, the beast...what was it? As I walked along the dusty abandoned tracks, I wondered if the beast would have harmed me. A thing that gave the tower such a sad, desolate air somehow didn't seem very dangerous to me. Even with my back turned to it, I hadn't felt threatened. If the shadow creature hadn't pushed me down the portal maybe I would have found out more.

I was so lost in my thoughts that I did not notice the thick grey fog that had enveloped the surroundings. The sun went down, leaving behind a smudge of red and the fog swirled around me as I trudged on. It was only when my Yakshi sense bristled again that I stopped.

Everything was quiet...too quiet. A deathly stillness that smelled of fear.

I rose in the air, deciding flight would be the best option in case I encountered something dangerous. I glided along the tracks until I heard a familiar sound.

I rose a little higher to see what could have caused it, hoping it wasn't what I thought it was.

Perched on a lamp post, sepulchral, unflinching, sullen, was the one-eyed raven, Gaggii.

If she was here then that could only mean one thing.

✦ 11 ✦

A flash of light and my core exploded. I clutched my chest, trying to breathe. Something grabbed my throat, choking the life out of me. I wrestled with it but there was nothing to fight against. I fell to the ground, gasping for breath, this unseen force still at my throat.

I tried to scream but no sound would come out. I didn't want to give up but my core was weakening. *This is it*, I thought. *I'm going to die…*

Another flash of purple light flooded my face and the grip on my throat loosened. My breath came back in slow, painful gasps.

Gaggii swooped down and circled above me. She let out a guttural caw and swooped out of sight. I sat up, dreading what was coming. And then I saw her, standing next to the lamp post.

Hera.

She had the force of a thousand desert storms.

She smiled at me as I slowly got up. The smile sent an unholy shiver down my spine.

'Did you feel the pain?' she asked in a mock concerned voice.

'Did I... Oh yes, I did,' I gasped.

Hera circled me, her long purple robes billowing in the wind. She resembled a mythical sea goddess – I half expected her tongue to be forked and filled with venom.

'Good! My new spell worked then. Isn't it a wonderful feeling when that happens?' She laughed, a tinkling, derisive noise.

I looked at her disbelievingly, still panting.

After a pause, she said, raising an eyebrow, 'I'm not sure I trained my girls to lurk and listen in corridors.'

'I wasn't lurking...'

'Of course you were...except, of course, my secrets aren't yours for the taking.'

'I didn't hear any of your secrets, Hera...'

'What did you hear exactly? Tell me and I will...'

'Let me go?'

'*Let you go?*' she laughed again. 'Of course not. Depending on what you tell me, I will decide whether it will be your life or your freedom...'

'Isn't that the same thing?'

'Don't play with me, you silly girl!'

She looked at me through her cold crystal eyes and I felt a kind of fear I had never felt before. And yet the words that came out of my mouth were reckless.

'Then while we are answering questions, I want to know... why can't you retrieve secrets on a blood moon night?'

She raised her eyebrows and then sighed. 'Ardra, my darling, you were not even supposed to go out that night. There must have been some mistake.'

She must have seen the shock on my face because she took

a step towards me slowly. 'What happened that night?' she asked gritting her teeth.

'I…I went out. I met someone…and I took his secrets.'

'You TOOK secrets that night?'

'Yes.'

'Where are they?'

I fell silent. I was going to die anyway, why make it worse by telling her that something went wrong?

Her eyes bored into me. 'You didn't take any secrets that night.'

Her words felt like a whiplash across my core.

'I did! I did what I always do and I came away with that man's secrets – '

'You didn't take any secrets, Ardra. I would know instantly if one of my Yakshis had succeeded in secret-taking. I made you, remember?'

I fell silent. It had only then dawned on me that I hadn't really taken any secrets from Dwai. Which explained how strange I was feeling. But…but if I didn't take any secrets from him, then that meant…

'HE IS ALIVE, Ardra. Because you made a silly mistake, he is alive. If you don't take someone's secrets they don't die, you fool!' she screamed.

I looked up at her.

'You silly girl, do you realize what you have done? *You let a human live.* Now what do you think he is going to do. He is going TO TALK ABOUT IT!'

'I'll find him tonight. And I'll kill him…'

'Are you utterly brainless?' Hera's eyes were red with anger, their irises gleaming like opals.

'If you couldn't kill him once, you can't kill him. EVER. AGAIN.'

53

I was stunned. How is it that no one had ever told me any of this?

Gaggii cawed and circled Hera. She shook her head in what I assumed was sadness.

'This is all so tragic. First, I find you lurking like a lowly spy outside my door and then I realize you can't even do your job…'

'But why would it have been fatal if you had come that day to retreive secrets?' I interrupted. 'Is it because of your spell gone wrong or is it something to do with the blood moon?'

Hera's eyes widened in shock.

'Stupid succubus…how dare you question me!' she snarled.

I rose in the air again. I was feeling very reckless. If I must die, I decided, then I would do it in style. She raised her head and looked at me, her eyes narrowing. Then she spoke, her voice unusually low. 'I could fly once, a long time ago… I can't anymore. I have to rely on Gaggii for aerial transportation. I can't fly because of a stupid mistake years ago…'

I circled her cautiously, expecting an attack any minute. But she had grown strangely pensive. She looked at me again and said quietly, 'Even your memories belong to me. Every one of them. I take them away and you will be reduced to a mere husk. It is a particularly joyful way of killing a Yakshi. Take all her memories, all the residue of the secrets within her and watch her die…slowly, as her core shrivels and runs out of life force.'

'Is that an Unspeakable act too?' I said casually, and my words had the effect I desired.

'You wormy little thing!' she spat. 'If you knew what the Unspeakable was…if you knew what it did…to me… how dare you speak of it so lightly?'

'I'm curious,' I said. 'You're going to kill me anyway. Tell me what the Unspeakable is. It's my…dying wish.'

Her eyes narrowed. 'Dying wish…' she repeated softly. And then she laughed, a bitter, mirthless sound. In a lightning strike of a second, she lunged forward, grabbing my throat. I could feel her demonic fire singeing my skin.

'Stupid Yakshi. You want to pit your pitiful life of 500 years against mine? Do you know how long I have been around? There isn't a measure of time for it. That's how long!'

I could see into the depths of Hera's mad eyes. I could see her skin, shining like glass, unreal in its sheen. And yet, underneath the sheen was a crumbly dryness. Up close, it wasn't very beautiful. It was as if she was slowly withering, falling apart. *What was keeping her together, then, for all these years?*

'So many secrets, Hera, curdling your soul like poison…' I gasped.

She let go of my throat and I fell back, struggling for breath.

'You can rot forever in the dungeons,' she whispered. I shivered a little, not from fear but from the force of her hate, emanating from her half-hooded eyes.

The snake glided down Hera's hair and raised its head, poised at her shoulder. It seemed to whisper something into her ear. Gaggii cawed again and flew to her shoulder. In that moment, she looked every inch the ancient myth that she was. Snake on one shoulder. Raven on the other. Beautiful, terrible, deathly.

Then, the air shook with a strange electricity. She looked up sharply. Something – or was it someone? – had caught her attention.

Gaggii flew off Hera's shoulder, circling the spot we were in. I felt a sudden lightness in the air and the thick blanket of fog that was surrounding us started thinning. A circular orb of light slowly wafted in, glowing, crackling, and sending off little lightning shafts of phosphorescent energy into the air around it. Gaggii circled above the orb uncertainly. After a moment, she screeched in warning. Hera stiffened and drew in a deep breath.

He stepped out of the orb like a God, his aura captivating, an air of determination about him. His eyes, his beautiful jewel-blue eyes, looked straight at Hera. There was no hate in them, just an unsettling cold anger.

'Aah, what timing…' she muttered. 'Dara.'

It was the monster slayer. *What was he doing here?* My core started pounding as the faint whisper of a memory returned.

'I have waited very long for this moment,' he said. His eyes stayed on Hera, unflinching. Never looking at me.

Hera snorted in disgust. She held up a hand as if to dismiss Dara but he didn't budge. They stood there facing each other like two Gods in some fantastical battle that seemed a little incongruous, by a deserted railway track. They belonged to another time, surrounded by strange beasts in armour and a storm of weapons raining from the sky.

'Okay, so you know where all my portals are. Took you centuries to figure it out, didn't it? Pathetic, that you wait around wondering how you can get in. Capturing my Yakshis didn't work either. You are so useless. Nothing has changed.'

'Nothing?' he asked quietly.

Hera sniffed in disdain.

'Let her go,' he said, to my surprise. He still wouldn't look at me.

'She is just an inconsequential Yakshi,' said Hera, malice evident in her tone. 'Why do you care?'

His eyes narrowed and he repeated, 'I said, let her go. Let

her go and we can get on with settling old dues.'

Hera laughed. 'I have no time for old dues, you fool. Don't you know who I am, what I have become. Be gone. I have things to take care of.'

Dara smiled. It was a sad smile, tinged with a kind of terrible truth.

'Let her go.'

Hera laughed cruelly and shook her head. She turned to look at me and the pain in my core began once more. Deep, excruciating pain. Perhaps I was screaming but I couldn't be sure. I crumbled to my knees, clutching my head. I wasn't sure I could hold on any longer.

Finally our eyes met – Dara's and mine. In that moment, I noticed something in them that I hadn't noticed before – heartbreak. Deep, soul-crushing heartbreak. He looked at me with an understanding of something that bound us, and I felt it too.

Oddly, I felt a sense of having been here before. I felt like I had stepped into some dusty long-forgotten passage of my own memory. I wanted to stay here, in this place, walk a little further towards this strange story at the end of the passage, but my mind was beginning to cloud over with pain...

Hera let out a cruel laugh and Dara's eyes turned from me to her. I watched out of my half-shut eyes as the evil goddess and the slayer turned to face each other.

Then, as abruptly as it had begun, the pain in my head stopped in a burst of silver light. There was that light again, streaming from him like a river. It was sharp and piercing, invading Hera's skin. It passed through mine too but it didn't seem to affect me the way it did her. She turned opaque. Her mouth opened in a scream but it only sounded like a faint echo.

He watched her unemotionally for a few seconds and then turned his eyes towards me.

'Go,' he urged.

'What about you?' I blurted.

'I said go.'

I wanted to stay. I wanted to know what was in that dark forgotten passage of my memory.

'GO!'

I got up slowly, my core still shaky as Hera crumbled to the ground. She was now a ghost, an echo, a shape of nothingness. She looked at me, her crystal irises cloudy. I could see the questions in her eyes. I had questions of my own, but right then, I knew I had to I turn and walk away. This ghost Hera, powerless and pale, would not come after me, I knew. It was as if her life force was fading out of her in waves.

Dara turned to me. I looked into his jewel eyes, hoping to find some answers, but all I could see was sadness. He nodded his head curtly, a command to leave. I walked away swiftly, not looking back even though I was hoping he would call me back.

'Dara,' I turned again, changing my mind. He seemed to sense it.

A sudden wave of light and suddenly I couldn't see them anymore. He had put up a force field of some sort, blocking me out. I had no choice but to leave. When I had gained some distance, I took flight. Mid-air, I could feel the tears streaming down my cheeks. Maybe I would never find the answers I wanted. Maybe I had imagined it all. But in that moment, mid-flight, while moondust scattered all around me, I felt that my strange life was about to get stranger.

If only I had known how much.

The wings of Gaggii brought her back to Atala. She was almost lifeless, drained of light and her eyes were weak and watery like the crone's. The one-eyed raven dropped her gently in the garden, where the frangipanis shrank back in terror at the sight of her. The black sun receded into its shell. The jewelled trees stopped whispering.

'The mirror,' she gasped.

Gaggii cawed.

'Take me to the mirror, you stupid bird.'

The bird circled her and flapped its wings.

'I want to see what I look like. Take me to the mirror!' she commanded, her breath coming in gasps.

Gaggii flew lower and Hera touched her wing. The bird rose again, carrying her mistress into the Palace of Vishara. A few Yakshis walking down the halls gasped at the sight of their mistress. Mantri, who was in his chambers, heard the flapping of Gaggii's wings and he also heard his mistress wail. He rushed out of his room in search of her.

He found her in front of her mirror, a deformed squishy orb ever since she had shattered it. It had managed to put itself back, even save some of its creatures, who skulked into the shadows when they saw her.

Hera, weak, unable to stand, collapsed on the rug on the floor. The mirror curved low to meet her. Gaggii watched them, mirror and mistress, with her one eye, silent and knowing.

Hera peered into the foggy quicksilver. The mirror shuddered. The creatures inside whined and wept.

'Tell them to stop whining,' she clenched her teeth.

Something within the mirror sighed. 'I wish I could, O Queen of Desire. But they won't stop until you do...they are but a reflection of you. It is not their fault.'

She let out a snarl of derision and then touched the mirror. The surface quivered and the creatures within hid their faces and retreated further into the blackness.

She began to weep, her head between her hands, while Gaggi circled her, pecking at her robes in concern.

'My sweet mistress...' Mantri drawled, keeping a safe distance.

She looked up at him and he struggled to not flinch. Her ageless, perfect face was a tattered ruin. Her skin sagged like rotting fish and her hair, once flaming fire, was a dead river of sooty hue. But it was her mouth that terrified him. It had lost its fullness, the ruby red seductiveness and the power of its deadly smile... Mantri coughed and his twin head closed its eyes dramatically and sighed.

'My sweet mistress...' he repeated softly.

'I can't stop it,' she sobbed, her rage flowing out in salt and water. 'I can't stop it anymore, Mantri. I'm doomed. Even Dara got the better of me today. All because of that...' she trailed off. 'I should have known...' She let out a harsh cry and buried her face in her hands.

'Shall I summon the crone, O Queen?'

'Dakini! Useless hag. No, I have to find other means. I have to...'

'She could be right, my mistress. Perhaps the only way is the Unspeakable. Destiny does repeat itself,' his drawl was quiet, carefully injected with Mantri's wisdom.

'I took destiny by its scrawny neck and threw it into the Black Dwarf Sea once, remember?'

'Of course, but the fate stars…they are infinite, O Queen. And they yield to temptation – the temptation of magic.'

'The Unspeakable isn't magic. And I have paid the price for it once already – this, here, everything around me is the price. Including *you*,' she spat.

The insult wasn't lost on Mantri. His twin head rolled its eyes and his own mouth twitched in anger.

'You are distraught right now, O Queen. Give it time and we will find a way – '

'THERE IS NO WAY! I'm *doomed.*'

The mirror sighed and spoke in a tone tinged with melancholy. Its language was old and not of any of the worlds known or unknown.

What you dream, what you darkly desire,
Find it by trial or by fire.
Seek it high and seek it low,
Search the skies or the realms below.
Look everywhere but beware,
The deepest magic, the strongest spell
Will not change what the stars foretell.

'See, my mistress? Even the mirror agrees. What you seek, what your heart truly desires, will not come by easily.'

'It sounded more like a warning to me,' said Hera. 'And the magic,' she continued in a low voice, 'for want of a better name, was thwarted, you know that. We need to undo it. And for that I will need something that shouldn't exist anymore, anywhere. Do I have to spell all this out to you, you twin-headed git?'

'No, sweet mistress,' Mantri said, his fists clenched behind his back. 'But there is always a way. If there is anything our long and arduous lives have taught us, it is that there is always a way…'

'Everything has changed. The doors have been shut and boarded. I can't travel freely anymore to another world if I wish to. I cannot do anything, anymore because of the infernal rules.'

'Rules are meant to be bent, O Queen. Let me go out and find what you seek. We will reverse this magic…'

She didn't even seem to be listening to him. She was watching the mirror intently, and the creatures within stared at her, fearful and cowering. The mirror sighed and fogged over again.

'The girl, the succubus…she has escaped, I presume?' Mantri asked cautiously.

'The girl…and him… He has returned, Mantri. After all this time…'

Mantri flinched. 'You mean…'

'Yes, Dara. This is his work,' her hands smeared her face. 'He seems more powerful than ever before. If not for the force field I managed to put up and for Gaggii, I'm sure he would have killed me. If he manages to find passage into Atala…'

'He won't,' said Mantri. 'Unless…'

'NO!' she shouted. 'I will *not* let her. Mantri, it was humiliating to watch him help her escape. She has no idea, does she, of what he and I share? I will destroy both of them. I will.'

'You might want to keep her alive, O Queen.'

She threw him a glance. 'Yes, alive, but she will wish she were dead. Prepare the dungeons. And she found the portal in the tower – do you realize how dangerous that is? I want a Rakshasa stationed outside the tower.'

'Yes, O Queen, but even they…'

'Do it! I don't care how many it takes to keep it contained.'

Mantri nodded. There was a significant pause before she

spoke next, almost as if she was afraid of what she was going to say. 'Do you think they…they crossed paths?' she asked without looking at her two-headed minister.

'I doubt it, O Queen. If they did, the story might have turned out differently. She may have…'

She put up a hand and he fell silent.

'Find me what I need, Mantri, and I will reverse this cruel affliction of yours.'

He nodded, his eyes brightening with greed.

'Meanwhile, I will travel to the only place that might give me some answers…'

She dismissed him with a flick of her hand. He bowed low and backed out of the room. After he left, Gaggii swooped down on Hera's shoulder. She stroked the bird absently.

'Gaggii, I have never lost, but I have never really won either. Perhaps it is time to change that. But, for now, some potion to revive my beauty. Without it I am just an ordinary queen. Tell the healers to send me some.'

The bird cawed and flew out of the room. The mirror sighed once again. The black sun outside glowered and sent off sparks of soot. Atala shuddered in the memory of a story that was about to be retold.

❧ 13 ❧

The sea had swallowed him whole. He fought for air, grasped at strange creatures gliding past him, watched rainbows of light shimmer around him underwater. She was there; she floated alongside him, her dark-as-night hair enveloping them like a cloud. He looked into her eyes and he saw someone else… It was her, the girl from his sketch. No, it couldn't be.

He hit the bottom of the water with a soft thud and wafted like a weightless doll among the seaweed. He didn't mind drowning, he realized. He wafted towards the dream; it was a shimmering light with a song. Could light sing? He didn't know. He didn't want to know. The music seemed to come from within him. He opened his eyes…and there she was, the girl from his sketch. The music was her, her eyes were full of the strange creatures in the sea, green like new magic from the skies…no, they were brown and soft like earth that had just made love to rain. Why did he say that? How did he know that?

The feeling engulfed him while she smiled. It was her, the nymph with green eyes; her magic was this sea. He wanted to smile back but instead he fell into her eyes. Bottomless, unfathomable, he swirled in its depths. Something pulled him back to the top…or was it the shore? It was her.

The witch…her lips pressed against his. They were on the glistening sand, her long fingers entwined in his. He could still hear the music, her music. He could feel it rising like a sad forlorn beast within him, and he wanted to weep. She kissed his silver tears and when he looked at her through his wet lashes, she was someone else…and he knew her and yet didn't know her.

He wept on that shore, each teardrop becoming a memory…

He was still weeping when he woke up. When he closed his eyes, there she was, a glimmer of green-eyed magic from that night. No, he hadn't made her up. He couldn't have, because he had a sketch of her. But no, that was the other girl and they looked nothing alike. And yet…

He knew he had seen them both in whatever he had experienced while he was sleeping. He wasn't even sure he *had* been sleeping. She had come home with him and from the moment she had pulled him down on the rug, everything was a blur. He felt like she had tried to unlock him, to find something, and he wasn't sure what. She had touched him, kissed him, and he remembered the electricity of her skin. She had claimed him, and looked within and he wasn't sure what she had found.

The girl from the fair and the girl at the hotel. They were the same. He knew it. He knew how they were the same and he could tell the difference – a little like the difference between a dream and its memory.

The difference between a dream and its memory?

These words were not his, he was sure. He had heard them somewhere else. Someone else had uttered them, but he couldn't remember who it was. Who was this girl? And what had she done to him? He glanced at his phone and realized he had been sleeping for three days.

He managed to shower and cook himself an omelette. He was ravenous. The omelette was swiftly followed by yoghurt, three-day-old parathas he scrounged from the fridge, week-old cupcakes and an entire carton of milk.

His hunger somewhat satiated, he rummaged in his bag for the sketch. 'Keep it,' she had said. 'I have me.'

He stared at his charcoal version of the strange girl whose seduction had almost killed him. *How are you sure those two girls are the same?* a little voice inside him asked. But he knew. He just knew. Something had stretched, yawned and awakened once more inside him. His memory of knowing magic. Of seeing it even when it wasn't visible. He knew she had bewitched him, just like he had known that the sounds in his grandmother's attic were not made by a stray cat. He knew it the way he had known what crows said to each other. And cats. He knew it the way he had been able to recognize people from his dreams in real life.

Strange things had been happening to him all his life. Still, this was outside the realm of strangeness he was used to. This wasn't the odd whispers heard under the bed, or butterflies vanishing mid-air. This wasn't like the old woman by the river who never spoke because when she did, they were prophecies that came true.

He had to find this girl. He needed answers, even though he knew they would not be real or the 'truth', as it was known in this world. He knew the answers lay in a different reality, a whole new world. The world he had been waiting to discover all his life.

He folded the sketch and put it in his pocket. He realized that as the day passed, his memory of the green-eyed girl was diminishing. He couldn't remember her face. But he did remember her bewitching. It still made his blood race. He had to find her.

Maybe grandma would know what to do, he thought. She usually did.

❧ 14 ❧

'A dream and a memory you say? That sounds like old magic.'

Dwai looked at his grandmother, wizened, sharp and toothless at ninety-five, with all the tenacity of an old banyan tree.

'Magic...' he repeated uncertainly. It still seemed absurd. His mind was still struggling against years of living in the mundane.

'Now, boy, don't tell me you don't believe in magic. It has been around you ever since you were born.'

Dwai considered this. Yes, he had been the boy strange things happened to. And the only person who had never seemed surprised by this was his grandmother. His father had died when he was a year old. And his mother...well, no one really spoke of her, so he wasn't sure what had happened to her. Even his grandmother wouldn't speak of her.

And so he grew up an orphan, in an old rambling house with its resident ghosts and talking crows, and a grandmother who was seldom fazed by anything. Not even by his story of the vanishing butterflies. 'It happens sometimes,' was all she had said, neither refuting nor validating his story. 'Children understand magic better than adults,' she said to the crows when no one was looking. 'But alas they do not remain children always.'

He grew up caught in a haze of half-reality, not sure what was considered real by the world and what wasn't, and more often than not he was left alone by other boys his age.

And then when he turned 16, the unrealness of his life vanished, just like the butterflies. On the day of his birthday, he tried to listen in on the crows and all he could hear was a coarse cawing and nothing else. The ghost in the attic seemed to have fled too and he was only left with the ordinariness of the world. With each passing day from then on, he forgot. He forgot that he knew. That he had once put his foot through the door to other worlds. The world he lived in consumed him, making him one of its own, someone unable to recognize magic even if it was right under his nose. He became an adult, the way adults do in this world, and all he had were his dreams – full of creatures, butterflies and rattling old treasure chests – to remind him of the magic he had so easily felt in his younger days.

Ten years on, magic had come calling in a way that he couldn't ignore. He had known it the second he had set his eyes on her in the hotel. It had drawn him in like an old memory and he hadn't resisted it.

'One doesn't have to believe in magic to know that it exists,' his grandmother said, while grinding tobacco between her palms. 'Most people,' she continued, 'will not see good magic even if it waved an umbrella at them from atop an elephant. The not-so-good magic? Now that everyone is quick to grasp. They need something to blame for their troubles.' She inserted the tobacco into her toothless mouth. 'Now what happened to you? Is it the good kind or the pesky kind?'

'I don't know. It's this girl. She…' he began.

'A girl? There is always a girl where a nice robust man in his prime is concerned!' she spat. 'Are you confusing a girl for actual enchantment?'

'No, well, she did something to me. I know it,' he said.

He stopped. It was awkward if not outright embarrassing to tell his grandmother about the girl without leaving out details. And so, haltingly, blushing violently, he managed to tell her the whole story.

'You have been bewitched,' she said simply. 'And you survived. I'm not surprised.'

He didn't ask her why she wasn't surprised. He didn't ask her what being bewitched really meant either. All he knew was that something terrifying had happened to him and he couldn't undo it. Or understand it.

'Is it bad, what happened to me?'

She looked at him, her once black eyes watery and grey

now. 'It's not good or bad. It just is. It depends on whether you are ready or not.'

'Ready for what?'

She wouldn't say any more. She hobbled to the old teak cupboard in her room and took out a carved wooden box. When he was a child she had told him the box was cursed and if he ever touched it he would turn to stone. So he had never gone near it. Now he saw that it was just an old box with a rickety lid and rusty, crumbling hinges. She took something out of the box and pressed it into his palm.

'Wear it. It's time.'

He opened his palm and recognized the stone beaded onto a black thread. He had found it years ago, a week before his seventh birthday, inside a fish that had been washed ashore on the river. He had spotted the fish, dead and faintly glowing, and he had ripped it open to find this stone. It was dark blue with an opaque centre and if you stared at it long enough, it seemed as if the centre rippled. He had carried it about in his pocket for a week and then, on his seventh birthday, he had fainted. His grandmother had found this stone in his pocket and taken it away. When he had come back to consciousness, he had told her he dreamt that the stone fell from the sky and the fish rose up from the water and swallowed it. The old lady had said nothing. He had forgotten about the stone a few weeks later but the dream of the fish recurred until his sixteenth birthday.

Now the stone was once again in his possession. He ran his thumb over it. It felt smooth, yet he could feel its rippling core. He strung it around his neck. He liked how it felt against his skin, not warm, not cold, just a stone that seemed to belong with his skin.

His grandmother put the box back in the cupboard and

locked it. 'Someday when I'm dead, you can have the box. If you can open the cupboard that is,' she said.

When he left her – lying on the bed, her white hair straggling on the pillow – he knew he wasn't supposed to understand any of it just then.

Later, on the airplane back to the island city he lived in, he fell asleep. This time it was dreamless and when he woke up, the clouds outside looked grey and ghostly. And then he saw her. He hadn't seen her get on the plane and he was pretty sure he would have noticed her at the ticketing counter or in the lounge. She wasn't the kind of woman you wouldn't notice. She was so *present*. And yet, there she was, occupying that window seat at the opposite end of the aisle. It was almost as if she had appeared mid-air inside the cabin.

He watched as she stared out the window at the clouds as if they were something she intensely disliked. She turned around as if she could feel his stare and he saw her eyes, slanting and cold, and beautiful, almost cruel cheekbones. For a second he thought her irises were white but he gave his head a little shake to dismiss that thought. *How could anyone have white irises? Or lashes that seemed to flicker, for that matter?*

A tiny shaft of lightning passed through him as she stared back at him and then, just like one flicks a fly away, she looked away and the lightning stopped too. From that minute on, Dwai was restless, uncomfortable. He tried to hold on to a memory triggered by seeing her. He was filled with a deep sense of dread, a feeling that seemed...well-known, ancient. It felt forgotten and remembered all at once. *But how is that possible?* 'It depends on whether you are ready,' his grandmother had said. Ready for what? This dread? This woman with the white irises? The green-eyed girl? He wished he had pressed his grandmother for more information, but he also knew she wouldn't have said anything.

Out of the corner of his eye he saw her get up. She was so tall. There was an announcement about turbulent weather and everyone scrambled to fasten their seat belts. The plane rumbled a bit and then wobbled, causing some of the passengers to exclaim nervously. He was wide awake now and he realized that the tall woman was still standing at the end of the aisle, looking down at the rows and rows of people in front of her. For a wild second he wondered if she was going to hijack the plane. Just then, an airhostess came up to her and said tersely, 'Ma'am, you have to go back to your seat. The seatbelt sign is on.'

She turned to look at the airhostess, a slender girl in her twenties, and smiled. She then lifted a hand and brushed the girl's cheek. The young girl dropped to the ground without a word.

There was a bolt of lightning outside. He looked around and realized that everyone seemed to be in some sort of deep sleep all of a sudden. A deathly silence had fallen upon the plane. He gently nudged the woman next to him but she slumped over against his shoulder, as if in a coma.

The woman, tall, cold and terrifying, ran her eyes over the sleeping passengers in front of her and he quickly shut his eyes, afraid she would know – know that whatever was happening had not happened to him. Somehow he was the only one on the whole airplane who hadn't been put to sleep by this woman. A deep unsettling seized him and he wasn't feeling as brave as he told himself he was. For a second he wondered if he was in a dream again, where strange things happened, where light could sing and two totally different girls could be one, but he knew this was real. His grandmother had asked him if he was ready and he hadn't known what she had meant. But right then, on that plane, when he was pretending to be asleep because something told him it was all the difference between life and death, he thought he was beginning to understand.

Out of the corner of his eye he saw her walk down the aisle, carefully surveying her handiwork. She looked pleased. The plane seemed to be flying normally and he wondered if the pilot had been excluded from this slumber party or if she was flying the plane herself. Somehow, he thought, it seemed like she could control anything she pleased.

She paused by his row. He shut his eyes tightly and let his head drop. *Roll over and play dead or you will die*, he thought.

He could feel her standing there as if she was waiting for the right moment... *The right moment for what?* Then she took a few steps backwards and he stole a glance at her again.

The sky blackened outside and lightning ripped through it again. The plane did a tumultuous turn and he wondered if this was what she had wanted all along – for the plane to plummet into the sea below.

And then she did it, and he knew this wasn't her first time. Her power was centuries old, tried and perfected over time. And even though nothing seemed to happen to him, he saw everyone twitch. A flip-flop dying-goldfish twitch. She threw her head back and laughed, mirthless and yet gleeful.

Dwai, terrified and still, watched as she seemed to grow more alive – as if spirals of light had uncoiled within her. She looked younger, no, older, no, *ageless* as she laughed and the people twitched and writhed around her.

It lasted for a few seconds and in that time Dwai watched her spread her arms like a giant gleaming bird, her robes flapping like massive wings. When she brought them together again everything seemed still and airless as if the world had suddenly lost sound. Dwai felt like he couldn't hold on much longer; he was going to scream and this woman, whoever, *whatever* she was, would kill him. Then all the people twitched again and were awake. They didn't look surprised or scared, and Dwai realized they hadn't noticed a thing. Most of them looked perfectly happy, rummaging around for their bags – the plane had landed and he hadn't even noticed.

Dwai looked around in the aircraft for the woman but couldn't spot her anywhere. She had disappeared just as she had appeared – out of thin air. Announcements were made and everything seemed so normal that he wanted to scream at the stark ordinariness of it all. The past few days had been a tightrope-walk between the real and the unreal and he felt that if he fell, there would be no safety net to save him.

Outside the airport, Dwai waited in queue for the cab service, and when one pulled up next to him, he hurriedly opened the door, wanting to be home as soon as possible.

Suddenly, something cold and soft clamped over his own hand. When he looked up in shock, it was her…her hand was over his.

He let go of the handle and blinked confusedly. She stared back at him with her cold white irises and smiled, and then he knew where he knew her from – he had seen her in his dreams. No, hadn't it been a nightmare? He could recall being afraid, but the feeling paled in comparison to what he was feeling now.

She lifted her long white hand off his and smiled.

'Take this one. I'll wait for another,' she said. Her voice was pleasant, in a cold, sweet way, and it left the sort of feeling you got when you swallowed ice cream too fast. When she stepped back on the curb, he felt like she had glided into place, her feet disappearing in the movement. And was that a raven on her shoulder? Surely it couldn't be. She smiled at him again, in a disconnected moviestar-like manner.

Then her gaze travelled from his face to his neck and he saw her eyes narrow. Instantly, the stone he was wearing around his neck scorched through his skin. He wanted to cry out in pain, rip it off, but something told him to stay calm. He smiled back at her and got into the cab as if he had all the time in the world, even though his heart was pounding wildly against his chest. As it drove away, he looked back to catch a glimpse of her, but she had vanished. For a second, he wasn't sure if she had been real or whether he had imagined her.

He clutched the stone and took it off his neck – it still felt warm against his palm. The centre was rippling as if something had disturbed it. He put it in his pocket. Something about the stone had caught that woman's attention. Whatever it was, he didn't want to think about it just now.

He didn't hear the raven flying down and perching atop the cab. He didn't feel it watching him with its single eye, silent and sinister, until he reached the door of his apartment. He didn't see it flying away, its shiny black wings moving faster than was possible for any bird of the mortal world.

❖

They found his grandmother's body the next day, lying face down under the frangipani tree. When they turned her on her back, her eyes were wide open and in her hand was a crushed yellow and white flower.

I felt alien, like the monster I was. The creature I was meant to be. You see, I couldn't go without killing for too long. I didn't even mean to kill, really. What I wanted was to seduce, use my power.

I had felt pretty powerless the last few days. Everything that had happened to me had been out of my control. I was Hera's plaything, to be tossed away the minute she didn't need me. I couldn't return to Atala, although if I were to be really honest with myself, I didn't mind not returning. Living in Atala felt like I was living in the belly of a beautiful monster that was alive and could feel my core at all times. I felt like Atala wasn't really my home. Odd, because it was.

Normally I was told when to do what. Now I was free. I could pick my prey and do as I pleased.

I walked around in the city for a while, aimless, a bloodthirsty vagabond. Eventually I hit one of the hotels and found a prey. It was most often very easy, sometimes even ridiculously so. Even the last one, Dwai, hadn't been difficult to lure. But with him I had experienced hesitation. Something about that boy had made me not want to kill him. If Hera was right, maybe he wasn't dead, and I had taken nothing from him. But how was that possible? Over the last twenty-four hours I had gone over all the peculiar events that had occurred. The thing in the tower, Hera's conversation with the crone, the human corpse portal, Hera's outright hatred for me, the mystery of the blood moon, Dara…the list was endless. I had a whole sea of questions and not a glimmer of clarity in sight. I would perhaps never know what had happened to Dara, or to Hera. I wondered about their connection, clearly a past that was stained with some betrayal. Whatever he was, Dara was powerful. He had practically killed Hera. Though I doubted she was dead. She was too old and too evil to die so easily. And if she had survived, she wouldn't rest until she found me. If she came looking for me again, though, I wouldn't go down without a fight.

Why had he come to my rescue? Why had he stalked me all these years and why did he choose to rescue me when I was injured? I wasn't sure how I felt about him, except that he had an effect on my core that I simply couldn't understand. I remembered how he smelled of sunshine – this ruthless monster slayer with his sad eyes seemed out of place in the darkness. He belonged naturally to the light, I knew this. And, yet, he didn't seem to belong anywhere. Just like me. I didn't

belong to anything or anywhere either. Not anymore.

I couldn't shake off the feeling of loneliness. An abandoned runaway Yakshi who knew only one thing. As I entered the hotel in a dark defiant mood, I knew my kill today would be particularly enjoyable.

I saw him from across the room. Tall, handsome, dressed in an impeccable black suit. I could see the expensively tailored lines of his shoulders, the elegant fall of the trousers, the fun yet classy golf ball cuffs. His shoes reflected light as he walked towards me. I casually turned my back to him and tapped my martini glass, smiling lightly at the bartender. I could feel his gaze on my back, taking me in from head to toe.

I kept my back towards him, smiling again at the bartender, who almost dropped his cocktail mixer. Taking a long unhurried sip of my poison – Purple Passion, the cocktail was called – I kept my expression neutral as he appeared beside me. His eyes, a lovely, soft brown, locked with my sea-blue ones. I had picked blue for today, remembering Dara and his jewel-blue eyes. He whispered something in my ear. I smiled in response. I knew that look on men, the one that said, 'Wow, that was easy!'

Yes, it *was* that easy. For me.

We left the bar together. No one seemed to notice. He had a swagger now; he had scored with a girl so out of his league and he couldn't wait to call and tell his friends. I walked just a few steps ahead of him, and I could feel his eyes on me as I moved my hips seductively. He asked me where I was taking him. I turned around and placed a finger on his lips. He tried to grab my hand but I pulled away playfully. Not yet. My imprint glowed gleefully.

The hotel had 366 rooms. We occupied the last but one. I entered and dimmed the lights. This was the best part of the process. He inched closer, I stepped back. Not yet.

I unzipped my dress and let it fall in a satin puddle on the carpet. Earlier that day, I had walked into a mall and picked it off the mannequin. No one had stopped me. Magic could be fun sometimes.

I slid into the bed and he followed, tearing off his clothes like his life depended on it.

'Wanna know a secret?' he whispered thickly.

'Always,' I whispered back.

'I have a thing for girls with blue eyes,' he said, burying his head in my hair.

'Tell me more,' I said, kissing his lips.

There was a mad flicker in his eyes as I dug my nails into his back...

Afterwards, I slipped back into my dress, straightened out my hair and walked out. I took one last look at the man sprawled out on the bed. He looked peaceful, curled up like a foetus and you really couldn't tell that he was dead unless you felt his pulse. Just a few seconds after I drew the life out of him, I closed his eyes. Nobody needed to see the manic expression in them.

I left the hotel, humming to myself. The recklessness I had been feeling for the last few days returned. The secrets were within me. I wanted to see what they would do to me now that there was no one to retrieve them. No evil goddess to take them and use them to fuel her own power. I wanted to see if I would die, or just go mad.

This should be fun.

⚜ 16 ⚜

I walked into a shop and picked up some clothes for myself and then found myself an empty apartment for the night to sleep in. This was pretty easy, as I could glide in through the balcony.

I looked at the moon outside. A burnished, waning crescent. I thought of all the times Vina and I would go for moonlit flying sprees, laughing, our hair flying like sheets of darkness, two monsters who let themselves be a little less so on nights like this. I never got to say goodbye to Vina. Maybe she was also here in these hotels, seducing her prey in some dazzling form she managed to conjure up every single time.

Yakshis were shape-shifters but the rules decreed that we

couldn't transform into animals or birds anymore. We could only take on different human forms. This power was essential to what we did. We shape-shifted so humans wouldn't see through our disguise. But other supernaturals could tell who we were, no matter how we looked. It was an aura that we emanated, which made us recognizable to similar monsters. I couldn't fool another Yakshi with my disguise. We would know each other instantly. I knew I had to be very careful in case I am spotted by my kind and Hera learns of my whereabouts, and yet last night I had been reckless in a way that surprised even me.

I went to the bathroom and stared at myself in the mirror. A tall, pale girl with sea-blue eyes and a sad mouth. I blinked and they were back to brown. A deep, liquid brown. I liked my eyes to be brown. When Hera created me I don't know what colour she gave my eyes. All I could remember was waking up as if I had been asleep for a very long time. She had stared at me for a while and then commanded me to shape-shift. When I did, there had been a flare of triumph in her eyes. I remember that dark room in Atala which was later used to create more Yakshis; I remember being naked, with a burning feeling in my core. No one ever asked how she did this, how she brought us into this world. All we knew was that it was some deep intricate magic and that we were bound to her by it.

Right then, in that strange apartment, in a bathroom that didn't belong to me, I didn't feel bound by anything. My life was mine for the first time ever. To live or die…it was mine. I was free.

And yet the price of my freedom haunted me. With a heavy heart I lay down to sleep. I wanted to be blissfully unaware for a few hours.

The waning moon wafted into the clouds as I slipped into my dreams. I dreamt of tall slayers with jewel blue eyes and snakes that rose out of Hera's hair, hissing at me.

I woke up the next day feeling perfectly fine. No death by secrets unretrieved. No impending madness due to darkness of the core. Perhaps I really was free.

The bathroom mirror in this apartment was dull, silent. I longed for some company. I longed for Vina and her incessant chatter. 'I am never going to see her again, am I?' I asked the mirror unnecessarily. A pale, sullen Yakshi with a foggy future stared back at me in reply. The mirrors in Prithvi didn't speak to you. I missed my little hand mirror and its gentle reassurances. 'You are a pretty bit of dark magic,' it had said to me once, sleepily. This mirror stayed mute and unmoving. I tapped the surface lightly like I would my hand mirror but of course nothing happened. This was Prithvi. Magic was at its weakest here. People had long chosen not to recognize it in their lives. Even the objects most vulnerable to magic, like mirrors, wells, cupboards and dolls, had grown immune, rarely absorbing the magic of the universe.

I stared at the mirror for a while. If the old mirror that belonged to Hera was out on one of its jaunts there was a one-in-a-million chance it would see me. But I wasn't worried. Given the number of mirrors on Prithvi, I would have to be very unlucky to be caught out just then.

I sighed. I was stuck in a world of no imagination. As I began to turn away from the mirror, I saw a flicker from the corner of my eye. I swung around swiftly, wondering if the mirror had its own creature after all. But there was nothing, no one. Just me.

I walked into the other room. The sun wasn't up yet. The sky outside was a brooding inky blue. I felt a little shiver go up my spine and I turned. It was that flicker again. This time I saw it clearly, a sliver of crackling static.

It was a girl, and she wasn't a ghost.

She was nothing like anyone I had ever seen before. She flickered in front of me in a billowing white robe, making my core tingle. I wasn't afraid. I was a monster myself, after all. I couldn't see her features clearly; all I knew was that she belonged to a time long past. I had lived through that time but my memory was hazy. I put a hand out and reached out to her but she crackled and disappeared. A sudden stab of sadness overtook me. It passed as abruptly as it had arrived.

My core was alive now and I felt an odd sort of restlessness. I sat in that apartment all day waiting to see if the girl would show up again; if she was a resident ghost of some kind or if she had something to tell me.

Night fell and there was no sign of her. Finally, I decided to leave the apartment and the flickering girl behind. She was so faint, so unfinished, like a story abandoned by its teller. As I flew out of the window and into the moonlight, I knew how that felt, deep down, in the forgotten recesses of my core.

⚘ 17 ⚘

He couldn't sleep and he couldn't stay awake. He felt haunted. If he slept, he dreamt of the woman with the icy white irises.

She exploded planes, swallowed oceans and crumpled skies in her palm in his dreams. Sometimes she and the green-eyed girl were one. At other times, the green-eyed girl was alone, a gaping hole where her heart should have been. At all times he could hear the woman's cold, low laughter. It swept across his consciousness like a hailstorm.

When he woke up, he thought he was going mad. The stone he wore around his neck rippled and scorched his skin constantly.

And then he started seeing her. The faint imprint of young girl that appeared around him all the time. He wasn't sure if he was imagining her or if she was inside his mind, designed to drive him crazy.

He had first seen her in the mirror in his bedroom and his heart had leapt to his throat. He thought for a second that the green-eyed witch had found him and she was going to try to kill him, for the second time.

This girl, a blurry shimmer of static, had floated in the mirror briefly and disappeared. He had gotten into bed and pulled the sheets over his head, wanting to fall asleep for a few hours without any dreams and without this bizarre reality. His sleep had been dreamless but when he woke up, she was standing by his bed, her silver hair billowing around her like waves. He couldn't really see her face or features but she was dressed like she belonged to another era, in a white off-shoulder wrap-around robe.

'Are you my madness?' he asked her. She remained silent and shimmering and he knew then that he had nothing to be afraid of. Except maybe of what was happening inside of him.

He walked around the city for hours. He noted the waning crescent and the purple sky it came with. But there was no respite from his thoughts. And the girl, the silvery thing full of static and confusion, followed him around, hovering in the air with an uncertainty that was heartbreaking. She even sat next to him in the rickshaw as he rode home and her silent quivering presence filled him with a deep unknown grief. He wasn't afraid. If this girl had visited him before he had turned 16, he wouldn't have even thought it strange. But now, the unrealness of it was too much for him.

'Maybe I *am* going mad,' he said out loud. The rickshawvala turned to look at him in alarm and Dwai laughed. He really couldn't blame the chap for hurriedly stopping the vehicle citing a burst tyre and driving off without accepting any fare.

He walked the rest of the way home, the girl following, a soft, surreal apparition by his side.

Dwai thought of his grandmother and her strange words. No, he wasn't ready. He wasn't ready for this sort of nightmare. He wanted to rewind to the day he had met the green-eyed girl. He wanted to erase her from his life.

He closed his eyes. When he opened them again, he found himself facing the apparition again, her translucent form unsettling.

'Stop haunting me,' Dwai murmured. 'Go find someone else's mind to inhabit.' She, of course, stayed where she was.

Later in the night, he fell asleep for a bit and when he woke up she wasn't there. He approached his relief with caution – nothing normal seemed to last for long these days. Getting up from bed, Dwai walked into the drawing room, and found a shimmery figure there – but this time it wasn't the girl. It was a man, tall and handsome even through his blurry features.

'Great, now there are two of you,' Dwai murmured. 'Unless you had a gender change overnight…'

He took a bottle of beer from the refrigerator and settled down on the sofa with it. He took in the figure opposite him and chuckled. If he was going mad he might as well enjoy it.

'It's rude you know, breaking and entering someone's mind like this,' he said to the figure. 'It's even more impolite when you just stand there and don't say a word. The least you could do is be entertaining.'

The figure glowed faintly. He watched as the girl appeared, right next to the man.

'Who are you guys?' he asked, almost to himself.

Unexpectedly, they answered, their weak, quavering voices echoing inside his head:

'We are the Forgotten.'

'I have no clue what that means,' he said, sighing, taking another swig of the beer.

'You wouldn't know us, but she does.'

'Who is "she"?'

The figures shook their heads sadly. Dwai sighed and leaned back on the couch. If this was insanity, it felt pretty sane. Everything that had happened so far seemed to be real, and yet he knew that the chances of that were slim at best. *Maybe I AM mad. Maybe I'm in an asylum*, he thought.

'We don't know who you are,' said the girl. 'We knew her. We have been with her for so long. Where is she?'

'I haven't the faintest clue who you are talking about,' he said. 'Would you like some beer though?'

'It is the difference between a dream and its memory, isn't it?' asked the girl instead, her voice like a distant echo.

'What did you just say?' Dwai sat up.

'That's what this is, isn't it? The difference between a dream and its memory. I have felt this before,' said the girl. And as she spoke, she seemed to grow stronger at the edges. He caught a hint of gleaming caramel skin and eyes shining with the light of a thousand stars.

'Who *are* you?' he asked, clenching the bottle.

The man glowed like a dying firefly and said, 'The Forgotten. Even she doesn't remember us.'

Dwai threw his bottle at the figures. They disappeared as it hurtled towards them and hit the floor, smashing into pieces. He let out a snarl of despair and clutched his head. He walked to the fridge and took out another bottle.

The front door behind him flew open with a bang. He turned around in surprise, expecting to see the apparitions standing outside.

But it wasn't them.

'I believe you have my memories,' she said, looking into his eyes.

⚜ 18 ⚜

It was her. She wasn't green-eyed and she didn't look like the girl he had met at the hotel or the art fair, but it was her.

'I believe you have my memories,' she repeated. It wasn't a question.

For the second time that night, Dwai laughed. The girl looked baffled.

'What's so funny?'

'Everything is funny,' he said wryly. Silence shrouded the room for a few seconds as they regarded one another. He took her in, tall, pale, with brown eyes – the same eyes he had seen in his dream. She looked lost and defiant. She could kill him if she chose to, he knew this. And yet, when she had burst through that door, he knew it wasn't his life she was after.

She stared back, unflinching. Dwai! Maybe she could finally ask him what it was short for. It seemed like everything had come full circle, standing in this very room, on the very rug where she had pulled him down, seized him into her bewitching, but somehow failed to kill him and take his secrets. That night had changed her life. She saw the wild look in his black pearl eyes and the hysteria in his smile and she knew: surviving her had been the toughest thing that he had ever had to do.

'May I sit down?'

He cocked his head to a side, moving to the couch, his mouth twisted in an unpleasant smile.

'Yes, you have my permission to sit down. Though strangely enough, I don't remember giving you the permission to ruin my life.'

'It's not personal.'

'Of course not, just an occupational hazard, I assume.'

Silence again. She didn't know where to begin, what to explain or how.

'What are you?'

She noticed he didn't say who. Fair enough.

'What *are* you?' he repeated. 'And why do I have your memories?'

She walked up to him. He didn't move. In fact he was hardly breathing though he barely noticed it. She did. She reached for the bottle in his hand and their fingers brushed. A familiar electricity passed through him and there was a tiny explosion inside his brain. She was close, so close. He could see her lashes, sooty, long, unreal. She took the bottle from his hand and drank from it. She handed it back to him and then sat down. 'I hope you are comfortable. This is going to take a while.'

'You should begin from the beginning,' he said.

'That is the problem. I don't know what the beginning is. I am afraid though, that whatever this is, we are right in the middle of it,' she replied.

I told him a story I didn't understand myself. Of succubi and secrets. Of Atala and its dark queen. I told him I was a Yakshi and he didn't blink an eye. I told him I was 500 years old and I had bewitched and killed countless humans in my lifetime and he didn't show any signs of emotion. I spoke of Hera and the corners of his mouth twisted into a smile. I told him how I was now homeless, with no past, no future, only a continuing meaningless present, and he said nothing. He asked no questions, he wanted no explanations. He listened to my story, to me, as if that was all he needed to make sense of what had happened to him, what *was* happening to him. When I thought I had reached the end of my story, I sat in front of him, silent, letting his eyes bore into me, questions and answers all colliding.

'So why didn't I die?'

'I don't know. Nobody does. Not even Hera. She was as puzzled as I was.'

'And I have your memories?'

'It seems like that. Though I don't recognize them at all.' I bit my lip in confusion.

'Then how do you know they are *your* memories?'

'Because they told me, the girl and that man.'

'They told me they are the Forgotten.'

'Yes, forgotten by me apparently.' There was a pause. 'Dwai, I don't understand this bit myself. In fact, there is a lot I don't understand.'

'Call them now! Ask them to come back to you.'

'I don't know how that works.'

As I said it I saw the apparitions appear. The girl and the man, slightly stronger round the edges than I remembered, but still shimmering. Instinctively, I held out my hand. They came towards me.

'Come back to me,' I said. 'I found you. You are not the Forgotten anymore.'

'We are still the Forgotten,' said the man. 'The day you know who we are we will cease to be.'

'Couldn't you just tell me?' I asked, frustrated.

The apparitions said nothing. My hand was still outstretched. They came closer and, in the blink of an eye, vanished. My eyes met Dwai's. His were expressionless.

'You won't be haunted anymore,' I said.

He laughed yet again. 'You have no idea what you have done to me, have you?' he asked casually. I shook my head. I genuinely didn't know; I had never left anyone alive for them to tell me how they felt. He scratched his stubble and looked out of the window. For a human who had just been told that monsters existed – and that one of those monsters, a shape-shifting Yakshi who had tried to kill him, was sitting in his drawing room – he was taking things extremely well. I wondered at his composure and then I remembered his laughter, tinged with madness.

'You smiled when I told you about Hera…'

He turned to look at me. 'I think I met her. I was on a plane. She did something to everyone on that plane but me. Whatever she did didn't affect me.'

'It could be because of whatever didn't kill you. After we…' I trailed off awkwardly.

'For some time I thought it was this,' he pointed to the

stone around his neck. 'She saw the stone and she seemed...
surprised. Maybe this protected me.'

'But you didn't have this when I met you,' I said. I went
closer and took it in my hand. It felt hot, almost singeing hot,
and I could feel a life force rippling through it.

'Where did you get this?'

'My grandmother gave it to me. Actually, I found it when
I was seven.'

'You found it?'

'Yes, inside a fish.' He said this as if it was completely normal
to find supernatural stones inside fish.

'It looks like one of those magical stones,' I said. 'Belonging
to divine beings. Or mythical ones, like Apsaras.'

'Apsaras! Those mythical sirens who live in heaven?' His
tone was incredulous.

'Exactly. Mythical. I doubt they exist.'

The irony wasn't lost on him. 'YOU exist but Apsaras are
mythical?'

'Well, no one has ever seen one in years. At least I haven't.
The Old Books speak of them, but for all you know they are
just stories meant to enchant children. Also, there is no heaven.
There hasn't been any sign of any life above for centuries. We
believe it is all a myth.'

'So Prithvi exists with humans, and Atala with you lot, but
none of that heavenly stuff is true?'

'Seems so,' I shrugged.

'Earth and the Underworld prosper while Heaven is a
fairytale,' he chuckled.

I didn't respond. Heaven might be a fairytale but I had seen
that portal in the sky with my own eyes. And the man who
flew right into it – a man who looked like Dara, it suddenly

struck me. It was now among the many things that didn't make sense to me.

There was a long pause as we sat watching the sleets of rain fall in bursts of thunder and lightning outside. It was a while before Dwai spoke.

'So, what of your memories? How did you know I had them?'

I told him. I had seen the girl in the mirror, and soon afterwards the man had appeared. They had followed me around like they had Dwai and finally the girl had spoken.

'We are yours,' she had said.

'What do you mean?' I had asked.

'We are the Forgotten. But we belong to you. We are memory ghosts. We are here to tell you that you have memories you don't know anything about.'

Then they told me that the man I couldn't kill had them in a sort of reverse magic. When the bewitching had taken place, my memories had gone to him, but his secrets had stayed.

'But we don't belong to him. We are yours. Go find him and take us back,' they said.

And so I had appeared at his apartment in the hope of finding him, my memories and perhaps some answers.

'You call them secrets when you refer to me. But yours are memories?'

I pondered over Dwai's question. I could feel his eyes on me, sharp, searching. 'I don't have secrets. I have never been allowed any,' I said after a pause. 'I don't know. Aren't secrets abandoned or forbidden memories in a way?'

'And which part of your dark, violent, bound-to-Hera monster life did you abandon?'

I said nothing. I wish I knew. Till yesterday, I had my life charted out for me; I had no destiny, no life outside of Hera's whimsy. Today, I was faced with a thousand new roads, all paved with questions, leading into the unknown.

'You have plans for the night?'

I didn't miss the tone or implication.

'None of your business, but no!'

'You can stay here,' he said.

'You don't have to…'

'I am not asking you to stay forever. Just until you figure out your shit.'

I nodded my thanks.

'You Yakshis sleep? I thought monsters didn't really need to.'

'Sleep for us is simply a mechanism to unwind. It wouldn't bode well for the world if we were Yakshis round the clock, would it?'

Dwai didn't respond. The rain continued to fall heavily outside but there was a silence between us I didn't know how to fill.

✢ 19 ✢

It was a strange night. I didn't sleep, and I knew Dwai didn't either. I could hear him tossing and turning in his bed. As the sun slanted into the little apartment, I could hear Dwai pottering around in the bathroom. He finally emerged, looking a lot cleaner and more sane than he had seemed when I had burst into his house last night. He still didn't look very friendly but I couldn't blame him for that.

'Coffee?' he asked, as he poured himself some.

I shook my head.

'Right! I forgot your poison is something else entirely,' he said casually.

Irritation flared in me and I stood up. 'I can't help it,' I snapped. 'Just like you can't help being an annoying human, I can't help being a Yakshi. I can't help who I am and how I am, but you, *you* could definitely improve that attitude.'

One of his eyebrows shot up. 'How grown-up of you. Sit down. I didn't mean to upset you.' He looked at me, his gaze frank and open. I stared back into his black pearl eyes and my anger abated.

I sat down.

'You must understand,' he said, 'there is still so much I don't get.'

'I don't either, if that helps,' I said.

There was a pause as he sipped his coffee, regarding me warily over the cup.

'So, what's your plan?' he asked.

My plan. I didn't have one. All I knew was, I was going to be on the run all my life. I could shape-shift and stay out of trouble but it was going to be tough.

I bit my lip in confusion. 'I wish I knew. I...'

'Don't you want answers?'

'I do. But I don't know where to start. And the answers I'm looking for are shrouded in danger. But this I know – nothing Hera does is free of evil.'

'There is evil on Prithvi, too,' murmured Dwai. 'We have forgotten what it is like to be human. Something is happening here too, Ardra. Sometimes there is no difference between humans and monsters; the lines are blurring. Prithvi is getting darker by the minute.'

He had uncannily echoed my feelings.

'I'm not surprised monsters exist,' he continued. 'I think they would fit in very well with this world and its penchant for cruelty.'

He tapped the newspaper in front of him. 'Look at this. This isn't normal. Whoever is doing this isn't human. Or normal.'

I picked up the paper. Another gruesome killing. 'An Animal Attack', screamed the headline. 'A Strange Animal on the Loose Is Killing People'. I read the whole piece and set the paper down.

'Animals don't rip hearts out or eat human innards. Nor do they peel the skin of people's faces and put them back on.'

'You don't think it's an animal?' asked Dwai. He looked curious, questioning.

'In the city? What are the chances, really? I don't know. Humans are capable of extreme violence, yes. But these killings, they reek of the supernatural. I just know it. And I think I know what it might be.'

I don't know why I said that. It was my Yakshi instinct, a sharp sliver of clairvoyance, that told me that the thing in the tower was responsible for this.

He set his cup down.

'Would you like to go for a walk?'

The question surprised me. I had thought that he would be eager to get rid of me.

'Sure,' I said.

We set out. It was a cold, crisp morning, and for a few minutes, I forgot my troubles as I walked alongside the tall, serious man whose life I had almost taken a few nights ago. I wondered how much of the bewitching he remembered, whether he remembered us, the way we were, that night. He was careful not to touch me as we walked, his arms locked tightly across his chest, determinedly looking straight ahead.

The sun warmed our skins. I wasn't used to this bright morning light. I had always crept away from Prithvi at the break of dawn. The sun was a happy thing, I decided, full of warmth and joy. I liked daytime – not as much as I loved the night, but it still filled me with a strange sense of hope. The dappled shadows of leaves gave Dwai's skin a strange sheen. His dark hair rippled in the wind and his jaw didn't look quite as obstinate in the beautiful light. He seemed unaware that I was staring at him as he walked on, a little ahead of me. And then he turned and smiled. He must have felt my gaze on him. I blushed under my succubus skin and was instantly thankful that it would never show.

We turned a corner and hit a beautifully kept promenade that rimmed the sea, a haven for lovers, clandestine couples and teenagers looking for a place to steal a quick kiss. The promenade was teeming with humans, all holding hands.

'Didi, please buy some flowers,' a young boy tugged at my clothes. He was holding a few roses in his hand.

I smiled at the boy and shook my head.

'Please, Didi, take two at least. One for you and one for your boyfriend.'

Dwai blushed. 'What the...' he started.

'How do you know he's my boyfriend?' I asked with a serious face.

'I know these things. It is my job. I sell flowers. Also see how he looks at you, Didi. Only a boyfriend can look at a girl like that.'

I burst out laughing. Dwai's expression was priceless.

'Here,' he said, hurriedly digging into his pocket for money. 'Here, take this and run away or I'll whack you.' The boy took the money, shoved two roses into Dwai's hands and ran away grinning.

Dwai laughed. 'I bought you flowers,' he said with a poker-straight face and held out his hand. I took them almost reflexively. They were wild blooms, the kind you found in forgotten cemeteries. Their petals spiralled into a deep, secret core. I slid my finger over the stem and a huge thorn that hadn't been snipped off plunged into my skin. Deep blue succubus blood oozed out. I put my finger to my mouth quickly, hoping Dwai wouldn't notice. But I wasn't quick enough.

He took my hand, the blood now a thin stream down my finger. 'You have blue blood,' he said quietly.

'Does it repel you?'

'Repel me? No, it's beautiful. In fact, you…'

He stopped, blushed furiously, and let go of my hand, picking up his pace until he was walking ahead of me. Then he paused and looked back, his black pearl eyes gleaming with a hint of a smile. I smiled back. We didn't say a word to each other, and yet the the silence between us was not uncomfortable, just shorn of the words we knew we didn't have.

'Aren't you afraid?' he asked suddenly.

'Of what?'

'Of everything that is happening. An evil queen is after you, and here you are, taking a walk on a busy promenade on Prithvi like any other person.'

'What would I do with fear?' I shrugged. 'It serves no purpose.'

More silence as we strolled along the concrete path. Around us, the sun grew bolder, its light glinting in his eyes. I looked up at the sky, scattered with clouds and swallows. I had never seen a sky so blue, so open and inviting.

'Would you like to go for a ride in the sky?' I asked, surprised at my own impulsiveness.

His eyes widened. I expected him to decline but he grinned instead. We walked away from the promenade and turned into an empty lane.

'You will have to take my hand.'

Without hesitation, he placed his hand in mine. I wound my other hand around it and rose. He steadied his body against mine with surprising grace. I picked up pace until the buildings turned into a blur. Next to me, Dwai laughed in delight. I turned sideways to steal a glance at him and his obvious pleasure was infectious.

'I had forgotten that this could be a thing of wonder,' I said, smiling.

'It's amazing,' he replied. 'Just amazing. How wonderful to be able to fly, to have invisible wings.'

I stopped flying and we hovered in mid-air, a Yakshi and a mortal, against an unending landscape of clouds.

'I've always wanted wings,' I said. 'Smooth, satiny wings. But only angels have those. I am too much of a dark thing to have wings of that kind, I suppose.'

'A beautiful dark thing,' he said. His eyes were steady and serious. I knew this wasn't the effect of my magic because it didn't work on him. This was...

The wind blew my hair right across my face and I was glad for it – I didn't want him to see the confusion I was feeling in that moment. It was all too much, too soon. I was still bruised from my previous encounter with a stranger, someone who had left me wanting and bewildered. Dwai, on the other hand...

A bird flew right between us like a feathery bullet and I was jolted out of my reverie.

'That, I can safely say, has never happened to me before,'

said Dwai, laughing. He reached out and plucked the feather that had settled on my shoulder.

The sky darkened suddenly and the white clouds slowly changed hue to a stormy grey. I began to descend without a word. Dwai had grown silent, too, perhaps baffled by my sudden silence. When we were low enough to see the top of buildings, I picked up speed and landed behind an old church.

'I want to be on my own for a bit,' I said. 'I'll see you at your apartment.'

He nodded. I rose in the air again. 'Don't be too late,' he called after me playfully. Not knowing how to respond, I merely smiled. Soon, he was a mere speck on the ground. I flew in and out of the turbulent clouds for a bit as rain started to fall. A bolt of lightning shot right past me on its way to earth.

'Don't think about anything right now,' I murmured to myself. After what seemed like hours, I finally began my descent, instinctively mapping out the way to Dwai's house in my head.

The air was swollen with rain, the city a mass of moving dots under me. One of them was Dwai. I wondered if he had gone back home or if he was still wandering around. I started to descend towards his building as the rain stung me, sharp and thin. I could see him walking home, his hands in his pockets, his dark head bent low in thought.

Another figure was right behind him, a person in a suit. An immaculate, expensive-looking suit. A strange vacuum had settled over the area; it had gone deathly quiet. I looked around and realized we were inside a force field of sorts. I was low enough to be inside it, but it was clear that was by accident – whoever had cast it hadn't noticed me in the sky. I knew this because the person walking behind Dwai seemed focused on him while keeping a safe distance but his gait was heavy. As heavy as...

I didn't have enough time to warn Dwai, just enough to change into my warrior aspect.

The Rakshasa looked up first. He was tall and tawny-skinned with a toothbrush moustache in his human form, but I could see the boiled candy-red pupils even from afar. I swooped down, surprising him and he let out a loud snort. That was when Dwai looked skywards. His eyes widened in surprise as I flew down towards earth.

The Rakshasa recovered quickly – he raised his arms and a row of neatly planted gulmohar trees by the road caught fire. He lunged forward as Dwai stayed rooted to his spot. I saw him take in the Rakshasa, a burly figure in his well-cut black suit, and I sensed his bewilderment.

I landed between Dwai and the Rakshasa just in time.

'Not here,' I said. 'This is an area with a lot of humans.'

The Rakshasa didn't respond. The tree tops crackled with fire.

'Leave,' I barked at the Rakshasa. 'Leave now. We are not supposed to do this in the open.'

He mumbled something incoherent. I was blocking him from Dwai. Without turning around, I said, 'Get away from here. Go and hide! RUN.'

Dwai didn't have the time to reply. The Rakshasa took a step forward and I made up my mind in that split second.

A ball of fire went hurtling towards the Rakshasa who was still in his human form. It hit him square in the chest. I rose in the air as he transformed, a huge craggy creature with bloodshot eyes and a heavy lumbering gait.

'Very bad move,' I muttered under my breath. The force field wouldn't last long and I had to act fast.

I sent another long ribbon of fire towards the Rakshasa as he lumbered towards me, his arms outstretched menacingly.

With a snarl of anger, he uprooted a tree and flung it at me. 'Such old moves,' I laughed as I rose above him and blasted the tree into bits. I did a quick scan for Dwai and found him still standing right there. He hadn't moved an inch.

'What is wrong with you?!' I screamed. 'Do you want to die?'

The Rakshasa answered for Dwai as he charged forward and dug his long nails into the surprised man's shoulder, picking him up as one would a toothpick.

I whirled around the Rakshasa, who was now holding Dwai in one huge fist. I couldn't send fire towards them now; it could injure Dwai.

I muttered an expletive under my breath. The Rakshasa ogled at Dwai and mumbled something. Unexpectedly, he changed back into his human form, now holding Dwai by the neck.

I still couldn't tackle the giant oaf because of Dwai. I circled them, just a few metres above the ground now. Dwai looked at me and then swiftly put his hand into his pocket.

A few seconds later, the Rakshasa in the immaculate black suit was clutching his face and roaring with pain. He let go of Dwai, who stumbled and swiftly backed away.

'MOVE! MOVE OUT OF THE WAY!' I shouted, as I flew towards the Rakshasa. My foot landed on his neck with tremendous force, snapping it in half, and his body fell back on the gravel, dead.

Dwai walked up to the Rakshasa's body and peered satisfactorily into his swollen, unrecognizable face.

'Pepper spray,' he said with a grin.

'Pepper spray?!'

'Yeah!' His black pearl eyes were twinkling.

'You beat a giant Rakshasa with pepper spray?' I couldn't believe my ears.

'Well, yes. I also added some chilli powder to it.'

I stepped over the Rakshasa as the force field around us vanished.

'Why the hell didn't you run when I asked you to?'

'Run? And leave you here to fight that thing?'

'YES! That thing was a murderous Rakshasa. You couldn't have possibly done anything to...'

'And yet...' he made a sweeping gesture towards the dead Rakshasa.

My furious face couldn't have had any effect on him because he was grinning. I clenched my fist.

'Of course I wasn't going to run, Ardra. When someone is trying to save your life you don't just run and leave them to it.'

He was smiling but his eyes were serious.

'We should go,' I said, exasperated. 'Come on.'

We walked rapidly away from the scene.

'Why on earth do you have pepper spray on you?'

He shrugged his shoulders. 'Since I can't turn into something like this,' he indicated my aspect, 'I just decided to keep some mortal defence handy. Good idea, don't you think?'

He grinned as I opened my mouth and shut it again. I had no idea what to say.

'Nice costume, by the way,' he smirked.

'Right,' I said walking ahead of him. 'Let's get away from here. I need to wrap my head around why a Rakshasa would attack you.'

'I guess I'm just really popular these days.'

I didn't reply. We walked up the stairs of his building in silence. I changed into my human form as we did and Dwai's eyebrows shot up again. I turned my face away as I suppressed a smile.

He couldn't sleep. He thought of the Rakshasa and how Ardra had tackled him. She had fought off a big lumbering beast by herself.

She, this delicate, wispy-looking…monster.

'Monster,' he whispered in the dark. That's what she was. A life-sucking secret-stealing monster. And then an image snuck into his mind. When they were flying, she had glanced at him sideways, a beautiful unreal creature with invisible wings and bits of storm in her hair. The sunlight had streamed into her eyes, her deep brown eyes tinged with sadness, and made her look like an angel. A monster who looked like an angel.

An angel with pointy teeth. And flame-winged eyes. And those talons, oh God, the talons. Or were they clawed fingers? Whatever they were, she really knew how to use them. Then there was her sheer strength as she took on the Rakshasa. He touched his shoulder, where the Rakshasa had ripped his skin, and winced. Clearly, wounds inflicted by demons hurt a lot more than human ones.

The rain started again, a gentle persistent tune outside his window, and his eyes started to close. His last thought before he fell asleep was of Ardra, awake and alone in the living room. *Maybe I should go give her company*, he thought, even as his body succumbed to exhaustion.

101

He murmured her name occasionally in his sleep and she, alone in the next room, heard him. A smile played at the corner of her lips as she slid down on the couch, hugging a cushion and staring at the rain.

He woke up with a start a little after 2 a.m. The rain hadn't stopped. Neither had his dreams. But then, he hadn't really been able to tell the difference between dream and reality for the past few days.

His shoulder was throbbing. He wondered if painkillers would help and then presumed that earthly medicines would probably have no effect on Rakshasa wounds. He would have to let it heal in its own time.

It was then that he noticed someone standing by the door, and he felt an old tingling up his spine. He had felt this before, this feeling of being reeled in, of being bewitched.

Ardra...

Passion overcame his confusion as she advanced. She seemed to gleam at the edges, her magic somehow seeming more powerful tonight. He gazed up at her silently as she bent down, her eyes iridescent indigo now, her skin shining like diamonds. She put out a hand and gently brushed his face. As she lowered her face to meet his, he saw that her irises had a mesmerizing icicle-like pattern. Her lips touched his and from then on he couldn't think of anything else. She kissed him deep and slow, and stars imploded in his brain. This was powerful bewitching, so much more forceful than last time. This was...

It happened so fast that his brain didn't fully comprehend it at first. Ardra was thrown off him by someone with such compelling force that she hit the wall. Sparks flew in all directions as she picked herself up and fought back against her unknown enemy. In the darkness, two figures duelled and the air was charged with angry magic. He watched helplessly as the two silhouettes, their auras violent and forceful, met each other's magic with equal fervour. He got out of bed, wondering if the Rakshasa had returned and reached for the bedside light. As soon as the light came on, the duelling stopped abruptly as both the assailant and Ardra paused to look at him. There she was, wrathful, still gasping from the power of her Yakshi force and, for some reason, fully drenched, and then his eyes fell on the other person in the room. A silent scream escaped his mouth and he wondered if his brain was playing tricks on him again.

It was Ardra.

☽ 21 ☾

I saw the look of utter shock on Dwai's face and I didn't blame him. There were two of us standing in that room. Two Ardras, duelling one another to possible death. And only one of them was real.

It had all happened so fast. I had been lying on the couch, listening to the rain and feeling just a tiny bit sorry for myself. I only allowed myself to wallow in self-pity in the still of the night. When I had heard Dwai murmuring my name in his sleep, it had made me oddly happy. Maybe, despite whatever he seemed to have against my kind, there were still some traces of my bewitching on him – that could be the only reason he was dreaming about me. I thought of how he had stayed and fought the Rakshasa with me. He could have run easily and he didn't.

I stepped out on the balcony, letting the rain wash over me, and that's when I heard her.

No, sensed her. I sensed her ancient siren energy as she entered the apartment. She glided across the living room and then paused. I knew instantly what she was looking for – something that belonged to me, so she could turn into me.

She spotted my jacket and turned, her feet never touching the ground, her sheet-like hair cascading to the floor. I averted my gaze. I knew to never set eyes on a Huldra's back. She held my jacket, caressing it, muttering something, and then suddenly, she liquefied and transformed into me. It was like looking into a mirror – a very creepy mirror.

The Huldra then glided into the bedroom. I wondered what she was doing here, in this apartment. If she had come looking for me, why transform into me?

And in that split second, I knew I had to do something. Her power was ancient and very potent but I was quite sure I could match it. It was night, the time when my magic was most powerful. But first I had to find out what she was up to.

I tiptoed across the room. I was surprised she hadn't sensed me yet but I decided to wonder about that later. She was bent over Dwai, her lips locked with his. That's when I made my move. I shot my strongest magic at her and she fell back against the wall.

It wasn't easy fighting her. She was strong, powerful, ancient. We might have killed each other tonight. Until I turned and looked at Dwai. The expression on his face drove me to stop. This sort of thing could drive any man crazy and I had already sent Dwai to the brink of insanity once. Not again.

I looked at the Huldra square in the eye, channelling my power in order to freeze her on the spot. I didn't normally use this magic because it took a lot of life force out of my core and I was left drained for hours afterwards, but just then, I knew it was the right move. As she froze, I sank to my knees, gasping.

After a few minutes, I pulled myself up with some effort and slowly walked up to Dwai. He was still sitting on the bed, shock in his eyes. I gently put my hand on his. 'Dwai, this is me, Ardra.'

He turned to look at me, a deep penetrating stare, and I knew he still couldn't tell it was really me. His expression was lined with disbelief and traces of fear.

'Okay,' I said. 'Let's try this. Ask me a question. Anything. Something only I would know.'

There was a long pause as his gaze travelled from me to the Huldra. She remained pinned against the wall, her breath coming in rasps. I ignored her. There would be enough time to ask her questions later.

His gaze stayed on her.

'Wait. Let me make this easier for you.'

I walked up to her and took the Huldra's face in my hands. She shivered again and began changing form. When it was done, she returned to her true self: a tall, pale siren with high cheekbones and silver hair that swept the floor, wearing a thin translucent gown so delicate it seemed to be made of spider thread.

'Better?' I asked Dwai.

He nodded. 'What is she?' he asked, his voice sounding strangled.

'She is a Huldra, a kind of siren. They are extremely powerful and can easily transform into other supernatural monsters, something we Yakshis can't do. Huldras also possess the power to control minds, albeit briefly. Judging by her magic, she also seems really old. She looks pretty now, but trust me, you don't ever want to look at her back. And, oh, you are lucky I came in when I did. Another three seconds and she would have possessed your mind.'

Dwai didn't react. He just stared at an imaginary spot in the distance.

'If you still think your eyes and brain are playing tricks on you, ask me a question.'

His gaze stayed on the Huldra as he spoke, 'What was the colour of your eyes the night you met me in the hotel?'

His gaze now turned to me and it was disconcerting and sharp.

'Green,' I said. 'I wore green eyes that night.'

The Huldra let out a noise of derision.

'Something funny?' I asked her sharply.

'Nothing,' she chuckled. 'This is such a tender scene. I am just not used to these.'

'Well, neither am I,' I said. 'Now, perhaps you will tell us who or what sent you here and why?'

'I thought that would be mighty obvious. Your mistress, of course.'

She smiled at both of us charmingly.

'Really? How does she know where I am?'

'Oh, she doesn't. You, my dear, are a pleasant surprise.'

'I don't understand,' I frowned. 'We were attacked by a Rakshasa just this evening.'

'Hmm, well, I'm not sure what is going on exactly but I think Gaggii the raven tailed you,' she said, looking at Dwai.

'A raven followed me? Why? How?'

'Who knows why Hera does anything?'

'Wait, so she doesn't know where I am but a Rakshasa turns up and, a few hours later, so do you? What is going on?'

The Huldra smirked, her sharp eyes gleaming.

'I'm not stupid enough to think she would just let me run,' I continued. 'But if she was after me, why did the Rakshasa attack Dwai? And what are you doing here?'

'Try using that sharp little succubus brain of yours. Go on,' she goaded.

'I think I know,' Dwai said slowly.

'What?'

His voice was level and calm as he said, 'She isn't after you. She is after me.'

❧ 22 ❧

The Huldra screeched with laughter. It wasn't a pleasant noise.

Dwai's eyes met mine as I tried to make sense of what he had said. And then the fragments began to piece themselves together.

'This human is clever, isn't he?' the Huldra smirked.

'What does Hera want him for?' I snapped.

'Search me,' she said.

'You're lying!' I screamed. 'And I am going to – '

'Stupid girl!' she interrupted sharply. 'I don't need to lie to *you*. That old bundle of evil that is your mistress, she knows that. I don't know why she wants this human, and trust me, sweetheart, I don't care.'

'Then why did you agree to come? And why did you turn into me?

'Because it's fun. Because life's been pretty boring lately, and pretending I am on assignment is the most interesting thing I've done in a while. I scoped this place for a while and I was surprised to see you, a Yakshi, with the human. I knew a Yakshi had escaped Atala and I deduced you were the one. I entered the house and realized that the best way to capture him was to turn into you and seduce him. The rest is history, as they say. Now, if you could unfreeze me, I'll be on my way. I have no doubt Hera will send along another creature to capture this poor human. Or she may even deign to do it herself. Either way, I'm glad I'm not in your place. Now, if you will please...'

'No,' I said. 'No, I need some answers. It can't be as easy as that.'

'You are banging on the wrong door. But, hell, even that can get you somewhere at times. Look, here's a deal for you. Unfreeze me, then tell me everything and I will try and decipher it.'

'Why should I trust you?'

'Strangely, for the exact reason that you don't trust me. I owe allegiance to no one. Not Hera, not anyone else. I have seen too much, lost too much, to pledge my loyalty to any one person. I'm free to do as I please. This is a pact with our kind that goes back centuries. And Hera knows that. She can't do anything. She doesn't own me. Sadly, in your case...'

'Listen, Huldra...'

'I have a name. And I promise you it's a pretty one.'

'Okay, Huldra, what is your name?'

'Morana. There! I said it was pretty, didn't I?'

Dwai got up from the bed.

'Right, Morana. Ardra will unfreeze you. But you can't leave until you give us some answers.'

She looked at both of us.

'Okay, but I can't promise anything.'

'I am not sure we should unfreeze her,' I said, still sceptical.

'Ardra, trust works both ways,' Dwai replied, laying his hand gently on my arm.

Morana smirked. I walked up to her and asked her to look into my eyes without blinking. A few seconds later she was strutting up to the bed and stretching out on it. She looked like a smug cat after a satisfying meal and I didn't like it. But endure her I would, for Dwai's sake.

When did it become 'for Dwai's sake'? I asked myself, the thought taking me by surprise. When did Dwai begin to matter so much to me? I wanted to think about it but I knew this was not the right time.

Dwai pulled up a couple of chairs and we sat facing her. He spoke first. He told Morana of the bewitching and how he had somehow survived. He spoke of his grandmother and her cryptic messages. But he didn't tell her about the memory ghosts and I was glad for it. That was our secret, something we had to decipher on our own, and I was happy he instinctively felt the same way.

'But none of this explains why Hera wants me,' said Dwai.

'You didn't die. That makes you special. She probably wants to use you as a lab rat or something,' Morana replied. 'The Rakshasa, I suspect, was an inelegant plan hatched by that two-headed idiot Mantri. He may have acted on his own.'

'There is something else,' said Dwai and he told Morana about the encounter with Hera on the plane.

'Where is the stone?' asked Morana. She had become more interested now and I could sense her rising excitement.

Morana held the stone in her hand. As she touched it, the surface scattered like sand in the desert wind. It was as if a storm was brewing within the stone.

'That has never happened before,' said Dwai, sounding surprised.

'And why would it?' Morana murmured.

'Ahem,' I said pointedly, glaring at her.

'Yes, Ardra?'

'Don't tease,' I said, 'tell us what you know.'

'What I know...' said Morana slowly, a sad, twisted smile on her face. 'What I know could destroy worlds.'

I stared at her disbelievingly. She was so full of herself.

Dwai inched closer to her. His face was serious and earnest and, despite my annoyance, I couldn't help but think how beautiful he looked.

'Morana, if this stone can tell me something, anything, about who I am, then please don't keep it from me.'

He placed his hand on hers and a great ugly beast flailed around angrily inside me. But his coaxing had its effect. Morana handed him back the stone and the storm within it stopped. It returned to its former state, rippling, emitting purple light.

'This stone belongs to an Apsara.'

'Apsaras don't exist,' I blurted. His hand was still on hers.

'Dear child, either you let me talk or I can leave — quite happily, I might add.'

Dwai threw me a glance and I sat back down. I was feeling sullen and childish. I was starting to actively dislike Morana but I was interested in her story.

'This stone belongs to an Apsara. She either lost it on earth or gave it someone willingly. I'm guessing the latter.'

'How do you know this?' Dwai asked.

'I have been around for longer than I'd like to remember,' said Morana.

'So Apsaras exist...' I said slowly.

'Yes.'

'So where are they? Why hasn't one been spotted for the last 500 years?'

Morana sighed.

'Child, I wish I could tell you, but there is a particularly charming head-exploding curse that will come true if I do. And I don't think I would look as enticing as I do now without my head.'

'But there is a sky portal that is still open,' I said.

Morana sat up. 'How do you know?' she asked sharply.

'Never mind how I know,' I said, noting Dwai's surprised expression from the corner of my eye. 'But the portal is open. And I saw someone fly into it. A man...'

'You saw a man fly into the sky portal?' she asked slowly.

'Yes. I don't know whether Aakasha exists but something does, up there. And since you say Apsaras exist, what about Gandharvas then?'

The Huldra stared at me intensely.

'Do Gandharvas exist too?' I persisted.

'Yes,' she said softly. 'They do.'

'And what do they look like?' I said, almost breathlessly.

She took a deep breath. 'Impossibly good-looking, most of them. Tall. And they have distinct individual markings on their faces.'

I drew in a sharp breath.

'As far as surprises go,' said the Huldra in a low, almost comforting voice, 'this may just be the beginning.'

'Can you tell me anything more about the stone?' Dwai cut in.

'I have an idea how and why you have the stone. And it is linked to why our kind don't affect you. But it is not within my power to reveal it to you.'

'Is there no one who can give me any answers without withholding some part of it?' said Dwai clenching his fists.

'Sorry, I really can't,' said Morana.

'Yeah, the head-exploding curse. You mentioned it.'

Morana turned to me. Her eyes were alight with a kind of emotion I couldn't place. 'If I could tell you how it all started, if only I could...'

Silence darkened the room like a rain cloud.

After a pause, Dwai spoke, 'Tell me what to do then.'

'Ask your grandmother.'

'My grandmother died a few days ago.' His voice was heavy with sadness.

'She may be dead. But she hasn't yet left.'

'What do you mean?'

'The dead, they have a sort of waiting period before they fully cross over. They wait by the river Tarini at the Edge of Prithvi.'

'The Edge of Prithvi? How do I get there?'

'Very easily, if you know how. The other option is to die, of course.'

'Still not funny, still not helping,' I muttered under my breath.

Dwai shot me a quelling glance. I could see Morana suppressing a smile.

'How do I get there? Can you take me there?'

'No. I'm not allowed passage. But there is someone who can.'

'Who?'

'This person called Dara...also known as the monster slayer.'

'I know who Dara is,' I said slowly.

Morana looked at me meaningfully. There was a hint of pain in her expression this time, followed by something else. Was it sympathy?

'Who is Dara?' asked Dwai.

Nobody answered him.

'You want me to ask Dara to help us? To take Dwai to the River of Death?'

'Well,' Morana shrugged. 'He is the only one who *can*. So find him.'

'Sure. Find Dara. Go to the River of Death. Ask your grandmother's spirit questions. Got it,' Dwai said sarcastically, shaking his head.

I ignored him. 'How does Dara have passage to the River?'

Morana sighed. 'Because he had to go there centuries ago; once you are given permission, you have it forever. Though few would want to return. It's not exactly a vacation spot.'

'Why did Dara need to go to the River of Death?' I persisted.

'Ask him yourself, why don't you?' she replied lightly. 'If you find him that is…'

'Right,' I said. 'What is his connection to Hera?'

'I can't really say, but why do you ask?' asked Morana, looking mildly taken aback.

'Well, Hera was about to kill me and he turned up. He… helped me escape.'

'He helped you escape?' Morana said softly. 'Why didn't you stick with him then?' Her voice did not mask her curiosity.

'I… He put up a force field. It was evident he didn't want me to linger. I had to leave.' I might have sounded mildly miserable.

She didn't say anything more but her silence was potent. I felt disconcerted. I wondered if I should tell Morana I had encountered Dara before but decided against it.

'I'm sorry, kids. This is all too much for you,' Morana said, turning her gaze towards Dwai.

There were lines on his forehead and his eyes held a slightly crazed look that was beginning to worry me.

'Has this happened before?' I asked.

Morana raised her eyebrows, questioningly.

'As in, has a monster not been able to kill a human after... after a bewitching?'

She smiled. That annoying, knowing smile.

'My dear girl. You are asking the wrong question.'

'What do you mean?' asked Dwai.

'That's all I can say for now,' she purred at him as she got up from the bed, ignoring me completely. 'I'll be on my way now. I'm sure our paths will cross again. That time has come.'

'Wait! Are you going back to Hera to tell her that I'm with him?'

'Go back to Hera? Why on earth would I do that? I don't live in that depressing place you call home and I don't owe Hera any answers. When she doesn't hear from me, she will know I couldn't capture the human. Unfortunately for you, that will only irk her more. And, trust me, she has ways of finding out where you are. Don't forget that ingenious mirror of hers that can travel to any home in Prithvi. I bet she has it keeping an eye on Dwai. It's only a matter of time before she knows you are here. Luckily, though, you have some time. She is off somewhere on a secret mission. You might be safe until she comes back. If I were you, I would leave this house and go elsewhere. As for me, I'm heading home. It's been a while since I was there. This place is too hot for me, anyway.'

She made her way to the balcony, her hair cascading down her back, her diaphanous gown so thin it hardly hid anything. She was beautiful, almost impossibly so, but she was also unreal, with an aura that was distinctly supernatural. A sudden burst of wind blew her hair to the side like a wave. In that moment, I wish I could have averted Dwai's eyes. But he saw it: her back, hollow like a tree trunk, the carved-out flesh within slimy and rotting. Pure revulsion flashed across his face. She had a tail too, a bovine one that swished from side to side when she walked. She carefully adjusted her hair so that it covered her back once more, turned to Dwai and said, 'Never trust absolute beauty. There is no such thing. Even the moon has shadows.'

She was gone in a vapour of white smoke, leaving us with more questions than before. I knew I had to find Dara. I had to find him, not just for myself but also for Dwai.

For Dwai. I whispered it to myself when I was alone and it seemed alien and odd. For someone else. To do something brave and selfless for another person seemed so human, so fragile. Hera would find it futile, even laughable. It went against everything she stood for. She would be utterly scornful that her carefully honed Yakshi, made of bloodlust and darkness, would make a choice so...mortal. But I would find Dara for Dwai. I had to. Even if it meant putting my own life at risk.

☩ 23 ☩

Dwai turned to me, his eyes full of questions. 'What should I do now? How do I find Dara?'

'I'll find him,' I said. 'I promise,' He nodded gratefully.

'Morana was right – it's not safe here anymore. It's stupid to stay and wait for her to find other ways to attack and capture you.'

'Where shall we go then?' he asked.

We. He said we.

'Anywhere but here. If I know Hera, as Morana said, she would have sent her mirror to spy on you. She will know I am with you. It will only make her more determined.'

Dwai nodded in agreement and started stuffing a few things into a rucksack. We left a little less than ten minutes later. I checked the stairway and the entrance for any lurking supernatural spies that Hera may have sent but the coast was clear. I considered flying but the skies were stirring up a storm. It wouldn't be safe for Dwai.

We walked together in the rain, knotted in our own riddles. I realized that I was no longer alone in my futureless existence – Dwai didn't know where his life was headed either.

After a while, we boarded a bus that took us to a sleepy little town. It had one derelict hotel whose beady-eyed owner stared at the two of us when we were checking in. He then winked at Dwai who, I was amused to note, looked suitably affronted.

As we entered our tiny room, we looked at each other and managed a little laugh. It consisted of one bed, one broken wooden chair, a threadbare carpet with some very suspicious stains on it, and a very old television. Thankfully, it had a small balcony whose doors I rushed to open, letting in the cool breeze.

'Take the bed,' said Dwai. 'I'll take the…floor.' He grinned.

'No,' I said firmly. 'I don't need sleep. You do.'

He didn't argue, and was soon curled up on the bed, fast asleep. I settled on the chair and watched him sleep. It was a comforting sight.

The next day dawned foggy and grim with only the occasional glimpse of sunlight. It was as if the world's weather was changing. The skies rumbled and growled, clouds moving across them like dark beasts, serving as an ominous backdrop for the birds. And, oh, there were so many birds – crows, vultures, ravens and even bats were circling the skies, as if waiting for a sign.

I could feel the tremors of magic in the air – I felt my own powers grow stronger. I wondered what Hera was up to.

A few hours later, Dwai woke up and rang for some tea that was brought to us by a curious young waiter. 'We should leave this place by tomorrow,' he said as he took a book out of his backpack. He retreated behind it and barely spoke for the rest of the morning.

I had some thinking of my own to do. I had to find Dara but I wasn't sure where to begin. The monster slayer could be anywhere. I didn't remember where his hideout was either, having run away blindly the last time. It seemed like a wild goose chase and I felt exhausted. I sighed and Dwai, who was now reading on the balcony, emerged from behind his book.

'All okay?'

'You think?'

He shrugged while I reached for the television remote.

I knew this thing existed, this contraption with picture and sound and stories. But I had no idea it told so many stories. I watched television all day on a low volume, trying to drown out my thoughts, and Dwai hardly paid attention to me except once when he stopped and stared at me, and then burst into laughter. 'Why, Ardra, you are almost a human now, glued to the idiot box.' I have no idea what he meant by that but I was just glad he was laughing.

I felt responsible for everything that had happened to him. It was my fault, my doing. If I hadn't picked him that night and bewitched him, he would have been a free human now, devoid of hallucinations, evil underworld monsters and memory ghosts. His life would have gone on like before, mostly unremarkable and uneventful. *But you don't know that*, said a voice inside me. *You don't know that at all. He had the stone. An Apsara's stone.*

Apsaras! Even for a 500-year-old Yakshi like me, they had been a grand myth – until two nights ago. I thought of what Morana had said about Apsaras and her heavy hints about knowing them. It was a small, strange world. I wondered if I would meet her again and decided I didn't really want to. Smug, superior Huldra with that horrible back and tail. And yet she had had that effect on Dwai. Somehow thinking of Dwai's hand on hers made me want to punch a hole in the wall.

Someone inside the television was singing – a beautiful love song, accompanied by a full orchestra. She was beautiful, more dazzling than any human I had seen before, though her cold and bright eyes reminded me oddly of Hera.

'*Asmaan se utri pari ho tum* (you are an angel descended from the sky)...' crooned a robust man to her as she stood atop a snow-capped mountain, her icy blue sari fluttering towards the sky.

'Who is she?' I called out to Dwai who was still ignoring both me and the 'idiot box' and reading in the balcony. He craned his neck to peek at the screen and said, 'Oh, that's Menaka Kapoor. Biggest film star in the country. Never had a flop.'

'A flop? What's a flop?'

He grinned and proceeded to explain the concept of hit

and flop movies to me. I tried to grasp the concept but mostly just stared at her.

'For a 500-year-old Yakshi with crazy powers, you know so little of life on Prithvi,' he remarked.

'That's how Hera wanted it. She barely let us out, and when she did, it was only to bewitch and take secrets. We have bewitched through wars and revolutions and plagues without really being a part of the conflicts. I think she didn't want us to get too familiar with life outside of Atala, in case we decided we wanted to be free.'

'No one has ever tried to run away before? From Atala? From her?'

I considered this. 'No. I don't think anyone ever knew they had another choice. Would you want to run away from Prithvi, from being a human? We didn't really know a life other than the one we had at Atala.'

'And yet your first instinct was to run,' he said.

'I think when your life is at stake, when you know you could end up as a head at the end of a spike, you will run. It's the oldest instinct known to both man and monsters.'

I absently flipped the channel. A morose-looking woman in a grey coat was talking about the gruesome murders that had been taking place in the city and other parts of Prithvi. It was the same story – bodies mutilated, intestines ripped out, faces torn out and placed back on, backwards. She spoke of the bodies being found in deserted areas, abandoned buildings and unused railway tracks.

I got up with a start. An idea had shot home like an arrow and the absolute inevitability of it sent a spark of pain through my core.

'What happened?' asked Dwai, surprised.

'Nothing.'

I sat down again. Dwai threw a suspicious glance at me. 'You're acting weirder than usual.'

'It's nothing,' I said casually, flipping channels again, my breath quickening as my mind played with an idea. He picked up his book and resumed reading. At some point he fell asleep, the book flopped over his face. As I watched him, I became more and more resolute.

Why are you doing this? a voice inside me asked. *You don't really need to. You need to keep running. Save this sad succubus life of yours.*

Run towards what?

Another life forever haunted by Hera? Another 500 years of loneliness and dreams full of riddles? Emptiness filled my core and I glided to the balcony. The moon was sulking behind the clouds and the night sky was thick, starless and sad. 'You are doing this because you owe it to him,' I said to myself.

'Nothing else. It's a debt,' and before that sneaky voice inside me could argue further, before it could tell me that Yakshis had no debts, that all we had was our bloodlust, I took to flight. I didn't turn back once. If I survived this mission, I could never go back to being who I was.

❖ 24 ❖

I was back at the same place I had been not so long ago, wondering if my evil mistress would spare my life or throw me into the dungeons. But strange things had happened since then and I was free now, whatever that meant.

But this was perhaps the stupidest thing I had ever done.

Wait by the deserted railway tracks that were known to be haunted by a supernatural beast for a monster slayer who I think has stalked me for half-a-century or so? Yes, this would certainly end well.

But it was the only hope I had of helping Dwai and of securing some answers for myself along the way.

I wasn't even sure he would come. All I had was an instinct based on something Hera had said: he waited by portals that could take him to Atala. And there was one here. He would come, sooner or later. I just had to wait, however long it took. I sat under a tree by the tracks and closed my eyes, my mind in turmoil.

I don't know whether I heard it first or sensed it deep within my core. It was a sound I remembered: the dry rustle of feet, the rough brush of scales, the sharp scratchy sound of claws – the Thing in the tower.

It was here, looking for new prey.

I stood up, my Yakshi sense bristling. Slipping behind the tree trunk, I peeked out. The air was rent with supernatural energy, a sort of negative electricity. Didn't this Thing just attack a human yesterday? I didn't expect it – whatever it was – to be back so soon.

Everything happened at once. A horde of rats suddenly emerged from the darkness, scurrying in all directions. I felt an unusual tension in my core and a memory ghost flickered in front me. It was the girl, and she looked stronger than before, like a sculpture made of hazy light.

'Why are you here?' I whispered. She said nothing but pointed to the Thing that was advancing along the railway tracks. I felt a flutter, an unexplained surge of emotion, and just as I was about to ask the memory ghost what it could have meant, I sensed someone behind me. Before I could blink,

I was pinned against the tree face-first, the bark splintering into my skin as I felt his force against my back. I didn't try to struggle; I had recognized the sensation within me and I knew I wasn't in danger. I turned and looked up. He put a finger to his lips, asking me to stay silent. His jewel-blue eyes bored into me, and my core did a slow, languorous flip-flop.

Dara.

✻

We stood there, his eyes locked with mine. I opened my mouth to say something but he shook his head. I heard a rustle behind us on the tracks, followed by a growl. For a few seconds, somehow, I had forgotten about the Thing altogether.

As I turned to face the tracks once again, my shoulder brushed against Dara's chest, making my core flutter like a butterfly in spring. No I didn't trust him, not yet, but I knew he wouldn't harm me. Not anymore.

Meanwhile, the memory ghost was standing in front of the tree and I wondered why Dara couldn't see her. Then I remembered: she was *my* memory. The only reason Dwai had been able to see her was because of the inexplicably reversed magic.

She remained there, shimmering like a young moon in the darkness, as I watched the creature approach. I still couldn't see what it really looked like, but I had the impression of it being a half-beast, half-man. The girl pointed to it again and I was about to ask her if she could tell me more when Dara whispered, 'We have to get you out of here.'

'Why?' I whispered back indignantly. 'I'm not a human. I'm not in any danger from whatever that is.' But even as I said it, I knew it wasn't true. I *was* in danger around that Thing —

perhaps not in mortal danger, but something about its energy undoubtedly affected me.

He muttered something through his clenched teeth that I didn't quite catch.

'Are you going to slay it?' I asked.

His face grew impassive, his eyes gleaming strangely.

'Well? Aren't you the famous monster slayer?'

'No,' he said curtly. 'I...don't have time right now. Also, it's none of your business.'

I bit back a retort; the advancing creature was making me breathless with its energy.

'Why are you here anyway?' I whispered.

'Can we save the questions for later? You need to get out of here. Now.'

I didn't argue. This was my chance to talk to him, to somehow get him to agree to what I wanted.

'Can you fly?' I asked casually. I knew perfectly well that he couldn't.

He gave me a sharp look. 'No.'

'Okay, hold on to me then,' I ordered. He reluctantly placed his hand on my shoulder. Right. I remembered how careful he was to not touch me. Ignoring the stab of annoyance I felt, I took flight. The memory ghost disappeared as I stepped off the ground and away from the tracks. I didn't look back; I had no desire to set my eyes on that Thing.

I didn't take him to Dwai straight away. I needed to talk to him first, to get him to promise me that he would help Dwai. I flew to the terrace of a skyscraper ninety floors high. As I landed, Dara immediately let go of me. He had barely touched me during our flight, choosing instead to hold on to my sleeve, and I was so annoyed that I wanted to shake him off mid-flight and watch him hurtle towards the earth. It wouldn't have killed him, of course, but it would have hurt. A lot.

He stood on the terrace uncertainly, the wind blowing his hair in all directions. The fact that this only made him look more beautiful infuriated me.

'I'm Ardra,' I said instead, trying to rein in my anger.

'I know,' he said shortly. He didn't bother to introduce himself. If he was expecting me to ask him how he knew my name, he was going to be disappointed.

'I want to trust you,' I said slowly.

He said nothing.

'I really do, and I may have no choice but to, because I need some answers.'

He raised an eyebrow but remained silent. I felt my anger rising once again.

'Why were you on the railway tracks?' I demanded. 'Tonight and…'

'It's simple, isn't it? I want to get into Atala.'

'So you wait around portals hoping you can capture some Yakshi who will take you down there?'

He nodded curtly.

'In that case…' I took a deep breath, 'I must ask again, why did you let me go?'

Was it a smile I imagined, a bitter hard smile, playing around the corner of his lips?

'Next question.'

'What's the connection between Hera and you?'

He laughed. It was a mirthless sound. 'That connection goes back centuries. We don't have time for that right now.'

'What happened after I…after you blocked me out and forced me to leave?' I asked.

'She disappeared. It is one of her talents. I suspect she

channelled her raven's energies and put up a force field against mine. She is an expert at those. I would have liked to settle our scores then but I suppose it must wait.'

He continued as I took in this information slowly. 'I suspect your presence at the railway tracks isn't just a coincidence. What do you really want?'

His jewel-blue eyes bore into me. 'You hoped to find me...' he said, carefully. 'Why?'

'Is it unusual to look for the man who saved your life twice?' I shot back. 'And because I also have a feeling you have been stalking me for years,' I continued recklessly. 'Ever since you first let me go. Why?'

This finally seemed to have hit home. His face crumbled in astonishment. He opened his mouth to say something but seemed to decide against it at the last minute.

I took a step closer to him and he instinctively took a step back.

Why don't you want to touch me?

'What do you want from me?' he asked. 'I'm sure it's something very important or you wouldn't have risked looking for me.'

I took in a deep breath. 'You need to take someone to the River of Death.'

Nothing could have prepared me for the look on his face. He looked so thunderstruck, so completely taken aback, that I thought he might faint.

'The River of Death?' he said under his breath. 'Why? Only the dead are allowed in that part of the universe. What makes you think I can go there?'

'I know you've been there before. Though I can't imagine why. I need you to take someone there. He needs to find a dead loved one and find some answers.'

'And this is important to you? And your life?'

'Yes, it is. I owe him.' I told him the whole story. When I got to the part about the Apsara's stone, he got up abruptly and walked around the terrace. His black leather trench coat billowed in the wind as he stood with his back to me.

'I want to see this stone before I do anything,' he said finally, turning to face me, his eyes gleaming strangely.

I nodded.

After a pause, I said, 'So, Apsaras exist then, as do Gandharvas.' It wasn't a question.

'Yes,' he said tightly.

'Should we just stop pretending then?

He tossed me a look.

'Dara...it's evident you are a Gandharva.'

I could see how surprised he was in his eyes. The markings on his face glowed beautifully in the moonlight.

'How do you know?' he asked finally, his voice barely audible.

'Long story,' I replied. 'But I started to figure it out when I chanced upon a flying man and discovered the sky portal. And then there was that battle with Hera. Any ordinary supernatural being could not have done what you did. So you ARE one, aren't you? If so, what are you doing on Prithvi?'

'I can't talk about that,' he said under his breath.

'Head-exploding curse?' I asked.

Despite himself he laughed. 'No. No head-exploding curse. I'm allowed to keep certain things to myself, I think.'

'Okay. But that other guy could fly. You can't.'

'Ardra...'

It was a clear command to stop talking. We stood there facing each other as silence stretched between us. Had it been any other time, I would have savoured it. Right then, though, I didn't have the luxury of time.

'Okay, so will you help me or not?' I asked finally.

'I want to see this stone,' repeated Dara. 'Also, I want something in return. Two things, actually.'

'What?'

'When this is done, I want you to help me get into Atala. You will help me get through one of the portals. This is non-negotiable.'

'And the other?'

'Once I'm down there, you will return to Prithvi and stay out of sight till you hear that she has been vanquished. Because I will do it, I will end her. I've been waiting for too long to take my revenge.'

'Why can't I help you?' I asked.

'I don't need help. I need your word on these two things and then I'm prepared to help you.' His tone had a finality to it that didn't encourage further debate.

I didn't see any reason to promise him anything, but I nodded anyway. I needed him to help Dwai. The wind whistled across the terrace, trying to fill the awkward silence that had settled between us. I was suddenly acutely aware that I was alone with him again. And the last time that had happened…

He seemed to be thinking along similar lines because he said unexpectedly, 'Why did you run away?'

I maintained my eye contact because I didn't want him to think I was afraid but my core was fluttering wildly. What could I say? That I had run because he unsettled me in a way I had never experienced before? That his eyes haunted me with secret stories? That I was deeply afraid of how he made me feel? My silence seemed to amuse him because he smiled again, the wry twisting of his lips saying more than his words ever did. It was in that moment I realized the difference between the way he made me feel and the effect Dwai had on me. And the knowledge made me sad somehow.

'I still don't know who you are,' I said. 'Who you *really* are.'

'I hope you never have to,' he said, his voice turning grim.

Heaving a secret sigh, I rose a few inches in the air, signalling that I was ready to take flight. He touched my shoulder with the same reluctance as before. We flew together once again, this time towards the hotel where I had left Dwai sleeping.

Even in the darkness, Dara smelt like warm sunshine and I couldn't get enough of it. I wondered what my fragrance was like to him, and whether he was attracted to it or not. *Not at all, judging by the way he refuses to touch you*, the voice inside me muttered snidely. *Well, we'll never know, shall we*, I thought. And I would rather face the Thing every day than ask him myself.

✢ 25 ✢

When they landed on the balcony, he instantly knew who the tall, absurdly beautiful man with Ardra was. Dara. She had returned with Dara. He had sensed her absence the instant she had flown away. The air had felt empty, devoid of her magic. He had seen a faint trail of bats in the sky behind her, and a river of windswept hair dipping in and out of the clouds.

Just then, he had wondered if she would ever come back. He didn't want to show her how glad he was that she had, so he remained stubbornly seated on the old chair, keeping his back to them.

'It's not polite to leave without a goodbye.'

She said nothing.

'I didn't think you were coming back,' he added after a pause.

'You should trust people more,' she replied as she came around to face him.

Their eyes met, her steadfast gaze meeting his frantic, searching stare.

The absurdly beautiful man stood around looking out of place. Dwai then shifted his gaze from Ardra and addressed Dara.

'We have to go on a trip together, apparently. I'm sure it will be a bonding experience for the both of us,' he mocked.

Dara stared at him without a word. Dwai stared back.

'Okayyy then, everyone is a winner in this staring match,' Ardra interjected. Both turned to her, the air heavy with awkwardness.

'Dwai, Dara wants to see the stone,' Ardra said quietly.

'Doesn't everyone these days,' he said lightly, removing the stone from around his neck and handing it to Dara.

Dara placed it on his palm. The surface changed texture and rippled into a sheer snowy white. Dwai whistled.

'How did you get this?' asked Dara quietly.

'I'm getting tired of repeating that story,' he replied pleasantly.

'Dara, I told you how he got it. He found it…'

'…inside a fish, yes,' finished Dara. His eyes narrowed as he seemed to gauge Dwai, assessing him. After several awkward minutes, he said, 'Come on, let's go. Let's get this over with. But I want you to know that, in exchange for this pleasant trip to the River of Death, Ardra has promised to go away forever and hide from Hera.'

He turned around. 'Oh, is that so? How interesting! What a pretty little barter all tied up with a fancy bow!'

'Don't make it sound like that!' Ardra said indignantly. 'What he has failed to mention is that I will also help him get into Atala.'

'No, that is not dangerous at all now,' said Dwai, his voice even but sharp.

Dara took a step closer to Dwai. His eyes glittered in a way Ardra had never seen before. 'She *has* to keep her promise. Am I making myself clear?'

'It seems to me that one promise might be more important to you than the other. Because once she is in Atala, who is to say what will happen?'

'I've made it very clear she will be safe. She has been safe before with me,' snarled Dara.

'Really?' started Dwai.

Before Dwai could do more, Ardra threw herself between them. 'Okay, that's enough. Let's get going please.'

Dara took a step back. Dwai inhaled deeply and laughed.

'I thought you couldn't come with us,' said Dwai. 'Don't get me wrong. I'm happy you want to,' he added.

'I can come with you till the Edge of Prithvi but only Dara is allowed passage from there on.'

'You didn't exactly tell me who Dara was, Ardra,' Dwai said.

'Right. Er, Dwai, he is a monster slayer. Also, he is a Gandharva who lives on Prithvi.'

'On Prithvi?' Dwai's eyebrows shot up. 'I thought Gandharvas lived in Aakasha.'

'They do. He doesn't. It's some big secret that he doesn't want to tell me.'

'Maybe if you two have finished discussing my life history, we could actually get a move on,' snapped Dara.

'So friendly,' whispered Dwai, as Dara walked forward and they followed. Ardra swallowed a chuckle despite everything.

They stood in the balcony, three of the unlikeliest people to be thrown together, tension rippling amongst them.

'Let's not waste any more time,' said Dara, clearly in command again.

'Take my hand,' she said to Dwai. 'And hold on tight.'

'I have done this before,' he smiled as he slipped his hand into hers. It felt warm and comforting. It belonged. She turned to Dara, who was as usual reluctant to put his hand on her shoulder. She noticed that he was careful to only touch her where there was a barrier of cloth between his skin and hers.

The Yakshi leapt into the sky. After a few minutes, she peeked a glance at Dwai and saw him looking delighted, his dark wavy hair swept back by the wind. The moon lit their path as they flew into the dark of the night – Yakshi, Gandharva and human – with bits of stardust in their hair.

⁂ 26 ⁂

It hadn't worked.

Hera took in a deep breath, a sharp knife of air, cold and stinging, and her eyes narrowed. The air turned into icicles of rage within her and she gasped from the pain of its impaling.

It hadn't worked.

She had gone all the way to that stupid ruin that passed off for a palace and it had all been in vain.

The old Blood Queen had laughed in her face. *Laughed.*

It was the price of failure. One stupid mistake years ago and she was still being laughed at. By a Blood Queen who didn't even deserve to be one. *She* did. She was *born* to be one. Did they even know what it meant to be one? No one did.

She wanted it. At any cost. She, Hera, Mistress of Phantoms, Queen of Desire, wanted to be Blood Queen. And she would be. She would rule over minds. She would possess dreams. There would be no one more powerful than her.

Hadn't she dreamt of this for longer than she could recall? Ever since the crone had first told her about the legend of the Blood Queen. It had all begun with when one of the earliest witches of the universe created the darkest, most powerful, spell of them all. Niara was her name, and she had been cursed by a hermit, doomed to darkness forever. Furious, she had channelled her powers and sliced darkness into three parts, swallowing one, throwing the other into the sky and the third into the earth. And from there had sprung the magic of the Blood Queen, a goddess who could choose what she wanted to rule over and nobody could stop her. However, the Blood Queen would only be as powerful as the magic that she channelled to make her one. The deeper, the more vile the spell, the stronger the Queen was. There could be more than one Queen at a time but how powerful you became depended on how deep your descent was into darkness.

Yes, she had wanted this for a very long time.

And that bitch, that ageing old *bitch*, that Skin Stealer, had laughed at her.

'Mistakes matter, Hera.' she had sniggered. 'Your mistakes will never let you be Blood Queen. The red moon has forever cast its shadow upon your ambitions. It will haunt you always.'

Even her Skull Dolls had grinned maliciously, nodding in unison.

'She doesn't even have style, does she, Gaggii?' Hera grit her teeth in frustration. They had flown for hours through difficult realms where she had to barter powerful magic spells in order to gain passage. This would have never happened had she been Blood Queen. Those idiots would have bowed their heads and let her pass, chanting her name.

'Silly white ice palace with all those Skull Dolls and that throne of fur. My eyes hurt,' she murmured. 'And I would NEVER steal skins to wear! It's *so* stone age. To wear something that once belonged to a human, of all things! Gaggii, we have magic, don't we, we have flourish. I could be a Blood Queen like the world has never seen before.'

Gaggii cocked her head to a side in apparent sympathy.

'I should have given you speech powers,' Hera said, stroking the bird absently. 'But then, you might have bored me to death. Everything bores me after a while.'

Which is why she loved her secrets. Oh, those secrets, streaming into her, brought to her by her faithful army of Yakshis. Delicious insidious bits of memory, sucked out of the human mind with magic only she could have conjured up. Her mouth watered. Her soul hungered.

'When is the next full moon, Gaggii?'

The bird cawed. Hera did the numbers on her long pale

fingers. A fortnight until the next full moon. Well, she would have to wait.

They were on top of a mountain where the wind coated in ice wound thick ribbons of ice around the landscape. Nothing passed through here; no living thing could survive in this cold. She, on the other hand, loved the cold which is why, the last time she had been passing through a tropical realm, she had spotted an airplane and had decided to hitch a ride on it. Gaggii's wings had grown tired of her weight and the raven had been happy to let go of her mistress for a while.

She had been hungry, she recalled. Far too ravenous to wait for the next full moon, her assassins to bring her what kept her powerful. She had taken a huge risk by taking the secrets of the humans on the airplane. Of course, she hadn't taken enough to kill them. A plane full of mysteriously dead humans would alert the Balance Keeper, the conscientious old fool. But she had taken enough to give her a high and that had kept her happy for a while.

Except she had been so delirious with the sudden rush of secrets within her that she hadn't paid attention, and that boy had slipped through her fingers. Something about him stirred a deep desire within her. She wanted him, the boy with those black pearl eyes and that strange indescribable pull. If she didn't know better, she would say he was...

No! That was impossible. But, then, how did he have the stone?

She had been so stupid, so slow to realize the full impact of what the stone around the boy's neck meant. How could she have been so blind? She should have captured him right there. This trip would then have been unnecessary; this begging and bowing to that horrible three-eyed queen on her silly chair made of bear fur.

She wondered if Mantri had found the boy yet. If he had, then this was over. A new era would start. Of her glory, her power.

But she couldn't be sure. She bit her lip in confusion as she recalled the stone, gleaming on that boy's neck. Was it a Jwala? But how? How was a stone like the Jwala found on earth? It had been centuries, hadn't it, since...

The memory of the past shot a fresh stab to her heart.

And that girl, that infernal succubus. She had almost ruined everything. The mirror, that old fool, had told her that Ardra and the boy were together when she had consulted it a couple of days ago. Clearly, the silly girl had gone looking for him. What a strange plot twist that was. Her mirror had also informed her that they were no longer in the boy's house. Which meant Morana had failed in her mission. Well, they couldn't hide from her for long; she would find them sooner or later. And she would deal with the girl once the boy was in her possession and she had had time to examine him. If he was what she suspected him to be, then... Her eyes shone with an unholy fire at the thought.

'Come on, Gaggii,' she said. 'We must look to the future. Not the past. The past is a graveyard, isn't it? Only fit to enter on rare occasions to revisit one's mistakes.'

The bird opened its wings in response and she touched one lightly. Soon they were airborne, a strange sight in the sky, a smear of witch and raven, full of darkness and magic, the sort children see and run to tell their mothers, who don't believe them.

'This is the Edge of Prithvi?' Ardra asked. Her tone was incredulous and not devoid of disdain.

'This is the door that leads to the Edge of Prithvi,' said Dara, long-suffering patience evident in his voice.

They were standing in front of a small, battered door with an iron handle. It was so low that only a dwarf could possibly pass comfortably through it.

'You can see it?' he asked Dwai, who nodded in response.

Dara frowned. 'That's strange,' he muttered, almost to himself.

'Why is it strange?' asked Ardra.

'Because humans should only be able to see a snowy landscape, bare and cold. But if they tried to walk off the edge of the mountain, they wouldn't be able to. The door is protected by an invisible barrier which ripples gently when touched.'

The three of them stared at it; it was the most unremarkable door in the whole world. They had travelled for most of the night using Ardra's powers of flight. When they had finally landed on top of the mountain that Dara had directed her to, Dwai noticed that, despite putting on a brave face, she was exhausted from bearing their weight for so long. As soon as he let go of her hand, all he wanted to do was hold it again and comfort her.

The mountain was ice-clad with no sign of life as far as the eye could see. Dwai shivered in the cold and pulled his jacket closer, his lips becoming bluer by the second. Ardra stayed close to him, trying to shield him from the freezing wind. Unlike Dara and her, he wasn't built to withstand the cold.

'So, what are we waiting for? Let's go in,' Dwai urged, trying very hard to keep the impatience out of his tone. It didn't help that his teeth were chattering noisily.

'We are waiting for the Keeper of the door. I've sent a signal across. It shouldn't be very long,' said Dara. He walked a little ahead, leaving Ardra and Dwai behind. Ardra watched him, a distant figure, hazy in the icy winds, aloof and quiet. He turned and caught her eye, and she noticed how warm he seemed. Even in that bracing cold, he looked like a mellow ray of sunshine.

'Get up,' she suddenly told Dwai, who was sitting on a rock, shivering. She held out her hand and he took it, hobbling in the cold, unable to speak. Walking purposefully towards Dara, to his great consternation, she put Dwai's hand into his.

'Hold it,' she said firmly when Dara raised his eyebrows at her. 'Dwai is bound to die in this cold otherwise.'

'Erm…' muttered Dara, but he didn't let go of Dwai's hand. Ardra looked fierce as she watched both of them closely. Uncomfortable seconds passed in silence, but slowly, Dwai's lips were returning to their normal colour. He seemed to be shivering less, too.

'It worked,' she said happily. 'I knew it would.'

'What would?' asked Dara dryly.

'Your warmth. You are as warm as…' she stopped, looking embarrassed.

'Well, I guess what she is saying is, you have your uses,' said Dwai, his eyes twinkling. 'But tell me, good sir, it wouldn't have hurt to warn me right? I don't have thermal superpowers like you and some layers would be nice right now.'

'Sorry, I didn't really think of it. I'm not used to dealing with humans,' was all Dara would say. But he didn't let go of Dwai's hand and Ardra smiled to herself.

The snow fell several inches thick as they waited for what seemed like hours. They made for a strange sight on top of the tallest mountain in Prithvi – a human holding hands with a man whose beauty seemed to belong to the tales of the Old Books, accompanied by a tall, pale girl dressed in black with storm-hued hair of the same colour. The snow seemed to fall around her with exceeding gentleness and the air around her was ethereal, speckled with white light. She suddenly twirled in mid-air and Dwai thought his heart might stop from the sudden unexpected beauty she emanated. A dark snowflake in a sheer white landscape, she twirled, mindless of her worries for that moment, the hail entangled in her hair giving the impression of an erratic constellation speckled against the night sky.

They couldn't take their eyes off her – neither human nor Gandharva. The Yakshi seemed unaware of their gaze as she twirled, chasing snowflakes as they fell to the ground. She picked up one and pressed it to her chest. It froze, like crystal, and she pocketed it.

They could have stood there forever, watching her, but the crunch of heavy footsteps coming up the narrow path pulled them back to reality.

'I think he's finally here,' said Dara. He let go of Dwai's hand. 'You will be all right now. The warmth should last until we get to the other side of the door.'

Dwai didn't respond. He was listening to the footsteps. They sounded like rumbling thunder as they inched nearer.

Then something enormous lumbered into sight, and Ardra and Dwai's jaws dropped. Dara, however, looked happier than he had in a long time.

'Izaru!' he shouted.

'Dara, is that you?' a squeaky voice replied.

Ardra and Dwai looked at each other.

Through the snow and fog emerged Izaru. He had the body of a human, covered in dirty golden hair and the head of the ugliest lion in the world. His mane was matted and mangy and fell on his shoulders in thin dirty ropes. Ardra noticed the tiny skulls of animals braided into his mane. Dressed in nothing but a pair of yak-hair trousers, he was seated atop a giant mountain goat with long white straggles of hair coming out of its humungous ears and a billy-goat moustache that scraped the ground. The goat plodded up the path with hooves the size of giant saucers. It was the hooves that were making the sound. Izaru, unable to control his excitement, stood on top of his mount and called out to Dara.

'Dara, you ugly old monkey! I'm so glad to see you again,' he squeaked, leaping off the goat which snorted in disdain and took a few steps back, kicking up snow as it did.

Dwai gulped, trying to swallow his laughter. Dara embraced his long lost friend but not before throwing Dwai a withering look over Izaru's scraggy shoulder.

The hug lasted a few minutes with Izaru gurgling with laughter and thumping Dara on the back numerous times in what was clearly an expression of joy. His goat harummphed and shook its head dolefully, stamping its massive hooves noisily into the ground.

When Izaru finally pulled back, tears of joy were streaming down his cheeks. He thumped his chest hard. 'Aah, such joy you bring to my life, my friend.' Eventually he spotted Dwai and Ardra standing on the side of the path, watching the whole spectacle, and his huge eyes narrowed.

'Who are they? This is not a place for humans, Dara. I thought you knew that.'

'Only the boy is human. She, Ardra, is a Yakshi.'

'A Yakshi, eh?' Izaru squeaked. 'Thank God I don't have any

secrets, or you might have found me irresistible!' he screeched with laughter at his own joke and Ardra smiled politely.

'Don't you give us that look, you two,' said Izaru, noting Dwai and Ardra's wry expressions. 'He and I, we've been through so much. We defeated the great beast of Razvang together. And such a great beast he was. Gave me this.' He parted his mangy hair and showed them a deep scarlet scar on his stomach. 'Enh, Dara, the realm of Razvang was a wonderful place, wasn't it? You remember the nymphs… aaah, those nymphs. Do they make them like that anymore? I don't think so, eh? Though this one here isn't so bad,' he added, waving a pudgy, furry hand towards Ardra. 'What say Dara, you monkey?'

All this was rattled off in one long squeaky breath after which Izaru thumped his chest again and screeched with laughter.

Dara, poker-faced, put his hand on Izaru's shoulder. 'Friend, I have come on a quest. And I hope you will help me.'

'Tell me, what can Izaru the Third, Keeper of the Edge of Prithvi, Warlord of the Mountains, do for you, my friend?' said Izaru pompously, dusting the snow off a couple of rocks with vigour so he and Dara could sit on them.

'It's a long story,' said Dara, 'but to cut it short, if you will not ask too many questions, I need to get to the River of Death.'

There was a deep silence as Izaru took in Dara's words. He scratched his mane and absently tugged at one of the skulls as he stared at Dara, not saying a word but shaking his head from time to time. Finally, he got up from the rock, sighed, and thumped his chest. Dwai and Ardra watched him, silent and hopeful.

'So,' said Dara, 'will you open the door?'

'I did it for you once, long ago, didn't I?' Izaru's squeak was pensive.

'You did. But let us not speak of that now. I need passage to the Tarini. And I need to take him with me.' He indicated Dwai.

'Take a human, a *living* human, down to the Tarini with you?! Dara, my friend, even if you managed it, he may not make it back alive!'

'That is a risk he has to take if he wants to find what he is looking for,' said Dara.

'And I'm prepared to take that risk,' said Dwai, sounding determined.

Dara's eyes flitted towards Ardra, who said nothing.

'You made it back last time, my brave friend. You may not be so lucky this time.'

'I will make it back,' said Dara. Izaru and he regarded each other for a while. Then the half-lion sighed and walked up the path towards the door. 'Remember,' he said as he fumbled for the key within his sheepskin coat, 'once I open the door, you will barely have seconds to get to the river. I suggest the human holds on to you so that you do not get separated. Once you are there...' He sighed and shook his head. 'Where's this damn key?' he muttered, searching the pockets of his trousers. 'There, found it,' he squeaked to no one in particular.

He gestured to Dara and Dwai and they walked up to the door. Ardra stayed where she was. Izaru fished out a key that was as ordinary as the door – iron-wrought, thick and dull.

'Right,' Izaru squeaked with a flustered air, 'let's do this. Though I don't know what kind of a friend I am, Dara, my brave brother, for letting you do this again.'

No one said anything as he fumbled with the key. Ardra took a few steps forward.

'I don't like goodbyes. So I won't say one. I'll be back soon,' Dwai said. She barely shook her head in response. Dara just nodded and then, without a backward glance, strode up to Izaru who was fitting the key into the keyhole.

'Be ready,' he said quietly to Dwai. 'We won't even have seconds.' They waited as the key turned by itself in the hole. Izaru stepped back. Dwai and Dara moved forward, readying themselves by bending to fit through the tiny frame. The wind howled, as if it knew something was about to happen.

Ardra stayed rooted where she was. No one said a word as the key turned seven times in the hole and then clattered to the ground. The door creaked open slowly. As it did, a blanket of darkness fell around them. Ardra couldn't see anything. It was as if she had gone blind.

'Dara,' she called out, panic rising within her. She couldn't even hear the sound of her own voice. The darkness swallowed it.

A few seconds later, the darkness ebbed.

Dwai and Dara had vanished. The door had shut again and Izaru stood pocketing the key. He didn't look at her as he walked past, a great big sigh escaping his lips. She stood frozen, staring at the door as if she could see beyond it and into where Dwai and Dara had gone.

✦ 28 ✦

The door creaked open and they ran through to the other side. Dwai stayed close to Dara as the Gandharva had ordered. What greeted them on the other side took his breath away.

Nothingness.

They were standing on the narrowest inch of earth and after that...nothing.

Nothing on top, nothing at the bottom, just a spiralling, colourless, airless void. It was if someone had taken an eraser and wiped out every hue, every shape, every texture from the universe, leaving a blank, lifeless landscape.

Dwai found it difficult to breathe.

'We have to jump,' said Dara. Before Dwai could give voice to his panic, Dara had propelled him forward and they sank speedily into the void. Even the airlessness had a force and it hit him square in the chest, leaving him gasping for breath. *This is probably what sinking into a marshland feels like*, thought Dwai, as he closed his eyes, taking in short gulps of air. They fell for what seemed like ages until his feet touched the ground abruptly. They seemed to be standing on what looked like vapour but felt like solid ground.

Dara took a deep breath and murmured. 'Almost there...'

'What do we do now?' whispered Dwai, not daring to raise his voice.

'Now we wait,' said Dara and his tone that sent a shiver down Dwai's spine. He didn't ask what they were waiting for. Something told him he was better off not knowing until it was absolutely inevitable.

A static emptiness stretched out in front of them. *The same way the television goes blank when the weather is bad*, Dwai thought. He felt disoriented and shaky on his feet.

'What happened the last time you were here?' he asked Dara, trying to distract himself. He was met with a stony silence.

'What on earth could have prompted you to come here?' he repeated.

Dara opened his mouth to reply and that's when they saw

the red dots in the distance. Not dots, flares. No, not flares, streaks. They inched closer, and Dara turned white.

'Whatever you do, do not look directly into their eyes,' Dara said between his teeth.

Dwai nodded. As the red streaks advanced closer, he felt like he was falling, even though he hadn't moved at all. Falling into an abyss, his head churning.

And then he saw them. They had skulls for heads and empty eye sockets. Their bodies were half-black, half-white and their skeletal hands held torches with red fire burning in them. He lost count of them after a while. There were hundreds.

'Nice welcome party,' he muttered under his breath. 'What are they?'

'Dutas,' replied Dara. 'The Dutas of the Death God. They don't negotiate. Just do as I say. Please,' he added.

Dwai merely nodded. He didn't trust his voice at this point.

The Dutas stopped when they saw Dara, but there was no greeting, no acknowledgement. Instead, they parted down the middle and waited in eerie silence. Dwai could see someone riding down the path made by the Dutas. A black fog enveloped him. He was seated on a skeleton horse which, Dwai noted, was made of bone but had a real shining mane and tail. The man on the horse was taller than the rest of the Dutas and had long, straight hair that fell below his half-black, half-white shoulders. He was holding a long white staff in his hand, a sceptre with a buffalo's head. When he spoke, Dwai felt a shiver of horror creeping up his spine. His tongue was human, but his voice was sepulchral, hollow and utterly unpleasant.

'You have returned, I see. No one alive has ever walked these parts twice. You are either brave or foolish, or both.'

Dara bowed in silence.

'And you have brought a human with you. A live one. Do you not realize the consequences of doing so? Only the dead pass through our world. I am surprised the Keeper let you through.'

'I do not expect a free pass. I will agree to your terms, whatever they are. But you must understand things are very different on Prithvi right now...the winds...'

'Yes,' the head Duta cut him off. 'I am aware of what is happening on Prithvi, and elsewhere. What brings you here?'

'The human, he is looking for someone. His grandmother. There are answers only she can give him. And these answers will affect the fabric of the world. Otherwise, I wouldn't be here.'

'The fabric had begun to tear ages ago, but something rips it apart with constant malevolence these days,' said the head Duta grimly. 'I am aware of the consequences of this, so I will allow him to pass if what you say is true. But in return...'

'In return,' Dara took a deep breath, 'in return, I am willing to pawn my soul.'

Dwai, who had been listening intently and quietly to the two, now started in shock.

'NO! Whatever that means, Dara, no!'

'Tell the human to hold his tongue,' spat the head Duta. Dara turned to Dwai who made a visible effort to quiet down, shaking his head in frustration.

'Gandharva, you do know what pawning your soul entails?'

'I am aware of what it entails,' said Dara, his voice devoid of any emotion.

'Oh yes, I forget you have done this before. But I have to warn you, I do not know anyone who has pawned their soul twice and survived. We must hope for the best.'

'Just get the human to his grandmother and back. Assure me that you will,' said Dara.

'You have my word. But once he is back here, I cannot help you return to the Edge. That is your concern alone.'

Dara nodded curtly.

'Take the boy,' the Duta leader barked at his comrades.

One of the Dutas skulked forward and signalled Dwai to step forward. He shot a nervous look at Dara, who nodded, and then walked towards the Duta horde.

'And now for the pawning...' said the head Duta. 'I will do this myself.'

'Listen,' said Dara, turning to Dwai, his tone urgent. 'If something happens to me...if I can't make it back...'

'What do you mean, you can't make it back?'

'Listen to me! If that happens, you will need to go back to the Edge by yourself. They may try to stop you. Use your stone.'

'Use the stone? How?'

'The boat is here. Let the pawning begin,' the head Duta cut in impatiently.

'Watch out for the Castaways. They will try to...' Dara said, but before he could finish, the Dutas clanked their spears impatiently, drowning out his words. The head Duta got off his horse and walked towards the Gandharva. In that second, Dwai realized what Ardra had meant by how warm Dara felt. Even in that airless, dank place, surrounded by these attendants of death, he seemed to emit a certain light, almost like the light of the sun, that emanated from him gently into the world.

The head Duta and Dara stood facing each other. The Gandharva seemed to stare at a point beyond the Duta's shoulder. He wasn't looking into his sockets. Dwai stayed transfixed on the Gandharva, his heart beating fast. What was going to happen? Why did he put himself up to this? For him, Dwai? No, surely not. For the fabric of the universe that was ripping away and changing everything in the world? Maybe. But this kind of sacrifice seemed extreme, even for the fate of the world. So then why would he do it?

Then he knew. He had seen it, known it on the snow-covered path, when a dark snowflake had swirled through the icy air, forgetting the world for a second. He had known what that look on Dara's face meant, because he was sure his own face had been mirroring the expression. Of wonder, of tenderness, of...

Ardra. He was doing it for Ardra. Despite the white hot flash of jealousy that shot through his body, Dwai saw a vision – a Gandharva and a Yakshi, flying together in the silver moonlight, their bodies entwined, a halo of stardust around them. It seemed possible. It seemed *right*. And, in that split second, he knew that he would have made the same choice as Dara if Ardra had asked him.

He was jolted back to the present by a clattering sound. The Duta was drumming the vapour-like ground with his sceptre, making a harsh metallic noise. Soon the other Dutas started doing it too, and the sound of a hundred staffs hitting the ground filled his ears.

Dara stood there, unmoving, expressionless. The Duta abruptly stopped the drumming and came even closer to the Gandharva, muttering an incantation under his breath. The energy of the chants sent a pang of hysteria through Dwai and he momentarily closed his eyes, trying to regain composure.

When he opened his eyes again, seconds later, Dara was on his knees. The Duta was standing over him, his skeletal head thrown back, immersed in his chants.

And then it happened.

The Duta extended his right hand. Dara gasped loudly as a circular orb of smoky light began streaming from him and into the Duta's palm. The light streamed fast and bright. Dara's face twisted in pain as he crumbled to the floor. Dwai tried to rush to him but one of the Dutas held him back firmly.

The head Duta extended his left arm and, on cue, one of his comrades came forward with a copper bowl. The Duta took it and started to guide the orb of light into the bowl. Dara now began to scream. His breath came in painful rasps and he writhed on the floor.

'Stop this, please! Someone…help him,' shouted Dwai, unable to bear Dara's agony.

But nobody did anything to help the Gandharva. The head Duta stood over him, unmoving, holding the bowl with stone-like impassiveness, not paying any heed to the writhing, screaming man at his feet.

Dwai covered his face with his hands. He couldn't take it anymore.

And then it was over. The writhing stopped. So did the streaming of the light. A gut-wrenching silence filled the place. Dwai looked up to see Dara twitching like a dying moth and then lying still, his hair slicked with sweat, his eyes closed, his mouth twisted in agony.

The head Duta looked into the urn and then passed it to one of the others before addressing Dwai.

'His soul will be in our keeping until you return. If you fail to return within two earthly days it becomes ours.'

'Is…is he dead?' whispered Dwai.

Some of the Dutas tittered.

'No,' said their leader. 'He is not dead. But his soul is separate from his body and that doesn't make him living either. Make haste, human. He has bought you passage into

Tarini, the River of Death, along with some time. Go find your grandmother.'

Dwai's eyes stayed on the unmoving Gandharva before one of the Dutas pulled him away.

29

After walking for what felt like hours, Dwai noticed that the ground beneath him had begun to change. The vapour was giving way to grass and mud and, in the distance, he could see something gleaming.

The River of Death.

As the scene changed, it took on a very theatrical feel. The sky, a glowing blood red above him, looked surreal. The trees, ghostly and gnarled, looked like props on the set of the mythological TV shows Dwai had watched as a child. The grass seemed too green to be real. Soon he could see the River clearly, its waters running oily and deep. A boat rested on the banks, bobbing gently even though there was no wind.

The Dutas walked him till the edge of the bank and then moved away wordlessly. For a second he wondered if someone else would come with instructions, and that's when he noticed her – a woman in billowing grey robes, wearing a mask, her hair flying in the non-existent wind. Her mask seemed to be made of ivory and had eyes painted on it. She hadn't been there a minute ago, he was sure of it. She was sitting in the boat and holding the oars with hands that were devoid of skin, just like the rest of the Dutas. She turned to look at him and, without a word, untied the boat. He hopped on just as it started moving, even though she didn't seem to be rowing, just holding on to the oars. As the boat glided over the oily waters, he started to hear whispers. He wasn't sure where they were coming from and he looked around, wondering if the shore was nearby. Shutting his eyes, he willed himself to remain calm as the whispers intensified. When he opened them again, there was someone sitting next to him – someone human, he realized with a start. As he watched, the boat filled up with silent, watchful people. They all seemed to just stare ahead, glassy-eyed and cadaverous.

'Let me guess,' said Dwai. 'You are all dead and are now being ferried across the River.'

They all turned to look at him at once and if this had been a scene from a horror film on television he might have laughed. But right then he didn't feel like laughing. He shut his eyes, wanting to block out everything – the dead people, the disconcerting woman at the oars and the whispers. And when he opened his eyes again, he realized they were coming from the banks on both sides. He could make out faint outlines of people who were watching the boat from the banks. Something told him that these were the Castaways that Dara had tried to warn him about – dead people who hadn't crossed over yet; who hadn't been allowed to cross over. He wondered what fate awaited them and if hell really existed. The whispers grew louder, and soon he could make out distinct voices. The outlines grew sharper, too, and he saw some of them enter the water, their bodies stiff and jerky. A sliver of panic flared in his gut as he looked around. The dead people in the boat continued to stare ahead while the woman steering paid him no attention, the eyes on her mask glassily fixed at a distant point on the banks.

The Castaways continued to enter the water in droves, their whispers growing louder and clearer. He could hear what they were saying now, all of them at once, like a chant:

Give me your soul. Give me your soul. Give me your soul. Give me your soul.

They could sense his soul; it was their only chance of crossing over again. The stone around his neck started to scorch his skin and he took it off and put it into his pocket. The people on the boat moved their glassy stare to the dead in the water. The boatwoman dropped one of the oars into the river. It sank without a ripple.

They were trying to get on the boat now, their stiff movements making it difficult for them to grab a hold. Dwai caught a glimpse of their hands and recoiled – they were grey and slimy, the flesh beginning to rot and fall off in places. One tried to grab his hand and he pulled away, standing up abruptly. The sudden movement caused the boat to rock wildly.

More hands reached out from all sides and the chants grew louder.

The boatwoman dropped the other oar into the water and Dwai watched it disappear into its inky depths.

As the oar vanished out of sight, the Castaways started to climb on board. Frantic, they reached for Dwai, plucking at his clothes, his hair, grabbing his legs, all the while chanting, '*Give me your soul...*'

Dwai fought back, lashing around, trying to fend them off. The people on the boat sat and watched, not moving, silent and expressionless. The boatwoman stood up and took a step forward. As she did, the vessel capsized. Screaming and groaning, the Castaways and the passengers fell into the water. The chants for Dwai's soul reached a hysterical octave.

Dwai hit the water head first. It was freezing and he could

feel slimy arms reach out for him. He swam ahead blindly, without really being able to see the shore. It was then that he felt the boatwoman right beside him. She wasn't swimming but gliding along the water that only came up to her waist. She took his hand and before he could react, he was gliding through the water with her. Her hand was skeletal and cold but he held tight, knowing that she was his only chance of escaping the dead.

'Are they ghosts?' he asked the boatwoman, surprised by how calm he sounded. She shook her head. They moved swiftly and silently for a while and then his feet scraped sand. Shore at last.

They were greeted by an unnaturally thick fog. When he looked back, he couldn't see the river anymore. The woman let go of his hand and by the time he turned to thank her for saving him, she was gone.

Uncertain of what to do next, he took a few steps forward. The mist swirled around him. He caught an unmistakably familiar whiff of sandalwood and ash – a fragrance that had filled his childhood. The mists gave way and he saw her, smiling, her eyes moist, dressed in her favourite white and gold sari – his grandmother. He reached out to touch her, but all he felt was the mist. He couldn't feel her, or hug her. She just stood there, smiling at him.

'We don't have much time, I am told,' she said in a distant, quavering voice. 'Ask me what you want to know, child.'

He wrapped his fingers around the stone in his pocket and took it out.

'Why do I have this Apsara's stone? What does it really mean, that I have it?'

The old lady smiled. 'You have the stone because you inherited it. It belonged to your mother.'

Dwai's fingers tightened around the stone as it singed his skin.

'My mother? But you said...I thought...' he trailed off. Actually, when he thought about it, his grandmother had never said anything specific about his mother, except an occasional 'She came from far away' or 'She lost her mind and couldn't look after you'.

'My mother...was an Apsara?' he whispered.

'Yes,' said his grandmother, 'she was. She barely held you, though. Madness claimed her.'

'How does an Apsara go mad?' he wanted to ask. But all he did was clench the stone tightly, as if he might lose it and it would take with it the memory of his mother.

'You must know,' continued the old woman, 'that it will help you survive what is to come.' She held out her wrinkled hand to him and he took it, expecting to feel the familiar wrinkled comfort he was used to. Instead, he felt a shaft of light pass through his palm.

'I don't know everything,' she said. 'But I will pass on whatever I do know. The rest the stone will tell you. Close your eyes, child...'

He did as he was told. The stone felt warm and alive in his palm. His grandmother caressed its surface and as she did, it seemed to implode, sending tiny shocks of electricity through him.

A lightning bolt passed through his brain and he felt as if he was on fire. And then he began to see:

She was in love, though she knew it was forbidden. But her heart wouldn't stop beating for him. They lay on the grass, counting invisible stars in a rainswept sky, their fingers entwined.

Her eyes, bright as sapphires, his earnest black pearls. They didn't need words to know they had created life. Her womb was a tiny heartbeat...

A sense that things were going to go horribly wrong. She knew deep in her soul that this could not end well. 'Take this,' she said, handing him her stone. 'Take this for our child. Someday he must have it and know who he is.'

She knew they had found out. She knew this was the end. They will banish her and she will never see her child or her lover again.

She fell from the sky. Banishment was her world now. She belonged neither to sky nor to earth. She was not allowed to belong to anything she loved. She crumpled to the ground and wept.

Her madness was a bird. It circled the sky crazily with broken wings. Her eyes were blank. She wandered around asking about her child. Her bare feet bled for they had never touched the ground before.

She walked to the river…she knew somewhere on the other side was her child and the man she loves. But she couldn't go to them. She walked into the river, her blank eyes fixed on a point in the distance. An old house with mud brown tiles and a broken heart within. The water embraced her, she welcomed its depths…

The visions stopped with a fizz and a crackle. Dwai opened his eyes, sweating and gasping for breath, the stone still in his hand. His grandmother stood over him, her aspect a little dimmer now.

'She killed herself…' he whispered. 'She drowned in the river that flows next to our home…'

The old lady was a faint smear of light. 'Yes, she had her powers wrenched away from her. She was a mere shell of a being when she gave birth to you, and then she jumped.'

She was beginning to fade now.

'No, wait. I want to know…does anyone else other than you and my father know I exist?'

His grandmother shook her head. 'Your mother lost her powers, but not the stone. The stone cast its protective shield around you. I doubt anyone else knew of your birth. But I am not so sure anymore. It is going to be tough for you.'

'Don't go!' he pleaded as his grandmother began to fade. 'Stay with me…'

'I am always with you, but now I have to leave. Blessed am I that I can move on.' Her eyes strayed to the far riverbanks where the dead who couldn't cross over waited.

'There are still so many things I don't know,' he said, desperate and sad. He took a step towards the fading light that was his grandmother and she seemed to diminish even more.

'Use the stone, it is yours. Your mother's powers are vested in that stone. Be safe, my child.'

She faded like a wisp of wind and Dwai stood staring at the spot she had stood on. The stone glowed in his palm; it had turned a deep purple. He closed his fist over it, remembering Dara's words.

Dara! He had to hurry back and make sure he was okay. He began making his way back to the river. The masked woman stood on the banks, the oars back in her skeletal hands.

She nodded silently as he approached and started gliding into the water. He paused briefly before following her into it, the stone tightly clasped in his fist. Waist deep in the water, he felt something solid under his feet. He looked down and realized he was standing on the boat. Taking a seat on a wooden plank, he looked away as the masked woman watched him, silent and ominous. The boat glided swiftly over the water. No dead waded into the river to claim his soul this time, though he could see their lifeless eyes watching him as they stood on the banks, forlorn, with no past, present or future, suspended for all eternity in a void by the River of Death.

30

Dwai soon spotted the Duta who had accompanied him waiting at the banks, his red torch flashing in the distance. He got off the boat and turned to look at the masked woman. 'Thank you,' he muttered.

She nodded slightly. The Duta stomped his spear on the ground impatiently and Dwai started walking towards him. A grey fog fell like a curtain between him and the river and, when he turned, there was nothing there but the now familiar vapour-like landscape. He walked quietly alongside the Duta, his heart beating furiously within his chest, wondering if he would find Dara alive at the end of his path. Was he late? Had two earthly days passed? The Duta who accompanied him strode on in stony silence.

When he saw Dara still lying crumpled on the floor, surrounded by silent Dutas, he broke into a run. The Gandharva's eyes were closed and his face looked far from peaceful. His eyelids were turning grey. He was beginning to look like those by the banks of the river, Dwai realized with horror.

The Dutas stood watching them. The head Duta was nowhere to be seen.

'Bring him back,' yelled Dwai. 'I have returned. Give his soul back to him.'

The Dutas started to stomp their spears on the ground again.

'Please do it quickly…' whispered Dwai, his voice frantic. 'Please…'

The stomping of spears continued. Dwai could hear the

156

click-clack of skeletal hooves and relief swept over him. The head Duta was here. Surely, surely, he would restore Dara's soul back into his body?

But the person on the horse was not the head Duta.

It was the masked woman. Dwai watched as she rode in, the Dutas making way for her. She got off the horse, her grey robes lapping around her like waves. The spears had now gone silent.

Something was different about her. With a jolt, Dwai realized that though her mask was still in place, her eyes were no longer painted on, but real, and piercing. He could see long lashes through the eye holes and when he looked into them, he felt a shiver pass through his gut. Later, he wouldn't remember this, his memory keeping this bit locked away from his reality forever, but in that moment he looked into those eyes and whispered, 'It is you. How is it possible?'

She said nothing but extended her hand towards him. A spherical ball of light bloomed out of her palm like a flower. It stayed suspended in the air for a bit before floating towards Dara's still, soulless body. Dwai watched as the light merged into the Gandharva's being.

It was like someone had switched on a light within Dara as he flickered to life. His skin slowly began to glow again and he opened his eyes.

'Thank God,' whispered Dwai as he helped Dara up. He was on his feet almost immediately, looking whole and divine, and a wave of relief swept through Dwai. By the time he looked around, the masked woman had disappeared, leaving only the Dutas with their skull heads and deathly eye sockets.

Dara turned to look at Dwai. 'Did you get the answers you wanted?'

Dwai nodded. He still had so many questions that were

still unanswered but right then, they had more pressing problems.

'We should go,' urged Dara almost under his breath. He nodded to the Dutas and then turned. 'Don't look back. Just keep walking,' he muttered, his voice low and tense.

'Keep walking where?' asked Dwai. They had fallen into this space out of nowhere. Off the Edge of Prithvi. How were they supposed to find their way back? Dara didn't answer. Instead, he quickened his pace as a dusty fog enveloped them. 'They sure love their fog around here, don't they?' said Dwai to no one in particular. They kept walking through the fog in silence. He wondered if Dara knew what he was doing.

There was something in the fog coming towards them. For a second Dwai wondered if they had somehow made it back to the snow-covered path on top of the mountain and the shapes belonged to Izaru and Ardra. But he dismissed the thought as soon as he saw that it was, in fact, not two but a throng of foggy outlines that was inching closer to them.

Dara stopped in his tracks.

'We've come the wrong way,' he said. As he spoke, the fog cleared a bit. Dwai took a step back.

The Castaways were advancing towards them – multitudes of them, abandoned, stranded, condemned to live on the banks of the Tarini. They had smelt the beautiful scent of souls. Souls that could ferry them across.

'Take out the Jwala,' said Dara quietly, his jaw set in a grim line.

Dwai took out his mother's stone from his pocket. 'Now what?'

'Think of where you need to go. Concentrate...'

He closed his eyes, trying not to think of the Castaways just inches away from him. He felt Dara's hand on his shoulder.

His mind filled with the thought of Ardra waiting by the door for them.

'Throw the stone up in the air,' said Dara, his voice ringing with quiet urgency.

Dwai didn't question him – there would be plenty of time for that later. Ignoring the thuds of the feet that seemed to be almost upon them, he flung the stone into the still air, his heart full of Ardra and his mind fixed on the door.

A purple light burst from the stone, coiling around the two of them. As hundreds of rotting arms reached out for them, a brilliant flash of light enveloped their bodies in an electric surge of energy.

❖ 31 ❖

It felt like the end of time. In reality, it had only been two days. Two days of sitting by the door, waiting for someone to pound on it from the other side. Waiting for Dwai, for Dara, to appear through the door. Dwai, with his beautiful black pearl eyes and that crooked smile. Dara, with his jewel-blue eyes and the aloof, ravaged air.

I would never forget what he had done for Dwai...and I will never understand why. Something told me it was much more than the barter promised to him. And now *my* end of the promise must be kept. I would lead him to Atala and then go away to be safe from Hera. The idea pierced my heart like a sword and I winced from the ache it brought.

To go away forever meant not seeing Dwai ever again. Or Dara...

Was it even possible that I thought about both of them? Did humans do that? Was it possible for your heart to be split into two wild halves? I put my hand to my chest. There was no heartbeat, of course. I had never had one. My heart would never pound against its walls upon the sight of someone. My core could do a slow waltz though.

As I sat there on that snow-covered rock while Izaru paced up and down, I realized that I wouldn't be able to keep my promise. I couldn't. I couldn't leave Dwai to fend for himself against Hera. And I couldn't bear the thought of never seeing Dara again. My decision wouldn't please Dara, I knew, but he couldn't force me to do anything either.

I know what humans call this sort of confusion, but I am too afraid to use the word. To say it out loud.

You don't know how Dwai feels, a voice inside me pointed out. *You don't even know what Dara really thinks of you.*

'Shut up,' I murmured, and Izaru looked at me. He had been throwing several sly glances my way as if he was assessing me, taking me in, wondering what I was doing on this strange quest with a human and a Gandharva.

A little after Dwai and Dara disappeared through that door, he had sat on his haunches in the snow, clutching his large head in his paw-like hands, and groaned, 'I shouldn't have let him go there again.'

I seized the opportunity. 'Why did Dara go there centuries ago, Izaru?' My tone was sweet and innocent.

He didn't fall for it.

'Ask him yourself,' he grunted.

That was pretty much all the conversation we had that day.

'What is down there?' I asked once, as Izaru continued his vigil.

'Nothing,' he grunted. 'It's a great big nothing down there. But I wouldn't really know. I hope I need to go there only when I am dead and gone.'

'Are they in danger?' I tried a few hours later. Panic was a constant butterfly in my core, with frail beating wings.

Izaru shook his head. 'Dara knows what to do. And if that stone really is what you say it is, they should be all right.'

'How long did it take for Dara to return last time?' I persisted.

A long, sad sigh escaped Izaru's lips. He scratched his mangy mane and replied, 'He came back after three days. I…I had lost all hope of seeing him again. He went in, a broken angry man with little hope left in him. When he returned, he…'

Izaru paused, realizing he had said too much.

'Please finish, Izaru,' I said gently.

He looked at me with his mournful golden-brown lion eyes. 'When he returned through that door, he was a man completely shorn of hope. He had nothing left to live for. It is no surprise what he became after. No surprise at all.'

Izaru's words created an ocean of sorrow within me. I didn't know why I was feeling this inexplicable grief for someone I barely knew.

'Was it…was it someone he loved?' My voice was almost inaudible.

Izaru nodded. 'And lost,' he added, as he walked away.

He didn't say a word to me after that for a while. And I didn't ask him anything. I sat with my back against the door hoping I would hear footsteps on the other side.

Dara had loved and lost someone. Had he crossed the River of Death in the hope of getting them back? Now I knew what the reason was for the sadness in his eyes. It was eternal heartbreak. My core swung on its axis wildly as I tried to grapple with how I felt. Something about Dara's heartbreak pierced my own being with an unbearable sorrow. I closed my eyes trying to fathom the depths of his grief, and failed. Why would a man who had once lost everything he ever loved down by the River of Death choose to return?

Izaru went hunting and returned with a wild deer on his shoulders. He lit a fire and began to skin the deer and roast it.

'It's not much,' he said gruffly. 'But I always carry salt and some spices with me. Should make it bearable.'

'I am sure it will be wonderful,' I said.

He grunted and went back to skinning the deer. His movements were deft and neat. Soon the deer was on a stick over the fire, the smell of freshly cooking meat wafting pleasantly in the air. When it was done, he took it down and tore the meat into smaller bits with his bare hands and handed me some. I took it with a smile. The meat tasted soft and salty.

'It's very good,' I said.

He nodded his head and didn't reply. I finished and sat back by the door watching him attack the meat with fervour. When he had stripped off the last bits of flesh from the bones, he threw them aside and wiped his mouth with relish. Then he sat down and tossed me a furtive glance. I raised an eyebrow.

'You are not like *her*,' he said finally.

'Who is *her*?'

'Her…that mad witch, Hera. I thought her girls would be like her. Dark bits of wicked and unkindness.'

I shook my head and smiled.

'Seems weird, though,' he continued. 'Legend goes that you were all made from her shadow. And yet…'

'Have you ever met her?' I asked.

He shuffled uncomfortably at the question.

'I did...a very long time ago. It wasn't a pleasant encounter. She didn't have the powers she does now, but she was still an unsettling presence. Devoid of humanity. She always had a way, I suppose, of shunning the light for the dark.'

'How did she get her powers, do you know?' I asked.

He made an unpleasant noise and said darkly, 'There are things that must not be spoken of, things that bear roots in betrayal and greed. She has her powers because she made choices that led to them. She and that crone...' he trailed off, shaking his head.

'You know her too?' I asked gently. If Izaru was in the mood to talk, then maybe I would get some of the answers I was looking for.

'That crone,' he spat on the ground with considerable violence. 'She's been cursed so many times I'm surprised she is still alive. She put a soul worm in one of my brothers once. Do you know what a soul worm does? It eats your soul bit by bit, silently. There is no way to take it out once it has infested your being. He died in a way I wouldn't wish upon anyone.'

'I am sorry,' I said, horrified. 'That seems like a horrible way to die.'

He snorted. 'Seems the pair of them have devised many more horrible ways for people to die.'

The implication wasn't lost on me but I decided to ignore it.

'That crone is the murkiest, filthiest bit of evil alive. Her realm was burned down long ago but she escaped by a whisker. She owes her life to Hera. Her loyalty, though staunch, is a terrible thing. It has led to such horror...'

'Like the Unspeakable act,' I prompted.

Izaru stood up, agitated, crunching his knuckles, each crunch setting off a minor explosive sound.

'One is not allowed to speak about the Unspeakable act,' he growled. 'It is a despicable act, beyond...'

'It involves a sacrifice of some kind, doesn't it? A sacrifice that enables you in some way...'

'You seem to know a lot about it,' he muttered. 'Yes, the Unspeakable act involves sorcery that is not even meant to be spoken of. The conjuring of spells that weaken the universe. Sacrifices that only the truly inhuman could think of. Yes, what she wants now involves a terrible sacrifice. She tried it once before and failed. Now I hear she is trying other methods, but none have succeeded so far. The last time she did this, it changed lives, *ruined* them.'

Izaru sighed deeply. 'You see, child,' he continued, 'there is no concept of absolute power anymore. The Gods have disappeared, leaving power scattered across the realms. But there are things one can control, I suppose, that makes them more powerful than the other. She wants to control something, something she already does in fragments through her army, you Yakshis. From whatever I hear, from the rumblings of rumours that reach my old tired ears, she wants to rule over the minds of mortals. And she will do anything to have that power in her grasp. She will even perform the Unspeakable act in order to achieve it.'

He turned to me then, his entire body shaking with emotion. 'Listen to me, girl. You seem different. You don't seem like you are the monster you were meant to be. Listen to me carefully. Let them return, these two. Let them return safe and then you disappear. Disappear with them. Don't let her shadow fall on you again...or him, Dara. He has suffered enough. My friend, my brother, he has suffered for too long now. Enough.'

Before I could respond, I heard a knock. Izaru jumped and scrambled towards the door, inserting the key with a little shout of joy.

The door opened.

Without a conscious thought, my feet lifted off the ground and I flew towards the two men emerging from the depths of hell. One of them ran towards me. The other stayed put.

My cheek brushed against Dwai's three-day old stubble as I threw my hands around his neck. It felt as if time had stopped. Or started again. I wasn't sure which.

I could hear Izaru sigh noisily with relief. In front me, still framed by the door and with dark half-moons under his eyes, stood Dara. As my eyes locked into his, I felt the same wave of sorrow flood through my being. I finally pulled away from Dwai.

I saw it in Dwai's eyes first – the heartbreak that a revelation brings. *Not all answers bring you peace, Dwai*, I wanted to tell him. I could see the chaos in those black pearl-like depths as the answers he had found settled on his shoulders like a burden you can never rid yourself of.

I took his hand and held out the other to Dara. He took a step forward, paused before me and then walked away towards Izaru.

The Keeper hugged him, tears streaming down his cheeks. When they pulled apart, even Dara's eyes were glistening.

'I don't know anyone like you,' spluttered Izaru. 'No one, my friend. When you were away I was telling Ardra about…'

He stopped. I could see a shadow pass over Dara's face.

'About Razvang,' I cut in. 'Izaru was telling me all about your exploits.'

Izaru nodded, looking towards me in gratitude, even as Dara seemed to relax.

'Got your answers, enh, boy? Are you happy?' roared Izaru at Dwai.

'Yes,' he replied. 'Though there is much to know yet...'

'I shall pray you find the answers, then. And as for you, my brother, I shall pray to the Gods that you may never have to go down to the River of Death again. I must take your leave now and go back to my people. May we meet again, my beloved friend. I shall wait for that day.'

After carefully pocketing the key, Izaru embraced Dara once more. He slapped Dwai on the back heartily and left the boy coughing his goodbye. He paused by me and his eyes held a strange gleam.

'Goodbye, Yakshi. I enjoyed your company while they were gone. I hope you find your answers soon, too.' He held out a huge paw and wrung my arm fervently. Turning away, he called out to his billy-goat who snorted and stamped the ground in impatience. Soon he was a blob in the distance, his mangy mane flying in the breeze, and we watched him go down the narrow winding path till he disappeared from sight.

Dara turned to Dwai. His stance had a certain purpose, a command, as he asked, 'So, what did you learn down there?'

'I am not sure I am ready to talk about it yet,' said Dwai almost under his breath. 'I need some time.'

'Dwai, Dara risked his life for you down there,' I said, slightly surprised by his sudden need for secrecy. 'I think he deserves to know.'

Dara took a step towards Dwai. 'You have a Jwala. That means something. I have to know because it may be important. For all of us.'

Dwai was about to answer when his eyes strayed to the horizon beyond. We all turned to look. The sky right above us had turned a deep, pure gold. Not a tangerine sunset gold, not a champagne sunrise gold, but the colour of molten fire.

'What the...' murmured Dwai and his grip on my hand tightened. Dara took a step forward, his markings suddenly gleaming, his whole being iridescent. He turned to look at me and, for the first time ever, I saw a glimmer of excitement in his eyes.

The sky now changed to a mellow copper – the pale, serene fire of twilight. The wind danced its way around us and the snow sparkled with unusual flicker.

And then I saw her. The girl simply stood there staring at us, her eyes the colour of water, her skin pale as the full moon, her limbs resembling young slender branches, and her face perfectly symmetrical and unlined. Later, when we talked about the moment we first saw her, we all remembered her differently. While to me she seemed like a young girl, Dara saw her as a beautiful woman, her womb brimming with life. Dwai, on the other hand, said she resembled his grandmother, except with flowing, rainbow-hued hair and an owl on her shoulder.

Whatever our first glimpse of her might have been, she soon melded into the strangest, most beautiful child in front of our eyes, her innocence startling, glorious. She looked sad and curious, her demeanour giving the impression of being utterly lost yet, at the same time, strangely confident, like she knew should be exactly there, with us, on that mountain top.

As we stood and watched her, the ground beneath us changed. I was suddenly standing at the brink of a meteor, watching new constellations burst into the galaxy and forge their incandescence through the velvety blue darkness. Dara was by the sea, the night moon reflected in its silvery waters, the sand soft and grainy under his bare feet. The earth beneath him sang poetry, Dwai later said to me, as he stood on a meadow, filled with golden blooms and birds that filled his heart with their music.

We were exactly where we were meant to be, in that billionth of a second, and my head tingled with the strange magic of this universe.

'Who is she?' asked Dwai, in awe.

She didn't look at anyone as she spoke in a voice that reminded me of crystal glasses clinking underwater, delicate, almost gurgling, musical.

'I am the Balance Keeper of the Universe, young and old as it is, and I have responded to your call.'

She raised her arms and everything went white.

⚜ 32 ⚜

Whiteness. Pure eternal whiteness. Dwai shielded his eyes and basked in it. *If there is a heaven, this is probably what it looks like*, he thought. When his eyes opened, he was in the meadow again. He looked around and saw Ardra and Dara's faces mirroring his own expression of peace and wonderment.

She spoke again. 'I would not have come but the universe told me I must. This time it may be important.'

Dara sank to his knees. 'I thought I would never see you again,' he whispered, his voice thick with emotion. The child walked up to him and gently caressed his face, making his markings glow. He bowed his head low and she smiled.

Then she sat down, like a child waiting to hear a story. And they all sat down too, Dwai on his grassy meadow, Ardra on a smooth spot on her meteor and Dara on the beach. The girl was surrounded by a halo of pure light and her branch-like limbs seem to glow and flower. She seemed ageless and yet somehow older than all the realms of the universe; untouched, untethered, pure.

'Why are you here?' Dara asked softly.

She looked at him this time when she replied, her eyes heavy with sadness. 'The fabric is ripping apart.'

Dara sighed and shook his head.

'Do you know how many times I have mended it myself, this fabric? I have sewn it whole again and again with the needle of time and the threads of space but this time...'

'You went to the River of Death.' It wasn't a question as much as a statement. Dara nodded.

She addressed Dwai next. 'Did you find what you were looking for?'

He nodded.

'Your story affects the fabric,' she said. 'Your knowledge of it will change the future.'

The little group was silent.

'Too much is changing, isn't it? The order of the universe is in chaos,' she said.

'I believe something disastrous is going to take place. It must be averted. It goes against all the laws of the universe,' she seemed to address Dara as she said this. 'Of course, the laws have become something of a cosmic joke, haven't they? Werewolves continue to breed, the monstrous killings of humans won't stop either, and there is still so much violence afoot... As for the underworld, the evil there cannot be contained in the Old Sea.'

'By the underworld, you mean Atala?' Ardra asked uncomfortably.

The child didn't answer her. Instead she said, 'Darkness must exist where light thrives. It is an Old World law, but the balance – that must be maintained. And as of now, I must say I am failing to do that on my own.'

Dara was about to speak when she continued, 'There was a manifesto, made when I was still young. I have it with me somewhere.' She patted about her wispy colourless gown and pulled out a weather-beaten parchment.

She started to read it out like a child reciting poetry in a classroom:

And evermore shall the passages between Aakasha and Prithvi be closed, for the heavenly have revoked their own rights to walk on earth. The Apsaras have thus been banned from procreating on Prithvi and creating Half-borns as the balance of the realms has shifted and magic has dispersed.

Dwai took in a sharp bolt of breath and Ardra looked at him curiously. Dara looked impassive and stiff.

'This was added a few years later,' she added, almost to herself.

'Following the regrettable events of the Great Dark, the Banished are forever condemned to Prithvi and Atala. The gates of Aakasha remain closed to them forever. The harbinger of the Great Dark shall remain in her base planet and never again attempt to disrupt the fabric of the realms. The dark things shall remain in Atala and if they wish so, roam on Prithvi, but shall not shape-shift into animals or kill without compunction. The ghosts shall have free passage between Atala and Prithvi but shall not haunt to kill. Supernatural ones possessing magic shall abstain from shape-shifting into animals as this further upsets the balance of the universe.'

She took a little pause.

'I don't...' began Dwai.

The child went on reading as though there had been no interruption.

'The Banished are banned from shape-shifting or using magic to fly or appear invisible. Furthermore, no living being shall be resurrected from the state of death in order to preserve the fabric of the realms and keep it intact for the times to come. The Unspeakable acts that will not be named here are forever banned from the surface of the realms and no living being, earthly or supernatural, shall resort to them in their quest for power or prosperity. All inhabitants shall adhere to these rules and peace shall prevail upon the universe.'

She took a deep breath, rolled up the scroll, put it back into the folds of her gown and surveyed the silent group sitting opposite her.

'Of course, no one takes the manifesto seriously,' she sighed. 'The rules are being broken and I, of course, look the other way most of the time, but now – '

'Who are the Banished?' asked Ardra.

There was a deep silence in the air before the Balance Keeper answered. 'There came a time when it was necessary to banish from the sky city Aakasha a few Gandharvas and...'

'Please,' Dara's tone was urgent, pleading. 'Please. Say no more.'

Ardra turned to him. 'So it is true. You *did* live in Aakasha. Why were you banished?' Her tone was incredulous.

Dara didn't meet her eyes.

'There are long stories and there are untellable stories,' said the child. 'This one is untellable.'

'Why?' asked Ardra. 'Why is it untellable? What happened

that a Gandharva, a heavenly being, is now a banished monster slayer on Prithvi? And who is the harbinger of the Great Dark?'

'Hera,' said the Balance Keeper. 'She committed an Unspeakable act and hence...'

Her gaze stayed on Ardra, and it was searching and sad.

'Please,' Dara's tone was beseeching. 'Please let us not speak of it.'

'Why NOT? I heard Hera mention the Unspeakable act. I heard her speak of it in connection with the blood moon. And that was the night I...'

She stopped. Talking about what she did in front of this child, this strange entity called the Balance Keeper, made her uncomfortable. It reminded her of what she was, how she had contributed to the rip in the fabric, how she had unknowingly helped spread Hera's evil.

'It is not that simple,' the child said gently. 'There is so much in the world that changes texture with time; stories that, like water, take on the shape of whatever holds them.'

'I want to know,' said Ardra, her tone insistent. 'I have to. You have not come here by chance. You have come here because you think we can, or at least one of us can stop this fabric from ripping. You think it is possible to stop whoever it is breaking your rules. I want to know.'

Dara stood up. He was shaking with anger. Ardra stood up too. She addressed him directly, 'Why can't I know anything about the history of the realms? Where you come from? Why is everything such a big secret?'

'Sit down,' commanded the Balance Keeper. Something in the child's voice told them not to argue.

'In order to find our way through the fog of future, we must understand the mysteries of our past. For we are all connected, aren't we? Connected inexplicably – man, beast, Gods – for the invisible chains of this universe bind us, weaving our stories through the loom of time and space. We must know the story of what lay behind us even if we do not fully understand it. I cannot speak of the Unspeakable,' she said. 'But I can tell you the story of the sun, moon and stars and their children.'

Dara sat down, his brow furrowed. Ardra inched closer to Dwai, who took her hand. Her eyes strayed over to Dara who stared into the distance obstinately.

'In the days when Prithvi was still young and Aakasha already a few millions years old, there was no sky separating the two. Just water the colour of smoke and twilight. Water that flowed from earth to sky and back. The stars floated in the ocean, shimmery sea creatures of light and ice. Then the old Gods created the sun and the moon and they created the sky, colourless and vast so they could live in it, and the ocean was sent to earth but leaving a part of it still in Aakasha, now known as the Old Sea.

'But the stars fell in love with the sky and wanted to stay there. So for many eons the sun, moon and stars lived in the sky, not knowing day, night or sly twilight.'

The Balance Keeper paused for breath.

'The sun and the moon fell in love and their ardour created sky storms all around. Their passion was so strong that sparks flew, bright as the sun, ethereal as the moon. These were the Gandharvas. Children of the skies, born of passion.

'The stars were jealous of the love between the sun and the moon, and beseeched the Gods to let them love each other too. The Gods relented, and their love brought forth children, glittering like crystals, filled with cold, eternal beauty and the icy core of their parents. The Apsaras.

'The sun and the moon loved the Apsaras as their own but

the stars were still filled with envy. They turned the sky against the sun and the moon and the sky split into two – day and night. The moon was too pale and powerless in the day and the sun burnt too strong at night, scorching the sky's walls. The Gods ordained that the sun belonged to the day sky and the moon to the night.

'The sun and moon couldn't bear to be parted but they couldn't defy the Gods either. And for some eons they lived apart, but the sun pined for his beloved so much he crept into the night sky and embraced her, causing her to turn dark and depthless. The offspring born of the union of the mad sun and the dark moon were different from other Gandharvas.

'The Gods punished the lovers and banished the moon to go live in the Old Sea. They created a new moon and it is she who now shines upon Prithvi. The old moon still lives at the bottom of the Old Sea, pining for her beloved and her sons.

'As for the sun, he mended his broken heart and continued to live in the day sky but he still occasionally creeps up on the new moon, his memory addled, confusing her for the old one.'

The Balance Keeper looked around the little group seated in their individual dream spaces.

Ardra spoke first.

'So...how did the Apsaras and Gandharvas...'

'Become consorts you mean?'

She nodded.

'It was, after all, inevitable. The fickle Gandharvas and the icy Apsaras belonged together just like the sun and the moon did. It worked in my favour that they would choose each other. With their volatile blood, any other union would challenge the universe.'

'And yet we seduce others for fun,' Dara said grimly.

The child laughed, a melodious tinkling sound. 'That is the curse of the Balance Keeper. It is my curse. You see, I saw what happened with the sun and the moon and the stars. And, like all unpredictable things in the universe, I overreacted.'

'You overreacted?'

'Well, I was an old grumpy woman then and lacked patience. I cursed the offspring of the union and decreed that, while they would find their partners, they would never fully be together. They would always be torn apart by their need to seduce mortals. Apologies if I have caused you any harm.'

'And the Gods didn't stop you?' asked Dwai indignantly.

'Aah, the Gods love a good curse,' said the Balance Keeper wryly. 'They loved the drama and the chaos... It amused them. And I was still new then, grappling with my job. Trust me, it's not an easy one.'

'I'm sure,' Dara muttered under his breath.

'What about here, on Prithvi?' asked Dwai heatedly. 'Everything is a mess and all I hear is some babble about the fabric of the universe.'

The Balance Keeper put a finger to her lips and he shut up. She stood up. The pale halo around her shimmered with energy. 'What do you know of this universe and its battles, boy? This is the battlefield. This is the soldier. They are not separate. What do you know of a universe that is fated to turn against itself every few million years or so? What do you know of Prithvi's lifelines, of Aakasha's fatestorms? What could you possibly know of me, as I create and detonate again and again on a loop. What do you know of my curse, of how I am damned by powers that are older than time itself?'

There was a quiet fury in the child's eyes and they held storms from a time that knew only of dust and black holes. Ardra placed a gentle hand over Dwai's, signalling him to stop.

Dara was mutinously silent and when she glanced at him, he was staring fixedly at a point on the ground.

'What about Atala?' Ardra asked. 'You have spoken of Prithvi and Aakasha but not a word about Atala or Hera.'

The Balance Keeper's face darkened, suddenly looking tired and ancient.

'Atala is a dark world that was never meant to exist. If there are dreams then there must be nightmares, and I cannot speak of Atala without speaking of these nightmares. I cannot tell its story without tearing asunder someone's memory, without resurrecting the mistakes made by those who chose to live in nightmares. Pardon me, but I cannot speak of it.'

Ardra stared at the Balance Keeper, a question churning in her mind. The child smiled and spoke, as if she had read the Yakshi's mind.

'You want to now know about your kind, don't you? The ones controlled by Hera. I cannot tell you, for it would mean digging up the grave of an old memory. Ask anything else, Ardra, but not this.'

'So how is it fair that werewolves roam the earth; the vampires of the north are acceptable; the ghosts, the Huldras and the sirens are allowed to exist, but we Yakshis are an anomaly?'

'You are an anomaly because of how you were created. Because Hera saw the loophole in the system. As ruler of Atala, I don't really control her. Nobody does. And she created you well within the mystifying laws. You don't consume human flesh, you don't maim, you don't torture...'

'And that is a consolation?' Ardra almost shouted.

'No, it isn't. But it doesn't mean what you do is acceptable. Each dark thing is different. The sort of violence vampires and werewolves have stained upon the world is unforgivable – the kind that is not only bloody but also devoid of any kind of human quality, born of a thirst to hurt and torture for pleasure. And yet there exist among them those who have sworn to not take a human life. Or drink human blood. Those who have never torn apart a mortal for pleasure. It is ultimately a choice. In my time, in these parts of the universe, I have seen monsters of many kinds inflicting unspeakable horrors on the beings of this earth. You Yakshis, however, do what you are told. But I doubt there is stark brutality in you. It is blurring and confusing, yes. As I said before, the laws decree that darkness and light must exist together. I have no choice but to accept you as part of the darkness now,' said the Balance Keeper evenly.

'What are Blood Queens? Are they things you accept as part of the darkness too?' asked Ardra, trembling in agitation.

Dara groaned, burying his face in his hands.

The child sighed, her rainbow hair flying softly in the breeze. 'Blood Queens…what can I say of things that take tumourous roots in the fabric? Perhaps that I have done nothing about it shows I'm growing weak. Perhaps it is a lesson for me that just because I despise something doesn't mean it won't exist or thrive.'

'Nothing makes sense, does it?' sighed Dwai. 'Nothing.'

The child directed her bright stare at Dwai and smiled. 'Nothing needs to make sense for a story to move forward. Use your knowledge and do what you must.'

'You want us to do something,' Ardra stated. 'Something to do with the universe and its fabric. What do you want from us?'

The child merely said, 'Ask yourself and you will find the answer within you.'

'Why choose *us*? Why tell us all this?' Ardra persisted. 'Why the three of us, of all the men and monsters in the world?'

'Because sometimes destiny chooses us, and not the other way around,' she said and walked away. She flew into the clouds, she melted into the landscape, she sank into the earth. They watched her meld into the universe.

She was born from it, and she once gave birth to it.

They watched her go and the questions didn't seem simpler or the answers clearer. But they felt a light streaming within them and for that second, just for that brief time in space, it seemed like all was right with the world.

⁂ **33** ⁂

The feeling of light and joy passed quickly. I turned to Dara, bristling with anger. All the feelings I had accumulated over the past few days, all the gratitude, seemed to drain out of me as frustration took over.

'What was that?'

He raised an eyebrow.

'What was that, Dara? The Balance Keeper of the entire bleeding universe shows up and you wouldn't let her give me any answers? What is the big secret about your banishment? What did you do?'

He stared into the horizon in mutinous silence.

'You belonged in Aakasha and you fell from grace. And then you roam Prithvi slaying monsters and seeking desperate revenge against Hera. Dara, *what happened*?'

He walked past me, almost jostling me in the process.

'I will not discuss it, Ardra.'

'WHY?'

'Because it is IRRELEVANT TO YOU!' He was shouting now. 'Anything to do with my life is irrelevant to you. I don't have to tell you anything.'

I glared at him, at a loss for words, wanting to throw something at him.

He walked back towards Dwai. 'You! Tell me what you learnt down there, now. The Balance Keeper seemed to think it was important. I think we all have a right to know.'

'Oh, right,' I said sarcastically. 'We all have a "right" to know about him but your life is off-limits?'

'Guys, it's okay,' interjected Dwai. 'I can tell you.'

His sudden calmness threw me off track. I wanted to stay angry and scream at Dara but looking at the earnestness on Dwai's face, I fell silent.

'It so happens that someone in Aakasha broke the rules twenty-five years ago,' he said quietly. 'An Apsara fell in love with a human and...let's just say that it didn't go very well after that. But she birthed a child. And, well...' He waved his hands, indicating himself.

I gaped at Dwai. Dara stayed rooted to where he was.

'My mother was an Apsara and she died of a broken heart,' Dwai said, his voice shaking just a little with sadness.

'Oh Dwai, that means...that means...'

'That means he is a Half-born,' finished Dara for me, a curious light in his eyes. 'A superior hybrid. With sky blood in him. It is one of the things banned in the manifesto.'

'I'm sorry, but I didn't really have a say in the matter,' Dwai said dryly. 'But this is the truth. My mother was an Apsara and they are forbidden to love humans. But she broke that rule and paid for it. It doesn't matter what that makes me.'

'It does,' said Dara, his voice strange and hard. 'It matters. This changes everything.'

'How?' asked Dwai. '*How* does it change anything? Except that Yakshis have no effect on me, what relevance does this have? I may have supernatural blood running through my veins but I have managed to live through twenty-five years without magic. I don't intend to use any power I might have.'

'You have sky blood in you, Dwai. You know what that makes you? It makes you a demigod of sorts.'

'Woah,' I said. 'A demigod?'

'It's not as fancy as it sounds,' said Dara tersely. 'Not any more. Over time, children with sky blood have become not all that different from human ones. What sets them apart, though, is their ability to channel their inner magic if they so choose to. That's why they are called Half-borns. They are not considered fully alive until they learn to access their magic entirely. It takes years of practice, and not all of them succeed. If Dwai truly wants to take advantage of his sky blood, he will have to work very hard.'

'I have no interest in being a Half-born or a demigod,' said Dwai hotly.

'You can choose what you want to be. You are a free man. But you still have the Jwala. It belongs to your mother who left it behind to protect you. Eventually, if you channel your magic, you won't need it,' said Dara. 'These are powerful stones. You have no idea what they can do.'

'And I don't intend to find out,' said Dwai tightly. 'The stone is something that belonged to my mother and I will cherish it forever. That's all there is to it.'

'No...' I said slowly. 'No, there must be more. Why is Hera after you?'

'I have no idea,' he said. 'And I don't care. Let's go, Ardra, let's go somewhere far from all of this. If you want me to come along, that is…'

A birdsong wafted through the short silence that followed his words. A nightingale somewhere in the heart of the wilds chose to serenade this moment, as imperfect as it was. I didn't say yes or no. I simply put my hand into his and we walked, past Dara, past everything I wanted to leave behind.

Dara followed us at a distance. I could feel his eyes on my back but I didn't turn back. The chasm between us seemed to have widened, our silence thickening and shaping itself into a cold white space between us.

'Where do we go now?' Dwai asked no one in particular. He turned to Dara. 'You look a little tired. Would you like to rest a bit before you go off on your path of revenge?'

Dara gave him a sharp look but saw that Dwai was earnest. Finally he nodded. 'The Forest of Fireflies,' he said. 'It's the safest place I can think of right now.'

I held out my other hand to Dara, a clear signal that I was ready to fly. He hesitated for a second and then walked up to us, delicately taking hold of my sleeve instead. I rolled my eyes, not caring if he noticed, and took to the sky.

'You'll have to direct me,' I said, not looking at Dara.

'I will,' he replied equally brusquely.

We flew for a few hours. At some point, Dara pointed towards a misty grove of green and I started descending.

We found a little thicket in the middle of the forest with a shimmering lake at the centre. It was set with strange trees whose branches seemed to fall all the way to the forest floor and snake their way around, looking unsettlingly alive. 'Are you sure we're safe here?' murmured Dwai. The air was cool and he pulled his jacket around him tighter. 'We should start a fire,' he suggested, and set off to find dry twigs, brushing off my idea that we use magic. I shrugged and settled down under a tree. We could spend the night here in this glade before deciding what to do next.

Next. It seemed like a myth – my future. Improbable and unstable. I wasn't sure where I was going or what I was supposed to do. After I had shown Dara the way to Atala perhaps, Dwai and I could go away as he had asked and I would never see Dara again. Ever. Despite my current cloud of anger, the thought brought me pain and I sighed.

He sat there opposite me, sullen and quiet, his jewel-blue eyes expressionless and cold. Dark tired patches had forged themselves under his eyes and his markings glowed only faintly. Whatever had happened to him down by the River of Death had taken its toll. He looked exhausted. I knew we would have to rest for a while before he was able to travel again.

A tiny speck of fluorescence floated through the air and Dara stretched out his palm. A firefly landed on it, and he smiled as his palm glowed incandescent. Soon, another one flew in and another... I watched as a hundred fireflies or more danced in a fiery pattern around the Gandharva. The little clearing lit up with an eerie green-blue light and as he sat there, the fireflies hovering around him lovingly, I felt my anger wash away. I smiled at him and even though he didn't return it, his eyes grew softer and the lines around his mouth eased. An errant firefly tussled with my hair and lost, glowing faintly within it, and I plucked it out. I didn't know what kind of magic this was – of feeling connected, of being one – and I knew then, no matter what, that I could never leave Dara in Atala and vanish.

Dara raised his hand and the fireflies swung themselves in the air into a curious pattern, weaving in and out around themselves, strobing the air with their sprinkly light. He continued to wave his hands like the conductor of an orchestra and I sat up, fascinated by the beauty of his magic. Finally, he swept his left hand in my direction with a flourish and the fireflies swirled towards me and came to rest just above my head. They had become an iridescent wreath of light and as I laughed in delight, Dara's mouth curved into a smile at the corners. He waved his hand once more, a mere flicker of magical flourish, and some more fireflies wound themselves around my wrist like a golden bracelet. His gaze lingered on my wrist where my frangipani imprint glowed.

'That's about as much magic as I can manage right now,' he said with a weak smile.

'It's beautiful,' I smiled back. A gentle river began to flow through the stony banks of our silence.

'I'm sorry. There is so much...' he began and I rose, wanting to sit next to him. The questions I had seemed a little less important right then and I gave up wanting to understand the draw this Gandharva had on me. Instead, I decided to just experience the moment. I felt the dew soak into my feet as I took a step forward and then I stopped.

Dwai had returned with some bracken and twigs in his hand. His eyes travelled from the wreath of light above my head down to the bracelet that fluttered around my wrist and he mouthed a faint 'wow'. It wasn't an exclamation of wonder as much as...

'Let's the start the fire, shall we?' Dara cut in.

'Without magic,' said Dwai firmly and started to rub the sticks together. Little sparks flew out of the dry twigs eventually and soon we were sitting around a little bonfire that infused the surroundings with a comforting glow.

There was so much to say, to discuss, but in that moment all I wanted was to bask in the warmth of the night and forget

I had an uninviting future to look forward to. Dara waved away my wreath but let the bracelet remain and Dwai relaxed a little. He even managed to collect a few wild berries and fruits which we ate after Dara had carefully examined each one of them.

'They could be poisonous. Or even worse, carnivorous. They start eating your insides once you swallow them,' he explained calmly, his eyes twinkling at Dwai's alarmed expression.

'The frangipanis back in Atala are always thirsting for blood,' I added, biting into a dark red berry shaped like a mango.

'You have frangipanis in Atala?' asked Dara.

'Yes, they like to drink blood so it's better not to get too close to them,' I said matter-of-factly. Dwai's expression was priceless and I couldn't help but laugh.

The fire flickered, emitting a comforting glow as we ate. Dwai took the Jwala out and turned it over in his palm. Its surface glowed like a starry night studded with constellations. He looked up and addressed Dara, his voice quiet, tremulous.

'Did you...know my mother? Do you have any idea who she was?'

Dara shook his head. 'I left Aakasha centuries ago. I have no idea which one of them...'

Dwai nodded.

'So,' he continued, 'do you know what exactly this stone does? As far I know, it gives me protection. And if I channel all my energy into it, it can transport me from one place to another.'

'An Apsara's stone,' said Dara, 'is not something you will find in any of the Old Books. The first of its kind was gifted to an Apsara by a sage who was besotted with her. He fashioned it from her own magical energy and she was so stunned by its beauty that she requested he make some for all the others. An Apsara's stone or a Jwala, as it is called, answers to the call of only its owner. Each stone is unique, mimicking the powers and aura of the Apsara who owned it. Because of this, every stone tends to have different powers. Some can help teleport, some can grant wishes and others can read minds. Of course, these kinds of stones are extremely rare since their power depends on the power of their owner. The more powerful the Apsara, the greater the ability of her stone. These stones can also become extremely belligerent if the owner doesn't take care of them or abandons them.'

'So my mother's Jwala is basically an imprint of who she was?' asked Dwai, clasping the stone tightly.

'Yes. And the only reason it answers to you is because she desired so. And it will cease to obey you if you ever decide you do not want its ownership.'

'Will we ever understand the true workings of this universe?' murmured Dwai. He looked helpless, lost in a world where a heavenly creature had died, leaving eternal protection for her son. A world he scarcely understood.

A peculiar music was streaming from somewhere in the glades. It sounded as if someone was playing the harp, the flute and the violin all from their throat – a distinctly otherworldly song that wove in and out of the forest.

'Wood nymphs,' explained Dara. 'They always sing during the waxing moon in order to help its womb grow.'

'It's beautiful,' said Dwai, closing his eyes.

'The Forest of Fireflies is an enchanted place,' Dara went on. 'Only a few are chosen to experience it. It allowed me in because I've been here before; it knows I'm not a threat.'

'What do you mean?' asked Dwai.

'The forest must decide whether it wants you or not. If it does invite you in, then you become a part of its enchantment. Usually it only allows children inside.'

'Maybe because the Balance Keeper is a little girl,' said Dwai.

Dara shook his head. 'The Balance Keeper is not just a little girl – she is so much more. But you wouldn't understand that.'

'Yeah, just as I don't get how stars are icy. Or how the sun and the moon fell in love. It was a fun story, though.'

I snorted. 'Says the non-believing son of an Apsara.'

'Hey, Apsaras are easier to believe in than some fantastical love story between the sun, moon and stars.'

'A story is only as true as you believe it to be,' said Dara. 'A myth is only as wondrous as the imagination of the people who pass it down through the ages. I don't know if the story of the sun, moon and stars is true. I don't know if the stars were once cold, in a time before time was even born; I don't know if the Sun pines for the Old Moon, my mother. But I know this – the universe is full of strange, beautiful stories, some untellable, some forgotten, and some written in a language that nobody can read, not even the Gods. These stories exist because the universe does, and the universe blazes on because these stories keep it alive. You and me, we are the stories. We live and so does the universe. One does not exist without the other.'

He paused. It was the most I had ever heard him speak. 'I don't know if the sun is my father, or the Old Moon my mother. But I know there *was* a moon in Aakasha. She rested in the Old Sea and when I lived there, I would walk down on nights when the stars had forsaken the sky and visit her. She shone there in those waters, and she shone with a sadness only a broken heart can bring.'

'You miss Aakasha,' I said quietly. 'Don't you?'

'I miss Aakasha like I left my soul behind there. Like I left my ability to love, to feel, in the only place I call home.'

'Tell us more about it,' I urged him.

His sad eyes gleamed. 'It is a strange place,' Dara said, almost haltingly. 'Nothing quite like what you might have read about in books. Living in Aakasha is a bit like living inside your own head. It is beautiful and calm and restless, all at the same time. We, the Gandharvas, and the Apsaras live…I mean, lived… in one big palace surrounded by numerous lakes and rivers. The Old Sea laces the whole city. We have our own sun and moon that rise and shine as they please. Sometimes they are both in the sky together, almost as if they believe in the old myth of their ancestors.'

'Sounds beautiful,' I said.

'It is,' Dara smiled. 'It is a pity, though, that I could tell you about the world I once lived in for endless hours and you would still not grasp the beauty of it. The skies, the music, the sunblooms…'

'Sunblooms?'

'My favourite flowers. It is said that the moon once cracked a joke so funny, the sun laughed till he had tears in his eyes. When those tears fell on Aakasha's soil, up sprung the sunblooms. I miss them the most. They gave me hope, happiness.'

His words seemed to take something out of him. He looked down, not meeting our eyes. 'I deserved to be banished,' he said, his voice barely audible now. 'I deserve my exile, my wretchedness. Don't feel sorry for me, Ardra. I don't deserve your pity.'

'I don't pity you,' I whispered. 'I just wish you would tell me how you feel.'

'What is banishment exactly?' Dwai interrupted.

There was a short silence before Dara spoke, his voice grim.

'It means I can never return to Aakasha. I can't fly. I must never contact my people. Even if I chance upon someone I know, I must maintain my distance.'

'I am so sorry,' I said.

'Don't.' He sounded tortured.

'Who else was banished along with you? Why aren't you allowed to contact them?' I pressed on. Now that he was talking about himself, I wanted to know as much as I could before he changed his mind.

But before he could answer, the nymph song stopped abruptly. The hair on my neck stood up.

'I wonder why...' Dara muttered to himself.

An animal growled somewhere and another answered.

'A wolf,' I said, relieved.

When Dwai looked at me incredulously, I laughed. 'Tonight this forest plays host to a Yakshi, a Gandharva and a Half-born. I doubt any of us will be eaten by a wolf,' I said. He grinned and sat back down against the tree trunk, his fingers absently plucking the dewy grass that surrounded us.

'Wolves are not allowed in here,' said Dara grimly. He got up, his hand on his sabre.

The animal sounds grew louder, coming in short bursts like signals or messages. 'Maybe I should go check,' Dara murmured.

His face tightened as he waved a hand over the fire, extinguishing it. Darkness fell over the little glade and with it, came an unnatural silence.

Dwai's voice shot through the dark like an arrow. 'I thought this forest was enchanted. What do you think is...'

'The forest is enchanted, but not invincible against evil spirits,' said Dara quietly. 'It's tough to keep the supernatural out of such places. Nobody abides by the ancient rules anymore.'

He took a step forward as I stood up. I could see clearly in the darkness, and what I saw made my core queasy. They were approaching steadily, a whole pack of them, skulking, menacing creatures. I could sense their glee from across the forest.

Werewolves.

✦ 34 ✦

Before I could say anything, I felt something shoot through the air and slide around my waist, binding me tightly. Dara and Dwai both shouted in alarm and I saw slimy rope-like things twisting around them, too, capturing all three of us in a tight hold.

'Werewolves,' gritted Dara through his teeth. 'The worst kind of hybrids.'

'No! And it's not even full moon. How are they – ' began Dwai.

'These ones don't need the moon to turn anymore. Bloody body vines,' said Dara through clenched teeth. Dwai tugged at the rope violently.

'Don't bother,' said Dara. 'These things get stronger if you struggle. They're impervious to our magic. Stay still and we'll find a way out.'

The body vines bound us together and began pulling us forward. 'Back to their master,' said Dara in a grim tone.

I could smell the blood on them as they neared. The body of a human with the head and feet of a wolf, their arms were long and sinuous with sharp nails. I could see dirty red stains on them. Their eyes were cruel, malicious.

The werewolf that led the pack caught the end of the body vine with an exaggerated flourish as it slithered back to him, and then threw it to one of the wolves behind him.

They walked right up to the glade and stopped, sneering at us, baring their irregular sharp yellow teeth.

The leader ran his eyes over us and whistled.

'Well, well, well, if it isn't the famous threesome everyone is looking for,' he said gleefully.

'What? You're surprised? You guys are faayymmouus,' he drawled. 'At least in some circles you are.'

'They call me Vrkayu,' he said with an exaggerated bow when none of us said anything. 'I thought I was famous too, but hey, there are always some ignoramuses who don't know of you. Dara, come on, I know you would ignore me if we met at a party, but here, in the Forest of Fireflies, we must try and be friends. Even if you have murdered many of my mates.'

Vrkayu's eyes travelled to the Gandharva's hilt where the long shining sabre rested.

'Tut tut,' he growled. 'Violence in the enchanted forest? What will those darling wood nymphs think?'

'I wonder what they think of their forest being infested with vermin like you,' I shot back. The body vine cut into my waist as I said it.

'Ooh, a retort. And from a Yakshi, no less! Slay me now,' he clutched his heart in mock agony.

'We were just passing by,' said Dara. 'We don't mean any harm. Let us go and there will be no trouble.'

'Sounds boring,' whined Vrkayu. 'All we get is wide-eyed children these days. No fun, no fun at all. We can't even turn them because of the stupid rules. All we get to do is eat them. The monotony is beginning to kill me. Come on, come on, let's have some fun. Come onnnn...'

'We're leaving,' said Dara, his fingers closing into fists.

Vrkayu smirked. His mean eyes travelled from Dwai to me. 'Not so easily. You know that mean mistress of yours? She wants the human. At any cost. She doesn't care that much about you two, though,' he indicated Dara and me. 'Although, I reckon if I do take you along, she will happily throw you into her infamous dungeons. I hear you will be upgraded to the luxury caves. The one with spikes.'

'You're lying,' said Dara calmly. 'Hera doesn't want any of us, least of all a mere human.'

Vrkayu laughed. It was a blood-curdling sound. 'You take me for a fool, Dara, don't you? Pity. Because you see, I am anything but one. This one here is a Half-born.'

'How can you tell?' spat Dwai.

'It takes one to know one. Of course, when it comes to Half-born pedigree, we are mere mongrels and you are of sky blood, but I can tell a Half-born when I see one and I haven't seen one in hundreds of years.'

He came an inch closer to Dwai. 'Now I can't, for the love of anything, fathom why Hera would want a Half-born, except that she loves all things forbidden. And she wants you before the Festival of Mara and that smells pretty bloody to me. She will be up to no good with you, that's for sure. I'm hearing rumours about her "big plans". But I don't give a hoot about that. There's a handsome reward waiting if I deliver you to her without a scratch. So let's get going.'

I laughed. He turned to me, his eyes narrowing, the hunger in them apparent. He clicked his nails together. I could see shreds of flesh in them. He would rip me apart just for the fun of it, I knew. Werewolf injuries were permanent and mostly fatal, even for the supernatural.

'What's so funny, succubus?' he rasped. He bared his canines, sharp and ruthless.

'Nothing,' I said airily. 'I am just amused you think you can take the Half-born away with me and him around.' I waved a hand towards Dara. The werewolf came closer. I could smell his breath, rank with stale blood. I held my stare. I wasn't going to show him I was afraid.

'Oh, what big eyes you have, Grandma,' he mocked, his voice cold. 'All the better to see you with, darling.' He gripped my jaw with his hands, the nails digging into my skin. My succubus blood dripped onto his hands, staining the dirty fur. 'What big hands you have, Grandma. All the better to...' his hands groped my chest.

I kicked him in the nuts. Hard. Vrkayu staggered back, howling in pain. The other werewolves howled back, their hackles raised.

'Distinctly stupid move, succubus,' panted Vrkayu. He strode up to Dara and signalled to two of his mates. 'Hold the bastard.' The werewolves caught and pinned Dara down to the ground. Vyakaru hovered above him and then kicked him viciously in the chest. Blood gushed out of Dara's mouth as he doubled over with pain.

'No!' I screamed. 'DON'T...'

'Keep quiet, Ardra,' shouted Dwai.

'Don't what,' said Vrkayu in a low, furious voice. 'Don't. What. Succubus? You mean this?' and he kicked Dara again, this time aiming for his face. The sharp nails scratched deep lines into the Gandharva's beautiful features, colouring them with blood.

Vrkayu knelt down beside the semi-conscious Gandharva, touching a dirty finger to the blood. Looking at me, he then put the finger in his mouth. 'Strange tasting, Gandharva blood. Though I do crave an Aakasha takeaway occasionally,' he said and kicked Dara again, this time in the head. Dara lost consciousness.

'Hurt me,' pleaded Dwai. 'Hurt me, you lowlife. Leave both of them alone.'

'Awww, how touching. The Half-born wants to saaaveee his girlfriend and the Gandharva,' chuckled Vrkayu.

His pack howled with laughter.

'Now!' the werewolf's voice was a whiplash. 'Search him for anything valuable and then we take him to that stupid witch. Dispose of the Gandharva. And as for her…' His mouth split into an ugly grin. 'Well, there's plenty of time for her later. Search him!'

One of the werewolves advanced towards Dwai. I struggled against the vine binding me but the more I did, the more it bit into my skin. Soon, deep gashes appeared on my wrists and neck. Vrkayu's eyes gleamed at the sight of my midnight-blue blood and he inched closer. 'Why wait?' he smirked. His long pink tongue darted out and he licked my neck. I struggled even more and the vine grew tighter, my blood now spilling into rivulets down my neck.

'Hmm…lowly succubus blood tastes better than that of those Aakasha snobs,' he said, his voice thick with lust and hunger.

Dwai let out a roar of rage.

'Search him, then bind him tightly. And wait here. The Yakshi and I are going on a quick date,' he snarled to his companions and then tugged at my body vine. I held my ground, and he lurched and stumbled because I didn't move.

He stopped and stared, anger and humiliation slashing across his face. My magic wouldn't work as long as I was bound by the vines so I couldn't turn into my warrior form or freeze him. But I still had my strength.

'We aren't going anywhere,' I said quietly. He tugged hard at the body vine but I wouldn't budge. He pulled at it harder just to see the blood ooze out of my sides as the vine sank deeper into my skin. I stood immovable, expressionless. He gauged me with narrow eyes for a few seconds and then addressed his companions who were watching us, hesitant. 'Search the Half-born, I said! Do it, and let's be on our way.'

One of the werewolves walked up to Dwai who began to struggle against the vine. It cut into his arms, his dark red blood dripping to the ground. 'No, no, don't tempt them with blood...' I murmured. The werewolf caught hold of Dwai's shoulder roughly in an attempt to steady him. Vrkayu snorted in impatience.

Then something strange happened. Though Dwai didn't look at me at all, my Yakshi sense flickered to life. It was as if his brain had signalled mine. My eyes travelled to the glint of steel on Dara's waist as he lay senseless on the forest floor.

A flash of a second later, the werewolf was howling in pain. Dwai was holding it up by its neck, the body vine now miraculously around the wolf's torso, cutting into its flesh. I saw Dwai tighten his hold, his eyes expressionless as the torso severed itself from the body and fell with a dull thud to the ground.

Vrkayu let out a snarl of rage as his other companions shrank back, suddenly looking frightened. Another second later, I was free. Dwai threw the body vine at the pack and I watched as it sailed through the air and whipped itself around them. He pulled the end that was still in his hand and, in an instant, the wolves' torsos disengaged from their lower halves and fell to the ground, their dirty brown blood staining the grass floor.

'And now,' Dwai said, his eyes cold and hard, his mouth set in a grim line, 'now for you!'

Vrkayu howled, a sound of fear, anger and frustration, and bounded on all fours towards Dwai who stayed where he was. I opened my mouth to scream but it got caught in my throat.

Time seemed to be shuffling its deck at an unreal speed for Dwai.

He knelt beside Dara and drew the sword out from its sheath. I didn't blink as he swung around with unexpected swiftness and neatly slid the steel tip into Vrkayu's heart. The werewolf buckled to his knees, his dying eyes wide open with shock, even as Dwai pulled out the blood-soaked sword and swung it towards the werewolf's head in a whirring motion. The steel flashed as it sliced through his head, which bounced to the floor, lifeless and ugly.

He looked up, his face spattered with werewolf blood, and shot me a wry smile. I think my mouth was still open in shock when he walked across, wiped the blood off his face, and kissed me.

☩ 35 ☩

The Forest of Fireflies seemed to glow as our lips met. If time had flown by at lightning speed when Dwai was slaying werewolves, it was now tiptoeing around us in gossamer stockings.

As I pulled away from Dwai, I could see the gold flecks in his eyes, wolf blood speckled all over his face. We stood there in that little clearing, surrounded by dismembered werewolves, as I tried to process the last few seconds. He looked different, like something had changed irreversibly within him, a splintered hardness shadowing his face. Yet, his pearl black eyes glowed with an emotion I didn't know I could have within me. It shot through my core, and old, tired and heartless as it was, it flooded with light, mellow and warm.

I could have stayed in this moment forever but I suddenly remembered the unconscious form on the forest floor.

'Dara,' I shouted as I darted across to him. He lay there, bruised and bloody, almost unrecognizable. I was about to scoop him up in my arms when I remembered he didn't want to touch my skin.

'We have to do something,' I said as Dwai knelt beside me. 'He looks pretty bad.'

'He will heal,' I replied, trying to sound reassuring. I wasn't sure who I was trying to comfort – Dwai or myself. 'Gandharvas are supposed to be natural healers. He will heal faster than most. But his magic is weak right now.'

'We have to get some bandages. Or medicines.'

'He is too weak to move,' I said. 'Besides, he is a Gandharva. Human medicines will have no effect on him. Let's find him a comfortable place here while he heals. We can wait until he's better and then get out of here.'

We moved him to the little clearing where the last embers of the bonfire glowed. Dwai took off his jacket and placed it under Dara's head.

'I feel responsible,' he said, sounding anguished. 'He was weak and defenceless because of what he did for me down by the Tarini.'

'I wish I knew of some way to help him heal,' I said, watching his markings gleam dimly, reminding me how weak his magic was.

As I said this, the strange music of the wood nymphs began again. This time, however, it sounded nearer. The whole forest seemed to whisper around me.

'Ardra, look,' Dwai whispered.

I looked in the direction he was pointing and saw them.

Wispy, with pale fluorescent hair and an almost liquid aspect, they floated through the glades, beautiful and airy. The wood nymphs. When they came closer, I could see the silver antlers on their head beautifully decorated with wildflowers. They were a joyful sight and their music filled my ears as they floated right up to us, hovering for a few seconds before they landed on the dewy forest floor.

They turned a shimmering green as they touched the grass and I realized they took on the colours of whatever they came into contact with.

'Thank you,' said one in a voice that seemed to ripple up from the bottom of the lake. 'Thank you for ridding the forest of them.' Her large marble-coloured eyes wandered over to the bodies of the dead werewolves. She sighed and closed her eyes.

A wind rose from the ground and swirled around the werewolves. When it left, their bodies had vanished.

The nymph who had spoken walked over to Dara, her glassy eyes loving. 'He will be okay. The water in the lake should help. Give him some of it.'

Dwai walked over to the lake and scooped up some of the water in his hands. He let a few drops fall on Dara's dry lips. The rest he used to dab the Gandharva's bruised face.

'He will heal by sunrise,' said the wood nymph. She then

turned to Dwai. 'It was you. It was your new magic that saved this forest from bloodspill tonight. For that we are ever grateful. But the forest continues to be plundered by those who do not understand or value it. You can help us.'

'How?' asked Dwai, looking baffled.

'You possess the Jwala. It has powers to bestow magical protection. Your mother…she loved these forests very much. She would want you to use it.'

Dwai's eyes met mine. I nodded slightly to encourage him.

He took the stone out of his pocket.

It flickered to life. Instinctively he placed the Jwala in the centre of the clearing and the nymphs gathered around it. A beam of light shot through the stone, took the shape of a flower, and then split into one more and another. Soon, hundreds of light-flowers flooded the air with their beauty as the fireflies flickered around them, their combined incandescence setting the whole forest on ethereal fire.

'The Forest of Fireflies is safe again,' warbled the wood nymph even as the light-flowers settled on everything, on tree tops, creepers, in the hollows of old trees, the lake.

'We shall sing in eternal gratitude tonight,' said the nymph, her translucent eyes looking deep into Dwai's pearl black ones.

'We seek permission to spend the night here,' said Dwai. 'Until the Gandharva is strong enough to move.'

'You can stay here for as long as you desire,' she smiled, some of the light-flowers entangling in her hair. She must have seen the shadow of confusion in my eyes. The forest had just been protected against my kind and I couldn't see why I was being allowed to stay. 'You are not like the rest of them,' she explained, her voice clear and low. 'There is something distinctly variant about you, and maybe someday you will learn what you truly are, deep inside. You are welcome here. The protective enchantments do not affect you, as you must have noticed already.'

'Thank you,' I whispered gratefully.

'We have to get back to our trees now,' said the nymph. 'You must return here whenever you feel the call of the Forest,' she said to both of us.

They left, fluttering through the air, and we settled down in the clearing with the nymph song floating over us from afar.

Dara was sleeping, looking more peaceful now, his wounds already beginning to fade.

'How did you do it?' I asked.

Dwai replied without taking his eyes off Dara. 'I don't know. I saw Vrkayu do that…to you…and something snapped in me. In that second, I knew what magic lay within me, what I was capable of.'

'I felt it too,' I said. 'I sensed it coursing through you.'

'Maybe it was the stone.'

'Maybe it was just you. We all have magic within us. You had just forgotten how to look for it.'

His eyes reflected the fluorescence of the forest. 'I don't trust this magic business,' he said, almost under his breath. 'So far I have only heard or seen it being used for evil.'

'Maybe how we use the magic is up to us.' Even as I said it, I realized that *I* had that choice too. It lay wide open in front of me.

The fireflies wove intricate patterns around us while Dwai fell asleep, his head resting on my shoulder. We hadn't discussed the kiss. Dwai had kissed me without any bewitching on my part and I had never dealt with something like that in my centuries-long life. I had no idea what it was like to be wanted by someone without my magic being involved. I glanced sideways at his dark head on my shoulder and I knew my life was propelling me towards choices I never knew I had. This thought that should have ideally made me restless and uncomfortable actually soothed me and I shut my eyes, but not without a glance towards Dara, who seemed to be sleeping now, his face slowly returning to normal. My last thought as I drifted off to sleep was that, despite its strangeness, this was one of the most perfect moments of my life and I wouldn't have traded it for anything in the world.

✤ 36 ✤

'Don't let her succeed...'

The voice woke me up. It seemed to have come from inside me and for a second I wondered if I was talking in my sleep.

Then I saw her, faint as a whisper, kneeling in front me on the grass — my memory ghost.

'She will do what she intends to. Don't let her...' she quavered.

'You mean Hera? Do you know what she's planning?'

She shimmered uncertainly. 'Time plays its songs on an infinite loop,' she said instead. 'You must stop her.'

'I don't know how.' I said. 'But I will try.'

I put my hand out to touch her but my hand shot right through her, as if it had passed through a shaft of fading moonlight.

'You are beginning to remember,' she said dreamily.

'But I don't know what I'm supposed to have forgotten in the first place,' I said, frustrated.

'The memory is a dark, dark thing...' she said, her voice shaking even more than usual. 'How can you not remember?'

'I'm so sorry,' I bit my lip. 'I've been around for too long. Did I hurt you in some way? I wish you would tell me.'

Her colourless eyes clouded with sorrow and she looked away. For the first time, I noticed a flower tucked into her flowing hair. A forgotten frangipani.

'That's my favourite flower, too,' I murmured, as sleep began to overpower me again.

'Sleep is sometimes the best way to be awake,' she said and melted into the dark.

I realized I was holding the forgotten flower in my palm. She must have somehow slipped it to me. I curled my fingers around it and glanced at Dara before my eyes shut themselves. He was fast asleep, his markings glowing again.

⚘ 37 ⚘

He fell asleep with his head on Ardra's shoulder. At some point he slid down on to the velvet grass in the glade and curled up, exhausted and unable to sleep peacefully. In his half-slumber he thought he heard Ardra talking to someone. Except there was no one around. Dara was sleeping; he had peeked at him just a moment ago. He turned on his back, his eyes closed, and the moment right after he had slayed the werewolves replayed itself in his mind.

Ardra...the expression on her face as he killed Vrkayu. Ardra, her eyes telling him more than even her own heart knew. No, *core*. She didn't have a heart. He was in love with someone whose heart would never beat loudly for him. But her eyes, her beautiful brown eyes, told him what he needed to know. And that kiss had sealed it. There had been magic in that kiss. Not the bewitching of the Yakshis, but the pure magic of the universe. He had felt it and he knew she had, too. When this was all over...

He never finished that thought.

A flash of steel charged through the air towards him. He threw himself across the ground and the sword caught his shoulder, piercing it in white hot pain.

He screamed in rage and turned wildly to look at his assailant and his brain clouded over in utter shock and confusion.

Dara.

Before he could react, the Gandharva, who seemed to have regained all his powers, aimed the sword at his heart yet again. Dwai ducked just in time, his new-found speed matching that of the Gandharva. The fireflies swarmed around them in hysteria.

The Gandharva's face was lined with a fierce, steely determination. He moved towards Dwai again, his feet noiseless on the forest floor, and it took every ounce of Dwai's nascent magic to swing out of his way even as the sword struck the ground where he had stood, missing him by less than a second.

Why was Dara trying to kill him?

He ducked again as the Gandharva circled him, his jewel-blue eyes darting towards the unaware, sleeping Yakshi on the grass. Dwai wanted to finish this before Ardra woke up. He didn't know how, but he wanted to make it go away so that she could never see that Dara…

The sword sliced through the air again and he avoided death by a whisker by throwing himself on the grass some distance away. And then, as he scrambled to his feet, he saw her.

She was standing where he had been a few seconds ago, bathed in firefly light, shaking with emotion. It was only when he looked at her face did he realize it was anger, even though tears were streaming down her cheeks. She had stopped the sword with her hand, her blue Yakshi blood dripping on to the ground.

Dara froze.

'Why?'

Her question cut through the air with violence. She caught hold of the sword's blade, now coloured midnight blue, plucked it out of Dara's hand and threw it with some force back at him. He picked it up slowly.

Dwai stumbled over to her side, clutching his bleeding shoulder.

'WHY?' This time she was shouting. 'WHY WOULD YOU DO THAT?'

'Maybe it was a mistake, Ardra,' Dwai interjected, his face screwed up with pain. 'Maybe it was his injuries.'

She ignored him. 'Answer me,' she said, her voice now cold and even. 'Why would you try and kill Dwai like a plunderer in the middle of the night?'

'Ardra…' said Dara, his voice strangled with pain. 'I…'

'What would you have done had you succeeded? Stolen away

like a murderer? Left me here with his dead body? WHAT WOULD YOU HAVE DONE?'

'I HAVE TO,' Dara shouted back.

'You *have* to? Why? After everything we have been through together, this is what you *have* to do?'

'I have to. He can't live. If he does, everything will burn. I can't let Hera have him. I can't. He is a liability, Ardra. I can't let Hera use him to...'

'To what? For once, Dara, complete your sentence!'

'She will use him,' he said under his breath, 'for evil beyond measure. She's been looking for a Half-born like him for centuries now. He cannot live. She will hunt him down wherever he goes and once she has him, she will be unstoppable.'

'So you decided to put your sword through his heart when he was sleeping?' The anger in her voice was cold and sharp.

'I had no choice,' he said between his teeth 'You heard the Balance Keeper. The universe is falling apart. If she gets hold of Dwai, the world will burn. I can't risk that.'

'You're a coward, Dara,' she spat.

'I HAVE NO OTHER OPTION,' he yelled. 'I don't. I will not spend another 500 years in regret that poisons every breath I take...not again. Not after – '

He stopped abruptly and turned away, his anguish visible in every fibre of his being.

'Complete your sentences,' she growled, her breath coming in angry rasps.

Dara clutched his head in despair.

'After *what*? What did you do, Dara? What happened to the girl you loved?

He turned, his eyes wide with shock.

She continued. 'What happened to her? The girl whose soul you attempted to retrieve?'

'How do you know about that?' he whispered in a cracked voice.

'Never mind how I know. Your wretched broken heart is not an excuse for you to do whatever you like! This is not how you redeem yourself.'

Dara let out a noise of torment.

'We had a pact. You help me and I help you get to Atala. I thought you were a decent man Hera had somehow wronged deeply, but now I'm not so sure. She is evil, yes, but you... What are you hiding, Dara?'

'I would never do anything to hurt you,' his voice was pleading. 'But...'

'But what? There you go again!' she yelled. 'You know what I think? I think you don't want to give me any answers because you are ashamed. You are ashamed of whatever it is you did.'

'Ardra, don't,' Dwai urged, trying to hold her hand. She wrestled out of his grip and walked towards Dara.

'Everything about you is shrouded in mystery, isn't it? Right down to why you stalked me for years. Why? I want to know...'

Dara buried his face in his hands.

'Leave,' she said, her voice devoid of emotion. 'Leave now, and don't ever come near Dwai and me again. Ever!'

'Ardra, try and understand. If I do that, he will die and you will too. She will not rest till she finds him.'

'I don't care! I will take care of him. And me. Hell, he can take care of himself. Who do you think got rid of the werewolves? Go, Dara. I never want to see you again. EVER!'

He took a step back. The loathing in her voice was so strong that even Dwai shivered a little from its force.

'Get away from my sight. I'm sorry I ever knew you.' She turned away from him, her hand still bleeding, her face hard. When she turned around again, he was gone. There was only a faint glimmer where the Gandharva had stood a few seconds ago. She then collapsed to her knees, her whole body racked with sobs.

Dwai remained rooted where he was. When he finally did hold her, her tears fell hot and angry on his shoulder and he knew – they both did – that something had changed irreversibly in their lives.

⤝ 38 ⤞

A day had passed in the glade. A wordless, tearless day, when both Dwai and she had walked around in the forest with their fingers interlocked.

She hadn't said a word. Not a single one since Dara had left. She had led Dwai to the lake where she had bathed his bloody shoulder with the magical water. Her face had shown no emotion as she had watched the shoulder heal inch by inch until the wound closed, leaving only a long, faint scar, a jagged reminder of that night.

He hadn't tried to coax her out of silence. He knew she didn't have the words to express her sorrow. He watched as she walked around the little clearing that had become their home for the last two days, a steady stream of fireflies following her wherever she went. She sat with her feet dipped in the lake, her dark hair clouding her face, shielding her eyes. She looked for him once in a while and when she found him sitting on the floor, leaning against a tree, she smiled faintly and he smiled back. He noticed she hadn't shape-shifted for a while. Her eyes had stayed brown for days now. Rich, brown, faraway eyes.

When twilight fell over the forest on the second evening, he walked up to her as she sat by the lake. Rolling up his trousers, he sat down next to her, dipping his feet in too.

They watched their feet float, misshapen and pale under water.

'I don't want to run anymore,' she said, almost to herself. It was the first thing she had said since Dara had left. He turned to look at her.

'There is just too much I don't know…too much that is still wrapped in riddles. And I don't want to run from it. I expected D…' she paused, as if even uttering Dara's name was physically painful, and then continued, 'I expected to find some answers but I haven't, and it's time I went after them.'

'That means putting your life in danger,' he said gently.

She shook her head. 'I don't care. I want to know what happened on the night of the blood moon. About the Thing in the tower and why it affects me the way it does. I want to know why I'm haunted by memory ghosts, what it is that I'm supposed to remember. I want to know why Hera needs a Half-born so badly. If I run I may still die and never know the answers. Let me die trying.'

He took her hand. It felt warm and loving over hers. She gripped it hard.

'You don't have to be a part of this,' she continued. 'We can find you a safehouse, somewhere faraway. You can be free.'

'But I wouldn't be with you,' he said softly. 'From the minute you picked me up in that hotel – actually, from the moment I sketched you – I think we were tied together in this...whatever this is. Maybe it was destiny.'

'I don't believe in destiny,' she said. 'I don't have a destiny. I never did. What I do have is my life and what lies ahead of me. And somehow my actions forced you to be in it too. I feel responsible for that.'

'If I am what Hera has been looking for centuries, she might have found me anyway,' he said.

'I have to find Vina. She will help me. I know she will. I have to find out more about what Hera has planned at the Festival of Mara. And whatever it is, I have to keep you safe from it. But running isn't an option anymore.'

'Then we will face it head on,' he said. 'But together.' There was strength in his voice.

She smiled at him. It was wistful and yet warm. Something soft and silken shaped itself into an emotion between them. It was unsure and unfamiliar even to itself, for it had never been experienced by a Yakshi. When it came into contact with her, it shivered in delight from the absolute strange beauty of her core.

He leaned forward and kissed her.

A curious scythe-shaped moon, bright and yellow, peeked out of the clouds, her light streaming into the Forest of Fireflies, onto the Yakshi and the human.

As they reached for each other, the Yakshi instinctively stirred her bewitching. He felt the tiny sparks of her magic and he shook his head. 'Just us...no magic,' he whispered, and she did something she had never done before. She chose the magic of her own being instead of the magic she was ordained to use against another. She awoke to the enchantment of her own mysteries, and as she did, she experienced a bewitching that stunned her, and she let herself be reeled in. This was the magic of the universe that was spun when two people decided to belong to each other, and it was greater than any other kind of sorcery, known and unknown.

Far away from the Forest of Fireflies, in the underbelly of the universe, the dark goddess felt the rumblings of change in her glittering palace of unearthly magic. She felt something detach itself from her and fly into an adventure of its own. She shuddered from the feeling as rage and fear coursed through her. She became profoundly aware that one of her creations, one of the dark things she thought she owned, had freed herself by choosing something she hadn't known she could. And as that freedom struck her cold heart like lightning, Hera shivered, for she knew then that the future was not something she could control anymore. The future was free to do as it pleased and her powers could do nothing to stop it.

✢ 39 ✢

Fairytales. Even a Yakshi like me knew what they were. The usual characters were a damsel; a prince; a dragon, beast or a creature of some sort; and an evil queen. If I didn't know better I would have said I was in a fairytale. A bloody, twisted one. Ever heard of a fairytale where the maiden was the monster? Monsters don't ride off into the sunset with Prince Charming. I was fooling myself by thinking that I was in the middle of a beautiful love story. I wasn't destined to love. My body, my core, would not recognize it. Give me blood, give me darkness, give me the twisted deliciousness of secrets. Give me hard cold passion, calculated seduction, bloodlust. I am the monster I was always fated to be.

And yet something happened last night. Something I wasn't even sure was possible. I was the bewitched one, captive to the spell of a strange creature that was alien to me. I dared not give it a name for then it would become familiar, real, something that would belong to me. Instead, I wished upon it like it was a star – distant, ephemeral, out of reach and yet full of hope.

We lay under the satin sky all night and watched the crescent moon wafting in and out of the clouds. I wasn't sure if I was imagining it but I thought her edges were turning red. A deep red, slowly staining her from the outside. I shut my eyes and opened them again and the moon seemed yellow and normal again. *It is almost time for another full moon,* I thought. A month since my life unravelled. I felt like a captive bird let out of its cage for the first time, flying though hills, brushing skies, kissing rivers, breathing in its freedom. I knew now there was another way to live and that I could choose it. I fell asleep with my head resting in the crook of Dwai's arm, my lashes brushing against his sooty ones as they closed.

I dreamt of her.

She flicked out her tongue, which was forked like a snake's, and swallowed a few sparrows. Stars crashed and died in her eyes. She had me tied to a burning tree. The flames kissed and licked my skin and when I tried to scream, not a sound would come out. Things started to emerge from the Black Dwarf Sea, things that didn't even belong in nightmares. Things that would send a shiver down my spine for years afterwards, but things I could never fully describe. Headless, limbless creatures spurting blood, feasting on the fears of children. And leading the pack was the Thing. It lumbered towards me while the tree burnt. I struggled against my ropes and Hera laughed. Behind her stood the ancient mirror, wringing its iron-wrought hands, its surface foggy and disturbed. Mirror creatures clung to my leg, moaning and wailing. Memory ghosts appeared next to me weeping, refusing to speak. The Thing advanced and I could look into its eyes. Depthless, they were darker than darkness itself – eyes that shunned light of any kind. Hera pointed a finger towards me and there opened a gaping hole in my chest where my heart should have been. I began to bleed, to scream.

I sat up, wide awake and shaking. I have had these dreams ever since I can remember. Hera's apocalyptic, nightmarish effect on my sleeping had always intrigued me. Now the Thing had been added to the horror of my nightmares.

I stared down at my chest. It glowed an eerie turquoise from the light of the forest. I traced my index finger down the faint silver line near my ribcage. The scar was exactly where my heart should have been.

'What happened?' Dwai said groggily, sitting up next to me.

'Bad dream. It's nothing. I have them often,' I shrugged.

'You were staring at that line on your chest.'

'It's been there forever. I don't know what it is.'

'It looks like a scar,' he said, following it with his eyes.

'I've never been hurt there,' I shook my head. It was an everyday reminder of the fact that I wasn't human. I was heartless, otherworldly – a monster.

Dawn was slowly stealing across the horizon. The time had come for us to leave the forest. I traced my finger over the wound on Dwai's shoulder. It had healed completely.

'Dwai,' I said, not sure how to say what I wanted to. He had an intent look on his face as he cocked his head to listen. In that moment, he looked terribly young and I felt very old.

'Dwai... I...I'm not human. I'm supernatural, a Yakshi to be precise.'

'Tell me something I don't know,' his mouth twisted into a boyish grin.

'No, what I am trying to say is...monsters don't fall in love. Monsters don't last very long in fairytales. Whatever I'm feeling right now...I don't know how to process it. I feel deeply for you. I feel something alien and wonderful within me, excited about the possibility of having a choice to love someone, but I am not sure how to do it.'

He opened his mouth to say something but I placed a finger over it. 'I'm without a past or a future, in a sense. I'm violent and filled with bloodlust. I'm programmed for destruction. Everything that is happening to me now is more unreal than what has happened to you over the past few days. It is unreal and scary. Love stories belong to moon maidens with stardust in their eyes and wild flowers in their hair. They belong to girls who are perfect and fragile and are destined to be rescued. Not to monsters like me. I don't even have fate lines. I am ordained to lust, not love. I don't know if I can be who you want me to be. And when I think of a life with you, I am afraid. Afraid that I won't love you the way you need me to. And...I think you deserve more than an imperfect love.'

'I'm going to assume you're trying to make a point,' he said quietly. He was serious now, his grin gone. There was a gentle passion in his eyes and I suddenly felt like I had been brought to a universe where a monster could be a thing of beauty, simply because he chose to see me that way.

'Human beings haven't exactly figured out love either,' he

said, taking my hand. 'We mess up all the time, just like the Gods, the Apsaras, the Gandharvas. Every living being deserves a chance at love and at messing it up. It makes the universe more beautiful, for these mistakes of the heart are as natural as the wind, the sun and the rain. I think we deserve to find for our own imperfection, especially after everything we've been through together.'

The fireflies danced around us in delight as we sat there holding hands, savouring the warmth and the quiet before the inevitable storm.

We left the forest some time later. I felt a strange sense of calm as I walked towards an uncertain future. I wanted a shot at this…imperfection, as he had put it. Because, as he had said, every living soul in this universe should be given a chance at love — their personal shot at having the most powerful and mysterious thing that ever existed. You could love forever, like Dara had loved the girl who had died, or your love could burn short and bright for just a few moments in the history of time. But however you did it, I supposed the idea was to make it count; to create a story worthy of a new fairytale, a poem, or a new constellation that would wind itself into an infinite thread of light in your name. Maybe that was the whole point of love — to create an eternal story of your own.

⚴ 40 ⚴

'We are running out of time,' hissed the crone.

Hera watched her with cold, unemotional eyes. 'I am aware,

Dakini. Don't bore me by stating the obvious every chance you get.'

The crone snorted and dug into her nose. Hera looked away in disgust. She was becoming increasingly anxious. The moon was getting fuller and the Half-born was still eluding capture. *If* he really was one, that is. But Vrkayu had failed to return and she had heard murmurs of the entire pack having been slain by something or someone. Their decapitated bodies had turned up by a riverside and their heads were found at the bottom of a ravine. Who could have managed to slay an entire pack of werewolves who were so strong they didn't even need the full moon to turn anymore?

This was the work of the Half-born with sky blood in him, on whose capture she had placed a reward. No one would confirm this but she had a feeling this was true.

She had summoned the crone back because she needed her. At least until the Festival of Mara was over. After that... She took a deep breath. After that, she would be the new Blood Queen. And she would be far superior and more powerful than that last one, who preferred her stupid palace of skulls and ice.

'I hope you are making the necessary preparations, O Queen of Desire,' cackled the crone. 'Once you are the Blood Queen, you will not need most of the things that surround you now. It will be a different life.'

'I know,' said Hera shortly. 'I plan to rule...' she paused for effect, '...from Aakasha.'

The crone drew in her breath sharply. 'O Queen of Phantoms, you are a true visionary. The absolute scale of your deviousness! But...'

'But nothing,' Hera cut her short. 'It has to work. If it does, conquering Aakasha is child's play. That stupid cow who is supposed to be in charge is never there, is she?'

'True, true,' cackled Dakini. 'A Blood Queen in the skies. Marvellous idea! Oh, I wish the Gods could hear this.' She laughed, a malicious sound, her bent figure convulsing with the effort.

'We must find the boy. I've made my plans,' said Hera, absently stroking Gaggii who was resting on her lap. 'I want that girl, too. But not during the blood moon. That would be – '

'Calamitous,' finished the crone. 'Positively calamitous. The Yakshi must be dealt with ONLY after the moon wanes. And the Gandharva?'

Hera sniffed in disdain. 'Dara... Maybe I will chain him to a post in Aakasha and he can watch my reign of glory forever.'

'Pardon me, O Queen of Desire, but what arrangement have you made for...it?' The crone's voice held scarcely disguised trepidation.

Hera fell silent. Her face darkened as Gaggi lifted her head to look at her mistress perhaps sensing her change of mood.

'Hmm...' she said slowly, as if speaking about him caused her physical pain. 'Perhaps I shall let him loose on Prithvi. He can do as he likes there. Who is to stop him, or me? It will be my reign after all, on all the realms.'

The crone scuttled about in excitement.

'And yet, Dakini,' said Hera rising, Gaggii fluttering to her shoulder. 'And yet I wonder about the legitimacy of your sorcery. The old Blood Queen was a Skin Stealer. She stole her own daughter's skin and murdered her to complete the magic. Are we doing enough? What if you are the blundering, blithering fool you look like?'

'You tried the Unspeakable once, didn't you?' hissed Dakini. 'And you blundered because you were so blinded by jealousy.

Where did that get you? You can either have faith in my magic or I can take it elsewhere. I am not answerable to you, O Queen.'

The old mirror sighed, deep and sad. Hera's eyes travelled to it and a shadow of uncertainty clouded those icy irises.

'What do you think?' she asked the mirror, whose surface instantly dissolved into a blur of shapes as the creatures within it scattered in fear. The mirror folded its arms and sighed again, this time deep in thought.

And then it spoke in a tongue only few could understand. Hera herself barely could.

'What I think is of no consequence, O Queen of Desire. I was there when you tried and failed last time. I am still here as you endeavour again. But remember, O Mistress of Phantoms, a bit of you lies in them. Those are the things that you will be forced to discard.'

'Does the mirror speak the truth, Dakini?' asked Hera.

'Yes,' the crone cackled. 'Yes, all your pieces of despair and defeat are in the things you created. You must leave them behind in order to be the Blood Queen.'

'Of course, incompetent as you are, you've failed to mention this of your own accord until now,' Hera said venomously.

The crone stood in the middle of the glittering diamond floor of Hera's chambers. She had the appearance of a mangy vulture, and her phlegmy eyes held an intense dislike that Hera failed to notice as she turned away towards a curious cage covered in a mesh of thorns stationed in a corner of the room. Something revolved in the middle of the cage in an orb of diamonds. Hera fingered the cage, pensive and quiet, as if a sudden memory had silenced her. It was a while before she turned back. The mirror straightened out its arms, clearly paying attention.

'She chose him. I felt it, Dakini. My Yakshi managed to free herself from the destiny I gave her when she was created. If that isn't a sign, nothing is. I *must* succeed. I dream of doom every night. I see it wherever I go. It fills my heart with dread, it laughs in my nightmares. I have to prepare for the worst. After my irreversible mistake last time, I must be careful.

'I have no choice but to trust you, Dakini. And we must get it right this time. But first, to find the Half-born. It shouldn't be hard, given Ardra's proclivity to walk right into the mouth of danger. It shouldn't be hard at all.'

The crone threw her hands up in the air and cackled.

'Such theatrics,' murmured Hera but the corners of her mouth twisted. Gaggii cawed, but Hera was too consumed by her thoughts to pay attention. It was the raven's signal that someone was outside the door, listening – someone who then crept away with muddled ideas in their head about the days to come.

⚹ 41 ⚹

In the beginning, there were 99 Yakshis in existence. We were all born together, we were told, but we didn't meet until we were ready to go out and retreive secrets. I remember waking up in what is known as the Retrieval Room today, naked and cold. Fully formed, in the presence of Hera, the mirror and Dakini, the crone. Before I could even think about what my original aspect was, Hera commanded me to shape-shift and I had, using magic I didn't even know existed within me. She had laughed triumphantly when I had followed her command. She had then asked me to fly. I remember her watching me intently, jealously shrouding her eyes as I took flight. She ordered me to come back down in a few seconds. I never asked who I was and what I was doing there. I just knew. It was as if the knowledge I needed about being a Yakshi and about Hera was already imprinted in my mind. Some say this is because Hera created us from her own shadow. She moulded us out of the darkest corners of her mind where desire mixed with magic.

In my early days, I remember her constantly testing me. I wrestled Rakshasas, fought off fire serpents, slew Raktarakshasas. She seemed pleased, and gave me and some others the warrior aspect that Dwai caught a glimpse of later.

She never created any more Yakshis after us. Maybe she didn't feel the need for it. Ninety-nine of us seemed like enough to extract secrets from humans. We had strength, guile, beauty and bloodlust. What we didn't have was freedom. What we lacked was destiny. The only past, present and future we were allowed was what Hera gave us. We were chained to her and the Palace of Vishara. We were only supposed to go out when we were given an assignment. I found that my turn often tended to come during full moon nights. I was sure there had been no other blood moons in the 500 years of my existence. I would have known if there had been, because Hera never missed a Retrieval.

The process, whatever it was, was conducted in oblivion. I never knew what happened to me while she retrieved the secrets I brought her from humans. I would wake up with my mind blank, as if someone had wiped my memory clean, and I could never remember the human I had seduced the night before. After the Retrieval, I would wander about the palace finding ways to amuse myself until my turn arrived once more. That was how my life had been designed for me.

Except Vina and I had found ways to go off on secret expeditions. She had a way of befriending or bribing the guards and had found out how to get past the skull gates without inspection. We would take short trips to Prithvi, exploring parts of that world which intrigued us. One of our favourite places to haunt was an abandoned temple on top of a craggy little hill that no one ever visited. It was old and made of stone; the idol within had crumbled and fallen to pieces years ago. But a curious creeper had made its home in the temple, its four-petalled blue flowers strewn like stars all over the temple ground. We had named this abandoned place the Temple of Flowers and had spent many an hour on its steep spiralling steps, or flying around the crumbling pillars in the hall outside the inner sanctum. It was a lonely spot with traces of old magic – *good* magic – and it made us happy to know that we had a place where we could just be two friends enjoying each another's company while wild peacocks haughtily strutted around us.

The idea was to bump into Vina there. Of course, this was hardly a concrete plan. It was not even a plan. Dwai had said as much when I had suggested it.

'You just want to go and hang around an abandoned temple?' he had asked, looking sceptical.

'Yes,' I had replied defiantly. 'I want to find Vina and I cannot think of a safer way to do that. Can you?'

He had shrugged his shoulders and quietly held on to my hand as we took flight.

'Why are you doing this, Ardra?' he had asked as we flew over a city made magical by its nightlights. I could smell the sea in the air and the salt against my skin. The wind carried his voice away but I could still make out the words. I brought our flight to a halt on top of an old building and settled him down on its terrace.

'Why am I doing this?' I repeated. 'I don't know, Dwai. Maybe because the Balance Keeper hinted we would have something to do with saving the fabric of the universe in some way or the other? Maybe I really do want to make sure you don't end up in a cauldron as a key ingredient in one of Hera's potions. Maybe I am...'

I paused. I didn't know how to say what I was about to without sounding selfish. Maybe I was doing this because for once I had a future of my own, made of my own choices, however disastrous they were. For once, my life wasn't on a loop that I couldn't escape from – of secrets and seduction, and Hera. Maybe this made me self-centred. Maybe it was reckless and selfish. But I wanted to do this. Even if it meant grave peril or certain death.

'You should think about this again,' I said instead. 'You have the stone. Go somewhere safe. You don't have to do any of this, Dwai. None of it. You can choose another way.'

'We've discussed this before,' he said, waving a weary hand. 'We are in this together. I just want to know why you seem hell-bent on running right into danger when you, too, could be somewhere safe.'

'It's just...'

'What?'

'It's just that I am tired of forgetting what I am supposed to remember,' I said. 'The memory ghosts keep asking me to remember. What have I forgotten, Dwai? I don't even know where to look for answers.'

'Maybe they start and end with Hera,' he replied. 'All the questions and all the answers.'

'The girl, she asked me to stop her.' I could hear the frustration in my voice. 'But stop her from what? What if I did something horrible, Dwai? I've taken secrets and ended the lives of hundreds in my time. But what if I did something terrible, even by Yakshi standards? What if I hurt those ghosts in some way, and now this is their way of avenging their own deaths? Is it possible I did something so heinous that my mind is blocking it out?'

'You can't misplace a piece of your memory like that, can you? How can you do something that horrible and not remember? I doubt it, Ardra. The answer has to lie somewhere else,' Dwai said.

I nodded, wanting – almost desperately – to believe him. 'Let's go,' I said after a pause and he nodded.

At some point, we were joined in the sky by silver geese. They flew behind us in their curious formation and Dwai laughed in delight. They finally left our side half-a-day later, scattering in the sky like sleek feathery clouds, and disappeared.

Somewhere over a very blue sea, where the waves formed lacy crests, we passed an entire village floating by in the sky. Dwai's jaw dropped in astonishment and I explained, 'Probably out of another dimension. Idiots lost their way, I expect.' Dwai shook his head and watched the village disappear behind pearly white clouds, the sunlight glinting on the thatched roofs.

After that we were alone for the rest of the expedition. I half expected to run into a Yakshi at some point but it never happened. Strange. My heart sank. *Maybe this is a wild goose chase*, I thought.

Dwai and I barely spoke through the course of the flight

save for the short stop on the terrace. We were both consumed by our riddles, together but separate in the journey inside our minds.

'I think I'm severely jet-lagged,' he groaned once we reached the temple. He stretched and then grinned at me, his eyes sparkling. I was happy to see him in a good mood. The next few days wouldn't exactly be fun, after all – camping out in the ruins of a temple waiting for a Yakshi who may or may not turn up was hardly *fun*.

We waited. We waited as squirrels scampered all over the ruins and allowed Dwai to feed them nuts, much to his delight. We waited as the sky changed colour rapidly, but no one stirred except us.

'I think the general idea is that this place is haunted,' I said as twilight stole in, casting its champagne glow over the faint stars.

'That explains the absolute absence of humans,' said Dwai. I could sense his growing impatience. And I didn't blame him. After all, he had come here following my whim.

I bit my lip nervously and Dwai raised an eyebrow. We were sitting at the edge of a dilapidated square with our legs dangling over the edge. It was a steep drop below. Lights danced at the foot of the cliff, a sign of unusual activity.

'What's with the enticing lip-biting?' he grinned.

I looked away. 'What if she never comes, Dwai? We may never get the clues we need. We may have to spend the rest of our lives hiding from Hera.'

'Ardra,' he said gently, placing his arm across my shoulders. 'The future is foggy enough right now. Don't worry so much. What has to happen will happen. Either way, we'll face it together.'

I almost choked with how his affectionate reassurance made me feel. His implicit conviction that I – *we* – would somehow find a way through all of this overwhelmed me. I took in a deep breath. The sun hung in the sky, low and bright, until the horizon pulled the orb into its smudgy walls. Almost as if on cue, the moon appeared, almost full and faintly red, still wistful and lonely.

'They really aren't destined to be together, are they?' I said. 'It's like they were torn apart because together their light would burn up the universe. It's the saddest story in the world. I haven't been able to get it out of my mind ever since I heard it.'

'It's a myth, Ardra,' said Dwai. 'The universe brims over with myths of this kind.'

'And yet there is a moon at the bottom of the Old Sea,' I said. 'She exists. And if she does, then...'

Dwai gazed at the moon as she scattered her light dreamily over the landscape.

'Did you believe in Yakshis?' I asked. 'Before you encountered me, did you believe that succubi of any kind existed?'

He shook his head.

'But I am real. And I am a myth. It's almost as if I exist in two different realities.'

'You are real because you are the most beautiful thing in the universe,' he said softly. 'You are monster and you are magic. Even the universe is surprised by how lovely you are. And, whatever happens, I'll always be glad there was us.'

Our kiss tasted of hope. The stars danced above us, waltzing into our private love song. I didn't dare believe any of this. I didn't have the courage to put my arms around this feeling and, yet, it had made its home within me. I didn't care about

forever anymore. I had experienced forever for a long time –
now all that mattered to me was the present. I wanted to spend
a lifetime in this moment. Time could rearrange its rules for
us. And the world could wait one more night.

❧ 42 ❧

I wandered around the ruins the next day while Dwai slept.
Despite how happy and comforted I had been the night before,
sleep had again brought with it dreams of Hera, Dara and the
Thing. In the end, I had stayed awake and spent the night
tracing the shapes of the clouds floating above us. As dawn
splashed its cold light over the world, I rose.

He slept peacefully, his face serene, even though he had
revealed two nights ago that he had been dreaming of his
mother and the River of Death. 'She warned me,' he said. 'She
was weeping, her face hidden in her hands, as she told me to
beware. Before I could ask her any questions, I woke up.'

Yet, despite how precariously perched his life was, at the
moment, Dwai seemed awfully happy. I wished I could imbibe
some of his free-spiritedness so I wouldn't be haunted all the
time.

I rose in the air and glided to the back of the broken
temple. Wild flowers grew stubbornly all over its floors and
walls. I bent down and picked a bright blue flower and tucked
it behind my hair. I wish I had my little hand mirror to tell
me how I looked. That little devilish piece of mercury almost

always knew what was on my mind. The other person who came close was Vina. She could tell what I was going to say or do most of the time.

'The Yakshi wore blue,' said a voice behind me.

I whipped around in disbelief. Vina stood there, looking like a bright flame with her flowing hair and shining skin.

I broke into a run just as she did. Throwing my arms around her, I tried hard to control my tears. 'I knew you would come,' I said again and again. 'I knew you would. I knew my plan wasn't so wild and idiotic after all.'

She pulled away from the hug, her eyes gleaming, full of an emotion I couldn't quite place. Before I could say anything she took the flower from my hair and tucked it into her own.

'I've missed you,' she said softly. 'Things have changed so much… I thought I would never see you again.'

'Me too, but I thought maybe if I took a chance and came here – '

'This is our place, isn't it, Ardra?' she interrupted, her eyes shining like stars. 'Our place of freedom, however brief.'

'How did you manage to steal away?' I whispered. I still couldn't believe she was here.

'Ever since you got away, I've been coming here whenever I could get past the guards. It has become tougher, I'm not going to lie. The skull gates don't let you pass unless one of the guards authorizes a pass. She…she's really determined.'

'Determined about what?' I linked my arm with hers and we glided into the air. The sun glinted off her hair as it flew in the wind.

'You *escaped*, Ardra. Have you ever heard of anyone escaping Atala without losing their life? You were her pet, her special pet. She was mad. There are so many rumours going around, I don't know which to believe.'

'Don't go back,' I said, squeezing her hand. 'Don't. We'll find a way to get away from all of this and be safe.'

'Are you alone? No...I heard the human was with you, too. Hera suspects he is a Half-born! And she...'

'She what, Vina?'

'She wants him for something...something very Hera-like. And she wants him for the Festival of Mara.'

'What *is* this festival? We've never had it before.'

'Lord Mara,' said Vina, her tone soaked in devotion. 'The God of Desire, of Lust. Hera draws her powers from his blessings.'

'I know who Lord Mara is. We have a statue of him in our chambers,' I cut in impatiently. 'But why a festival now?'

Vina shrugged. 'Maybe she wants something from him again. Hera never does anything without getting something in return, does she? But tell me, Ardra, is the human a Half-born? How is that even possible?'

I said nothing. I could sense a storm in the air.

'IS he?' she asked again, impatiently. I looked into her curious, eager face. Vina had always been interested in others — it was one of the things that made her a good Yakshi. She had a genuine hunger for secrets, however briefly she held them in her core.

'Is he what?'

We both swirled around. Dwai was standing a few feet below us. His hair was tousled, giving him a more boyish look than usual. He looked directly at Vina and grinned, 'So you're the famous best friend!'

She floated back to the temple floor. 'And you're the famous Half-born,' she smiled. 'Or so it is rumoured, anyway. In fact, the only hybrids I've seen are mangy werewolves. You are *so* much better looking.'

She laughed. I landed alongside her and walked up to Dwai.

'She came,' he said to me. 'You were right, Ardra. She came looking for you.'

'I told you she wouldn't let me down.'

'Ahem,' Vina cleared her throat. Her bright-as-stars eyes slowly took in the scene before her and I could see understanding dawning on her face.

'Really?' she gasped. 'Can we even do that? Are we...'

'Do what?' I asked, trying to not look as guilty as I felt. 'Don't be silly, Vina.'

'Okay, fine, I'll tactfully change the subject, then,' she giggled. Looking at Dwai as though suddenly seeing him in a new light, she said, 'Go on, tell me...are you really one?'

Dwai nodded. He put his hand inside his pocket and kept it there.

'Amazing! You know you are a rare specimen, right? There hasn't been a Half-born with sky blood in more than 500 years.' She walked up to him and surveyed him from head to toe.

'So he has the stone then?'

I nodded.

'Can I see it?' she asked, excitedly clapping her hands.

Clouds circled the sky, dark and heavy. The storm was coming closer. Vina smiled brightly at both of us, her eyes round and expectant.

I gestured to Dwai. He hesitated for a second and then reluctantly drew his hand out of his pocket along with the stone.

'Wow!' she said, taking it from him, her childlike enthusiasm making me smile. 'Ardra...the stories were true. Apsaras do exist. And these stones...'

'They're called Jwalas,' I explained.

'Oh, I know! Jwalas are powerful things,' she nodded.

'You knew about Jwalas?' I was surprised. 'I heard about them for the first time a few days ago.'

'Of course I knew about Jwalas. It's every girl's dream to possess one.'

'You've never mentioned them.'

'I'm sure I did. They have remarkable powers, these things, am I right? All those myths...'

'They do, yes.'

She nodded absently, hardly paying any attention to us now. When she turned with the stone in her palm, it turned a brooding grey. 'You know,' she said, not taking her eyes off the stone as its surface quivered, mirroring the angry sky looming over us. 'I was told these stones recognize intention. They won't work unless the owner wants them to.'

'Unless, I am told, the owner abandons the stone,' said Dwai.

'Amazing,' she repeated, mesmerized by the stone in her palm.

'So it won't work if you are stunned or unconscious?'

'I guess,' Dwai shrugged.

The sun seemed to shift its position just a little bit. The clouds, as if on cue, moved to cover it. Ghost clouds, wafting slow and silent. I felt the first droplets of rain hit me, cool against my skin.

'May I have my stone back now, please?' asked Dwai politely. He took a step forward.

Vina laughed. It was a tinkling sound, fickle and beautiful. She rose in the air playfully. 'Come and get it,' she said.

'Come on, Vina...' he said. 'Give it back.'

I watched as she rose a little higher in the air, now juggling the stone from one hand to another. 'Come and get it,' she repeated, giggling.

Something flared in my Yakshi core.

'Vina…' I called out. 'Give the stone back to him.'

She looked down at me. 'Come on, Ardra, come take it. Winner gets the stone, loser gets – '

I dashed into the sky after her. She shot right through the air, now thick with rain, like a sleek comet, the Jwala firmly in hand.

Let this just be a game…please, let this just be one of her stupid games. My mind raced as we somersaulted through the air, Vina's laughter ringing loudly even in the howling wind.

'Vina…' I called out. 'Come back! This is *not* a fun game.'

An unnatural darkness fell over the sky, over earth, over us, bringing with it a stifling silence. For a few seconds I could neither see nor hear anything. Then lightning splintered the sky, flooding it with its sharp white light.

She was hovering just above me and her aspect had changed. She was now a warrior, her lashes wing-tipped but aflame, her eyes larger, meaner, and her talons long, sharp, curved. I was filled with a deep sense of foreboding. This was not my friend.

'Vina!' I shouted. 'What…'

'I'm sorry, Ardra,' she said through the sheet of rain. 'I really am. But I have to – '

She didn't finish the sentence as, all of a sudden, shouts could be heard from down below. I could make out figures – larger, stronger than humans. I felt their feral energy and I could sense Dwai's confusion.

'Dwai!' I screamed, turning to dive back down.

Faster than I could blink, Vina flew in front of me, blocking my view. Her warrior aspect was terrible, emanating incredible power. 'Don't, Ardra. I'm too strong for you.'

'NO!' I screamed. 'No…'

I could hear faint noises of a scuffle below. Dwai wouldn't go easily, he wouldn't.

'Vina...' I shouted through the howling wind. 'Don't do this, please.'

Another sharp splinter of lightning cut through the sky and it highlighted the madness in her eyes. This wasn't the girl I knew...this wasn't...

I had no time to think.

I closed my eyes and my swelling rage exploded out of me. When I opened them again, there were little shards of fire everywhere. I had become a warrior, too.

'I'm too strong for you,' she said, her eyes dancing with wild excitement.

I wanted to fight her, yes. I wanted to beat her to pulp, oh, yes I did, but right now, she wasn't my first priority.

I went around her and she turned, expecting me to lash out. Instead, I dove towards earth and she let out a roar. I could feel her following me, her fire darting towards my back, stinging my skin. But I wouldn't stop.

'Ardra!' she screamed through the rain. 'I have his stone. It doesn't matter anymore.'

I turned in mid-air. She stopped mid-flight too.

'They will take him, Ardra...' she panted. 'You can't stop them. He can't either, without this.' She opened her palm to reveal the Jwala, now burning golden with an angry, bristling energy. 'He will not have the time to channel it. Don't bother really.'

I turned away from her and descended towards earth as fast as I could. The sounds from down below came nearer, and I finally caught a glimpse of the ambush before the clouds obscured my sight once again. The beastly forms were crowding in on Dwai while he was putting up a fight.

Oh, Dwai! Please let me get to him on time…please.

My feet touched the ground just as the moon blinked and vanished completely from the sky. The temple grounds were empty. There were no scuffling Rakshasas there. And no Dwai.

He was gone.

I stood there as the rain fell all around me and I forgot for a few seconds that my best friend-turned-foe was hurtling towards earth to fight me. I forgot everything except that he was gone and it was my fault.

But the unholy warmth that hit the rain-soaked surface shook me out of my reverie. Vina was back, but her face didn't belong to anyone I knew. This was someone else. Someone who fed on greed and fear. Someone who had traded a friendship of 500 years for…what?

'What did she promise you?' I asked. My voice sounded strange and unhinged.

She laughed shortly. 'Hera is going to be Blood Queen. Do you even know what that means? A BLOOD QUEEN.'

'It means she will become more evil than is now,' I shouted. 'Vina, how could you?'

'We are Yakshis, Ardra. This feeling of betrayal that courses through you…it's unnatural. We are not supposed to feel things like that. The only things we like are seduction, secrets and power.'

'We don't have any power,' I said bitterly.

'Oh we do, we do… At least I will, as a reward for taking the Half-born to her. Once she becomes Blood Queen, she will allow me to start my journey to become one, too. Eventually.'

'Hera promised to make you a Blood Queen one day?'

'Yes, there can be more than one. We can rule over different things. You are so boring, Ardra. You never wanted anything other than to be a Yakshi. There are things in the world that can be yours. You just have to *want* them.'

'Not the way you do,' I retorted. 'And if you really think Hera is going to let you be – '

'Stop it!' she shouted over me. 'She will. She promised. And if you aren't stupid enough to get yourself killed, you will be around to witness it someday.'

'I wouldn't hold my breath for it,' I said before I threw a ball of fire towards her. Surprised, she screamed as the fire caught her unawares.

What came back towards me wasn't just fire. It had a face. It was a pyromonster.

'Wow!' I shouted as I ducked. 'Fancy, aren't we?' I continued to shoot fire balls at her. The pyromonster roared and crashed into one of the pillars, setting the whole floor on fire.

'Vina,' I said, constantly moving so she wouldn't get a steady aim. 'Vina, listen to me. She is never going to keep her promise. Don't...'

'Keep quiet, Ardra!' she screamed. 'God, how are you so weak? We were all created together. How on earth could you have become so annoying and...human?'

Another pyromonster sped towards me. I shot up in the air and it hit one of the broken towers of the temple.

'I don't want to fight you, Vina,' I yelled. 'I need to find Dwai. Don't...'

'That Half-born is gone, Ardra. You will never see him again,' she smirked.

My core erupted in flames. Rage burnt my insides and dried up the tears that were on the verge of spilling out. A spiralling flash shot out of me, a long red ribbon of fire. I took a few steps back in the air as it sped towards Vina. Her eyes opened wide in surprise as the ribbon caught her around the waist, twisting itself around her.

She shrieked in pain and convulsed. I saw her unfurl her palm, the Jwala falling to the ground. I dashed towards it but a cloud of fire hit me square in the chest.

Everything turned to black nothingness.

✦ **43** ✦

He woke up, harsh dots of light stinging his eyes. The room was dim and shadows played on the walls. He wondered if he was in the famous dungeons Vrkayu had mentioned. When his eyes adjusted to the dim light, he realized he was definitely not in a dungeon. This was an expansive chamber, decorated almost entirely in gold. And were those real rubies studded on the ceiling?

He was lying on a bed that was as big as his bathroom back home. Dwai sat up, puzzled. His mind was a jumble of images. He remembered Vina and Ardra rising in the air, and he recalled the Rakshasas. There had been four of them, accompanied by terrifying dogs with scales and fins – the mer dogs Ardra had mentioned. He had a vague memory of trying to fight them off with a stick. Then there was a burst of lightning, some fire in the air that burnt despite the storm, and after that…blackness.

And now he was in this room. He wasn't shackled or bound

but there was probably no need for it, he thought dryly. A couple of those drooling, panting Rakshasas were no doubt stationed outside. He got out of the bed and winced. His leg had been injured in the scuffle. The pain brought some more images to his mind – Ardra speeding towards him like a falling star. Bursts of red fire all around. He had heard Vina shout, 'I have his stone...it doesn't matter anymore...', her words somehow reaching him through the din of the storm.

He didn't have the stone! Vina had taken it. He was stuck here, in this ridiculously decadent room possibly in Atala, and all he could do now was wait for his death. He wouldn't go quietly, he told himself. He wouldn't. He owed Ardra that much.

'Ardra,' he whispered. Saying her name out loud brought an unimaginably painful pang to his heart. Beautiful, wild, hopeful Ardra. He wondered how she was taking the betrayal by her best friend. 'You didn't let me down, Ardra,' he said out loud. 'You were only trying to save us...'

Something moved in a corner. Something dark and shapeless. But when he turned to look, there was nothing there. *I'm going crazy already*, he thought, shaking his head.

There was a table by a huge window with rich velvet drapings. It was full of food.

'Fattening up the sacrificial lamb, are you?' he muttered. He walked to the window, stopping at the table for a few seconds to take an apple. When he bit into it, he almost convulsed with joy. It tasted like no apple he had ever consumed in his whole life. It tasted of magic, if that was possible – sweet and rich and sinful. He took another bite, letting the taste course through his tired body.

He could see a shiny deep purple sky outside, the kind an imaginative child might draw. And then he caught sight of the black sun, suspended in the purple sky, glum and charred.

After a while, he fell back on the bed. The shadows on the walls were ever moving and changing. He closed his eyes, trying to block them out. When he opened them a few minutes later, she was standing in front of him. Raven on her shoulder, snake in her hair, just as Ardra had described her. Just as he had dreamt. The woman from the aeroplane. Cold, terrifyingly beautiful…and unquestionably evil. In fact, if evil had a face this would be it – magnetic, yet repelling, rippling with all the ungodly forces in the universe.

'We meet again,' she said in a low, cold voice. The golden snake hissed, its emerald eyes narrowing. He couldn't take his eyes off it. The raven flew off her shoulder and on to his bedstead, watching him with its glassy, ancient eye. He got up from the bed warily.

'She won't hurt you,' Hera said. 'She just likes intimidating people, don't you, Gaggii?'

The bird cawed in response. Hera laughed, the doting, indulgent laughter one reserves for a pet.

Her robes seemed to be made of something he had never seen before – the fabric flowed like dark water as she walked towards him. It seemed to be a part of her diamond-hued skin which, on close quarters, looked glassy and brittle.

'I believe your mother and I knew each other,' Hera said, her eyes boring into him, studying him keenly.

'You knew my mother?' he blurted out. 'How…?'

'I wonder which one of them it was,' she said, ignoring him. 'I wonder which one of those cold bitches actually found it in them to love a human. To make you…to protect you. Your father must have been very special.'

'How do you know my mother?' he asked again.

'I knew every one of those dancing girls,' she said, her voice hard as diamonds. 'All of them fickle-minded and useless for anything but having a good time.'

'What *are* you?' he asked.

'What are you?' she repeated. 'What am I, indeed. If I knew the answer to that...if only.'

She sighed.

'I am so many things in so many different stories. Different tribes know me as different things, myriad cultures fear me, some love me. I have been bird, goddess, spirit, angel... No story, no myth has ever bound me to any limitation. I always escaped my own myths, transcended my destinies. I have shed so many forms, so many roles, and here I am today, in my own custom-made hell. I rule here, I lord over desire, I own the power of secrets. I do not breathe, I do not sleep, I do not dream. What am I? I was something once, trapped in a myth for a long time, caught in a story that began to bore me. And I wanted more. I will always want more...'

Dwai flinched.

'Every timespan in the universe has its own mundane limitations. I could have been so much more if I was in some era of the past or the future. But I am here now, and this time will go on for a while. And here, in this space, I want to be a Blood Queen.

'And for that,' she cupped his face, 'I need you.' She pushed him back and he fell to the floor.

'What will I do to you? They call it the Unspeakable, because they are soft-hearted, they who made these useless rules. What they forget, what they refuse to understand, is that anyone thirsting for power will always be ready to commit the Unspeakable. I made a mistake the last time. And I have been trying ever since. All these years, I've experimented with all kinds of hybrids, but nothing's worked. So you see, I can't make a mistake this time. Keep yourself healthy, Half-born. Eat more than just apples, sleep well, for I need you to have all your strength on the night of the blood moon.'

'Night of the blood moon,' said Dwai. 'That's the night...'

'Your pretty little girlfriend loved her little conspiracies. The night of the blood moon has nothing to do with her, that inconsequential succubus. But it matters not. She is dead now. Vina saw to that.'

'NO!'

His shout sent Gaggii flapping around the room.

'Oh yes, she is. And she was so irrelevant to me, ultimately. But *you*, you are important. The powers you will give me on that night, as Lord Mara blesses me, ah...'

She shivered with delight. Gaggii cawed and flew to her shoulder. The snake writhed in her hair.

Dwai got up, his face brimming with loathing. 'Do what you think you can. Try. You want to be the most powerful thing on earth but your plan depends on the life of a powerless innocent? The irony is palpable, don't you think? That your power needs the weakness of others?'

'Hmm...' she said, stroking Gaggii, her eyes alight. 'Such wise words from a Half-born who will bleed to death for me in two days. Irony, indeed.'

And she struck him across the face. A long golden gash appeared where she had hit him. There was no blood, just a wound that stung with her magic. She looked at him intently for a few seconds, maybe searching for a reaction. But Dwai stood unblinking, defiant. If she was looking to discover fear in his eyes, she found none.

'Sky blood!' she said gleefully. 'Your wound is golden. Enjoy your time in Atala, Half-born. And don't try to escape. There are things here that will rip you to pieces in seconds and I couldn't stop them.'

She turned on her heel and strode out of the room, leaving behind a cold draught.

He sat on the edge of the bed and stared out of the window. There was not much else he could do except think of a girl with storm-coloured hair and brown eyes who was now perhaps dead.

☘ 44 ☘

238

'Asmaan se utri pari ho tum...
Kaun hoon main kaun hoon main kaun hoon main?
Apsara ho tum mere sapno kiiiii...'

My eyeballs felt like lead. My head was sore, blank and carved out. It was filled with the sort of emptiness that could drive a person crazy.

'Ooh, she's opening her eyes,' said a husky voice in an odd accent. 'Ila, look...'

Through the slits of my eyes, I saw two blurry heads leaning over me. As my vision cleared, I could see two sets of eyes, one light green, wide open in obvious curiosity, and the other a deep blue, cold and uninterested. Both reminded me of something – of somebody – but my brain was too tired to process the thought.

I could hear them talk in hushed tones to each other.

I strained my tired ears, hoping to hear snatches of their conversation. And as I did, I realized this was an entirely different tongue, not human, nor any kind of supernatural language I was used to. But somehow I could understand it.

'Her kind…'

'What if the humans had seen any of it?'

'No no, I don't think she's dangerous…it's okay. Shush, she seems to be waking up. Be a darling and get me a Starbucks. The set coffee is worse than drain water.'

I sat up. I was in what seemed like a tiny room, the highlight of which seemed to be an enormous mirror lined with lightbulbs next to which sat a stout little table. A television hung on the wall and it was there that the song had been playing.

The woman who was hovering over me a few seconds ago was on screen, twirling about in a bright pink Amrapali costume, while a guy dressed like a pirate was throwing flower petals at her. She watched the screen with me, almost as fascinated as I was. I took in her jewel-hued skin, her marble-like wide eyes and full lips. Her hair cascaded down her shoulders like a river in the monsoon. This woman was beautiful. Beautiful in a way that seemed almost unreal.

'You are Menaka, the movie star.'

'Among other things, yes.' She hadn't taken her eyes off the television.

'Thank you for…bringing me here,' I said awkwardly. I didn't know what else to say. I was in a ridiculous costume with clearly supernatural wounds and yet Menaka seemed nonplussed. Then I remembered.

Dwai. Oh my God, Dwai.

'Ineedtogo,' I said, the words tumbling out my mouth in a frenzy. I stood up and my legs turned to water. I sat down again. There was a pause while she smiled benevolently at me, like I was a puppy she had picked up from the roadside and decided to keep as a pet.

'Nice costume,' she said, showing off a set of impossibly white, pearly teeth.

'Yeah, it's, er…'

'It's a warrior costume, babe, I get it,' she said, still smiling brightly.

'Umm, yes,' I mumbled. 'I should go. Thank you for taking care of me.'

'Where would you go, babe, come on,' she said, looking at me through her mirror as she deftly applied mascara. She had finally wrenched herself away from the television which was now playing another song, also featuring her.

'Back home, I guess,' I muttered unconvincingly. She smirked at me in the mirror and I looked away.

'Sweetie, you can't go home. She'll kill you, no?'

'What?' I gasped. 'What did you just say?'

'That horrible bitch, ya. Hera. She won't stop until you're dead. You can't leave this van.'

The dull spots of light had returned, now dancing in front of my eyes.

'Right…and how do you know about Hera?'

'Everyone knows about Hera, darling,' said Menaka shrugging, waving a beautifully manicured hand at me.

'Erm, not on Prithvi they don't.'

She smiled again, sweet, benevolent, patting her hair as she did. 'Not on Prithvi, no, but her tales are the stuff of legends in Aakasha.'

'Who are you?' I asked slowly.

'Me? I am Menaka, chief of the Apsaras.'

She seemed to delight in what could only be an expression of jaw-dropping surprise on my face.

'Aakasha is boring, you know. At least, it got damn dull in the last few centuries, what with the Gods leaving and the demigods wandering off to other dimensions and leaving me in charge. Me. You know I do love a lot of things, but herding a bunch of self-involved cloud-brained Apsaras and Gandharvas is not one of them.'

'Right, so?'

'Yeah, so then some stuff happened that is a really long story, but after that, I decided to head to Prithvi. There was a restriction that was imposed on travelling between Aakasha and Prithvi but, come on, who takes notice of such things? Besides, I was in charge of Aakasha and people in charge normally do as they please, don't they? Anyway, I like it here. People have fun here. Amazing fun. And then the movies started in the 1900s. They needed pretty-looking girls to sing, dance, laugh and cry, and I thought to myself, "Hey, I can do that!" So here I am. I have been a movie star in both Hollywood and Bollywood for the last century.'

241

'But didn't the humans catch on?'

'Catch on to what? That I've been the same person all these years? Humans are blind. They want to just block out anything that makes them uncomfortable. In any case, after the talkies started, I moved to Bollywood. Because, you know, they continued to sing and dance here. Of course, I had different names in different eras. Let's see…in the 50s, I was Rupa Devi, and they loved me. Then I gave the 60s a miss – I couldn't stand most of those leading men – and returned in the 70s. I stayed for a bit, did some vamp roles. I went by the name Ruby. And then I skipped the 80s again – what a horrendous time. I ruled the 90s and the 2000s. Of course, they didn't know I was the same person. They thought I just looked like Natasha Kapoor, who has now married and retired to a life of reclusive domestic bliss in the UK. And now here I am – with different eyes and a cuter nose – as Menaka. I tricked a director into naming me that. He, of course, never caught on. Gives himself credit. Isn't that funny? Well, they loooove me.'

'Why do you have that accent?'

'Oh, these idiots. They love a girl with exotic looks and an accent they can't place.' She shrugged and laughed. 'It's fun, trust me. When you are young forever, life gets boring. And you have to constantly keep finding new stories to live in. But enough about me. What happened to you? We – Ila and I – found you on top of that abandoned temple. Clearly you got into some kind of catfight.'

I got up. 'Yes...er...catfight. I have to go.'

'You keep saying that. It's a stupid thing to do.'

'No, it isn't,' I clenched my teeth. 'Dwai...he...I have to go save someone.'

'All the portals to Atala are closed, my child,' she said. I swung around to look at her. She suddenly looked different, serious. 'You can't get in. And if I were you, I wouldn't try. I would try and make a new life for myself here, on Prithvi. It's a safer place than you think.'

'Really?' I said. 'It's a safer place? Is that because it has the likes of me running around seducing people, taking their secrets, killing them...'

'Tut, tut. There is the supernatural shit of your sort, and then there is evil of another kind. The kind that rips apart the fabric of the universe.'

'The Balance Keeper said exactly that,' I said.

'Oh, that old coot is still around? Haven't bumped into her in hundreds of years. Does she still have that funky rainbow hair? Maybe I should do that for a song or something...my fans will go crazy.'

I stared at her. She seemed crazy to me, unhinged from reality. If she was the person in charge of Aakasha, I really wondered about the state of things there. She seemed utterly disinterested in what was happening around her, unless, of course, it concerned her.

'How did you find me? And how did you know I wasn't human?' I asked.

'In that costume? In that place? It reeked of a supernatural tussle, my girl. *Reeked* of it. The air was full of your magic. And how did I find you? Well, these idiots took a lot of time setting up the props for a scene and I got bored. So Ila and I stole away. We were located just below the hill so we flew to its top and, lo and behold! Like a scene out of one of those apocalyptic movies – which I keep refusing, by the way – there you were, unconscious and wounded. So we smuggled you in here. I told the production team that you were a struggling actress who had fainted after a tedious audition. I hope you don't mind.'

'I have to go,' I said, for the millionth time.

Before she could respond, the door opened from outside. 'Aah, that must be Ila with my hazelnut cappuccino. How long does it take to fly from Starbucks to here really?' she whispered to me.

Ila wafted in pokerfaced and set the coffee down on the table.

'Thank you, Ila, my darling. What would I do without you?'

Ila sat down and started flipping through a magazine without responding.

'Babe, I am so lucky to have a friend *and* an Apsara for a manager. The humans I first hired were so slow that I wanted to stab myself in the eye. I brought Ila in, and wham! Life is so much easier. I couldn't do without her, really. I've thanked

243

her for every award I've won, haven't I, Ila?

The blue-eyed Apsara gave a slight nod.

'So you guys have been walking around Prithvi all these years?'

'Oh yes! Well, not all of us. Just some who tend to get bored and restless. The boys have to disguise themselves though, you know, to hide their markings. Some of them get really careless but...'

'So, er...if you are Apsaras then...then you must know Dara right?'

Ila looked up. The magazine fell from her hands. Menaka continued to preen in front of her mirror as she said, 'Daraaa... hmm... God, there were so many of them, babe. Which one was Dara again, Ila?'

She was clearly play-acting.

'Dara, Menaka, Dara,' Ila said with emphasis. 'He is sort of hard to forget.'

'Oh, Daraa! That whole horrid scandal that started everything...how could I forget? I must be getting old. And Ila here had a thing for Dara,' she chuckled.

Ila's mouth was set in a hard, straight line. Her eyes flickered towards me and then went back to the magazine, rather pointedly.

'What scandal?' I asked. 'Did that have something to do with his Banishing?'

'You know about that, babe?' Menaka turned around. 'So impressed. Most people don't mention it.'

'What happened?' I asked, pushing my luck.

'We are forbidden to talk about it,' snapped Ila.

'Well, I'm not forbidden to do anything, darling. But I consider it one of my personal failures,' said Menaka, pursing her lips prettily.

She rose from her chair. Her mood seemed to have shifted now, becoming more sombre as she absently played with the tassels on her costume.

'I should have been more aware of what was going on. It was my fault. Whether I liked my job or not, I should have kept a watch on all of them, especially her.'

'Her?' I asked.

'Hera, babe, Hera,' she said a little impatiently.

'Hera? But...I don't understand. How could you keep an eye on Hera when she was in Atala?'

Menaka turned to face me. Her eyes were gleaming strangely. 'Oh my God,' she said softly. 'You have no idea, do you?'

'No idea of what?'

Speaking as though she was delivering a key dialogue at the climax of a film, Menaka said, 'That bloodsucking, conniving, evil bitch was once an Apsara.' She snorted in disgust. 'Before she got kicked out on her perfect lil' ass, that is.'

For the second time that day, my jaw dropped, to her great delight.

⚡ 45 ⚡

'She was never really one of us to begin with,' Menaka continued. 'She was different. Possibly someone from another dimension who just managed to find a place in our throng. A darkling, always running off on forbidden adventures, cahooting with crones known to do the darkest, most unimaginable sorcery.

No one could control her. Not even that brooding boyfriend of hers.'

'Hera had a *boyfriend*?' I cut in, still trying to process all that I was hearing.

'She did. They belonged to each other, in a way. He was melancholic, dark, restless.'

'You shouldn't be telling her all this,' interrupted Ila.

'You and Dara should get together and form a "Let's not tell anyone anything" club,' I retorted, my tone belligerent.

We glared at each other.

'Tut tut, Ila, I'm not giving away anything I shouldn't be,' purred Menaka comfortingly. 'So, anyway, where was I, babe? Oh, yeah, Hera, the darkling Apsara. I should have guessed she was up to something. She…well, she wanted to be…'

'Ahem,' interjected Ila again.

'She wanted to be a Blood Queen.'

'She still wants to be a Blood Queen!' I almost yelled. 'So she didn't succeed then?'

'No. As far as I know, she and that crone bungled up the sorcery badly. She broke too many laws of the universe… someone died,' she paused for effect.

'A girl…' I said slowly. 'A girl died.'

'Yes, and it resulted in multiple banishments.'

'Why was Dara banished?' I asked. 'Why…I mean, this girl…' I couldn't finish the sentence. I could barely comprehend what all this meant. The stringing together of it was painful. For some reason, I could hardly breathe.

'Dara? Oh, he should have stopped it. He could have. He had a strong inkling she was up to something. You see, the Unspeakable had been committed. I should have stopped it too. She wanted to rule Aakasha, overthrow me. She wanted too many things…and what happened was – '

'Menaka!' Ila was on her feet now.

'She fell from grace. And, somehow, the next thing I know, she had created her own realm. And her powers grew stronger, if anything. And she created you lot. Though even that is shrouded in some sort of suspense because...'

'MENAKA, PLEASE! We are not allowed to talk about any of this!'

She sounded exactly like Dara, fearful of the story, petrified of the past. Menaka stood up, too. She was taller than even Hera.

'I know how it works, Ila. Some of these stories are secrets. And secrets are meant to be kept, not spilt carelessly.' She turned to me. 'You, of course, are a Yakshi. Who would know more about secrets than you?'

I didn't say anything.

'In a way,' she continued, throwing her hair back in a dramatic sweep, 'aren't we all secrets? Someone's own personal, living, breathing bit of hell or heaven as we see it? Aren't we both the sleep and sleeplessness, the dream and the nightmare, the memory and the forgetting?' Throwing a look towards Ila, who was trembling with trepidation, she said, 'Fear not, Ila, I'm not as crazy as you think I am. I know when to stop talking. As for you...'

'I need to get into Atala,' I cut in. 'Please help me.'

Menaka shook her head. She seemed sad. 'There is no portal open to Atala anymore, babe. It's futile to even try. And even if you do get there, it's stupid to think you can stop her. Don't get me wrong, if she succeeds I have more to lose than anyone. She will try and conquer Aakasha, I know it. Then I will have to stop her.'

'Why don't you stop her now?' I shouted. 'Why must you wait till she is invincible, more powerful than you, than everyone?'

'Because Atala is impenetrable. And because honestly...' she trailed quietly.

I understood. She didn't think she really had a chance against Hera. And she didn't want to get her hands dirty trying.

'If anyone can stop her, it's Dara. God knows he has been trying for ages. All he needed was passage to Atala and no supernatural creature was willing to risk their life by helping him. And you Yakshis had a way of exploding around him, didn't you? If someone could find him now, then maybe there could be a way out. But Dara knows very well how to hide. Even from himself.'

She threw a meaningful glance towards Ila. 'Someone must tell him I've lifted his Banishment. He's free to return to Aakasha now, and under these circumstances, I could certainly use him there, now that Hera is truly going batshit.'

I stood up.

'Right, I'm sure Dara will be happy to hear that, whenever he does,' I said. 'I'll be going then. I have to find a way into Atala to stop her. And save Dwai.'

Menaka sighed. 'Good luck, my girl. And do let me know if you succeed. If SHE does, I will know. It will just mean cancelling a whole shoot in Venice and heading to war. The horror...'

Ila and I exchanged glances.

'Wait a minute, how did you know Hera was after me? Who told you? When you found me, you didn't even know who I was. Or did you?'

Menaka regarded me with what seemed like kindness. 'Go back to the human's home and things will become a lot clearer. I would love to spend more time with you but you are in a tearing hurry...and rightly so.'

'Back to Dwai's house?' I asked, wondering if this was a trap of some kind.

'Yes, I assure you it's a safe place. Go. It will give you the time to think and plan.'

I murmured my thanks and headed for the door.

'Ardra...'

I turned back. I didn't ask how she knew my name. I hadn't told her what it was, and she hadn't asked me either.

'I wish I had met you before. So much could have been saved. You are a brave girl,' she said.

'I have no other choice,' I replied and exited the van.

❖ 46 ❖

The light of the moon seemed to taunt me as I walked away from Menaka's movie set. The crescent was giving way to what would soon be a full moon. A full blood moon. I didn't have much time. And I didn't know what to do.

As I stepped out of the brightly lit set swarming with people, most of whom didn't seem to find my appearance strange, I realized that the hill and the abandoned temple was situated right above us, up the steep craggy hill. I took to flight in the darkness. Before I did anything else, I wanted to find Dwai's stone. If Vina had indeed taken it, then things were worse than I imagined. Hera would destroy the stone and Dwai would never have a chance to fight or protect himself.

The moment I reached the top of the hill, I knew what Menaka had meant by the place reeking of magic. There was an unmistakable odour about it, like the smokiness of fireworks, except stronger, headier. I doubt humans could actually smell it but I was sure they could feel it. It would definitely contribute to the building's 'haunted' reputation. Our weapons had singed the grass, laid them black and charred, and some of the taller, drier grass was still smoking.

If I had a heart, it would have broken at the sight. This was where I hoped I would find answers. Find a way to protect Dwai, to unravel my own mystery. This was where Dwai had looked into my eyes and assured me that I wouldn't let him down. But I had. And now he was gone. I sank down on the grass and wept. The last time, I swore to myself. This was the last time I would pretend to be human and weep. Because

tears got you nowhere.

A little later, I wiped my tears and attempted to look for the stone. My vision was sharpest at night. 'Show yourself,' I repeated fervently. 'I am not an enemy. Show yourself, please.' Nothing glowed in the dark; nothing directed its strange rippling energy at me through the charred vegetation. The stone wasn't there. If that was the case, no one but Dwai could draw the Jwala to him from wherever it was hidden. It wouldn't respond to anyone else.

But what if Vina had managed to find it and take it with her back to Atala?

Worry coiled itself like a clammy snake around my core. If Hera had it, then all was over. I rose into the sky again, flying right past the moon and into the city.

I was about to find out if I could trust Menaka and that dour companion of hers. I was going to Dwai's house. The place where it all started.

There were traces of magic even on the staircase. I had landed directly outside his door but I could sense the magic in the air all the way down the crumbling stairway.

I wondered if I should break the door down and surprise whoever it was at the other end in case they had been sent by Hera, or whether I should enter quietly, using a spell to open the door. I decided on the second option. I didn't want to wake up any human neighbours. It was almost midnight.

The door clicked open gently and my senses bristled with the magic in the house – warring spells, duelling spells, killing curses.

Someone had died in here. I stepped in, wondering if I had walked into a trap of some kind.

I stepped on something glutinous and immediately recoiled. Rakshasa blood.

I cautiously lifted my feet into the air again, deciding that aerial was the way to go right now. As I did, I noticed a severed limb the size of a small tree trunk on the ground. It took up almost the entire room. And then I spotted a leg near the balcony. Ugh! This had been a bloodbath.

But who...

I got my answer about three seconds later. Someone emerged out of Dwai's bedroom. Someone who looked like...me.

'Morana! What the...'

'Come on, admit it. I do a better you than you. I give it... what's that human thing? Attitude.' She made no move to

251

transform into herself. Instead, she stood there smirking. She actually seemed a little pleased to see me.

'Right. Why are you wandering around pretending to be me?'

'It's fun. Plus I knew *this* snot-brained thing was skulking around. And he was looking for you.'

She gestured flamboyantly at the messy pieces of the Rakshasa strewn all over the room.

'Umm...thank you?' I murmured doubtfully.

She smirked in response.

'Okay, before we continue, could you please...' I gestured towards her.

She sighed and changed back to her original form, rippling as she did.

'You are the most humourless monster I have ever encountered,' she said. I could see her tail swishing behind her.

She looked as weirdly compelling as ever but tonight her aura was forceful. There were still traces of the strong magic she had used on her persona. Her eyes looked cold, determined; the pussycat smugness was missing from her demeanour.

'What happened here?' I asked, ignoring her comment.

'Well, this handsome troll was stationed here, clearly on the lookout for you. I spotted him and turned myself into you and he came right at me. The rest is...' she swung her eyes around the room.

I was impressed. She had vanquished a Rakshasa without a scratch on her. But I wasn't going to show it.

'Hmm...but what were you doing here in the first place?'

She surveyed me closely. Then she said, 'I was asked to come here. By Menaka,' she said, her eyes twinkling with amusement. 'I can see that your life has been changed forever from having been touched by her dazzling grace.'

I couldn't help myself and laughed out loud. 'Well, she was helpful, at least, I'll give her that.'

'Yes, she asked you to come here.'

'Please explain the connection between you two. Everything is so confusing right now.'

'Right after Hera sent me to capture Dwai, I knew he wasn't a normal human. I suspected he was a Half-born, just as she did. The minute you showed me the Jwala, I was sure. It belonged to an Apsara I knew long ago who had been banished for falling in love with a human. No one knew she had had a child with him. I couldn't tell you any of this without having my head blasted off my neck. But I did sound off Menaka. We have been in touch all this time, despite almost everything changing in the realms. She sent me back here to warn you guys, and perhaps to offer you protection, but by the time I got here you had disappeared. I heard rumours that Dara had joined you and Dwai. Then the next thing I hear is Vrkayu and his entire pack had been decimated. It wasn't hard to piece everything together, Ardra. I knew Hera was getting more and more hysterical with every passing day. She wanted him. And she wanted you and Dara imprisoned, too, but that was only second on her list of priorities. But, let me tell you this: your friend Vina could have taken you back to Atala. Instead, she left you behind. She may have done what she did, but I doubt she stopped caring about you entirely.'

'It's okay,' I managed to say. I wasn't ready to discuss Vina's betrayal yet.

'I'm sorry about Dwai,' she added softly. 'I know you really tried to fight her off. I'm sure he put up a good fight, too. Also, here...' she opened her fist to reveal the Jwala. 'I managed to retrieve it from the hill where we found you.'

I took it and slipped it into my pocket. The stone trembled with unstable energy. Dwai wasn't okay. I knew this in my core.

'So then, the three of you smelled the magic on top of the hill and found me there?'

'Yes. I must say I was surprised you even came back, though. I thought it would be easier to run. But now I know that's not what you would do. You seem to be a fighter.'

I floated over the Rakshasa's decimated body and into the balcony, which was still relatively clean. So much had changed since the last time I was here.

'What do I do?' I asked, not bothering to hide the desperation in my voice. 'It's the full moon in a few days. The blood moon, actually, and I know she's planning something horrible.'

'She is,' said Morana. 'If I were you, I would find Dara.'

'HOW? He and I…we…' I couldn't continue.

'I knew that would happen. Because he couldn't possibly have let a Half-born run around for Hera to capture and use for her own sorcery. I don't blame him, Ardra,' she said. 'In fact, I thought he would succeed. I liked Dwai, but a part of me wanted this madness to end. And if he didn't exist anymore, then Hera would likely give up.'

I didn't bother to correct her, to tell her that murdering Dwai would hardly stop Hera. I had known her for 500 years. She would simply plod on and look high and low in all the realms for another Half-born. She was unstoppable.

'What will happen if she succeeds?'

'The realms will go to ruin,' said Morana, matter-of-factly. 'There have been only two Blood Queens in the history of the universe before her, and more can come into existence while the old ones continue to dominate. The chain grows stronger depending on the power of each Blood Queen. And Hera…

her dark magic is already too powerful. It runs in her veins. She has consumed too much of it. She will be a Blood Queen like no other. She wants to rule Aakasha. It's her private vendetta. You know all about that now, I suppose. And however badly-run the place is, most of the rules of the universe still originate from there. Think of the chaos…think of what will happen once Hera starts to make the rules.'

'I also heard her talk about reversing the effects of a spell…'

'She seems sure she can kill two birds with one stone. In any case, it was the Blood Queen spell that went wrong. It not only resulted in her Banishment but she also seems to be withering away. Using Dwai will erase its negative effects and give her the power she needs.'

'I know she has tried the sacrifice before.' I told Morana about the mermaid I had seen long ago. She sighed.

'Whatever went wrong before involved a hybrid. She made a mistake. From what Menaka told me centuries ago, she accidentally created one.'

'She created a hybrid?' I asked, astounded. 'What kind of a hybrid?'

There was a pause before Morana responded. 'The kind that went against one of the most important laws of the universe. The crone deduced the damage could be undone if they could successfully use another hybrid in the Blood Queen spell. For the last 500 years, she has been trying to reverse the effects by murdering other hybrids, but it hasn't worked. The crone is convinced that a Half-born – who is a superior sort of a hybrid – will do the trick. And Dwai, unfortunately, is one.'

'She is *evil*,' I said unneccessarily, gritting my teeth in anger.

'I think I've said more than I should,' said Morana, looking uncomfortable for the first time.

'So has the head exploding curse been lifted?'

The Huldra grinned. 'Yes, by Menaka. The time has come to stop Hera.'

'You've known her and Atala for so long. I'm sure you know how to get there. Please, Morana.'

'I'm sorry,' she shook her head. 'I don't know of any hidden portals to Atala. If anyone does, it's Dara.'

'Dara doesn't! If he did, wouldn't he have got into Atala long ago?'

'Even if he knows of a hidden portal, he would still need someone who inhabits Atala to take him down there.'

'I don't know how to look for him,' I said, frowning.

'She won't stop until she has become Blood Queen,' Morana went on. 'Then she will come after you and Dara. You don't have much time, Ardra. Unless you fancy spending the rest of your life in one of Atala's dungeons.'

'I thought, perhaps, you would still be on Hera's side.'

Morana threw me a withering glance. 'Dear girl, haven't you understood by now the difference between being born a dark thing and allowing actual evil to fester and grow within you? I, for one, would have never come after Dwai had I known what her plans for him were. I am a nomadic mercenary, but there are some things I won't do. Everyone has a choice.'

'Dara does, too,' I said. 'And if everything I have come to know about him is true, even a little bit, he will not sit still while this happens. I'm going to go and wait by the Yakshi portal in the old house. He frequented that one the most. It's my only hope – that he will find me there. He can't have left Prithvi, can he? Menaka said he isn't Banished anymore.'

'Yes. Now that war is imminent, she needs him. Everyone is either on Hera's side or against her.'

'I told him never to come in front of me again.' I almost choked on my words.

'It must have hurt him, yes,' she said. 'But I think even he will know you didn't mean it, deep down.'

I made up my mind in that instant. 'Thank you for finding and keeping the Jwala safe for me. If I can get to Atala and somehow pass it on to Dwai, I know he has a chance of surviving. I must go and wait by the portal now.'

'And I have a hunch. I shall go act on it,' said Morana.

'What hunch?' I asked.

'Don't want to get your hopes up, girl,' she said. 'But I will try my best. You go ahead to the portal. I will join you eventually.'

I lifted my feet off the floor.

'Ardra…' I turned. 'There is so much that must seem so strange still. Even about yourself. I don't know if the time has come, but when it does, you will know the truth. Trust your instincts and your core. Sometimes the answers lie right where we've forgotten to look.'

With that, she shimmered and vanished. And as she did, the room cleared of the dismembered Rakshasa. I took to flight, but not without casting one backward glance towards the moon. She was almost full, with a womb brimming with blood and dark sorcery.

✢ 48 ✣

The raven watched over him day and night, but it wasn't really necessary. He wasn't going to try and escape – it was impossible to even try. Moreover, his own life was the last thing on his mind.

He couldn't believe Ardra was gone. He wouldn't. It wasn't possible. That was not how a story ended. The hero of the story didn't just die, murdered by a minor character. Ardra had pointed out to him that she was the monster in the story, not the maiden. 'Monsters don't usually triumph in fairytales,' she had said. 'Dragons don't walk away into the sunset having won the love of their lives.' But his heart didn't believe that.

'No,' he said out loud to Gaggii. 'It isn't true. She is alive, isn't she?' The bird merely blinked and continued to watch him, beady-eyed.

Vina had visited him once. She looked twitchy and gaunt, as if she hadn't been sleeping. She had silently walked in and, despite his resistance, tied a tiny string to his arm with a little bundle attached to it. He hadn't asked what it was, assuming it was part of the great ritual that was to take place in a couple of days when he would be sacrificed.

'How's your conscience doing?' he had asked her lightly, hate coating his words.

She hadn't replied. Instead, averting her gaze, she had quickly shuffled away.

He had tried to untie the little amulet but it wouldn't budge. Eventually he had fallen into uneasy sleep, Gaggi watching over him.

The next day (or was it night? He wasn't sure. In Atala, time was relative) he was moved from the gold room into a larger room with diamond encrusted floors and jewelled thrones. There was no bed.

'It's because I don't sleep,' said Hera as she strode in, her aura emanating fire. 'You shall stay in my chambers now, under my watch, until it is time. It won't be long now, my dear Half-born. The wait is almost over.'

The crone cackled in glee and stirred something in a cauldron in a corner of the room. She watched him with her one eye and muttered to herself.

'Rest, Half-born, for soon you will be eternally alive in my bones,' said Hera, the excitement in her voice almost vulgar.

After that, sleep evaded him. He was living in a nightmare now, as time danced on gleefully, reminding him he had only a few hours to live.

He tried to rest on the ruby and emerald studded thrones, but they made him uncomfortable. They prickled with a strange energy. The room itself, vast and unreal as it was, was too bright with artificial light, too brittle for his eyes. *Maybe this is what hell really looks like,* he thought.

Shadows danced on the walls, but one seemed different from the others. It sort of scampered from one corner to another like a little mouse, and he watched it hide and pounce on itself, playing a lonely little game to amuse itself. Finally, it came out of its hiding place, a squishy dark shape that had mournful saucer-shaped eyes.

'You are Ardra's shadow creature,' Dwai said softly. 'You've been shadowing me since I arrived here, haven't you?'

The creature mewed in response. It scurried away into the darkness of the thick velvet drapes and reappeared at the other end of the room. He got up and followed it.

In the corner of the room, he noticed an unlikely cage of thorns. Diamonds circled its insides as if providing an extra layer of protection for what it was guarding. At its centre rested what looked like a large, oddly-shaped red jewel, emanating sorcery.

He inched closer to the cage, not daring to breathe. The air seemed thick with suspense.

He set his eyes on the strange inhabitant of the cage and let out a low gasp. He took a few steps back, horror and fascination melding into a strange wild rhythm in his heart.

And, suddenly, he knew. He knew the story that was now forbidden. It made him so sad that he thought his heart would break from the burden of it.

He sank to his knees by the cage wishing this was a dream, even if it was a horrible one with no end in sight.

❧ 49 ❧

Waiting is a storm that sometimes doesn't pass. Time becomes a haunting that racks your spirit with each passing second. It had been a little over a day since I had taken up post by the old house. I hoped Dara would come, even though I knew I had driven him away with my words. Words could be weapons, causing wounds that seldom healed. You could fill them with stardust and seal them, but they would still glow as reminders under your skin. I wondered how Dara had dealt with the wounds I had inflicted upon him. I myself had attempted to understand his actions, to some success.

The dilapidated house that had served as a portal for Yakshis for the last 100 years wasn't exactly a pleasant spot. The air inside was thick with malevolent energies. My uneasiness was made worse by the constant jabs I felt from the Jwala in my pocket. Perhaps Dwai was trying to send me a message. Or the stone was simply so agitated and tortured that it couldn't stay still.

I wandered around the compound, trying not to pay heed to the bustle of energies around me. I even considered asking the rats if they knew anything about another portal but they seemed to have disappeared, too. It was distinctly weird that everything connected to Atala had vanished from Prithvi. Only earthbound ghosts and spirits seemed to be afoot but they were of no consequence to my world.

A familiar fragrance led me to a corner of the garden, where pushing its way through an old crumbling brick wall was a frangipani tree in full bloom. I loved this flower. If I had a soul, I reckon it might have been shaped like a frangipani. I always stopped to look at them on my short sojourns to Prithvi. The carnivorous ones in Atala made me uncomfortable. Now, I plucked one off its thick branch and tucked it behind my ear. The fragrance of the sun-drenched bloom filled my senses.

When I turned, someone was standing there. Someone who had the strangest look on his face as his eyes travelled to the flower tucked behind my ear. He took in a deep, sharp breath.

'Dara...' I whispered, scarcely able to believe my eyes.

Neither of us moved.

The thing about distance between two people is that it devours silence with beastly ferocity. The more it consumes, the wider the chasm between them gets. Dara and I were separated by distance and silence, and soon one was indistinguishable from the other. It didn't matter that he was standing right in front me, beautiful and ravaged by his mysterious grief. Silence still stretched out its hands, keeping us at bay from each other.

Until I broke into a run and rushed towards him. I would

have dived straight into his arms, except I remembered just in time that he didn't really like to touch me. I stopped myself just an inch away from him, looking up at his beautifully sculpted face. I had never seen his eyes so up close before. They were jewel-blue and flecked with silver – unreal, unearthly, with a fragility about them. Unbearable heartbreak seemed to have made its home in his eyes. A familiar wave of grief washed over me, and something inside me shattered.

A tear rolled off my cheek and he caught it on his fingertip. My breath caught in my throat at the intimacy of the gesture. The teardrop stayed on his fingertip, a glistening orb of my vulnerability, and I took a step back, not daring to be so close to him.

'I'm sorry,' he said simply.

'You shouldn't have left. You shouldn't have. No matter what I said…'

'You asked me to go away,' he said, his voice so quiet that I scarcely heard him. 'And you were right. I did do something unforgivable.'

'She took him.' I broke into uncontrollable sobs. 'She took him. And I've been all alone.'

'I'm sorry,' he repeated. 'I truly am.'

'I've been waiting here for two days, hoping against hope that you would come. And that we could save Dwai. Even though I know you want him dead. Maybe he is already…'

'He's alive,' Dara said, his voice grim. 'She won't do anything until the moon is full.'

'It *is* full,' I replied, agitated. 'And red. I am now ready to keep my end of the promise. I'll take you to Atala. But you have to help me get Dwai out of there.'

He watched me for a few seconds and then nodded slowly.

'Why *are* you here?' I asked.

'Same reason as you,' he said, and then hesitated. 'I thought I might find you here.'

'Why?'

'I wanted to explain...'

'Why didn't you tell me Hera was an Apsara?' I interrupted, folding my arms. 'Oh, wait, you don't tell me anything. I forgot. My mistake.'

'I would have told you,' he replied, not meeting my eyes. 'Eventually...'

'I also know she is one of the Banished,' I said. 'I know she committed the Unspeakable, creating some kind of hybrid. And a girl died...but there is still so much I don't understand.'

Silence fell like a thick curtain between us. He knew what I wanted to ask next. And I wanted to, except...

'Dara, I'm afraid we're running out of time. Do you know how we could get to Atala?'

'It wouldn't be of any use if I asked you to return to Prithvi immediately after we get there so that I could go and bring Dwai back, would it?'

'No.'

'Not even if I said I want to face Hera alone? It is what I've waited for, for centuries.'

'I would still come with you...'

He sighed. 'She is even more bloodthirsty than usual, Ardra. If she succeeds...'

'I will die, too, I know. She won't spare me. But I have to go back. For Dwai.'

'I know,' he said. 'I know you want to go back for him. But...'

'It's what you would do, Dara. It is what you did. You tried to bring back the girl you loved from the River of Death.'

'And failed, let us not forget.' He turned, perhaps so that I would not see his face, and walked towards the old well. I followed him.

'This well will take us to Atala?' I asked, trying hard to mask my impatience.

'Something like that,' he murmured. 'I've had my eye on it for years and it is not a regular portal but…'

Before I could ask what he meant, he looked up. I felt a distinctly supernatural presence, but nothing that raised the hair at the back of my head. Whatever or whoever this was, they weren't malevolent. 'Who…' I began.

Someone came in through the old rusty gate. I craned my neck, both impatient and curious. She wafted in looking as lost as she had the last time I had seen her, although some of her dourness seemed to have evaporated.

Ila.

She advanced towards us, and as her eyes travelled to Dara, there was a look of such utter devotion in them that an ugly stab of jealousy pierced my core.

'Ila…' said Dara, and strode towards her. They looked like two people out of a painting, distinctly otherworldly and ethereal. I felt another childish prick of jealousy as he hugged her. When they pulled apart, Ila's eyes were strangely agleam.

'Were you planning to leave without telling me?' she said, her soft voice laced with indignation. Her auburn hair rippled in the wind in a way that Menaka would have loved to copy for a scene.

'No, of course not. I was going to wait for you so I could tell you myself,' he said evenly.

I raised my eyebrows, looking first at the Gandharva and then the Apsara.

'Oh, ahem,' Dara cleared his throat. 'So…while I was on the run, after er…I left the Forest of Fireflies, I ran into Ila. She was kind enough to shelter me.'

'But the rules of Banishment don't allow you to mingle with your kind anymore.'

'I chose to ignore that bit,' he said. 'In any case, this was the first time in 500 years that I had broken any of the rules. I didn't even try to meet Ila in all these centuries.'

'It has been hard,' she said, not taking her eyes off Dara.

I shot her a look. 'So when I met Menaka and you were there…you knew where Dara was?'

'Yes, but it was not my business to give him away,' she said staunchly. She ran her eyes over me, taking in my tear-splotched appearance. 'But then, yesterday, Morana suddenly appeared. She seemed to think I was harbouring him and she was right. I don't know what she said to him, but he was convinced he should come and find you. Of course, despite everything we've shared, he didn't think to involve me in the decision.'

She looked away haughtily.

'Ila…I would have done this anyway. With or without Morana's urging. I just wasn't sure…of anything. I'm not sure of my own choices and actions anymore,' Dara said.

'And correctly so. You are dabbling in things that are too dangerous. They will do irreparable harm to you,' she said, still not looking at either of us.

'Be that as it may, I've made my choice.' He sounded gentle yet firm.

A long, uncomfortable pause stretched between us.

'Right, then. Shall we go?' I asked Dara pointedly.

He nodded. After a moment of deliberation, he turned to Ila. 'Go to Aakasha. Prepare reinforcements. Convince Menaka. She cannot be in denial anymore. And take Morana with you.

She will not be safe from Hera after all the help she has given Ardra and me.'

Ila took a step towards him as she said, 'Yes, I will. Dara, you're in grave danger. I don't trust that bitch, Hera. I hope…' Her voice shook a little. 'I will pray for your safety.'

Dara said nothing. She took his hand. Without taking any notice of me, she leaned forward and kissed him on the cheek. 'Soon, this will all be over and I will see you in Aakasha. You are not banished anymore. Maybe we can dream of happiness again,' she said. Then she turned and walked away without a backward glance.

He watched her go and only turned back to me after she had shimmered out of sight.

'So,' I asked as casually as I could. 'That's your girlfriend? I thought you were heartbroken and single.'

Ignoring me, he walked around the rim of the well as though studying it.

'Is the well a portal?' I asked again, unable to keep the impatience out of my voice this time.

'No,' he said. 'It's not a portal. All portals in and out of Atala have been secured and are under watch. They will not present themselves to anyone from the outside. This well, on the other hand…'

His eyes narrowed. 'I discovered this well years ago. One of your kind was nice enough to show me. Soon after that, she exploded. It's a passage between here and the Black Dwarf Sea.'

'The Black Dwarf Sea! How the hell are we supposed to get to Vishara after that? The sea is full of monsters, isn't it?'

'That's a lovely old myth,' he said. 'The sea has no monsters, that much I know. What I don't know is what exactly is in it. Ardra, if you mean to do this, then this well is the only way to get to Atala. We fall into the Black Dwarf Sea and swim our way out to Vishara. It's dangerous, but this is the only way.'

'Let's do it,' I said grimly. 'I have to get to Dwai.'

'Right,' he said. 'So we climb right in and...'

'And?'

'I have no clue. I'm making this up as we go along,' he shrugged and climbed over the rim of the well. I followed suit.

The well looked dank, overgrown with creepers and bottomless. As I looked down, I got the impression that it was the inside of a reptile, dark and slimy. I took one last look at the Prithvi sky – it glowed with a strange light, the moon that had emerged from the clouds. Something within me coiled in fear, although I had no idea why.

'Is it even normal,' I asked, 'that the full moon glows scarlet twice in a row?'

Dara glanced at the moon and said, 'Strange is the magic of the moon. And powerful to those who can channel it. Hera will harness the powers of this red moon. If you really mean to stop her, we must hurry.'

'I intend to try,' I said, tearing my eyes from the sky and gazing into the sticky depths of the well. 'Dara, whatever it is that you seek revenge for, it involves the girl who died?'

His eyes were distant and sad. 'Perhaps when this is over, you will know. But now is not the time.'

'Right...'

'Shall we, then?'

I nodded.

'Dara...I know why I'm doing this. For Dwai, for myself. But why are *you* risking your life?'

There was a short pause before he said quietly, 'A chance at redemption is rare, Ardra. We must take it when it comes our way.'

I didn't know what to say so I just nodded.

'Right,' breathed in Dara. 'On the count of three. One, two...'

We jumped.

The shores of the Black Dwarf Sea were not sandy. Instead, they were alive with jewels of all sorts, including crystals that killed and stones that were so full of venom that stepping on them meant instant death. The shores seemed to stretch endlessly into a dull grey horizon, but that was an illusion. In reality, or what passed for that in Atala, the Black Dwarf Sea was a lake. It was in these torrid, oily waters that planets came to die. It was what the stars hurtled towards at suicidal speeds to their ends. Within the depths of this unusual lake were all the secrets that Hera had considered too weak or too boring. Its waters were the colour of old wine and it had pieces of dead planets bobbing on its surface like debris. Shards of stars floated just below the surface.

Ardra pulled out one such shard from the sole of her foot and let out a profanity as blue blood oozed out and fell on the jewelled shore. She was wet and tired. She looked sideways at the Gandharva who had literally pulled her out of the waters and was now lying on his back, gasping for breath.

'Thank you,' she managed to say after a while. 'I think it was all those secrets in the water. It was as if they wanted to crawl inside me...' She shuddered. 'It was horrible.'

It had been. They had jumped into the well on Prithvi and had travelled down its dank coils for what seemed like eons. They had passed many a long dead and decaying creatures entangled in the vines climbing against the sides of the well. They also spotted a Gandharva or two, and even a valkyrie whose skin had started to drip off her bones. 'Must have jumped in to see where it leads,' Dara shouted, his voice throwing back eerie echoes. Soon, it had become evident that the well didn't want them to pass. It kept obstructing their path with thorny creepers and once even pushed out cadaverous hands from its walls that tried to grab hold of them. Dara had to pull out his sabre and chop away as many as he could before the well finally seemed to give up. The rest of their journey was uneventful, if tedious. They couldn't even really talk to each other because the echoes were overwhelming.

Then they hit the surface of water – hard and cold as it was – and sunk into it for a while before they gained enough control to swim back upwards. And that was when the secrets had tried to hold Ardra back. They had whispered to her, tried to crawl inside her and her core had almost exploded in panic. She had fallen into a semi-conscious state and it had taken all of Dara's strength to pull her weight as well as his own while he swam towards the shore. Finally, he had managed to claw his way up the jewel sands, an almost unconscious Ardra by his side. Then he, too, had passed out for a few seconds.

Now Ardra threw the star shard back into the sea where it hit the surface with a little spark and disappeared below the surface.

'Now what?' Ardra asked, wincing as she got to her feet. When Dara regarded her with concern, she added hastily, 'I'm okay, don't worry.'

'I couldn't even sense the secrets,' he said, sounding worried. 'You seemed possessed...'

'Well, it's over now. So...' She could hardly disguise her urgency. 'What do we do next?'

The look on his face was intense. His eyes narrowed as he took in the place, the beach and the palace in the distance.

'How long I have waited,' he said drawing in his breath sharply.

'Welcome to Atala,' she said lightly. He tossed her a twisted smile and looked around. 'We have to find a way to get into Vishara without being detected.'

She was about to reply when she spotted something floating in the water, bloated and shapeless. For a second she wondered if it was a particularly ugly planet that had crashed headlong into the sea. When it bobbed closer to the shore, she took a step forward, unable to believe her eyes.

'What...' started Dara and then his gaze followed hers.

She reached closer to the thing, and when she turned, Dara saw her face lined with shock.

'It's Mantri,' she said. 'Her minister. How could she... Dara, it's Mantri.'

Hera's faithful two-headed minister was floating in the sea of waste, dead and discarded. His second head was missing; his bloated body was revolting as it made little squelching sounds in the water. They both stared at him for a few seconds and then Dara spoke. 'Come on, we don't have any time to waste.'

'How...why,' Ardra said, bewildered, as they walked carefully over the bejewelled shore, looking for a gap in the spiked fences that cordoned off the Black Dwarf Sea from the Palace of Vishara.

'She's readying herself,' he replied grimly. 'Getting rid of everything she doesn't need once she becomes Blood Queen.'

He looked around. 'Strange,' he murmured. 'I thought there would be guards everywhere.'

'Dara,' whispered Ardra. 'Dara, look…'

He took a step back as he cursed. 'Bloody mer dogs…of course, I've heard of them.'

Ardra instinctively lifted her feet off the ground. 'Come on, Dara,' she urged. He took hold of her sleeve and they flew into the air, out of reach of the sniffing, growling mer dogs.

'This is right where I don't want to be,' she clenched her teeth. 'In the air, where some Yakshi can spot me.'

They hovered above the mer dogs as the mutant canines lunged at them, their gills flaring and their mer tails swishing in the air.

'Let's go,' said Dara. 'There has to be a way for these dogs to come and go. Let's find it.'

They glided along in the air while the dogs snapped at them, frustrated.

'I still can't get over Mantri,' Ardra said.

'I'm not surprised,' replied Dara. 'I'm just wondering what else she has in store.'

They flew in silence, looking for the opening through which the mer dogs might have come to the shore. But there was none.

'Can't we just fly over the fence?' she asked, frustrated.

'Not unless you want to die horribly.'

She tossed him a questioning look.

'Give me something to throw at it,' he said. She reached into her hair and pulled out a pin.

He threw it at the fence. It burst into flames instantly.

'Nice demo,' she murmured. They hovered in the air uncertainly.

'Dara!' exclaimed Ardra. 'Dwai's stone!'

'What about it?'

'Well, the stone has been very unstable. It clearly senses Dwai isn't happy. But now we are in his vicinity. What if… what if the stone can help us get to him?'

Dara frowned. 'No one has ever tried it before. I don't know if the stone works by proxy like that.'

'No, not by proxy. Dwai is inside Vishara. I'm merely going to send the stone towards Dwai. Over the fence. Maybe it will clear the path for us?'

Dara looked doubtful. 'Try it,' he said.

Ardra took out the Jwala from her pocket. She held to her mouth and whispered. 'Go to Dwai, he's inside the palace.'

'Er…' mumbled Dara. 'I don't think…'

She ignored him and flung the stone on to the fence. The Jwala hit the spiked fence and bounced back into Ardra's palm.

There was a second where absolutely nothing happened, and then there was a ripple in the air. An invisible shudder later, the fence collapsed to the ground.

Ardra grinned as Dara shook his head in amazement.

'Now to find Dwai and return you to him,' she said to the Jwala determinedly.

They flew right over the demolished fence and into the gardens of Vishara. Ardra landed on the ground again.

'Where *is* everyone?' said Ardra. 'This is really odd. There isn't a ghost in sight. Nor is there any sign of the guards at the main entrance… Where do you think she will be keeping him?' she asked.

'Knowing her, I think he would be in her chambers, right under her nose,' he said grimly.

'Wow, that's not at all complicated,' she sighed. The Jwala felt warm in her pocket. Perhaps it sensed Dwai was nearby.

She felt a slight movement in the thick shrubbery to her left. When she turned to looked into the green thicket, she flinched.

'Dara…'

He turned.

'Something is watching us…'

The Gandharva slowly directed his gaze towards the green thicket.

A pair of yellow eyes was looking straight at them.

✢ 51 ✢

They stood frozen as the reptilian eyes moved from Dara to Ardra. Something fluttered in her core and she almost took a step forward. Dara sensed her movement. 'No,' he said under his breath, 'Ardra…no.'

But she wanted to. She wanted to go towards those eyes, inexplicably drawn to them. A pair of wings flapped in her core. She wasn't sure if it was fear or excitement.

She took a step forward, forgetting for a second what she had come back to Atala for. Reality blurred and spots of colour waved in front of her. She took another step.

A hand curled around her arm. She stopped.

Aromal…wait…

A flash of white. A jumble of images.

A girl and a man running through a meadow as lightning struck.

'What was that?' she gasped. Dara recoiled. He let go of her arm as if it had scalded his fingers.

When she turned again towards the shrubbery, her brain fuzzy, the eyes had disappeared.

'What was that?' she repeated.

'I don't know what you mean.' Dara's voice was devoid of emotion.

'I mean, you touched me for the first time and something happened. I saw something...'

'What did you see?'

She took a step back as she said, 'I saw my memory ghosts.'

'What is a memory ghost?' His tone was flat, as if he was deliberately trying to avoid emotion.

'I don't know... They just appear...a girl and a man, and they tell me to remember. Except I don't know what I'm supposed to have forgotten.'

They looked at each other for a few seconds. Dara seemed to be barely breathing. Finally, he turned on his heel saying, 'Let's go.'

She followed him. 'You touch me and I actually see flashes of something that happened to these memory ghosts.'

He didn't break his stride.

'Dara!'

He stopped. His back was still turned to her. They had reached a little covered path full of carnivorous frangipanis. They hissed at her lustily. He turned slowly to face her.

'Dara, I'm begging you. Do you know anything about these memory ghosts?'

'How long have you been haunted by them?'

'Ever since Dwai and I... Ever since we met.'

'I have no idea what they could be,' he said tightly.

'You're lying again. I can sense it. Dara, for once, just *tell* me.'

She walked up to him until they were so close they could

hear the other breathe. She put her hand on his cheek and closed her eyes. He didn't draw back.

Electricity flashed through her veins and the memory snaked its way in with a stinging intensity.

Moonlight. Dew drops in her hair, bafflement in her eyes.

'Like the difference between a dream and its memory,' she whispered, her cinnamon skin shining in the light. He smiled.

'Your eyes are blue like a summer sky,' she said. 'Bright blue…'

She opened her eyes. His eyes were a stormy shade of azure now.

'No,' she whispered. 'No…'

'Ardra!'

She broke into a run. She ran past him through the frangipanis and blindly dashed into the palace. She had no idea where she was going but she knew she had to keep moving. Staying still meant she would have to process what her memory meant.

Blue eyes…lightning…the difference between a dream and its memory.

The difference between a dream and its memory…

She kept going, her core in turmoil, her mind flashing images.

An elephant, a thousand lights, the sound of anklets…

A kiss, an embrace…

An old woman. 'Take this talisman, child, it will protect you…'

Heartbeats, then nothingness. Just endless sorrow.

She stopped to catch her breath. *Am I going mad?* she asked herself. *Is it possible for a monster to go mad?*

She shut her eyes in the hope that the images would go away. She breathed in deeply and they slowly faded. When she opened her eyes, she realized that she was outside the Retrieval Room. There was no time to collect her thoughts. She could hear voices inside.

'Well, well, my Yakshis, the time has now come for you to prove your worth to me. After centuries of what I could easily call penance, the moment has arrived.'

Ardra peeked in through the door. All the Yakshis were lined up, Vina heading the pack. She looked excited, despite how gaunt and drawn she was.

Hera was seated on the Retrieval Throne, its arms clasped in a folded gesture above her head. She looked magnificent in a flowing ox-blood-hued gown and a huge bird-crested headdress. The plumes trailed dramatically down her shoulders while the headdress, golden and rich – a bit like a hunter's trophy – sat on her flowing hair. Her aura was more potent than ever, sending slivers of energy all around. Her eyes were thickly lined with kohl, setting off the crystal gleam in them. They flickered over her army of Yakshis, all of them holding their breath inside the room, and one outside of it.

'Lord Mara is pleased,' she said, her voice sonorous and clear. 'Lord Mara has always been so benevolent towards me, his favourite devotee. How ardently I worship at his altar, how deeply I adore his magic.'

She made a sweeping gesture with her hand. A thick curtain behind her parted revealing a huge statue of the God of Desire. He was a boyish God with a bow in one hand, arrow in another. Cherubic, devious, fickle…he was the perfect God for Hera to worship.

'Of course,' she said, rising from her throne, 'like all Gods, he demands proof of my devotion. He wants the blood of my penance, a sacrifice…'

There was deafening silence among the Yakshis. Only Vina seemed to move, holding her head high, eager to be noticed.

Ardra listened, horror creeping through her core. Dwai…

oh, how was she to stop this from happening? Where was he? He wasn't to be seen anywhere in the room.

'And a sacrifice he shall have, my beloved Lord Mara.' Hera's voice drifted through the door.

'Millions of moons ago, I built Atala and this bejewelled abode of mine in the hope of a new start. And I created you, my beautiful dark things, glittering with sin and seduction to serve a certain purpose.'

The crone, who was crouching in a corner, cackled in glee. Ardra could now sense a certain uneasiness creeping into her fellow Yakshis' cores.

'Now I must endeavour to make yet another new start. One that truly honours who I am, my powers, my vision. And for that... Vina, my dear, come to me,' she extended her hand. A trembling Vina, unable to contain her excitement, stepped up to the pedestal on which the throne sat.

'And for that,' said Hera, now almost lazily, 'I must not carry with me any burden of the past. You wouldn't want that for me, would you? I must walk into my new future free of encumbrances. I must be truly free...'

There was a significant pause. She laughed. It was a sound infused with the horror of a hundred nightmares. Then she pulled Vina's head back and neatly snapped it into two.

Ardra cupped a hand over her mouth to stop the scream from escaping. *No no no no... Oh, Vina...*

The Yakshi slumped to the floor lifeless, her eyes still reflecting surprise. Hera walked over her body and surveyed the remaining Yakshis, all of whom looked terrified of their creator.

'Give me, one final time, the power you have streamed into me so faithfully for 500 years,' she roared.

Ardra drew in her breath.

Inside the Retrieval Room, there was an ominous silence. Hera opened out her arms. Her face changed. It was something else now, demonic, base, a thing that fed on the fears of others, their darkest secrets.

She opened her mouth wide. Ardra watched as, for a final time, the Yakshis passed on every fragment of any secret they may have carried within them to their dark mistress. Ardra's core recoiled as the Yakshis fell to the floor silently as Hera extracted their life force out of them.

Every single Yakshi lifeless.

Except...

Ardra stood behind the door, numb, as her sisters in sin fell to the floor. She wondered if she was dead too – if this is what it meant to have a still core. But it still felt alive within her. It was fluttering madly, asking her to run.

Stunned and paralyzed by shock as she was, she slowly turned. The crone was standing right behind her.

'You're not dead, are you?' Her sickly white eyes gleamed.

Ardra backed away against the wall. The crone advanced. 'All of them are dead. Except you. Why? Do you not want to know why?' she hissed, her voice quivering with excitement. 'Ask yourself, succubus, why do you live while the others are gone?'

'Dakini!' Hera's voice rung out into the hallway, bristling with anger.

'Dakini, Gaggii tells me he's out of the tower. We must rush or he will –'

She walked out of the room to find the crone standing there alone, silently chuckling to herself.

'Have you completely lost your senses?' she snapped. 'There

is still the blood sacrifice to be made. I do not need this complication. Come on, let's get going.'

The crone laughed. It was a malicious noise and Hera threw her a wary look. 'What is it?'

'You are a foolish, blind woman. Always were...'

'Why? Why do you say that, you old bag of rubbish?'

'Go...go to your chambers first, why don't you? And ask that thing in the cage why.'

Something dawned on Hera's face. A shadow of doubt, misshapen and sharp. Without another word, she walked away, her stride quick and urgent. She could still hear the crone sniggering behind her.

☥ 52 ☥

The long corridors of Vishara seemed to writhe and move as I ran along them. My brain couldn't process anything that just happened.

All the Yakshis...gone! All of them. She had killed them in cold blood. She had sucked out their life force without a trace of regret.

But I was still alive, the only surviving Yakshi in the universe. How? More importantly, *why*?

I ran along, my thoughts colliding against one another. The walls whispered things to me, the floor kept moving under my feet. The pillars swayed precariously. It was as if Atala itself had come alive.

I swung around a corner and something shapeless and familiar engulfed me. My shadow creature!

It tugged at my hand and I followed it blindly. It would lead me to Dwai, I was sure of it.

The walls called out in hushed tones. 'We know things,' they hissed. 'We know things. Ask us...ask us about you. Ask us and we shall tell you about the cage... The past lies trapped in a cage...'

I paid no heed to them and sped along. But they called out constantly, taunting me, telling me I could ask them anything.

I didn't know what I was supposed to ask. I didn't know where I was going. We turned another sharp corner and the thick magic in the air hit my core.

We were near Hera's chambers.

Whatever this was – this unending riddle with myriad heads – I knew then that the answer lay within her chambers.

I walked in. Dwai wasn't there. The old mirror leaning against a wall sighed.

The shadow creature squeaked. 'Find Dwai,' I whispered. 'Find him for me, please.' It blinked its mournful saucer eyes and bounded away.

I stood in the middle of the room, not sure what to do or where to look. Then I heard a curious ticking sound echoing faintly in the silence.

The sound seemed to come from a distant corner of the room. Slightly breathless, I followed it, the ticking growing louder as I approached it.

The mirror behind me sighed noisily and said, to no one in particular, 'Destiny is doom and doom is destiny...'

Something glimmered in the corner, something that was ensconced in a cage. The cage itself seemed like a living thing. Covered with thorns, it flickered with a strange, sad energy.

I went closer, curious and afraid at the same time. Afraid of something that seemed so familiar and yet so alien. I peered slowly inside the cage.

It was a heart. A human heart in a tiny nest. It was suspended at the centre of the cage, hanging in mid-air, surrounded by an orb of diamonds. It was what had been making the ticking sound – a sound that had stopped as soon as I was near the cage.

I felt a wave of enigmatic sadness and rage all at once. I wanted to move but I stood transfixed, momentarily forgetting everything else. The heart hovered inside its thorny cage like a beautiful bird, trapped and sad…and dead, I soon realized. I must have put a hand out to touch it because blood was dripping from my fingers and on to the floor. Drip, drip, drip, the only sound in that large glittering room, cold and beautiful just like its owner. I stared at my bloody fingers and was about to take a step back when…

'Beautiful, isn't it?'

She stood at the entrance like a sharp, glittering star. Her eyes, silvery, tinged with a kind of inexplicable emotion, travelled from the heart to my fingers.

'Beautiful?' I asked. 'You think this is beautiful?'

'Hearts are beautiful. Those who possess them are lucky…' she said in a low, quiet voice, and took a step forward. I stayed where I was.

'Unfortunately, this one is utterly useless to anyone. Not me…' her eyes flickered over me, 'not you.'

'Who does it belong to?' I asked, a little breathlessly, afraid to know the answer.

She was close now, dangerously close, and yet she made no move to attack. I remained where I was. Both of us watched the hovering heart for a few seconds – its deep redness, the skein of diamonds revolving around it with a throbbing energy – and then she sighed. It was a sigh of sadness. I had never ever seen Hera sad before.

'This heart belonged to a beautiful girl. A beautiful, innocent, annoying girl, impossibly in love. It was pure, it was untouched, it was perfect.'

She reached within the thorn cage and took the heart out. It nestled in her white hands like a dead little bird. I was starting to feel sick but I couldn't suppress my curiosity.

'Lovely heart, so gentle, so true, so kind,' she murmured to herself.

'Do you know how tiresome it is to be kind?' she asked me, suddenly. 'So tiresome to be good, to have people love you, to…to…be someone who will never let anyone down, never do anything wrong…'

'It's bloody awful, that's what it is,' she suddenly shouted. 'And yet, that was the kind of heart I required. The kind I desired. So you know what I did?'

She came a little closer, the heart still in her hands.

'I took it,' she whispered, her white irises bright with madness. 'I ripped it out of her chest while she was still alive…'

I took a step back and my shoes squeaked on the marble floors, echoing in the horrifying silence of the room.

'I don't want to know anymore,' I said, not sure how my voice sounded.

'Why, succubus? Does this horrify you, this story of mine? You are a monster and this story of a silly human and her heart scares you? Don't you want to know how it ended?'

'NO,' I said, suddenly aware that I was shouting. 'I don't. I…'

She lunged forward, letting the heart fall to the floor, and grabbed me. I could feel her demonic madness rip through my core. I struggled but she was too strong for me. She put a hand to my chest and pulled down my clothes to reveal that curious silver line down my chest. She placed a finger on it and my core screamed in fear. I didn't want to hear what she had to say next.

She ran her nail down the line on my chest and I screamed in pain, a storm of memories piercing my mind like shrapnel, my head exploding with images.

'I did this,' she whispered. 'I did the Unspeakable. I ripped your heart out, Ardra. I plucked it out of your chest and the worlds changed forever. Because no one, not the Gods, not the Balance Keeper, not anyone in Aakasha or Prithvi could understand…'

She threw me back with inhuman force and I fell on her dazzling diamond floor, still convulsing with memories I didn't know I had. The heart lay at a distance and I turned my eyes away, not able to look. I couldn't understand what she was saying. My heart…but Yakshis don't have hearts…

Another turbulence of memories rocked my core and I knew what I had always known. In some forgotten recess of my mind, I had *known*.

Her eyes slid down to the caged heart. 'For all that you lived for, Ardra, and all that you died for, it proved useless to me. And for years now I have looked for another like you, a pure-heart, and look at the irony of your sad little life – you led me right to him.' She laughed – a maniacal, mirthless laugh.

'But you messed up,' said a familiar voice from behind her. Dara stood at the door, quiet fury emanating from him.

Hera whipped around. 'So,' she whispered, 'you are finally here. Strange, but I have waited for this moment.'

'You messed up then and you messed up now, Hera,' he

said quietly. 'Everything will burn in front of your eyes now, everything you think you own will cease to be.'

He walked across the room towards me. When he held out his hand, I didn't take it, choosing to rise to my feet on my own. His gaze, sad and wistful, moved from me to Hera and turned hard.

'Was it you, Dara?' Hera spat out. 'Did you let him out?' She flung the heart to the floor with violence.

He didn't answer. His eyes travelled to the heart and he picked it up, cradling it tenderly, before returning it to its resting place in the cage.

'You shouldn't have told her, Hera,' he said sadly. 'You really shouldn't have.'

'Why NOT?' I screamed. 'How long would you have kept it from me? All of you? For how long? A million years?'

Rage surged within me until I was shaking from its force.

'Is this why I didn't die along with the others? Is it because I was already dead once? Am I the hybrid that ruined your spell? Tell me. I WANT TO KNOW!'

'How does it matter now?' said Hera, clenching her teeth. 'The past is a useless instrument. All it is good for is to churn out regret. I belong to the future. I will use the Half-born and become the Blood Queen.'

'So you can continue on this soulless quest for power?' asked Dara. 'Not anymore, Hera. I – '

'It is *not* soulless,' she screamed. 'You stupid, weak man, do you not see? Nothing comes out of letting your heart rule your life. I will be Blood Queen and all of you will bow to me. How does it matter what I did 500 years ago to a stupid girl who was foolish enough to love a Gandharva?'

Blue eyes...the scent of frangipani...a kiss under a star-strewn sky...a cry of horror...someone holding her, holding her close...'I don't want to die...'

'Was it you?' I asked Dara. 'Was it you I loved? Is that why...?'

A scaly rustle interrupted my sentence. Something had entered the room, something so beastly, so monstrous, and yet so familiar, that my core flinched. The Thing in the tower. It was here.

Hera drew in a sharp breath.

'Dakini!' she screamed.

'Don't,' said Dara, quietly. 'Let him...'

'Let him WHAT?' Her voice was trembling. She staggered back as the Thing moved towards me.

'Bael!' she called out sharply.

The Thing turned to look at her and snarled in warning. She backed away a little further.

Bael...the Thing had a name. Did beasts have names usually reserved for humans or Gods?

He moved towards me, a twisted thing crawling back from a forbidden memory. I looked at his face, scaly and repulsive, with leathery skin stretched out like lines. I shrank back a little as he crawled towards me.

Dara took a step forward and then stopped. Hera took in a deep breath.

'Aromal...' Bael said, his voice a rumbling rasp.

The name rattled something inside me, like finding an old love letter from a long-lost lover. A fluttering rose in my chest.

He put out a scaly hand not unlike a claw and ran it down my cheek. I wanted to pull away but some instinct held me in place.

'Aromal, you are back,' he rasped. 'Aromal…'

Then I looked into his yellow and reptilian eyes. He was gazing at me with unmistakeable tenderness.

And it all came back. Like a song that hadn't been heard in ages. Because the past never leaves. We might tumble into the future like comets but the past trails along like a tail behind us. It is that untellable story that binds our tired, bleached bones with invisible threads.

The memory ghosts reappeared. And I recognized them now. And so we stood there, all of us, bound by our untellable story.

And I remembered…

⁕ 52 ⁕

'I want to live forever,' she said.

He turned to her. 'Forever is a long time, little fawn.'

'Forever is not enough if it means being with you,' she said, sitting up on the grass, her hair studded with dewdrops, her eyes afire with starlight.

It had been seven days since he first set eyes on her. Seven days since he had decided she would be his. A ruthless romance for a few days, and then…

And then what? He had never really thought of what happened to the girls once he left them. Once the magic lifted. Gandharvas were rarely built for regret.

He sat up, too, weaving his fingers into her hair and delicately holding a dewdrop on his fingertip. It glistened, an ephemeral universe that wasn't aware of infinity.

He tucked a frangipani blossom into her dark night tresses and ran a long pale finger over her hair ornaments. She blushed as his finger travelled down to her ear lobe, decorated with emerald and ruby earrings.

'Shy little fawn...' he said softly.

The princess fought hard to stay haughty but her heart was racing too fast for her to breathe.

The Gandharva inched closer to her.

She murmured, 'If someone sees...'

'...us there will be hell to pay. Your nose will be cut off. They will hang me from the tamarind tree and beat me till I die,' he smiled.

'Then I will die with you.'

She meant it. He knew that. His magic was potent.

'Aromal, nobody will see us. Or know about us.'

He took her hand in his. 'I promise.'

He slowly lifted her hand to his mouth but she drew it away, blushing.

For the love of Aakasha, he thought to himself, *the virgin ones are such joy but also such exasperating agony.*

'What is this, little fawn? Has no one ever kissed your hand?'

She shook her head in horror.

'Really? No enthusiastic temple light-bearer, no twinkle-eyed lad from music school, no Romeo sneaking into your room at night?'

'I am a *princess*!'

The haughtiness was back.

'I am a princess. My father is the king. My heart is not to

be given away in vain. Besides, what do you take me for? I am not that kind of a girl.'

'No, you are not. You are...my kind of girl.'

The temple gong sounded in the distance and she rose in panic.

'It's time to light the lamps. I must go. Goodness! What will I say if Mother asks me where I was?'

And with that she bounded away without a backward glance at him, her feet making no sound on the soft grass.

He watched her go and leaned back on his elbows, watching as twilight arched itself slowly over the temple tower.

The first time he had laid eyes on her was in the light of the brass lamps that burned tall and bright at the temple festival.

He watched as she flitted from one towering lamp to the other. He watched until he could watch no more, his eyes singeing with her radiance.

'Aromal...' someone had called out.

She turned and smiled.

Aromal. It meant 'my beloved'. He smiled and whispered her name to himself. It tasted like wild honey on his lips.

Her bare cinnamon-hued shoulders gleamed in the copper light of the lamps. Her hair was coiled in a thick bun on the top of her head, angled to the side the way aristocratic women wore it. He wondered what it would look like loose, a tangled night river flowing down her back...

He could have used his magic to seduce her that very night. He wanted to. But he waited. He wanted the thrill of the chase.

He watched as she folded her hands and closed her eyes, praying to the stone goddess she believed would grant her everything her heart desired. He saw a smile unfurl gently on her face as her lips moved in prayer.

When she opened her eyes and turned, he was standing in front of her. She locked eyes with his for a fraction of a second and then walked past him, her chin in the air, her young figure straight with haughty grace.

'Princess…' the priest called after her, 'you forgot to take your offering.'

She turned back and held out her hand.

'I have made an offering to the Goddess in your name,' he said, smiling, 'in the benevolence of the star under which you were born – Aathira, the brightest star. Your birthday is in a few days. Tell your mother to make an offering again then.'

'She will come with enough gold and bananas to outweigh the whole temple,' laughed the girl. The Gandharva shut his eyes, drinking in the music of her voice.

The drums and the cymbals reached a deafening crescendo as the elephants began their procession through the roads, going all the way up to the palace where the king was waiting. The king of the land they called Gods' own. And she was the princess, his only child, the apple of his eye.

She walked ahead of the procession with three companions. Kesava, her elephant, lead the pack, a magnificent animal decked in gold. She turned to look at the animal a few times, her eyes gleaming with love.

Laughter, chatter, noise rang across the town. The cymbals and the drums began again, their rhythmic explosions searing the air. Someone broke a coconut in front of Kesava, offering a prayer.

Kesava raised its trunk high and let out a loud trumpet, almost drowning out the drums. The elephant stopped and then swayed gently from side to side. His mahout turned sharply even as the animal let out another sound, an unnatural, violent bellow.

Only the Gandharva could see that the elephant, Aromal's pet, had started oozing a sweet liquid out of the sides of its head. Sweet, liquid madness...

Aromal turned to look at her usually gentle pet as it picked the mahout off the ground, hoisting him high above his head, the sweet scent of his madness floating through the air.

The princess's lips parted in horror.

Kesava bucked and then brought its mahout crashing to the ground. The man lay writhing in pain, screaming for help as the elephant raised his foot, ready to bring it down on his terrified face.

'Kesava!'

The elephant paused and the crowd drew in a collective breath. Kesava's mad eyes swung wildly until they found its mistress. She stood fearless, unflinching, her chest rising and falling with emotion as she gazed at her beloved pet descend into a state she couldn't explain.

'Kesava...NO!'

The crowds gasped as the elephant lowered its foot gently, away from the mahout on to the ground. It let out a kind of whimper as it buckled to all fours, as if begging for forgiveness.

Aromal walked up to the whimpering animal ignoring her companions who were calling out in alarm, asking her to stay back. A few palace guards came running with torches, ropes and spears.

He took a step towards them.

Her eyes turned to him as the Gandharva moved towards her pet before she could. She paused, watching this extraordinarily beautiful man put his hand on Kesava and stroke its head. He seemed to whisper something into its ear as a result of which the madness ebbed, as if a gentle magic had overcome it. She thought she imagined a golden shimmer where the man's fingers had touched her pet's head.

Kesava wound its trunk gently around her waist as she stroked its head. But she kept her eyes steadily away from the stranger who stood just inches from her, gazing at her while she soothed her pet.

He watched as the palace guards slowly took away the injured mahout whose face was twisted in pain.

He watched as Kesava lifted her, like a tendril, between the coils of his trunk, and placed her on his back. The crowds erupted with relief, joy, wonder...

He watched as Aromal looked down at him, a whisper of a smile flitting across her lips. She gently patted Kesava, giving it the signal to move on, but the elephant paused and turned its trunk towards him. He moved forward, allowing Kesava to lift him up and place him behind Aromal.

He could feel her stiffen against his chest; he was close enough to notice the dark wisps of hair resting on her neck, the ones that escaped the elaborate do on her head. He studied her shoulder blades, bare, burnished and smooth, and he gazed at her earlobes, twinkling with diamonds.

They rode along, the crowds walking on either side and cheering, Aromal never once turning to look at him or uttering a word.

He wanted her. He had decided it the second he had set his eyes on her. He would seduce her and leave her possibly on the brink of madness, because that was what he was ordained to do.

What he did not know was that, before Aromal's birth, it

had been prophesied by a powerful astrologer that she wouldn't last beyond seventeen years. That she would be consumed by magic, evil and conniving, and it would result in her death. The king and queen, alarmed by their daughter's dark destiny, had summoned priests from across the land. These priests had chanted mantras for twelve days and nights and, at the end, produced a talisman that would protect the princess from magic or bewitchery of any sort. No man or woman could penetrate these barriers they had erected around Aromal through her talisman. Aromal herself would tell him this later, in the throes of love, and it would sow the seed of his betrayal.

That night she lay in bed, safe from danger of any kind, or so thought her father. No magic could pass through her.

But magic finds its own little skylights in the soul. It seeped into her like moonlight slides in through a half-shut window at midnight. It ran through her veins, glimmering and shining, making her blood run like the moon-rivers of Aakasha, laced with dreamdust and desire.

It wasn't the magic of his lust. This was an equally powerful and ancient magic – the spell of the sun and the moon before they knew betrayal. It was the enchantment of the wildest nights and purest days. This was a magic called love and, unknown to the Gandharva, it had nothing to do with his own powers.

That night, Aromal couldn't sleep until the faint smudges of dawn had appeared on the horizon. When she did fall asleep, she dreamt of silver creatures bounding through glistening woodlands, and of a strange land where the sun shone in a dark purple sky.

That night, another meteor tumbled out of the heavens and disappeared somewhere on earth. The blazing light in the sky curved and fell, embedding itself softly on the dewy grass outside the temple.

Another Gandharva had decided to walk the earth in search of maidens waiting to be seduced in the dark shimmer of the night.

He looked around and smiled. Prithvi always held the promise of pleasure and fun.

'Is she beautiful?'

He watched her in amusement as jealousy coloured her cheeks. The sun flirted its way through the walls of their private chamber in one of the glass palaces of Aakasha. The sky outside was a dark purple, studded with stars. He stretched out lazily, his translucent skin gleaming as it did when he was back home, where his magic was strongest.

'The first rule of Gandharva seduction: pick the pretty ones. Otherwise it's a waste of time.'

'So, she is pretty?' Her tone was hard, persistent.

'Why does this bother you? It hasn't in a thousand years.'

'Because this is the first time in a thousand years that I've seen such a sickening smile on your face. It's disgusting.'

'Don't be ordinary, Hera. It doesn't become you. Go find some earthling to amuse yourself with. Just…return to me.'

He leaned forward and pulled her towards him. She wrestled herself out of his clutches and walked over to the window.

'When will she change this stupid sky? I'm sick of this purple.'

'You are in some mood.'

She turned to look at her heavenly lover. One she had been with for thousands of years in human time. In Apsara time…

goodness, she didn't even want to think about how long it had been. It made her feel old.

'Mood? Yes, I am. Who does she think she is? Bitch of the heavens. Preening and pouting. Lording over me. Who died and left her in charge? Oh wait, I know…'

The Gandharva laughed. 'You are funny when you are angry.'

'And you are annoying when you are trying to be funny.'

'Come here to me.'

'No.' She drew in a sharp breath. 'I can't do this much longer.'

'What do you mean?'

'I mean… I'm going to do something and…'

'Be queen of the heavens?' he asked softly.

Her eyes were afire, hard like jewels. 'I'm going to use my powers.'

'Hera, that is a banned power… You can't!'

'I will,' she cut him short. 'She will ban anything that harms her darling humans. She, and that rainbow-haired Balance Keeper. They think they know what's good for the realms now that the Gods have taken off. It's a joke. Look at what we've become ever since we held back on our primal powers. We've become…'

'Human,' he said softly.

She made a derisive noise.

'Remember the times when we could use our gifts? When we could curse and bless and read minds? It was *useful*. Now we are mere courtesans and playthings.'

'We can still seduce.'

'Take that away, and I would kill myself.'

He looked at her, beautiful, angry, glittering with dangerous desire. He loved her. He always had. But now…he found himself wondering what she was becoming.

'Hera…'

'Tell me something,' she turned to him. 'What of your own gift?'

'It's hardly a gift. I never used it. It is the shadow of my parents' union. I'm glad it is banned.'

'You don't want to use it then?'

'No, never! It horrifies me. I wonder if it is a gift or a curse. I have overcome my desire for it…it's for the better. Nothing good ever came out of a need that resulted in the death of others, Hera.'

She wasn't even listening to him anymore.

'I'm not like the others, I'm not. I never have been. I'm not an assembly-line puppet-variety Apsara. I'm not just "a heavenly creature who can sing and dance". Unlike her, the silly bitch, I can actually think for myself.'

'That's what I'm worried about.'

He walked up to her and held her by her cold alabaster shoulders.

'Hera, life is good as it is. Don't go chasing dark things.'

She didn't respond. Instead, she turned to face him.

'What is her name?'

'Whose?'

'The earthling's…'

'Aromal. It means beloved.'

'Aromal,' she repeated. Her eyes darkened, storm clouds brewing within.

Seven days of enchantment. A week of slow seduction. It was Gandharva rule-of-thumb that you never stayed long enough to make a human connection once you had seduced the girl. And when you left, the magic was lifted, leaving the girl to deal with what had happened to her. Sometimes they remembered what had happened in flashes, enough to wonder if they were going mad. But most just forgot about it. After all, Gandharva magic rarely lingered beyond a few weeks. He had seduced thousands of girls in his very long lifetime – most he had forgotten instantly, moving on to the next with a certain heartlessness. Some he recalled with fondness, even mild regret. But he had never ever revisited any of them. Ever.

He thought of Aromal. She thought she loved him, this mysterious, handsome stranger, but this wasn't love. It never was. It was just deep, ancient, ruthless magic. It was the law of the old world, the way of the old Gods.

The old Gods had warred, seduced, killed, betrayed and moved on without compunction. That was what had made them powerless in the first place, this reckless disregard for their own worth. Their rules, magic, divinity, all came with a price. The price of humanity. There was always a cruel barter involved. And, as always, the innocent were the currency.

Like Aromal, who was waiting for the love of her life. What she had got instead was a Gandharva – cold, calculating and slave to his primal desires. He couldn't reject what he was ordained for, even if he wanted to.

And he didn't want to. Not with Aromal. Soon, she would be his...

Twilight swept the landscape as he sat by the deserted temple pond. He thought of Hera, his Goddess of Desire. Darkened by her jealousy, burnished by her anger, poisoned by her hunger for power. He thought of her gift and what it could lead to. He thought of his, and the dark depthless end that it was in itself. It made him base, brutal. He had subdued his need to feed his gift a long while ago. He wasn't about to succumb now, simply because Hera wanted to be chief of the Apsaras.

He had seen a storm in her eyes that night. He knew it could finish him. His gut told him that things were about to change. Very fast. And very badly.

He walked back to the rest house he was staying at. He had become something of a local hero ever since he had charmed the berserk elephant into dull benignity. It hadn't been hard to cook up a story about being a wandering temple drum player. This was the season of festivals. A lot of musicians went from town to town looking for work.

He walked into his room and stopped. Standing in a corner, lighting it up like a lamp, was the last man he wanted to see. His own reflection. His twin. His nemesis.

The twin smiled. It was a sweet, affectionate smile, almost teasing. It annoyed his brother.

If one could see both of them in their Gandharva forms, the only thing distinguishing them would be their individual markings. Otherwise, they looked like two blazing suns in one universe. In their human forms, they looked different. Perhaps like brothers, not twins.

'Greetings, brother.'

The older one didn't return the greeting. 'What are you doing here?'

'The same thing you are,' he smirked.

'Copycat.'

The twin laughed. 'No, dear brother, we just seem to have the same ideas at the same time.'

'And usually I beat you to it. Which means, darling twin, light of my life, jewel of the heavens, you must stay far away from it.'

'Hmm...boring. I know you secretly covet the competition.'

The elder looked at his twin with scarcely concealed dislike.

'Leave. Now. The girl is mine.'

'Ooh, there is a girl already? I didn't know. I just happened to saunter by and I saw your mark on this place. For some reason, I felt this intense desire to visit you. I beseech you, brother, don't throw me out.'

'When will you grow up?'

'Well, if it hasn't happened in a few eons, I doubt it will happen now.'

'Stay AWAY from her. She's mine.'

'Tsk tsk...what would Hera say, I wonder, about that tone in your voice? You sound – and I hope I am wrong, brother – like you are in the throes of agonizing mortal *love*.'

The twin stressed the last word with a stinging sarcasm that wasn't lost on his elder.

'Love? You think this is love?' he laughed. 'Have you forgotten what it is to be a Gandharva? We don't love mortals. It's a sheer waste of time. But that girl...she's beautiful. She has this force, this *desire* to live, to love, to be loved, that I can't describe. I am drawn to that.'

'Fascinating. Who did you say she was?'

'I didn't.'

'Don't be cruel, brother.'

'Listen, just leave. Find another girl, another place on earth. Anywhere but here. And if you are horribly bored, go back to Aakasha and keep an eye on Hera for me. She is...up to something.'

'Hera is always up to something.'

'There is no love lost between the two of you, I know. But

I need you to help me with this. It's a command. An elder's command.'

'Tsk...you do know that is a mere technicality, don't you? Elder, younger. We are twins – you were born a mere whisper of a second before me.'

'Yes. Our mad father impregnated our mother in the night sky after they had been separated. I was the first to be born of her lightless despair. That is why I am the dark one. Considered unlucky, capable of...evil.' He paused, his face like a thundercloud, his blue eyes shadowed.

'And you have always wondered if Hera is attracted to you because of this – this dark side of yours.'

The elder said nothing. The arrow had shot home.

The twin threw his brother a glance and then said, in a gentler tone. 'You have never been capable of evil. You possess the means for it, yes. But you have made the choice to not use it. It is a noble choice. And a difficult one.'

The elder remained silent.

'Come on, take me with you tomorrow. I promise to remain invisible. Show me this bright, beautiful thing you will love and I will leave very soon.'

The elder looked at his twin. He knew his sudden appearance here wasn't a coincidence. The twin knew how he, the elder, was always precariously close to using his accursed gift. How it took every ounce of his willpower *not* to. How he clung to every shred of his God-given humanity to push the gift into the darkest corner of his aura. Let loose, the world would be a frightening place.

Yes, the twin knew. The twin understood.

As for Hera, she watched him the way the sun watches the moon on the verge of an eclipse. She watched, waiting for the slightest sign of weakness. Then she would push...

until he turned. Until his magic broke, and he unleashed the horror within.

He couldn't allow it. And as much as he disliked his brother, he was the best person to watch over him.

'Okay,' he said. 'Come with me tomorrow. I shall show you who she is. But promise me you will not go looking for her later. Promise me.'

The twin smiled and nodded. He felt an odd thrill in his heart. It reminded him of a time when they had hunted in pairs. When seduction was a war, waged only by one side... won always by that side.

He didn't keep his promise. He never had any intention to. Promises meant very little to heavenly creatures, toys that were given and broken without remorse.

He had gone with the elder the next day, staying out of sight the entire time. And he had watched the girl his brother had chosen for seduction. And then, just like he knew would happen, he wanted her.

He wanted her with every ounce of his sunblood.

He watched her taking a stroll in her garden. He watched through the moss-stained hole in the wall as she walked around barefoot, her long hair whipping around her. She had braided some wild flowers in them and they shone like stars. Her mouth was brooding and petulant, her eyes shining with an uncertain love. He continued to watch her for hours, utterly spellbound, as she wafted around in her garden, conversing with the birds and the flowers. He could sense the impact of his brother's magic on her.

She had the chaos of a young star within her.

He couldn't take his eyes off her.

He couldn't take his mind off her.

And he couldn't keep his promise.

Lightning struck, splitting the sky into two halves. The stars appeared like fireflies, blinking through the storm clouds.

'Aromal…'

He ran after her. She was darting across the meadow like a fawn, frightened, confused. He caught up with her and grabbed her by the arm.

'Aromal…stop! What is it?'

'I don't know,' she sobbed. 'Something very strange is happening. I can't tell if I'm dreaming or awake.'

He tenderly lifted her chin and kissed away her teardrops. She freed herself and took a few steps away from him.

She was confused. She had given away her heart to a man who didn't look dissimilar to the one who stood in front of her now. She couldn't understand what was different about them, and what was similar. A little like the difference between a dream and its memory.

She couldn't tell if it was the same person, and if perhaps love had addled her mind. He pulled her close to him, and she shut her eyes, swimming in his magic, even though her heart told her something wasn't right. Rain started to fall around them.

'I told you not to!' The elder was furious. He clenched his fists to prevent himself from using magic on his twin. But he wanted to cause him pain. He did.

'I couldn't help it,' said the twin. 'She is unlike any girl I've ever come across. She responds to starlight and fireflies. She watches the moon endlessly, she speaks the language of fire and rain...'

'ENOUGH!' His face was twisted in jealousy. 'She said she loved me. She said it a hundred times...'

'Despite everything, elder, I believe she has given away her heart to you. And you alone. Our magic seems to have confused her. It's not her fault.'

'If it was true love, she wouldn't be confused,' said the elder. 'Do you love her? Have you fallen for a mortal in spite of yourself?'

The twin didn't say anything.

'Your silence says it all,' said the elder, his voice hard. He felt something wrong and heavy filling him up. He closed his eyes, fighting it.

'Elder...I withdraw. She is yours.' The twin searched his brother's face worriedly. He seemed more angry than usual.

'What is the use now? She has almost been driven to madness.'

The elder walked away, bitter and heartbroken. And afraid. Afraid that Hera had been right all along. That he had managed to fall for the girl. He didn't think such a thing could happen. But he hadn't bargained for the magic of the heart to be stronger than his Gandharva lust.

They came in storms. Hundreds of them. They formed dark, sharp smudges in the sky, until the sky itself looked like a great monster rising from the sea, billowing smoke and dust and throwing up strange creatures.

One-eyed ravens, a vast unkindness, plummeting from the sky. Unimaginable, gut-curdling, poison-feathered.

She watched as they landed around her, cawing guttural and

deep, flapping their inky black wings. She held her hand out, a long sinewy thing that seemed to shimmer at the edges. The ravens cawed and circled her like dark moons and she stood at the centre, tall, terrifying, full of fury.

One left the circle and flew to her extended hand – a big, one-eyed, night-hued sliver of unkindness. She drew her hand close to her chest and the bird fluttered wildly, as if her heartbeats were hurting it. Then it crawled up her chest bat-like and nestled on her shoulder.

'This is the one…Gaggii.' The voice had the rumbling disquiet of a landslide.

Gaggii and her new mistress turned to face the crone. She was a withered thing, with bulging phlegm-coloured eyes and a mean, crooked mouth. She slid one gnarled dirty fingernail into her bulbous nose as she sniggered.

'The perfect pet for a Blood Queen.'

303

'Not yet, Dakini. You said it yourself, I have some way to go before becoming one.'

'Aah, the bittersweet price for becoming a Blood Queen…' the crone paused for effect.

'What is it?' she snarled, Gaggii almost falling off her shoulder. 'What is this price you keep speaking of?'

The crone giggled unpleasantly.

'Blood,' she cackled, stamping her stick gleefully to the ground.

'Blood?' she repeated in a half-whisper. 'But…'

'But? There is no "but" anymore. You have let loose the unkindness. The Dark, oh, the great big Dark, is now afoot in the world. You are on your path now and there is no going back, my dear. There is only what you desire. Speak it and it becomes true. It becomes true and stronger every time you speak it.'

She looked into the sickly whites of the crone's eyes and she saw in them what she feared the most. And what she desired.

'Whose blood? And how much?'

'*Now* you are talking,' the crone said gleefully.

Gaggii shifted uneasily on her shoulder. Her mistress lifted a shimmering hand and stroked the bird absently.

'Tell me, you horrible hag!'

The crone lifted her hands to the sky which instantly became darker. The air suddenly grew thick with locusts. The other ravens gathered closer. The crone advanced towards her and Gaggii's mistress took a small step back. The smell of her! The stench of a rotten soul emanated from her mean mouth.

'And so it shall be…Queen of Desire, Mistress of Phantoms, Harbinger of Snake Storms, hold close to your heart, the beating heart of a young girl, plucked from her chest before she dies. Hold it close to your heart and let my magic make it one with yours. When the innocence weeps into your blood, when the sacrifice is complete, you will be the most powerful Blood Queen the realms have ever witnessed.'

Everything was silent, even the ravens. Gaggii lifted a wing and then let it fall.

Hera stared at Dakini.

'The heart of a young girl? That is forbidden magic. It is Unspeakable sorcery. The price for that…'

'The price for that,' hissed the crone, 'is that you get what you desire.'

'It's *murder*. That is an Unspeakable act. I can't…'

'Then go back to your miserable existence,' spat the crone. 'Go back to your second-best life. Go back and desire nothing evermore.'

'NO! I can't bear to. I've come this far…'

'Then do it. It's just a teensy weensy heart. Of a teensy

weensy girl. There are thousands of girls. Find the one whose heart beats the loudest, find the one with the purest love, and then....' she made a squelching noise and Hera shrank back in disgust.

'Do it when the moon is next full. My magic is strongest then.'

'Don't call what you do magic. It's unspeakable. And you know it.'

Hera began to walk away, Gaggii on her shoulder.

'Mistress of Phantoms, one last word, if I may...'

Hera turned.

The crone hobbled up to her. 'The new moon that comes is extraordinary. It carries in its womb a full moon that bleeds blood. A blood moon and a bleeding heart – oh, Blood Queen, you will be born in scarlet glory. Do it then.'

Hera gave her the slightest of nods and walked away, shimmering at the edges like a forest fire burning bright.

The crone, witch of the wicked, invoker of soul worms, watched her go.

'You are brooding,' she crooned into his ear.

He turned to face his consort of many centuries.

'I'm just preoccupied.'

'By the girl, I assume.'

He glanced at her sharply. Her face was a picture of sweetness.

'I don't mind. I really don't,' she purred. 'I was foolish to be so jealous before. I'm bigger than that, aren't I? All these human emotions like jealousy don't befit me.'

'Hmm,' he said. He couldn't get the girl out of his mind. She had bewitched his body and soul. He was consumed by thoughts of her day and night, racked by human feelings of jealousy and, more pitifully, by love. He loved her. And he wanted her. His face darkened as these thoughts grew more intense.

'Dakini was telling me about a potion,' she said, stroking his hair. 'It's for eternal beauty. Even we heavenly girls need it once in a while, you know. But I need one ingredient and I'm not sure how to get it.'

'What ingredient?' he asked suspiciously.

Her eyes were wide and innocent. 'Well, it really is a very harmless potion. Just crushed flowers and a bit of forest fire. I also need a tiny drop of a young girl's blood.'

He sat up. 'Hera, any potion that requires blood is not "harmless". What are you up to?'

'I swear,' she squealed petulantly. 'I swear it is a potion for beauty. Trust me, won't you, love?'

'Why are you asking me, anyway?'

'Well, you do know a young girl whose heart is pure and good, don't you? Just one drop of her blood is all I need.'

'And you expect me to do this for you? For this silly sorcery of yours? Hera, I don't trust that crone. She is always up to no good.'

'She's just a silly old woman. But she is *so* good at potions. Please, love, help me. Imagine if I looked more divine than I do now. It wouldn't hurt your blue eyes would it, to look at me?'

She was demure like a kitten. She stretched out on the bed and held out her arms. He sighed. He may have been in love with someone else, but he couldn't resist Hera's charms.

'Okay. You shall have your drop of blood,' he said. 'But it will not be easy to procure. She told me she is protected by a powerful talisman. She wears it all the time.'

'I shall find a way,' she said sweetly as he closed his eyes, burying his head in her flaming hair. He didn't catch the wicked gleam in her eyes.

Hera gazed into the huge mirror in front of her. It lifted one of its brawny arms to absently scratch the wolf-head crest on top of its wrought-iron frame.

'So...what did you find out?'

'Well, mistress, we mirrors are sly. We are so cunning...'

'Stop rambling and tell me what I need to know. Is she pretty? Is she prettier than me?'

'O mistress,' rasped the mirror in a throaty, servile tone. 'How can anyone in any of the realms be as beautiful as you? But...'

'But? But what?' Her flame-tipped lashes flickered.

'She gazed into me as I replaced one of my own in her chambers. Pure of heart, made of fire and flowers, she is like no other, O mistress. Her eyes see things that no one else does. Her heart beats in a rhythm of rivers and rain. She is...unusual.'

'I see.'

She picked up a goblet and flung it at the mirror. It ducked. The goblet hit its wrought-iron edge and clanged to the floor.

'Out!' she snapped. 'Out, and do not present yourself unless I command it.'

The mirror bowed and wheeled out of the room.

'Pure heart made of fire and flowers,' she muttered. 'I must have a glimpse of it myself, I must.'

A gnarled finger traced the lifelines on her outstretched palm. Aromal had found the old fortune teller lurking outside the palace gates. She was older than it seemed possible and she had eyes that seemed to change colour in the fading light.

'Such a bright burning star your fortune is, princess,' she croaked. 'I see a long life, many travels...and what is THIS? Oh, oh...a *man*...'

Aromal had the grace to blush.

'Ah, princess, a man, tall and handsome as the Gods. But beware, he is as fickle as he is ardent.'

'Why do you say that?' asked Aromal, frown lines appearing on her forehead.

'It is the nature of men to be fickle with beautiful women. But fear not, let me give you something for it. Something that will bind you to him.'

Hera took out a little black thread. Her fingers were adorned with numerous rings. A large star-shaped one with sharp edges and an emerald in the middle stood out on her index finger.

'Hold out your hand, princess,' she rasped. 'This is a tiny talisman, filled with the love of the sun, moon and stars. Wear it and be lucky in love.'

'I already have a talisman,' hesitated the princess.

'Oh, what match would that be against this one? This black thread here is for love. Is there anything greater? We must take off the other one, sweet princess, and let this work its charm.'

Aromal paused for a few seconds, unsure, and then held out her hand. Hera pulled back a few bangles and tied the thread to her wrist. She quickly pocketed the discarded talisman, intending to burn it later.

'That's a nice ring,' said Aromal, indicating the star-shaped ornament.

'You like it? Here, see how it looks on your beautiful finger. Go on, try it.'

Aromal shyly took the ring from the fortune teller and

slipped in on her ring finger. It was loose. As she took it out, it cut into her skin. Three drops of blood fell to the ground.

'Ouch,' she gasped.

'Oh, princess, a thousand apologies. Gypsy rings are too rough for delicate girls like you. Here, let me stem the flow of blood.'

'N-no...it's okay. I will go and apply some turmeric on it,' said Aromal, getting up. 'You must go now. Thank you for the talisman. Here, take this,' she held out a few silver coins.

'Oh, no, princess, I desire no money from you. You have paid me richly in blood.'

And with that, the old woman hobbled away, leaving the girl a little baffled. She regarded the black thread on her wrist and then covered it up with her bangles. She didn't want her mother to see it.

'The full moon is almost here,' cackled the crone.

'And I have her blood,' said Hera, tossing the ring towards the crone. The old hag caught it and gleefully dropped it into a boiling cauldron. It bubbled noisily on the surface for a few moments before disappearing.

'I was almost afraid she would ask for this,' said Hera, fingering a ring with a blood red stone set in it.

'Your Jwala, O mistress. You won't need it once our endeavour is successful. You will be a hundred times more powerful than any stone can make you.'

'Hmm. What was the thread for? She took it readily.'

'That thread has now bound her to our magic irreversibly. She can't run even if she chooses. Her heart, O mistress, her pure heart is yours now.'

'The rules ban all of this.' For the first time, Hera's voice held doubt. 'And if Menaka gets a whiff of what I am up to…'

'Hah! Before she does, you would have overthrown her. Aakasha will be yours to rule before that silly woman even catches on. Do not worry yourself, O mistress. It is all going according to plan. Now the only thing left is to make sure the girl comes out on the night of the full moon. She needs to be inside the circle I create. You will have to enlist the help of your consort…'

'He may refuse,' said Hera. 'He imagines he loves her.' She could barely hide how bitter she was, how consumed by jealousy.

'Oh, you must try, O mistress. It is of dire importance that she arrives that night. Everything has been planned to the last second.'

'All right. I'll think of something,' said Hera.

'You and he will rule all the realms once this is done. Your gifts are truly unique.'

'He refuses to use his. He thinks it's a curse. How do I convince him that anything that makes him powerful, even if they are the dying wishes of people, he should embrace as I have? All he needs to do is channel his magic and feed on them. Feed on the dying wishes of mortals and, oh, he could be so much more! Even the stars can't comprehend that kind of power. I can know a person's deepest secrets. I can delve into the darkest parts of someone's heart. Of course, I have to channel my powers and that makes it exhausting, but still, I know it's a gift. But he…'

'He will realize its potency when the time is ripe. You must be patient.'

'Patience!' murmured Hera. 'I hate patience.' She glanced at the moon as it bloomed into fullness.

He watched her sleep. He had been away for too long. Racked by jealousy, he had stayed away. He had watched from afar as she wandered, teary and heartbroken, in her garden. 'Where are you?' she had whispered to the wind. 'Why have you gone away?' He knew then that his twin hadn't approached her either. He had kept his word.

Moonbeams flitted across her skin, making her look almost divine. He gently brushed his fingers against her bare shoulder. She smelt like a fresh breeze, carrying with it the scent of jasmine. He inhaled her fragrance deeply.

Her eyes fluttered open. 'You,' she murmured sleepily. 'Is it really you? Am I dreaming?'

'No,' he whispered. 'It really is me.'

She gazed into his jewel-blue eyes and smiled. 'It really is you. For the past few days, I thought I was going mad. I thought there was someone else… I couldn't understand…'

'Shh…don't speak of it now,' he said. 'Think of it as a strange dream.' He kissed her.

Below her room, standing right by the frangipani tree, was the twin. He had come to see her, having pined for her for days. He was having trouble keeping his word. But now, he sensed his elder brother's potent aura. With a broken heart, he walked away, but he knew he would return every night, if only to stand below her room in the hope that he would appear in her dreams.

'Why do you want *her* for your "little spell", as you call it?'

'Darling, she is pure of heart. I just need to channel her aura. No harm will come to her.'

'What is this spell for?'

'Oh…just something I'm planning. Don't be surprised if Menaka ends up looking like a bullfrog at the end of it.' She laughed. It was too bright and innocent a sound for it to be real.

He could sense the storm in her mind. It wouldn't retreat. Instead, it would take everything around her with it, including him. But he didn't know how to stop her. All he could do was make sure no harm befell Aromal.

'You promise me no harm will come to her?'

'I promise with all my heart…which is yours, in any case.'

She placed her beautiful head on his chest. He closed his eyes.

The elder stayed back in Aakasha that night. The twin, however, still stood under the frangipani tree. He couldn't help the wild drumming in his heart. In a flash, he was by her bedside.

She was wide awake.

'You!'

The odd feeling of walking a tightrope between real and the make-believe was back. The eyes were the same: deep, passionate, blue eyes. But something told her this was someone else.

'You are not him. I know it in my heart.'

'Perhaps he is not me.'

She gazed at him with her large faraway brown eyes. 'Maybe it is all a dream,' she said.

The moon wove silken patterns on her skin. She looked fragile and ephemeral, different from anyone he had ever come across. He realized he didn't want to play any more games with her. She would be driven to madness, like many girls before her. And he didn't want that for her.

'This is a dream,' he said softly. 'There is only one man that you love. I am your illusion. Sleep, and when you awake, I will be gone.'

She closed her eyes. He stayed and watched her sleep till the first lines of tangerine streaked the night sky and then he shimmered away.

He hoped his heart would free him of the guilt now.

'She is up to something,' the Apsara who stood before him looked worried.

'She is always up to something. Doesn't mean she will actually succeed,' he replied.

'No. This time is different. I tried warning Menaka but she's too distracted by all the festivals on Prithvi to care.'

'I will find out,' he said.

'Before it is too late, please.'

She laid a hand on his cheek. 'I barely see you anymore. Have you found someone on earth? Who is she?'

'No,' he said shortly. 'There is no one.'

She wanted to believe him but his eyes gave him away. He looked heartbroken and lovelorn. Broken.

They met by twilight on the steps of the temple pond. To a human, they seemed like two young men whiling away a lazy hour of the evening.

'Tell me, elder! What is Hera up to?'

'It doesn't concern you.'

'Excuse me?'

'It really doesn't. When this is over, and she has what she wants, she has promised Aromal can be mine. She won't be jealous. She took a vow of fire.'

'And you believe her?'

'I do.'

'And you will let her do this, whatever it is, simply so Aromal can be yours?'

'Yes.'

The elder's obstinacy was unflappable. The twin swore under his breath.

'We are all going to regret this, brother. All of us. And if something happens to Aromal...'

'Why do you care?' snapped the elder. 'She means nothing to you. I'm there to protect her. And Hera has given me her word.'

'What word? What are you dragging Aromal into? Elder, you should know better!'

The elder wouldn't meet his eyes.

'I won't let it happen,' said the twin. 'I will do everything within my power to stop her. And you, if need be.'

The elder said nothing. They stood facing each other for a while, steeped in mutinous silence. The moon rose above them, full, almost ready to swallow their future.

'I can't let you do it,' said the twin. 'My heart tells me there is unbelievable evil in Hera's plan. And you are too blind, too weak, to see it.'

'I am *not* weak,' said the elder between his teeth. 'Don't thwart me, brother. Step aside and let me go.'

'No.'

The twin made a slight move. A wave of energy bolted towards the elder, who ducked.

'How DARE you?' he roared in anger. 'How dare you draw me into battle like this? NO, I refuse to...' He started to walk away.

'Brother, please,' pleaded the twin, anger and sorrow coursing through his voice.

The elder didn't look back. The twin closed his eyes and drew in his breath. 'I'm sorry,' he muttered.

The next bolt of energy that hit the elder knocked him down into the dust.

'I warned you,' he snarled, his breath coming in gasps, his eyes blazing with rage. 'I want Aromal and this is the only way...you can't stop me!' He flung his arm forward, unleashing a lightning rope of energy towards his twin.

The twin rose up in the air to avoid it, but the force of his elder's magic was too strong for him. The rope caught him and sparks flew. He screamed and fell to the ground.

The elder gazed at his brother's unconscious body for a few seconds before he walked away, his mouth set in a determined line and his thoughts full of Aromal.

'Where are they?' hissed the crone impatiently.

The moon was swollen, stained scarlet. A large white circle had been drawn using the crushed bone powder of sky horses. A cauldron was simmering with an oily fluid, occasional whispers emanating from it. The sky was darker than usual. They were at the top of a little hill on Prithvi where the wind howled their names in a hundred different languages.

'They will come,' said Hera. 'He has promised me he will bring her. And he has promised that his twin will not come anywhere close to this place. He will see to it.'

'You know what to do, O Mistress of Desire. Once the spell is complete, you must – '

'I know,' cut in Hera impatiently. 'I must pluck her heart out and consume it. Your black thread ensures she will stay alive till I am done. Then I must dip my hand into the cauldron... I know all of this. We've been through this a hundred times.'

'Nothing must go wrong. It must be precise, down to the last minute. I fret, oh, I worry...'

Hera didn't bother responding. Instead, she turned away and walked to the edge of the hill from where the palace could be seen, glimmering with the light of brass lamps.

'Do not let me down,' she muttered to herself.

'It is a compelling full moon night,' said the crone. Her voice held a kind of temptation that got Hera's attention. 'A scarlet moon and irreversible sorcery that only few are capable of. If only he would harness his powers tonight... You would be invincible together, O mistress.'

Hera turned to the crone. She was framed against the blood moon, a gleaming otherwordly siren. She was about to say something when her eyes travelled beyond the crone and lit up.

'You are here,' she said. 'You kept your promise.'

Bael, her lover of countless centuries, stood shrouded by darkness. Hera's eyes strayed to the frail body lying limp in his arms.

'I kept my promise,' he said. 'Now you must keep yours. Use her aura for your spell and then I will return her to her bed. I gave her a sleeping draught some time ago. She will be unaware of whatever happens here.'

'The sleeping draught will cease to affect her once the spell begins,' whispered the crone to Hera. The Apsara held up a hand to silence her.

'Bring her to the centre of the circle.'

He did.

'Place her down and exit the circle.'

She sensed his hesitation.

'Do as I say, Bael. Do you not trust me?'

He didn't reply. Instead, he laid the mortal girl he had given his heart to on the ground in order to please the Apsara he had belonged to since time began.

'Good,' she said, her eyes fixed on Aromal as she lay in the middle of the circle, unconscious, perhaps dreaming of a man with jewel-blue eyes.

'Let us begin, Dakini.'

Bael waited outside the circle, feeling increasingly uneasy. Dakini dragged the cauldron into the centre of the circle, muttering an incantation under her breath.

She placed a few droplets of the inky fluid on Aromal's forehead.

'Wait,' said Bael.

'What is it, darling?' Hera's tone was sweet but hard. He fell silent again.

The crone danced around the cauldron, chanting incantations that grew louder by the second.

The moon seemed to grow bigger suddenly, the scarlet staining darker across its surface. The cauldron began to emit red smoke. Hera's eyes began to bleed.

'Now, O Mistress… Now is the time… The moon will emit its light…'

Hera's eyes rolled back into themselves, her cheeks were bloody as her body grew rigid and her feet rose a few inches off the ground. Bael tried to take a step inside the circle but he couldn't. There was an invisible fence around it.

'Hera,' he called out. 'Stop this now!'

She swayed from side to side, her flaming hair swirling around her. The crone chanted relentlessly, throwing things into the cauldron.

'Where am I...'

On hearing Aromal's faint voice, a deathly silence fell upon the gathering.

'She is awake,' rasped the crone, shivering in excitement. 'The moment has come!'

'Where am I? What is this?' She stood up, shaking in fear and surprise. Then she saw Bael outside the circle.

'What is going on?'

The crone resumed her chants. Hera moved towards Aromal.

Bael's heart contracted with dread. 'No! Hera...' he shouted. 'HERA, STOP!'

She was an inch away from the girl now. Her eyes were aflame with demonic fire. If the end of the world had a form, it would have looked like her in that moment. Aromal's eyes widened in shock.

'Who are you?' she asked.

Hera laughed.

When it happened, when she did it, the moon skulked into the clouds. The only sound in the utter darkness was the sound of skin and flesh ripping.

Aromal didn't even scream. She looked down at the gaping hole in her chest, her face registering puzzlement.

'AROMAL! NO, HERA, PLEASE NO...'

It was too late. Aromal sank to the ground, not unlike a butterfly spiralling to earth. The fence around the circle disappeared and the world quietened in mourning.

Bael rushed to her. 'Aromal...'

He caught her just as she crashed to the earth and gathered

her close, her delicate body limp in his arms. Hera towered over them, blood dripping from her hands as she clutched a pure heart, watching her lover weep inconsolably for the dying girl. An ugly shadow gripped her heart.

'What did you do, Hera?' Bael could hardly speak.

'I did what I had to do. Now I will be Blood Queen, and you can return with me to Aakasha, where we will rule.'

She moved closer to him, where he clutched Aromal to his body like a baby. He was convulsed with sorrow, tears streaming down his cheeks.

'She isn't dead yet, you know,' she said softly, her voice holding the dangerous quietude of a sleeping volcano. She still clutched the heart in her hand.

The crone scuttled around, nervous and impatient.

He looked up, anger rising within him like a firestorm.

'You are despicable,' he spat.

'Maybe,' she said, still softly, as if gently coaxing a child to drink his milk. 'Maybe, but you want to... Deep inside, you do...'

His eyes met hers and for a second she thought she saw something stir within him. Something that had been asleep for years.

'It is Aromal, after all,' she said, her eyes sliding to the dying girl, whose breath was now coming in slow, painful gasps.

'Don't you dare speak her name,' he said sharply. 'Don't you dare, Hera.'

He looked down at the only person he had felt anything for by way of love, and held her close.

'Don't let me die...' she murmured, her voice like a whisper in the wind.

He kissed her cheeks madly as she repeated, 'Don't let me die... I don't want to die...'

Hera made a slight noise. When her lover of a thousand years looked up at her, his vision blurry with tears, there was a strange compassion in her gaze.

'She doesn't *wish* to die... She doesn't...' she muttered almost under her breath, the gentle coaxing melded into her tone like honey in milk.

The crone clicked her tongue. 'O mistress, do not worry about him. He will change. But you must consume the heart now.'

'Shush.' She was watching him now, the heart in her hand forgotten.

'No, no, no...' He was inconsolable now, shaking his head violently, fighting it. Fighting it with every ounce of his godly strength. And yet the monster inside him was on its haunches now, finding steady ground. He could feel its evil breath on the walls of his soul.

'What are you doing, Hera?' he whispered, his eyes red and bleary as he clung to the almost-dead girl.

'I'm bringing you to your true self,' she said, advancing a little and yet keeping her distance as one would from a wounded lion. 'Your true self, my darling...and mine. Together we could rule the world.'

The dying girl, his Aromal, still alive due to the dark spell that bound her, heaved violently as her last breaths came out in little ruptures of air. She dug her frail fingers into his chest, trying to sit up, and he buried his head in her hair, still faintly fragrant from the frangipani blossom in it.

The monster clawed at the wall of his soul, ripping and shredding them with bestial ferocity and he could feel his strength ebb. He couldn't hold on much longer...

'I don't want to die...' Aromal repeated faintly.

There was a sudden flash of red, and then the monster leaped out from within him. All that he had held back for centuries, that which was imprisoned within him, crashed noisily into the world and he buckled to his knees from the sheer force of it. He was the monster and the beast was him…there was nothing to tell them apart.

Aromal's dying wish escaped her lips and into the jaws of the monster. It stuck out a forked tongue and licked the wish, roaring with glee. Bael, the Gandharva, had given in to his dark side.

'I don't want to die…' *Lick, rip, devour.*

'I want to live… Save me…' *Lick, rip, devour.*

He fed on his beloved's dying wish and, from then on, there would be no return.

Hera watched her lover's manifestation, her sapphire eyes gleaming with an unnatural emotion. He was what she wanted him to be. A beast with the power to control humanity. To feed from it.

She threw her head back and laughed. Bael let the girl slide from his arm and fall to the ground. He rose, his face twisted in deviant power. He stepped over Aromal as if she were a dead branch in his way. He walked past Hera and then stopped dead in his tracks.

His twin. His nemesis. The lucky one, who missed the darkness of the moon by the sliver of a second.

Dara.

The twin surveyed the scene with hollow eyes. All the light had gone out of them.

'I knew…' he whispered, sorrow rising in his voice. 'I knew it. I knew you would do something like this,' he lashed out at Hera. 'You evil witch!'

He crumbled to his knees and scooped up the bloodstained dead girl into his arms.

'WHY?'

'Why?' she said, her voice stone cold. 'Because I am meant to be great. I know I am. Of what consequence is one heart belonging to a foolish girl if it helps me on the path to greatness?'

'Great?' he spat. 'You are not great. You are worse than vermin. You feed on life itself. You hateful, evil devil...'

She was about to say something when, suddenly, she felt as though an invisible force was choking her. Clutching her throat, she sputtered, 'Dakini...what...'

The crone advanced, pointing at the moon with her bony finger. 'The magic, o mistress...it has gone wrong!'

'Wha...ttt...' Hera choked and buckled to her knees.

'O mistress, the spell has turned. You failed to consume the heart in time. You were so taken up by what your lover was doing that it is now useless to you. The girl should have been alive when you consumed her heart. Now you must reverse the spell to save yourself.'

'Reverse it?' gasped Hera. 'How? It is against the laws...'

'Then you will die.'

'DO IT THEN,' she screamed, her breath coming in painful gasps. 'Do it, you stupid crone.'

'You cannot reawaken the dead!'

Dara's voice was a like a whiplash on the empty hilltop.

'Hera, you cannot! It is against the laws of this universe. It is against everything our Gods fought for. You cannot bring back the dead. It tears the very fabric of this world, it upsets the balance. You cannot.'

'Don't you want her back? You loved her, didn't you? Both of you did.'

'And yet...' Tears streamed down his face as he turned to face his elder...no, not his elder, the base creature that had taken his place. He watched as the half-man-half-monster circled Aromal's body.

'And yet...he did this to her,' he caressed Aromal's cheek, tears falling on her eyelids, falling faster and faster until his entire body was racked by sobs.

'How can you love a dead thing?' Her voice was a mere whisper, cold and unbelieving. 'How can you love someone who can't love you back?'

He rose. 'You can love someone who is a star in the sky. You can love them till the worlds turn and die and new ones rise. You wouldn't understand this, Hera, because you have never loved anyone.'

'Maybe my love is a war,' she said, almost under her breath. 'Maybe my love is poison, maybe it is meant to conquer.'

'Go forth and conquer, Hera, your dark kingdom awaits you, your realm of ruin. GO. And take this thing with you. He once loved you. You conquered him. He is your beast now, your burden. He is your poison and I hope you choke to death one day because of him.'

'Words, all words...useless words. For once, why don't you do something? You couldn't stop your brother from handing her over to me. And you were too late in stopping me either. You are...' she gasped, clutching her throat once again.

The crone strode up to Dara. 'Bring her back you must. You must...or Hera's life is at stake. The spell has turned on itself.'

'I don't care about her,' said Dara coldly, tears still gushing from his eyes.

'You don't have to reawaken her, Gandharva. You can put her soul back in her body. Ask the Death God. He has allowed it before. Her soul will return to her body and she will be whole again.'

'And how is that different from reawakening her?' asked Dara.

'Reawakening takes dark magic. It doesn't involve the soul. What you are doing is giving her life back to her.'

'*Do* something!' Hera screamed, her face turning blue.

'Think about it,' the crone rasped. 'You will get Aromal back... The Death God will give her soul back. The Old Books tell of many such tales.'

'No one has succeeded in recent times,' said Dara, his eyes fixed on Hera.

'That is because no one, no matter how brave, has dared to go down to the River of Death. This act requires some sacrifice. Only the purest of beings can survive it. You are pure, Dara. I have looked within. Your soul gleams like the rivers of Aakasha. You can do this.'

The beast that was once his brother growled. Dara walked up to the girl he loved, the dead girl whose pure, beautiful heart had been plucked from her chest just minutes ago, and knelt beside her. Her face looked serene now.

'Will it work?' he whispered. Hera was still slumped on the ground, her hands around her throat, her eyes beginning to bulge. The crone hobbled up to him.

'You can try, can't you? Isn't that what this love you talk of is all about? Doing anything you can for the one who claims your heart...'

Dara stood up.

'You will go then?' asked the crone, her eyes gleaming with something resembling hope.

He nodded.

'I will try and keep her alive till you return...' she called after him, indicating Hera.

'I don't give a damn about her. She can rot to pieces,' he

said, as he walked away without a backward glance at the Apsara who had ruined his life.

'He didn't succeed, O Dark Mistress,' said the crone. Hera was lying on the grass still clutching the heart, her breath rough and irregular. Aromal lay close to her with the serenity of a sleeping child. 'And I bring worse news.'

'What could be worse?' coughed Hera.

The crone averted her eyes and stepped back. 'Banishment. Menaka has heard. So has the Balance Keeper. The price of this Unspeakable failure is Banishment. For all three of you. You are realmless now…'

And as the crone spoke, Hera felt a burden settle on her shoulders. She knew she would never fly now. She was bound to earth. *Earth!* she thought bitterly. No, it wouldn't do. She wanted a realm of her own. If the life she was born into was forbidden to her now, she would create another one for herself. And no one could stop her.

'Do something,' she said, sitting up. 'Do something. Invoke the darkest sorcery. But do it. I cannot let Menaka win. I must be queen.'

'Of what?' sniggered the crone.

Hera lunged at her and caught her by the throat. 'You are the cause of this. Now undo it. Create a new realm for me. Where I will rule, where I will be queen.'

'And what is a queen good for if she has no one but a beast to rule over? Funny sort of kingdom that would be.'

'Then create an army for me. And make sure Dara can never find us. Do it before he returns from the Tarini. Create an army from my shadow. Create ones who desire secrets, who will covet them as I do and bring them for me. Create dark things made of sin and shadows. Go on, do it!'

'That still doesn't reverse the spell. You need to bring her back to life, O Dark Mistress. Otherwise you will be the dead queen of a ghost kingdom.'

'Then do it. Bring her back to life however you can. Even better, infuse my shadow into her. Make her my first Yakshi.'

'She will then be a hybrid, O Dark Mistress. That is banned, too.'

'Nothing I desire is banned in my own kingdom,' she screamed. 'DO IT! Turn her into my own little monster. Do it *now.*'

She spat in disgust. 'Banished, indeed!' Ripping the ruby-studded ring off her finger, she flung it to the ground. 'I will not be needing this anymore, now that I am no longer an Apsara.'

The crone hobbled away muttering, 'You will never be Blood Queen now, as you intend to bring another curse upon yourself. Creating a hybrid monster? Pure dumb genius, O Queen.'

Hera lay back in the grass a little distance away from the innocent girl who had proved to be her nemesis. 'You shall live forever now,' she said. 'Forever, in darkness, and in my shadow.'

The blood moon shimmered ominously and vanished out of sight. The beast who was once a Gandharva named Bael hovered near the girl he had betrayed, growling and snarling as his life sunk into the dark depths below earth.

When Dara came back, there was no one around save a melting cauldron full of dark magic. The girl he had loved was gone, even her lifeless body was missing. His brother, the dark one who had turned into the beast that fed on the dying wishes of mortals, had vanished along with the girl he had once loved. And the dark Goddess who had ruined his life seemed to have vanished from the face of the earth.

He let out a roar of rage and sorrow.

'I will find you,' he screamed between his sobs. 'I will find you and destroy you, Hera. Even if it means waiting till the end of time to do it...'

The wind rattled around him as he sunk to his knees, his face buried in his hands.

The room was cold. It seemed lit from within and shone with an eerie glow. She sat on a throne made of a metal unknown to earth or heaven. Her face had turned cadaverous, diseased. She was holding on to her life force with all the magical vigour she had left. Her eyes, cold and narrow, bloodshot from the spell gone wrong, stayed fixed on the crone.

A girl lay on the floor, naked, faceless, a withered frangipani tangled in her hair. She had a gaping hole where her heart should have been. The blood had crusted and dried around the wound. Hera still held the heart she had plucked from the girl's chest tightly in her fist.

The crone stood in a corner muttering under her breath. She finally lifted her hands high in the air. 'It's done. The spell is complete. Give your order now, O Dark Queen...'

Hera rose. Gaggii, her raven, flew to her shoulder. A golden snake slithered in her flaming hair.

'Rise,' she commanded. The girl stirred and sat up. She was devoid of expression as her features slowly formed. Hera's mouth twisted into a smile.

'Wonderful. Now, shape-shift.'

And she did.

53

I finally understood what I had felt all my life without understanding what it had meant. It was the loneliness of being trapped in someone's memory. How could I have known? No one tells you, however strange your life is, whether human or monster, that you could be somebody's darkest secret.

I never fully remembered what was said to me afterwards. But it didn't matter. I remembered how I felt when I saw myself in Dara's eyes. In Hera's rage. In Bael's beastliness. I pieced myself together with jumbled memories spiked with sleeplessness and guilt. This was what it was like to haunt other people's minds. This is what I had felt all my life without understanding it.

I saw for a few seconds a part of me that was a forbidden story. It was but a few seconds of remembering. But it consumed a lifetime in its depths.

It consumed us.

The Forgotten returned to their rightful place in her memory. They never appeared again, for after wandering in a lost land of forgetting for centuries, they had found their final resting place.

I was brought back to cruel reality when Hera laughed. It was a cold and remorseless sound.

'Well,' she said, 'now that little Ardra remembers everything, shall we get on with it?'

I was human once. I was murdered by Hera.

Suddenly in the distance, there was a hissing and crackling sound, followed by rumblings of what seemed like thunder. But Atala didn't have thunder...

'What is that noise?' Hera said. Her eyes narrowed. The room was getting hotter and hotter.

'That is the noise of your private hell crumbling,' said Dara, his voice dangerously even. 'I will make you burn with it.'

She drew in a sharp breath. But before anyone could say anything, the crone came into the room with Dwai.

'Fire!' she screeched. 'Fire, O Queen! Atala burns. We must leave at once.'

'No,' said Hera. 'We will not leave. We will stay and complete the sacrifice. You think I cannot stop a mere fire? Or for that matter, him?' She threw Dara a dark look.

Dara took a step forward.

'Don't you dare,' said Hera. 'Try anything and I will rip his heart out now, right in front of you.'

I shook my head at Dara imploringly. He stopped in his tracks, his face burning with rage.

'It's not a mere fire, O Queen,' said Dakini. 'The Gandharva has started it. His magic is powerful. Only he can stop the ruin of your realm if he chooses to. .'

As she said this, her crafty eyes darted towards me. It was evident she knew that the past had come tumbling out of its secret world. Dwai's eyes met mine. I took an unsteady step forward. He shook his head in warning.

'He will not stop me,' scoffed Hera. 'Nor he, nor this succubus. Bring the Half-born to me. Now!'

'NO, my Queen. Atala's magic runs low now. We cannot complete the sacrifice here. It won't work!' screeched Dakini. 'Prithvi is not strong enough to sustain the magic required by this sacrifice either. It must happen in Aakasha,' she announced merrily, as if she was merely changing the venue for somebody's birthday party. 'What started there must end there. I have seen it in the runes.'

Nobody saw what happened next. Dara moved towards Dwai just as the crone flung her hands forward and a black sooty smoke rose from the ground, engulfing us all.

'Dwai!' I shouted. I couldn't see anything.

The room spun around. Dwai...Dara...Hera...Bael...Dakini...all became swirling shapes around me. My core churned. The last thing I remembered before sinking into nothingness was the void of Bael's yellow eyes.

It was a strange song that woke me up. A song of sorrow and regret. It seemed to come from a voice not human but old, so old, it had seen things more terrible than my own story. It was the mirror. The walls of the room seemed to shake as I sat up, trying to focus. Dara was kneeling beside me, watching me keenly. As I opened my eyes, he averted his and stood up.

The mirror, or what was left of it, was on the floor, a wreckage of mercurial magic and metal. It was bent out of shape, a twisted puddle that still had some life in it. Some of its creatures lay around it, writhing and gasping.

'Where are they?' I asked. A low snarl behind me indicated that Bael was still around.

Tired and withdrawn, Dara replied, 'You fainted. It must have been the after-effect of... She seized the opportunity and vanished with Dwai. She used the mirror as a portal to Aakasha.'

'But how? Isn't Hera banned from entering Aakasha?'

'You forget that she has with her a Half-born with sky blood in him. However unwilling, he can get her in,' he said grimly.

They were gone. The crone, Hera and Dwai. I hadn't been able to stop Hera from taking my Dwai towards his inevitable death.

In a realm burning to the ground, I was alone with the two brothers – one, a beast created by Hera, the other, a Gandharva consumed by regret. I had loved both of them a lifetime ago. And I still loved one of them.

'Dara,' I said, urgently, 'what do we do? We have no time!'

Bael growled behind us.

'We can't take him with us,' said Dara, finally.

'We can't leave him here to die!' I exclaimed. 'The fire will raze Atala to the ground.'

'I'll put it out,' he said. He closed his eyes, the marks on his neck glowing brighter than ever before. A few minutes later, I could indeed sense the fire dying out. Atala would stand, broken and charred.

'Let's waste no more time then. I can get you and me to Aakasha,' he said, sounding tired. The powerful magic seemed to have taken a toll on him.

'How?'

He held out his hand. 'I'm not Banished anymore, remember? I can transport myself to Aakasha now.'

'Too late…' rasped an ancient voice behind us.

It was the mirror. 'Too late,' it said again. 'If you need to get there soon enough, use me. Whatever is left of me.'

I stared at the dying thing. 'But why…' I began.

'She used me for centuries and destroyed me on her path to power. Let me go with an ounce of repentance. Waste no more time…'

I looked at Dara and he nodded.

I had no one to say goodbye to. No Yakshis, no Vina, nobody. The shadow creature scampered around my feet. I scooped it up with one hand while placing the other in Dara's. I realized I had never held his hand before, at least not in my life as a Yakshi. It felt firm and reassuring around mine.

'*Wait…*'

Bael slouched towards me slowly, uncertain and mournful. Dara shifted to shield me but I stopped him. I watched as Bael extended his hand to me. For a second, I wondered if he was mirroring his twin but then he placed something in my palm. It felt cold and still against my skin. My eyes met his reptilian ones. Something had changed in them. They held a lifetime of heartbreak and regret. I wanted to hug him but instead I squeezed his scaly hand. He let go and took a step back.

I looked around. I would never return to Atala. I wouldn't miss it but something in me still felt carved out and empty.

Dara and I stepped into the mirror. The room spun around for the second time.

Aakasha. If Atala was unreal in a cold, brittle, nightmarish way, then Aakasha was a dreamscape. It was dreamy, phantasmagorical, ever-changing, even a little uncomfortable to the senses. It felt as if one was in the middle of a very vivid, very lucid dream.

We tumbled out of a mirror that looked a lot like the one in Atala, into a long shimmery passage. Getting to our feet, we stood still for a few seconds, unsure.

'Let's go towards the entrance,' said Dara, finally. I could see how difficult this was for him. He was back home after centuries, with the person who was the reason behind him leaving it.

I had so many things to say to him, to ask him. So many centuries of regret and longing to comprehend. Instead, we moved swiftly and silently down the corridor.

'I hope we're not too late,' I said, anxiously.

'We would know if we were,' he replied.

'Do you think we'll be able to stop her?'

'I don't know. I intend to try.'

The corridor seemed unending, its walls shifting like waves and changing colour ever so often. The windows were large like the ones in Atala, but framed in pale gold. I could see the sun in the distance, pale and fragile in comparison to the moon that shone beside it. A blood moon of ferocious intensity.

I set the shadow creature down, and it bounded away, finding new corners to inhabit. I let it go, knowing it would return to me later. I glanced sideways at Dara as we glided as

333

fast as we could. His sculpted face held a look of inevitable determination. He would finish this, I knew that much. Somehow, anyhow, he would. The thought made me feel cold and warm at the same time.

'Why did you let me go?' I asked at last. 'You can surely answer me now.'

'It was your imprint,' he said. 'Don't ask me how I knew what it was, except I did. I was sure only one Yakshi could have a frangipani as her imprint. I just *knew*…'

I didn't question that feeling. It was exactly what had violently unsettled me when he had come to my rescue as I was bleeding out. It was because of this feeling that I knew my bonds with Dara ran deeper in some way.

'I know you did your best to save her…*me*,' I said softly. 'You couldn't have known.'

The haunted look in his eyes was heartbreaking. 'And yet I lost you,' he said.

I wondered if this guilt would ever leave him, whether he would ever have a chance at happiness. At peace. Whether we would ever be okay. Was it possible?

Rather abruptly, the corridor opened up into a huge hall. I could see light outside. Something was happening just outside its walls, on a massive porch with marble steps. I could see Menaka, Morana, Ila, a few other Apsaras and Gandharvas, including the one I had followed towards the sky portal.

I could sense him now. Dwai. His mother's Jwala in my pocket burned.

I took a deep breath.

'Ardra…' Dara's jewel-blue eyes were fogged over. 'When this is over, we shall talk. I…'

'I know,' I said. 'We will.'

We wouldn't. I knew that. When this was over, I knew

neither of us would go back into that memory. It was an untellable story. We would never pass it on.

I could hear the commotion and chaos outside, shouts of fear, anger and desperation ringing inside the empty hall we passed through.

A crackling energy spurted around the entrance. As we ran towards it, we realized it was a circle of protection. Inside it was the palace with its inmates. And us. Outside the circle were Hera, the crone and Dwai.

I turned to Morana, panic drumming at my core. 'What's...'

'It's Dwai,' she said, her voice low and breathless. 'He seems to have channelled his powers somehow, even without the Jwala.'

'WHAT?'

'Yes,' added Menaka. 'The three of them landed in the palace. We tried to stop them but she is too powerful right now. When she realized that there were too many of us, she decided to head outside to complete the sacrifice.'

'She invited us to watch,' said Ila grimly.

But I wasn't really listening. I rushed down the steps and towards Dwai but fell back. I could see him outside the circle, looking utterly serene. None of the chaos or the impending doom seemed to affect him.

'Don't Ardra...don't,' his voice came through the protection of the circle like bubbling water.

'No, Dwai!' I shouted. 'Don't give up. You did this even without the stone...'

'He has sky blood in him. He doesn't need the stone while he is in Aakasha.' Dara stood behind me, utterly still, like a panther ready to spring.

'Is he powerful enough? Can he...?' My heart raced wildly with hope.

'I doubt it,' said Dara gently. 'He is still new to this. He may have exhausted his powers while setting up this protection. I think he knows that. He is just trying to protect everyone else while...'

'NO! I will never allow it. Not while I live.'

Outside the circle, I saw Hera prowling restlessly like a wild cat. The crone was chanting something, her hands raised above her head.

'She's going to do it. Dara!'

Hera looked straight at Dara, hate spilling out of her eyes. She muttered something to the crone. The crone stopped her incantations and drew a pattern in the air.

There was a minor explosion and the entire area was covered in thick smoke. Someone on the steps screamed.

The smoke cleared after a few minutes and Hera came into focus. The crone and Dwai were missing. Dara took a long look at Hera who shook her head menacingly and shimmered out of sight. He turned to Menaka and the others gathered on the steps.

'Go inside.' It was a command. 'All of you, get inside and close the doors.'

'What are you going to do?' asked Ila, her voice trembling.

'I have to stop her. This has to stop. I don't want any of you hurt. Go inside. Please, Menaka...'

The chief of the Apsaras and the Gandharva regarded each other for a few seconds and then she said, 'This is not how I would have liked to meet you again, Dara. I wish it had been under better circumstances. But if there is anyone who can stop her, it is you...'

She turned to the others, motioning them to go inside the palace. Ila hesitated for a second and then went in.

'Let me come with you,' said Morana, with some force. 'I know I can be useful. Let me…'

'No. Your supernatural powers will be mild at best in Aakasha,' Dara was emphatic. 'Nobody else needs to put themselves in danger. Stay here, Morana, and guard the palace.'

She nodded reluctantly.

'I would ask you to go too…' he said to me.

I laughed. 'That's Dwai out there, Dara. I am going with you whether I can channel my magic or not.'

'You would do anything you could to save Dwai, wouldn't you?'

His jewel-blue eyes were strangely unreadable.

'Yes,' I said. 'I would. Even if it meant I die in his place.'

It was just a few seconds but it felt like a lifetime in which we stood there, contemplating each other. In the end, he said, 'I'm going to pull down the protection just in time for us to get outside.'

He stretched out his arm. I felt the crackle in the air, and then stillness.

'Step outside,' he said. We quickly descended the steps and out on to the grounds of Aakasha.

⚸ 57 ⚸

'The old battlefield,' Dara said quietly. I looked around. Long ago, divine battles had been fought here, and kingdoms of skies and earth had been won and lost on this field. Now it was just a vast, beautiful expanse, covered with golden grass and flowers I had never seen on earth or Atala. Strange trees with wispy branches and luminous fruit laced the landscape – cloud trees, or as they were known in Aakasha, megh vrikshas. Peculiar blooms sprung up from the ground to greet Dara. They were his favourite flowers, the sunblooms – little orb-like things with a rich gold centre and hazy petals resembling the rays of the afternoon sun. They climbed up his wrist and, as they did, they changed colour from yellow to a deep orange.

Something rose behind us – the scarlet full moon, now looking like a gigantic ball of blood.

'It's time,' I said, trying to keep the panic out of my voice.

He looked into the distance where Hera, Dakini and Dwai stood, and started to glide.

Hera was naked, the snake wrapped around her waist. Gaggii flew around her, silently watching.

The crone had resumed her chanting, her hands high up in the air, her pupils receded into her eyelids.

'Dwai!' I shouted.

Hera turned before he did. She looked even more terrifying in her nakedness, a rogue force of nature that was raw and unbridled in its turbulence.

She looked mildly surprised to see us but it didn't seem to bother her at all.

'Welcome to the party. I thought you might skip it but I suppose it is irresistible to watch your lover die for my cause. Like you did, a long while ago. Perhaps you two *do* belong together.'

Her words came at me like a torrent of hate, but they meant nothing. I didn't take my eyes off Dwai, who kept his steady gaze on me as well. He looked a little tired and I knew that

Dara was right – putting up that protective circle had weakened him. Yet, he had done it to keep us from danger. He hadn't thought of saving his power to fight Hera.

'What shall we do?' I asked desperately. 'He isn't strong enough.'

Dara was silent, as if he was weighing the whole situation. 'I'm going in,' I said. 'I want to get in somehow and…'

He placed his hand on my arm. I fell quiet. He looked at me, his jewel-blue eyes blazing. I knew he wanted to say so much more, but the words wouldn't come. Perhaps he would find the strength to say them later, when this was over.

There was a flash of light and, for a second, everything around us froze. Except Dara. He walked over to Dwai swiftly. Rooted to my spot, I watched as a haze of smoke appeared seemingly out of nowhere and the landscape blurred. I realized then that this was Dara's magic at the place of his origin – more potent, more powerful than ever.

When the haze cleared, Dwai was standing beside me outside the protective circle. Dara had taken his place inside and it was he who was now facing Hera.

Her flame-winged lashes breathed fury. If Dara's magic was stronger in Aakasha, so was hers.

'Dara, Dara,' she muttered. 'Always putting a spoke in the wheel. You are so useless.' Hate was now spilling out of her voice. 'Ask Ardra. I'm sure even she thinks so. You couldn't save her 500 years ago and you will fail again today!'

He said nothing but took a deliberate step in her direction. Furious, she sent a black ball of magic towards him. He obstructed it, sending back an invisible orb of his own energy. The air exploded under the pressure of their magic.

Something fluttered wildly in my chest – a scream. I suppressed it with difficulty.

'Dara!' I called out instead.

He didn't turn. He didn't look at me.

'You can't even bear to look at her, can you?' taunted Hera. 'You and your brother...you did nothing. There is no redemption for you, Dara. None.'

'That isn't true, Dara,' I shouted, the wind carrying my voice. 'Don't listen to her...please...'

This time he turned. His eyes, those jewel-blue eyes, were filled with torment. He looked at me and I fought back the tears that were threatening to spill out. He didn't say a word, but his gaze begged for my forgiveness. I wanted to tell him it was okay, to hold him and tell him to forgive himself. That there could be a new beginning...

I took a step forward, and then started running. The air in front of me rippled like a wave and seemed to implode with a quiet force. I fell back to the ground.

Hera's force field. She must have put it up just a few seconds ago. She smiled, satisfied. I pounded against the invisible wall but Dara turned his back to me.

'There must be a way,' he said. 'There must be an end. I have looked for it, Hera. And whatever it is, the answer, the end, it isn't within you. You aren't capable of anything decent. You never have been. You are not capable of peace.'

'Peace?' she snorted. 'There is no such thing. There is power and those who yield to it. Peace is a delusion, you foolish Gandharva. So is love.'

'You have ruined everything. My family, my love, me...'

'I loathe self-pity,' she snarled. 'Don't waste my time, Dara. Begone. All I want is the Half-born.'

'Not while I live,' said Dara and raised his hand. His magic hit her being with so much force, she gasped. Her life force began to stream out of her.

'Not so easily,' she snarled as the crone chanted something hysterically. The life force streamed back into her. She rose, baring her teeth like a wild monster.

Her shadow splintered and broke away into writhing fragments. Black forms rose from them, hissing and snapping at Dara. He rose in the air and whipped out his sabre. It gleamed sharp and ruthless in the blood-moon light. He lashed out at the things that had emerged from her shadow, battling in mid-air. Hera watched intently as the things clawed at him and his blood spilled on to the sunblooms below. He let out a roar of rage and hurled his sabre at them with unbelievable force. The weapon slit the air and through the creatures in one neat stroke. They howled and vanished.

As he returned to the ground, he lurched. The movement was so slight that only I saw this.

'Dara...' I called out. I wanted him to return. He didn't respond. I knew it was deliberate. His sabre was flung far away in the distance.

Dwai gripped my hand tightly. I knew it wasn't out of fear. Fear had fled from his soul long ago. This was something else.

Inside the force field, sparks flew as Hera raised her hand, but he blocked her attack almost effortlessly. She then took a deep breath and closed her eyes. When she opened them again, she was smiling. Then she uttered something under her breath and flashed her hands at him again.

There was a second when it felt like all the silence in the world had blanketed that one spot. Nothing made a sound. Nothing stirred.

There was no blood.

He simply crumpled to the ground, a wingless angel, his eyes empty.

58

The air was a noiseless vacuum as I broke into a run. But I was stopped by the hand I was holding.

I turned to look at Dwai, and all I could see was the deep, angry slash across his cheek and the rage burning in his eyes. I was numb, but I wanted to soak up the rage, the sorrow, and make it my own.

'I'm not leaving him, Dwai.' My voice sounded like a stranger's to my own ears.

'No. He wouldn't leave you here either,' he said, his face taut.

There was so much noise around me. There was so much unbearable silence. I blinked and my cheeks flooded with hot tears.

He was gone.

Hera threw back her head and laughed.

The sound hit me like a whiplash. It was like the world had snapped back into place as I felt my senses returning to me. I could feel her evil pulsating around me, fuelling my rage.

The crone cackled as Hera said something to her.

No.

Not Dwai...not anyone else...ever again.

When her head whipped around, I realized I had said it out loud. Her eyebrows rose.

'What?' she spat. 'What did you say, you succubus?'

'No one else, ever again,' I repeated.

A grieving wind blew across the battlefield. Of course, one couldn't really call it that. There were no soldiers hacking one another to death. No elephants trampling enemy troops. No decapitated horses, capsized chariots. No widows' cries to rent the air. No losers. No winners.

Just one fallen warrior.

I watched her walk towards me, the snake in her hair hissing ominously. The crone followed her, giggling madly to herself.

'It's over, Ardra. The Half-born is mine. Nothing can stop me now. Not you, not that Gandharva.' Her eyes strayed to Dara. There was a despicable glint in them – nothing and no one mattered to her now.

'It's over,' cackled the crone. 'What started centuries ago is over today… You, O Mistress of Phantoms, you…'

'Don't call me that ever again, you old hag,' spat Hera.

'Apologies, Your Highness. You are now to be the Blood Queen. Everything else falls short for your power, O Queen of the Underworld, Ruler of the Realms, Chief of the…'

'Enough! Bring the Half-born to me.'

'No.'

I wasn't sure how my voice sounded but it sparked surprise in Hera's eyes.

She laughed. 'Come on, Ardra, it is getting a bit boring now. Even the Gandharva is dead. Hand over the human and be gone. I will spare you your lowly life.'

'How kind,' hissed the crone.

'Not really,' I said slowly. 'Magic goes wrong all the time. Unfortunately, this one binds me to you. I die and you will never be Blood Queen.'

Hera's cold eyes widened. 'Stupid girl – ' she began, her face alive with hate.

I shook my head and raised a hand.

'It's true, but having my life is not the same as having my freedom, is it? I doubt you will let me go. The other Yakshis died in vain, after all. You can't call them back. They transferred their power over to you and now they are gone forever. But I didn't die. Don't you find that odd, Hera? You won't kill me, I am certain. I will be imprisoned in the dungeons of Vishara forever, while you become Blood Queen or whatever evil title you prefer, and…do what, exactly?' I asked.

'Do WHAT? Your stupid mind cannot even conceive what that means, can it? What it means to be a Blood Queen…to have the world bow to me, to own whatever I choose to.'

'Not everything,' I said. 'Not love, not freedom, not happiness – the only things that matter in this world and all others.'

'I AM FREE!' she screamed. 'I am HERA, the next Ruler of the Realms. I am free, you stupid succubus.'

'And, yet, you are a prisoner of your own ugliness, your evil, your wretched need to conquer. It cripples you, Hera.'

As I spoke, her face twisted into something beastly, all traces of beauty vanishing from her being. She was an empty ornament now, brimming with dark, repugnant magic. She made a noise of derision, malice in her eyes.

Something turned within me. It was ugly, horrible, angry. *No,* I reasoned. *Not this way. Not like her. There must be a better way.*

'Ardra.'

It was Dwai. There was no fear in his eyes. He simply looked determined. 'Take the stone and go. I…'

'No. Running away isn't my thing anymore,' I said. 'And giving up isn't yours.'

'Maisha's stone won't work once he hands himself over,' said Hera, her irises gleaming. 'The stone only works…'

'…if the owner wants it to,' I cut in. 'I know. It recognizes freedom. Giving himself up will send a signal to the stone that he doesn't want ownership anymore.'

'You *do* know your myths then, Ardra,' she laughed. 'Come on, my Half-born…it is time.'

Dwai's eyes locked with mine. There was a finality there, heartbreaking and empowering at the same time.

He took a step forward.

'Wait.'

Hera shook her head with impatience. 'Now what, Ardra?'

'Do we know what happens when a stone is abandoned by its owner? These stones hold intense emotion. I wonder what happens if…'

I put my hand into my pocket and pulled something out.

'I believe this belongs to you?'

I extended my palm. On it shone the blood red stone, shaking with belligerent energy.

'Where did you get this?' she gasped. 'WHERE? DAKINI!'

'O mistress, this is…unexpected,' croaked the crone.

'I thought you found it and destroyed it, you useless bag of bones!' she shouted.

The crone lifted her face towards Hera's. It was lit with an unholy sense of glee. 'I lied,' she said and broke into laughter, her whole body convulsing.

Hera struck her across the face. The crone fell to the ground, her bones making a brittle snapping sound.

'Ardra,' Hera's voice was low and desperate. 'Give that to me.'

'No.'

'Ardra…?' Dwai took a step towards me, his eyes alight with curiosity.

'Where did you get this? How…?'

'Bael gave it to me.'

'Bael! What?'

'The night of the blood moon 500 years ago when you murdered me, the night you turned him into...what he is today, something else happened. You fell from the heavens and, in your rage, you flung away your stone. Someone picked it up...and kept it. Kept it for centuries, hidden from you. You didn't need it all this time, did you? You had your dark magic and the power we Yakshis gave you. You thought the stone had been destroyed. But Bael had it – even his monster mind knew it was important. And today, he gave it to me. I didn't even realize what it was until now.'

Hera clenched her fists.

'I didn't really know what this stone did, what it meant to have it. But now I have an idea, Hera. I have an inkling.'

'ARDRA!'

The crone, still on the ground, spat. 'Damned you are, you evil Mistress of Phantoms. And that's what you will remain. You can't own power infinitely. It is a sly, fickle thing that runs to the highest bidder that will have it, and right now, Hera...'

Her laughter rang loud and sickly.

'What will you do with that stone once I am the Blood Queen, you silly girl?' scoffed Hera.

'Once? *If*, Hera. Look at the sky. The moon is red again. We have been here before, haven't we? You and I...'

A shadow fell over her diamond-hued face. I closed my fist over the stone.

'I now know why you couldn't meet me during red moon nights. Your power would diminish if you took anything from me. Because the stains of what you did run deep and stubborn, don't they?'

'Ardra...' she whispered.

'The last time, you plucked my heart out and I died, while

two people who loved me watched helpless. One of them is dead now, and the other...'

I trailed off. The moon bloomed violent and rich, staining the sapphire-tinged Aakasha sky with its blood. It looked huge, unbearably alive...and ready.

I flung the stone into the sky, towards the red moon. It rose in the air like a scarlet star, a dying comet flung into the firmament. I watched as it hit the surface of the blood moon, which rippled violently. The crone gasped with pleasure as the stone then plunged into the moon's heart and disappeared.

Hera screamed with rage.

Her face twisted in demonic pain as it began to crack, her hair burning to soot. Blood gushed from her eyes, her crystal irises fighting for light as she screamed and Aakasha trembled with the evil that emanated from her being.

She crumpled to the ground.

'She cannot die,' rasped the crone. 'She will never die. She has too much magic in her veins.'

'There are things worse than death,' I said, my eyes on the blood moon as it continued to ripple with the force of the stone. 'And that is something neither you nor she will ever understand.'

On the ground, Hera's screams had turned into sobs as her skin withered, turning into an ugly and barren landscape.

'Help me,' she croaked.

'No one can help you now, Hera. Go back to your burnt hellhole, and never return to Prithvi or Aakasha,' I said.

Her body racked with angry sobs, Hera slumped to the ground. The crone hobbled away, muttering gleeful curses. There was a hollow sound, like the crumbling of a wall, as Hera started to disintegrate. She turned faint, a mere outline, as parts of her floated away like bits of burnt paper. With one last cry of fury and sorrow, she disappeared completely. Perhaps she would reappear in Atala, a shadow Goddess, inconsequential and powerless.

I turned and walked to where Dara lay, my hand encased in Dwai's.

59

Everything was quiet. Even the moon bled crimson tears of sorrow. I sat next to Dwai as I cradled Dara's head on my lap. The battle was over and Aakasha's moon was giving way to soft sunlight.

'We must put him to rest,' said Dwai gently. 'You can't hold him forever, Ardra. You have to let go.'

His eyes were steadfast and sad.

'We have to let Ila know,' I said, numb with sorrow. But he wouldn't leave me alone on the battlefield. He continued to sit next to me, his arm around my shoulder.

As the pale sun rose over Aakasha, I saw Menaka, Ila and Morana rushing towards us.

The Huldra broke into a run as soon as she saw us. She knelt beside me, her eyes agleam with tears.

'He is at peace now,' she whispered. 'He isn't tormented anymore.'

Menaka took his cold golden cheeks into her hands. She sank to the ground without a word, shaking her head.

Ila stood rooted to where she was, a few feet away from us.

She wouldn't move. In fact, she didn't move until darkness fell again when, finally, she knelt slowly beside the still Gandharva. I rose, transferring Dara's head to her lap.

'He must rest now...' she said to no one in particular. 'We must find a place for him to rest.'

She caressed the ground. As her hand touched the grass, sunblooms sprang up, long and graceful, their heads glowing and burnished. Their glow seemed to light up Dara's face.

'He can rest right here,' Ila said. 'He doesn't have to move until he's ready.'

The earth flowered with sunblooms all around the Gandharva. A diffused light filled the place. Everything seemed serene, but my insides were in turmoil. I wasn't sure how I would ever quiet that beast. It was angry, wounded and unforgiving. I was wondering how I would suppress the feeling when I suddenly felt something touch my wrist tenderly.

It was a sunbloom. It wound its way up my wrist and arm and crept around my neck. I gently plucked it and wore it in my hair. A lightness engulfed me...a warm feeling of hope. *Now I know, Dara*, I thought, *now I know why you loved these flowers. They helped you hope.*

Hope. It was the only thing in the world that mattered. It could be both frail and invincible, fleeting and infinite. It never made sense to hope madly, ceaselessly, against all odds, and yet that was the only thing that dispelled the darkness.

✦ ENDINGS AND BEGINNINGS ✦

In the end, what should matter is the living. Those who survive the storm carry with them scars that never heal.

And yet the dead sing their life song forever. The dead never let us forget. The war lives on through them. They, who died in sacrifice, and they who unflinchingly murdered without mercy.

The day after the New War, as she insisted on calling it, Menaka asked me to go for a walk with her. She seemed totally unaffected by everything that had happened and spoke incessantly, while I listened half-heartedly, my mind and spirit elsewhere. Then she asked me if I wanted to stay and rule as her deputy and, despite everything, I laughed.

'You are a very funny girl, you know. Most people would kill for the job,' she said, mildly indignant.

'They did,' I reminded her. She shrugged her shoulders and walked away.

She then decided to return to Prithvi, stating Union issues with the Producers' Guild. 'I can't waste any more dates. I will be sued.'

I promised I would come and see her when I returned to Prithvi, but I knew I wouldn't. She knew it, too.

I have tried to enjoy my time in Aakasha. The megh vrikshas have started blooming and they produce fruit not unlike polished full moons. Morana insists they are made of moonlight and honey. We sit under the trees, eating the fruit, her long tail swishing in pleasure. She will return to her land, too, eventually, but she isn't in any hurry.

She, Dwai and I often walk around the burnished lanes of Aakasha, so different from the glittering bejewelled ones in Atala. We speak of everything but never of what happened. And never of Dara. I'm not ready yet.

Dara seems at peace among his favourite flowers. They reach out to him lovingly, with their tendrils rippling like crooked lines of sunlight. They gently caress his face, his arms, his eyes.

After that night, Ila sat by him for three days and three nights. She wouldn't move and I didn't have the heart to make her. Finally, on the third night, she rose and walked into the Old Sea. We didn't stop her. She would find her peace there, at the bottom, in the lap of the Old Moon. For a few days, I went to shores of the sea, expecting to find Dara there. I couldn't help thinking he might follow Ila into the waters.

But Dara was never made for water. He was made for fire. Someday, when he is truly ready, he will combust into the final fire and fade into starlight.

Until then he will be safe here, where he will be remembered and loved forever, for the sunblooms never sleep.

My memories keep me awake at night, like they have for the last 500 years. A part of me was always awake, I think – the part that was the sad love song of a girl who had died in the arms of the man who had betrayed her.

The night after the war, I lay in Dwai's arms, wondering if the rage within me would ever quieten. When morning came, I went to visit Dara in his sunbloom-serenity, and I knew then that I shouldn't look for the answer. It will come and speak to me when the time is ready. Like my story. After all, both past and present hadn't met a second sooner than they had to. As for the future...

Dwai...gentle, steadfast Dwai with the scar across his cheek. The scar would never fully fade as it was marked by evil beyond comprehension. I see him look at it every day in the mirror, the jagged lines of skin and blood slowly and steadily closing into one translucent golden line.

He is still coming to terms with the magic in his blood. He prefers to be human, not caring much for that which makes him 'special'. I know he will always try to fight it, to stay human in his choices.

He looks at me like I am a dream – one that imprinted itself in his mind but that he couldn't remember fully when he woke up. I don't blame him. I am driftwood now, cast out into starspace, and all my parts are still searching.

His love is my solace. In his eyes, I can see that if he could fall in love with a dangerous supernatural assassin, he will stay in love with me as I am now. But it will take me a while to love him the way he loves me.

Perhaps I will never find it in me. I think of Dara and how he carried his broken love for me in his heart for five centuries and I feel an emptiness that cannot be filled.

As for Bael, I have vowed to forget him with a vengeance. Betrayal is love's evil twin and sometimes it is remorseless. Perhaps he did love me in his own weak way. For if there is one thing I have learnt in my long time on earth, it is that love is a strange creature, defying true definition.

I still dream of Hera. It is the same dream I have had for centuries. Hera, with her raven and her snake, and I, with the gaping hole in my chest. But my last dream was a little different. In it, I walked towards her, wounded, scraped out, and as I did, she faded into a scream. I woke up with the echo of the scream still ringing in my ears. I think of her sometimes, wandering around an Atala that is empty of its people, stripped of her power, her beauty, her fire. A ghost Goddess devoid of light and redemption.

I will return to Prithvi soon with Dwai. It is my home now. I will take a few sunblooms with me and plant them there, on earth soil. They will remind me of Dara.

The blood moon dissolved into dust a day after it had consumed Hera's Jwala. And in its place rose a shimmering young moon, full of joy. Aakasha is alight with the joy of the new moon. She shines forth like a good omen.

Of new beginnings. And new stories.

As for the untellable stories, like mine, they will always cling to the world in places intended for the lost...only to be found again by a new teller.

ACKNOWLEDGMENTS

Dark Things started off as a mad flicker of an idea and it can only end in humble gratitude.

My first thanks to my parents, Jaya Nagarajan and T.S. Nagarajan, for giving me the gift of living with books; my grandparents, Seetha and P. Subramanian, Rajalakshmi Swaminathan, and especially T.B. Swaminathan, teller of endless stories, who introduced me to the magic of storytelling. All my teachers, in particular, Nalini Chandran, Jaya Narayanan, Professor Nandakumar and, again, my mother for nurturing the writer (and reader) in me.

Jitesh Pillai, mentor and friend, you were the first person to actually believe I would be published one day, thank you. Anuradha Choudhary, my own thing of light, for the love you have shown me and my characters.

Sejal Mehta, traveller to strange worlds, for urging me to set off on my own adventure with words. Jason Menezes, mad poet and wizard of the weird, whose twelve-page, 4,000-word feedback truly made the book what it is today. Nikita Deshpande, for being a fearless fellow adventurer in this book-writing business. Parvathy Girish, for being the kind of joyful early reader only a childhood friend can be.

Krishna Udayasankar, endless gratitude for being the best

hand-holder I could have imagined through this process. Thank you for letting me blubber and rant on long international phone calls.

My brother, Shyaam, and sister-in-law, Aparna, for kindly letting me skulk around your house while I searched for words that refused to come out of hiding.

Ruchika Roy, that amazing writer friend everyone should have.

Shruti Haasan, for being a creature of true fantasy. I have a feeling Ardra dreams of you often. Ishaan Nair, my fellow lover of odd, beautiful things, for that gorgeous author picture in which I clearly seem to have shape-shifted.

My sincere thanks to the entire team at Hachette India. Poulomi Chatterjee, thank you for letting me take my time with the book and putting the needs of a writer above all. It has been a pleasure writing *Dark Things* for you. Prerna Vohra, editor, fearless nitpicker, I promise you the goat was fed. (Yes, there is a goat in the book, however briefly.) Asma Kazi for the magical cover art, the kind that appears in my dreams.

Bouquets of thanks to Anupama Vikramadityan, Swarnima Deepak, Rashmi Praveen, Thushara Thomas, Jayati Bose, Sandhya Menon, Visha Suchde, Tanuja Dabir, Shraddha Soni, Danesh Kumar, my in-laws Savitri and P. Sahasranaman, and anyone else I may have missed out for being there through this enchanted adventure, whether you know it or not.

My husband, Venkatraghavan S., my not-so-invisible wings, how do I thank you for the unbelievable love, support and patience you have shown me? Well, I could let you edit another book of mine, mwahahaha.

Lastly, thank you, gentle reader, for choosing this book. My worlds tend to be weird but they are also happy to have you live in them. You are at the right place.